SOUL BOUND

DAWN OF THE CURSE BOOK 1

A PACK BOUND PREQUEL SERIES

LEISL LEIGHTON

PERMIEN PRESS

Published by Leisl Leighton as Permien Press.

For more information, email: leisl@leislleighton.com

Epub: 978-0-6451089-2-7

Print: 978-0-6451089-3-4

Cover design by Samantha Marshall

Edited by Marnie St Clair

 Formatted with Vellum

PRAISE FOR SOUL BOUND

Wow what a start. This was magical and captivating throughout. Thoroughly enjoyed the storyline and characters and how they overcome things.

— PAT'S REVIEWS - GOODREADS REVIEWER

I loved this! ... I loved reading about the history and what happened to set things in motion. This is a very good book and is most definitely worth reading.

— A SCHOFIELD - GOODREADS & BOOKBUB
REVIEWER

Great start to the prequel series ... Beautifully written and moving ... I look forward to reading the next one.

— N PARKER - GOODREADS REVIEWER

This is so good! I found myself swept away in the magical and captivating story ... I'm hooked and so looking forward to the next book.

— DEBBIE EYRE - GOODREADS & BOOKBUB
REVIEWER

I loved the way Leisl Leighton wrote this, it was what I was hoping for in this type of book. The characters were what I was hoping for. I was invested in the plot and really glad I read this.

— K LEER - GOODREADS REVIEWER

SOUL BOUND

To my soul-mate, Mark, who helps to make this writing thing possible. And to my boys , Jacob and Nathaniel, who make me laugh every day, especially when I need it.

I love you

THE PACT

The Pact was created, the Darkness was banished
Magical beings no longer vanish
In the fire and flame of power vast and killing
Now they share with the Were and are willing
To bless the future and worship the sun
Giving thanks for the freedom granted by the One
The first and true Goddess who looks after thee
Blessed be her glory and the power of three
Pack Witch Blessing to the Goddess
Anonymous

1

Scottish Highlands—1493

'Out ye get, Frenchie.'

Alistair Sinoir nodded at the farmer who'd rowed him across the loch then swung himself out of the boat. Water lapped over his boots, wetting his breeches. He cursed to himself as he turned to haul his pack out of the boat—he was in for an uncomfortable walk unless he soon found a patch of sun in which to dry off.

He glanced up at the sky and frowned at the grey clouds lowering above the mountains surrounding the loch. He didn't fancy his chances of finding any sun in this wild place. It was more likely he'd end up wetter than he already was if the heavy scent of rain in the air was anything to go by.

Not that he wasn't used to living rough. He'd put up with worse in the years after his parents were killed. Their deaths had forced him to do things he'd never thought to endure since fleeing their small cottage in southern France—all in an effort to keep his siblings safe, fed and dry. At least, that's what he told himself.

'It looks like a storm is coming o'er the loch yonder. I hope yer not plannin' to go into the hills thata way. The storms when they come at this time o' the year can be mighty fierce.'

Alistair looked to where the farmer pointed—the exact direction the never-ceasing compulsion pushed him towards. *Merde.* The urge was only an uncomfortable prickling across his chest though, so maybe he could find another way out of this valley and over the mountains. Surely the voice behind the force that made him travel from his home to this strange country would give him some leeway to—

The prickling became a blaze; agony spiked through his head, squeezing his chest. His wolf whimpered.

He refocused on the mountain the farmer had pointed to and the pain twinging his nerves began to fade—as it always did when he made the correct decision on which way to go. Right. So, he was going to get wet. And cold. 'Is there shelter in that direction?' he asked the farmer.

'There might be some caves up in yon hills behind the woods. But I wouldna be going there if I were ye.'

'Pourquoi? Why?'

'There be wolves in those hills.'

Alistair snorted. 'I am not afraid of wolves.' They were usually afraid of him. As were most humans—although, he'd managed to lessen that impression somewhat in the search for foster parents for his brother and sister, Frederique and Amandine. In fact, his younger siblings had been his teachers there. They smiled in a friendly unassuming way and struck up general chit-chat easily even though both of them were a bit shy. But it worked because people took to them. He'd mostly let them take the lead when entering new villages and meeting new people, because even though he practiced what he saw them do, he still wasn't as good at it as they were.

When he left them though, he'd had to use what he'd learned during that time. It was essential to appear more human on his travels to this land if he was to gain people's help and trust. He'd managed to get their help, but trust was another thing. Something inside them obviously told them he was still a predator; but he had found this was soon overwhelmed by the coin he placed in their hands. It was amazing how pieces of metal could make a human ignore their instincts.

But who was he to talk? Since coming to him six months ago, the voice and its compulsion had made him ignore every instinct he had. He'd wanted to stay with his siblings, to make certain they were safe and happy. But the voice impelled him to travel, leaving all he'd loved and worked for far behind.

The farmer eyed him up and down as he stood in the waves, the older man's gaze taking in the breadth and height of Alistair. Finally his mouth quirked and he nodded. 'Mayhap ye have the right to no' be afeared o' wild critters, but there be many more things to be afeard of in yon hills, as I tried to tell ye across the loch.'

'Like what?'

The old farmer leaned in closer, his voice a harsh whisper. 'The faeries dwell there. Beyond yon crag there be an old place: their sacred Dance. It no' be a place any man of sense would wander. Especially with such weather lowering o'er the crag.' He looked up at the darkening sky, his eyes twinkling with the horror of the tale he told. 'Tuatha de Dannon—the insane faeries o' the Wild Hunt—will be riding the storm clouds and could take ye for their Queen's slave. Young Euan McBane went into yon hills on an afternoon such as this 'un, and ne'er came back.'

Alistair hid his amusement at the old man's superstitions. In all his years roaming the woods of France and Europe he'd heard many tales of the faeries and their terrors; not once had he come across any sign of them. The only magical beings he'd ever come across were his father's coven and his mother's pack—both far more dangerous to wandering souls than imaginary faeries and their Wild Hunt. 'I think I will be safe from faeries. *Merci* for your concern.' He bowed his head slightly. 'But this is the way I must go.'

The old farmer glowered, obviously annoyed his warnings had not been heeded, but then, after hocking up phlegm and spitting it over the side of the boat, said, 'Well, tha's yer business then, isna it? Ye've been warned and I've done my duty. Now, give me the rest o' the payment, laddie, then push me off, would ye? Ye ken I dinna want to get caught in the rain, and my Agatha has supper waiting for me.'

Alistair sighed and dug into the purse he kept inside his shirt, handing over the rest of the payment for the provisions they'd spared him, and for rowing him across the loch. It was the last of his coin. He would have walked around the body of water, should have, but the compulsion to move only in the direction the mysterious voice wished him to move wouldn't have it when he'd tried. The torture it inflicted on his nerves had almost driven him to his knees. It had forced him to turn towards the farmhouse to seek faster passage.

'Use your coin. It will be of little use to you where you are going,' the voice had whispered to him, its feminine tone soft yet unyielding; he knew from experience to disobey was to court pain; to question a futility he still struggled to accept. Acceptance of the inevitable apparently wasn't in his or his wolf's nature.

He still wanted to know why the voice and its compulsion had forced him to leave Frederique and Amandine before seeing them fully settled. It was a question it had never answered. He only had his guesses, and they were wild and fanciful: no matter how he wished the voice was leading him to the woman in his dreams, he knew it could not be so.

The girl, with her violet eyes, shining black hair and gentle voice, had grown into a woman in his dreams as he'd grown into a man. And while those dreams had become more ... sensual in the last six months, completely ousting the nightmares that had most often been his constant companion, they were nothing more than they'd ever been: an escape from the daily toll of a life on the run, the only protector of his younger siblings. A creation of a mind in desperate need of someone to lean on, someone to rely on, someone to keep him strong, even if it was only in his sleep that he could share his burdens on the nights the nightmares didn't take him over.

No, the compulsion to travel here was more likely to do with his magic, given the voice resonated with a power he felt in every fibre of his being; a vast power that revived him just enough to keep going when exhaustion overwhelmed him, and punished him whenever he challenged it.

It had come upon him suddenly—another reason it could not be his dream woman. He'd seen her all his life, whereas the voice had only come upon him just after Frederique and Amandine had been settled with the kind baker and his wife.

But whether it had something to do with his magic or not, one thing was certain: the closer he got to his unknown destination, the greater the compulsion to get there faster.

And as that compulsion grew, so had his wolf's need to be allowed free. Certainly, there were parts of the journey that would have been easier if he could have travelled in wolf form but giving it such freedom could not be allowed.

For years he'd only released his wolf when necessary, not trusting its violent urges beyond the need to bring down game to feed himself and his siblings or stave off attack by other wild animals; and occasionally roving bands of bandits. Even though the freedom that washed over him every time he let his wolf out was glorious, he couldn't trust it. He'd seen the damage others of his kind had done in years past—which paled in comparison to what it had done to those humans who had threatened the safety of his brother and sisters. He didn't want to be responsible for more of that violence and horror than he already had been.

'Laddie, yer eyes.'

The farmer skittered back in the boat, dropping one of the oars, his horror prickling stabs in Alistair's heart. *Merde*—his animal must be showing in his eyes. He was right not to trust his wolf when it had this effect on humans even when it only showed in his eyes. He shoved it down where it belonged, deep inside, then before he could give the farmer more reason to fear him, picked up the oar, handed it to the old man, then pushed the boat back into the loch, his strength sending it and the scared farmer well on their way.

'*Merci*,' he called out. The old man didn't respond, just rowed frantically, putting as much distance between them as possible.

Sadness washed over him but he didn't have time to give in to it. A little reminder stab of pain fired through his nerves, forcing him to turn and head ever on.

He waded out of the water and up the embankment. The shale and stones of the small beach crunched under his feet as he was pulled towards the darkest section of forest that skirted the highest mountain and its craggy peak. He hoped he could find a path over those crags because he didn't fancy mountain climbing in this weather.

Sighing, he made his way from the beach to the long grass and into the dark woods.

Not long after, rain swept down, hard and cold. Despite the fact it was summer, it chilled him to the bone within minutes.

His wolf growled to be let out—it could handle the wet and cold better than his human side would. But Alistair couldn't risk it. There was a familiar scent in the air here, one he could smell even through the drowning rain. It made him reluctant to let his wolf out, no matter how much it insisted. Werepeople had been through here at some stage in the last few weeks and he could not chance meeting them in wolf form if they were still around. Meetings with full-bloods never went well.

He trudged on, through the woods, the thickening canopy overhead slightly lessening the stinging impact of the rain.

There was no sign of any life in the woods around him; not even the small animals that called this place home were foolish enough to be out in this. His only company was the pounding of the rain and the sloshing thumps of his boots on the leaf-strewn ground. And his wolf. It wasn't letting up, pushing, pushing.

'No. I cannot let you free,' he said out loud. 'It is not safe.'

The wolf kept trying, claws spiking out of his fingertips, fur scratching under his skin. He stopped, needing to be still to get his wolf under control.

Agony spiked through his entire body, driving him to his knees. His wolf whimpered and pulled back as Alistair tried to stand, hand against a tree; the rough bark scraped against his skin, cutting his palm.

But the pain was nothing to the bright torment that started to punish him for stopping. It flared in his mind, blinding him; squeezed his chest, making him gasp for breath.

Panting as if he'd run for miles, he cried out into the cold darkness around him. 'Please. Let me rest for a moment. I am losing control over my wolf.'

'*Let it be free and you will feel no more pain.*'

'No!' He lurched to his feet, stumbling forward. Freeing his wolf was not the answer to his problems—it would only make things worse.

Instead, he dug inside his mind, using his power in a way that sickened him. Pulling on threads of magic, he quickly wove an internal shield over and around his wolf before it could know what he was doing; an iridescent cage stronger than the strongest stone or metal. He could not keep it up forever, but it would at least allow him a little breather so he was not fighting his wolf and the voice's compulsion at the same time. If the violence of the urge was anything to go by, he was close to his destination and should be able to release the cage then. 'It's only for a little while,' he whispered to his wolf.

Understanding dawned in his wolf and it howled then began to fling itself against the shield; but due to the shield, its distress was a distant thing. Even so, it made his heart ache. If only …

But no. There was no use wishing for a past that was long gone.

He stumbled on, shivering with cold as the rain whipped into his face. Thunder rumbled overhead, followed by a bright crack of lightning that zigzagged across the sky.

Damn. The lightning made it dangerous to be under these trees. He should find shelter, maybe those caves the farmer had spoken of. But the voice, merciless in its wish for him to keep going, wouldn't let him.

'Why can you not let me rest? Why am I doing this?' he cried out, his voice almost lost in the noise of the storm.

'*You know.*'

'You answered me,' surprise had him blurting out.

'*It seemed necessary.*'

'But why?'

'Why what?'

'Why now? Why not before?'

A pause, then, *'Your destination is your salvation. There you will find the reward you have long sought to relieve all your years of suffering.'*

Not an answer to his question, but it was an answer that forced him on. For the only reward he could think would ever be worth this was to know his siblings were safe, happy and accepted.

Would he ever know whether all his sacrifice had come to fruition? He could tell by the utter silence in his mind that if he asked, the voice wouldn't continue to answer.

Rather than play into its cruel games, he simply trudged on, trying not to think of the words that had brought fragile hope fluttering into his heart.

2

'What a sheep's arse.'

Morghanna Cantrae stared between her sister, Morrigan, and the Were-male who was now hurrying away from them, tail quite literally between his legs.

Then she burst into laughter.

She knew she shouldn't, but she couldn't help it. Even the expression on Morrigan's face wasn't enough to stop her laughter ringing out over the fields and echoing back at her from the well.

Her sister crossed her arms and glared at her. 'It is not funny.'

'You are right. Not funny at all,' Morghanna said lips twitching uncontrollably.

'Stop laughing at me.'

'I am not laughing at you. Just ... the look on his face was price-less.' She schooled her face to seriousness as Morrigan continued to scowl at her. 'But you are right, I should not have laughed.'

'No. You should not. I am sick of it.'

'I can see that.'

'He told me I was going to lay with him and grabbed my arm. As if it was not my choice what I did with my body and with whom. What was I expected to do?'

'Tell him you did not wish to lay with him.'

'I did tell him. Every time he brought me flowers or tried to strike up his version of conversation. But like most of the fur-balls we now live with, he thought I was playing hard to get. What is it with these Were?'

'They are not used to dealing with humans.'

'We are not humans.'

'You know what I mean,' Morghanna said softly. 'They are far more used to dealing with their own kind. And remember, up until the Pact was spelled half a year hence, they were subject to the Darkness and its influence on their wolves. Now they and their wolves are suddenly free. It is only natural that they want to be more at one with their animal side after centuries of practically being at war with it.'

'That is no excuse to act like a pushy bore. They have to learn things are different now.'

'Perhaps so do we.'

Morrigan shoved her hands on her hips and glared at Morghanna. 'Are you telling me that I should have allowed that excuse for a male to put his hands on me and do as he wished? Would you allow Lachlan such freedoms?'

Morghanna shuddered but veered away from thinking about that particular Were and his "attentions". All humour faded as she said softly, 'No, I would not.' Clearing her throat, she spoke more firmly. 'Nor am I telling you to lay with a male you do not wish to lay with simply to keep the peace. But this is a period of adjustment for us all. We need to be ... gentle with how we go about educating them.'

The Werepeople were very sensitive to the intimacy of the new bond with their pack's witches and warlocks, but many of them—the horny young Were-males in particular—were having trouble distinguishing the intimacy of shared power with the intimacy of sexual desire. It was a side-effect of the Pact that she and Bridgette hadn't considered when coming up with their plan to save both their peoples.

She really needed to have another talk with the pack's Alpha, Iain MacCrae, and his second, Dougal, who'd been helping to keep

Lachlan busy. This was going beyond her own little annoyance over Lachlan's proprietorial claim on her.

Morrigan chewed her lip for a moment before responding to Morghanna's words in a sullen tone. 'I *was* gentle.'

Morghanna snorted. 'You told him if he touched you again his balls would shrink to the size of squirrel droppings. He thought you cursed him.'

Morrigan snorted. 'He is an idiot if he thought *that* was a curse.' Her eyes began to glint as her lips quirked into a mischievous smile. 'If I had *actually* cursed him, I would have called on our Goddess, raised my hands like so and said—'

'Morrigan!' Morghanna shouted as magic gathered and prickled in the air, any last vestige of humour fleeing with her sister's threat to misuse her astonishing powers.

Morrigan's hands dropped to her side, smile turning to a pout. 'You are no fun.'

'Fun?' She stared at her sister, anger sparking. After all she'd been through these recent years ... 'You think this is fun for me? You do know I am going to have to go to our Alpha and smooth things over once again? Is it too much to ask that you not make my life harder?'

Morrigan's mouth dropped open, the quick-fire of ire lighting her eyes. 'Your life? Harder?' She turned away, kicked at a plant and shouted up at the sky, 'What about *my* life?'

Crows burst from the fields they'd been working, their caws drowning the echo of her shout as they lifted in a fear-driven flurry into the late-summer sky.

Morrigan swung back around, eyes ablaze with the passion that was an essential part of her nature. 'I never asked for this, sister,' she shouted over the noise of the crows.

She began to pace, magnificent in her anger.

What Morghanna would give to feel the intensity of emotions her sister did, even if it caused problems much of the time. Just a little taste would be nice—but it wasn't to be. Her talents with the spirits did not allow for displays of emotion like Morrigan was free to give in to. Nor did her new position as Coven leader of Pack MacCrae. So, instead of firing up to match Morrigan's anger, she said quietly, 'I know you did not choose this. You have made your position quite clear.'

'Have I? I don't think I have if you can think to bring me to task for my behaviour today. You and Bridgette decided for us all. *You* wanted this. Not me. Do not try to make *me* feel sorry for the burdens *you* must carry.'

'I am not trying to make you feel sorry for me.' She strode to her sister's side and grasped her hands. 'But please, Morrigan, understand that I need your help, not your sulks and ire. This position is lonely and difficult and I am not made for it. I have no idea why Bridgette ever thought me capable of leading a pack's coven. I need you, my sister—your strength, your passion for the wellbeing of our people, your flare with your magics, your support and friendship. Now, more than ever.'

She had thought her plea would touch her sister's loving, loyal nature, but instead, Morrigan's frown lines deepened, anger now more than a spark in her eyes as she pulled her hands from Morghanna's to gesticulate with.

'What nonsense is this? You are plenty strong enough. Plenty capable. In fact, you're the most capable witch of my acquaintance. The entire coven has looked to you ever since our parents were killed by their power. We would have fallen if not for you.'

'That was mostly Bridgette's doing.'

'No, it was not. It was you. Bridgette did nothing except continue to give of her friendship. It was not until after her husband took nearly the entire Council of Elders with him that she decided action must be taken. And even then, she was only able to do what she did because of you. Do not underestimate who you are and what you mean to our people. You are one of the best of our kind.'

Not a little floored at her sister's estimation of her talents, Morghanna waved away her compliments. 'You overestimate me, sister. The uselessness of my powers when it comes to handling this kind of thing would suggest I am lacking.'

'Your power is one of the most important that we have,' Morrigan said with stunning intensity as she grasped Morghanna's hands. 'It keeps us connected to our ancestors, keeps us in contact with the older magics and—'

'Yes, yes,' Morghanna said, this time being the one to pull her hands from her sister's. She turned away to look out over the field. 'My power is fine for talking to the spirits and accomplishing small Healings, maybe even making the Were feel more empathetically inclined to us, but beyond that very minimal offering, I need help. I thought you would back me up.'

'You do not need me to back you up. Or anyone for that matter.' Morrigan's face set in lines of fury. 'Who put this doubt in your head? If it was that blow-hard Alpha you must deal with day in and day out, I will not just threaten, I will curse him and his entire pack for real.'

'Morrigan!' She spun around, grabbed her sister's arm. 'That is the last thing I need.'

'You do not know what you need. Which makes this entire thing even more infuriating. You never questioned the veracity of your powers before this. To see you brought this low ... You know, I just ... I just ...' She threw her hands up. 'I am done.'

Morghanna stilled. 'What? What do you mean by that?'

Morrigan breathed hard and fast as she stared at her sister for a long moment before saying, 'I cannot do this anymore. I cannot watch you drive yourself into the ground worrying about things that are not true. I cannot pretend I am capable of helping you when I believe with every fibre of my being that this is a mistake, that our way of life has been destroyed. I cannot. I will not.'

'Morrigan.' She tried to grasp her sister's hands again, but Morrigan flinched away. Worry curdling her stomach, Morghanna rung her hands together as she said, 'Do not speak so. Please, let us talk about this. I know you are frustrated.'

Morrigan made a low, growling sound. 'Frustrated does not come close to what I am.' With a toss of her head, Morrigan turned and stomped away from the well where they'd been quenching their thirst. They'd been enjoying the warmth of the sun after a day's harvesting the lavender that was at the heart of Pack MacCrae's—and now their—future prosperity. They'd been chatting, enjoying a cool drink and the freedom of the outdoors, before one stupid and infuriatingly persistent Were-male came along—one more catalyst to set Morrigan off. Blast and double blast.

Morghanna took up her skirts and followed her sister through the lavender field. 'Morrigan, wait.'

'No.'

'Where are you going?' They'd had plans to go to the hot springs to bathe after their drink, but Morrigan was headed in the wrong direction.

'Away from here.'

'You are being ridiculous.' Morrigan had threatened to leave many times. Had stomped off into the forest around MacCrae Packlands countless times in the last six months but had always come back. Because the truth was, they had nowhere else to go. Nowhere safe at least. Not with the Church stirring up more and more fear and the Witch Finders scouring the lands for anyone they could call a witch to put through their trials—trials that meant torture and a horrible painful death. Morrigan wouldn't willingly put herself through such danger. Not after everything they'd lost. 'Go. Walk it off in the woods,' Morghanna said, softly, soothingly. 'I will wait here until you calm down.'

'Do not bother. I will not return this time.'

'Do not say such a thing when you cannot possibly mean it.'

'Do not tell me what I cannot possibly mean!' Morrigan said as she swung to face her sister, eyes sparking with an intensity and fervour Morghanna had never seen in her before.

Fear skated up Morghanna's spine. Her sister wouldn't leave her —would she? 'Please, Morrigan. Do not be like this. You know you cannot leave.'

'I have no choice.'

'Of course you have a choice.'

Morrigan smiled bitterly. 'Yes, you are right. I have the choice to stay and bind myself to those animals, as you and Bridgette and all the covens you have talked into your insane plan have done. Or I have the choice to find my own path. I choose the latter.' So saying, she turned and continued stomping off towards the heather-covered moors that lay beyond the lavender fields.

Morghanna's mouth moved over words and arguments as she hurried after Morrigan, but all she finally said was, 'If you think to go to our old home, you know you cannot do that.'

Morrigan stopped, turned, grief and pain a bitter flame in her eyes. 'Of course I know I cannot go there. I am not an idiot.'

'Good.' At least she knew she couldn't return to their family estate. It wasn't only that it was a ruin, destroyed when their grandfather, St John Cantrae, lost control of his power, the resulting fire destroying much of the rest of the village where the coven had lived for centuries. It was the danger that lay in wait for them there.

The Inquisitor would not forget and would be on the lookout for any Cantrae to show her face. They had only just escaped him and his Witch Finders by mere days when their parents had packed up their grieving people and fled the destruction, heading off into the wilds of the Lake country.

Their parents had gone the way of their grandfather a few years later. Rather than staying as they felt the build-up of their powers and taking the risk of killing more of their people, they took off one night deep into the Forest of Deane before their powers exploded. Even so, the explosion of their death had been felt by the rest of the coven at the camp miles away.

For some reason, the rest of the coven had looked to her to lead them. She'd had to put aside her grief—helped a little by her ability to see and talk to her parents when they came to her in spirit-form—and lead her people to safety before the Witch Finders heard-tell of the explosion deep in the heart of the forest and came hunting.

Her decision to meet up with her friend, Bridgette, and travel with her coven had been the only thing that saved them. Even so, they'd lived a nomadic life for years, never settling, travelling constantly, always looking over their shoulders—much the same as many covens had been forced to do.

Until the Pact with the Were had once again given them a home.

A beautiful home of lakes and mountains and forest and fields. A home that called to her soul.

She couldn't understand why Morrigan didn't feel the same.

Meeting her sister's angry and agonised stare, she pressed on in the hopes of making Morrigan see reason. 'But if not home, where would you go? To another coven?'

Morrigan snorted. 'Hardly. Why would I jump from one hell to another?'

'Then where? Will you live alone in the hills? Will you try to hide in a city and hope your power doesn't give you away? Think Morrigan. Do not make a rash decision that will put you in danger simply because you are angry.'

'I am not. I have felt this way for some time. But I do not expect you to understand.'

'Then help me. Understand.'

'I do not want to be here. I cannot be here. Watching you, watching all of you give away what is yours to these animals and do so happily ... it eats away at my soul. I cannot bear it. I cannot.' Morrigan turned away then, her shoulders hunched tight, skirts twitching angrily as she stomped down the row through the lavender plants. 'I cannot say for certain exactly where I will go, other than the fact that anywhere, even a place dripping with Witch Finders, is better than here. Anywhere far from these animals and your Pact is better than here.'

Morghanna halted, her sister's words and the passion she had said them with hitting her in the chest, momentarily stealing her breath, her words. But desperation to stop her sister from going, from putting herself in danger, had her moving again, rushing to catch up with her Morrigan's long-legged stride, uncaring that she damaged the plants they'd spent the day nurturing in her rush. 'There is nothing but the mountains and highlands that way,' she said, her voice a breathless puff.

'Sounds perfect.'

'Morrigan, stop,' she shouted, fear overriding the need to be sensible and gently reassuring.

'I will not. I have been stopped for too long. Now it is time I take flight and go.'

Tears prickled her eyes, she said, 'Be reasonable. Things will get better. I promise. We just have to give it time.'

'It has been six months since you forced us to come here and bound our coven to this pack!' Morrigan stopped, pivoted, forcing Morghanna to come to an ungainly halt. 'I am not being unreasonable. I am finally setting myself free. It's something you should think of doing. Come with me.' She held out her hand.

Morghanna gaped at her. 'You know ... I cannot do that.'

'Why? Why not? There is nothing for us here.'

'There is everything for us here if only we are patient enough to carve it out for ourselves. It is why I need your strength—'

'Agh! No! I cannot hear any more of this. I am leaving.' She continued to trudge out beyond the field of lavender onto the thistle- and heather-crowded moor, seemingly unaware as her skirts caught on the brush and bramble she crushed under her sturdy boots.

'You will ruin your skirts going that way.'

Morrigan whipped around once more, brows a thunderstorm on her face. 'You think I care about ruined skirts? I can fix a tear with my magic. What I cannot fix is this ...' She pointed back to the pack's village with an angry jab. 'This doubt, caused by them. It is a constant sore within you, worrying away, making you unable to see things for what they truly are. It is hell, you know that? This "safety" you and Bridgette created for us all is actually hell.'

'It is not hell. It is necessity.'

'You and those animals you have tied yourself to can have your "necessity". I will have none of it. I will not be pawed and treated like property. I will not share my power with those who are undeserving of its beauty. I will not be stunted when I should be allowed to grow.'

'Nobody is stunting you, Morrigan. When you join the Pact, you will see that your power is still your own. It is just more ... manageable. The bond with the pack gives us a freedom we have not had for a very long time.'

'That is a lie. You and the others who have stupidly tied themselves to this Pact of yours have no choice but to give those animals power so they can stay in control. That is not freedom and I will have none of it. My power is my own and no-one else has a right to it.' She stepped back, chest heaving, nostrils flaring. 'I am leaving.'

'Morrigan no.' She tried to grip Morrigan's hands once more, as if she could keep her there just by holding on, but her sister flung her hands up as if to fend Morghanna off. Hurt a slash in her chest, she took a steadying breath and said, 'You know you cannot be out there alone. It is not safe for our kind.'

'It is safer out there than it is here at the mercy of those animals. Besides, I will not be alone.'

'What do you mean?' Everyone they knew, every family member, every coven they'd ever met with, were now tied to the packs throughout this country and across Europe to the great icy plains of the land that stretched far north and east of Europe. 'You have never been anywhere I have not.'

Something canny crossed Morrigan's face. 'I am not a fool. I did not wish to tell you of this, but I also do not wish you to cause you more worry than you already have. I will not be alone because I have been in touch with those you and your precious Bridgette abandoned: those whose magic was not deemed strong enough to tie into the Pact; those who were covenless; the Hedge witches; the Wiccan. All of them left to fend for themselves. Why do we need saving by these animals if the others do not?'

'Morrigan. You know it was not like that. Bridgette only tied the covens to the packs because it is our power that is most unstable, most likely to place us and others in the most danger. She did it to save us, not to reject others with a claim to magical powers. If they wish to join us, they are more than welcome.'

'Bridgette? Save us?' Morrigan's face twisted. 'She did not save us. She made us slaves. And I refuse to be a slave.' Morrigan swiped her hand down, as if cutting a bond—although, there was no bond to cut. She had not made the blood bond with Pack MacCrae and therefore was not tied into the Pact as yet. Morghanna had hoped she would be able to convince her sister to join them now that things had settled down somewhat, but Morrigan was so stubborn, clinging to the belief that they were giving away something important rather than gaining something essential.

And Morghanna had nothing but her belief as proof that she was right.

'I am not a slave,' Morghanna said softly, chin raising. 'I chose this freely.'

Morrigan poked the air in front of her. 'If you had, you would stand your ground with that Alpha and make him rein-in his horny Were. If you had, you would not doubt your ability to hold the peace.'

Morghanna's mouth opened and closed as she struggled for words. 'My doubt has nothing to do with the rightness of the Pact.'

Morrigan's face became a sneer. 'If you truly believe that, then go and be with the creatures you so love. But do not expect me to stay and give up all I am and all I believe. I will not allow myself to be used and abused by anyone ever again.'

There was so much to say to Morrigan about that, but the stubborn jut of her sister's chin indicated there was no way to get her to listen. Not now.

Instead, she asked softly, 'What do you expect to accomplish with those you say we left behind? What can they give you that we cannot?'

'They will offer me shelter and safety while I do what you and Bridgette could not.'

'And that is?'

'I will find another way to save our kind. We should never have tied ourselves to these beasts. Mark my words, it will bring nothing but grief.'

'You are wrong. We simply need to work things out.'

'Goodbye, sister. Go join your kind and leave me to join mine.'

Before Morghanna could beseech her further, Morrigan waved her hand, transforming into a raven as black as night, the sheen of blue and green and purple feathers a gleam in the sun as it lifted into the sky and flew away.

3

The sun hung overhead, indicating it was after noon. Hunger gnawed at Alistair's stomach and his entire body was chilled to the bone even though the rain had ceased just before dawn. He wanted to stop, to build a fire—he was a practiced woodsman and would be able to find some dry kindling somewhere—but even the thought of stopping had what felt like shards of lightning spike through his head, making his wolf leap against the shield once more after hours of silence.

He dug out the last of the food the farmer and his wife had sold to him and ate it as he walked; as he'd done all through the night. The food was barely enough to sustain him; not that the voice cared beyond driving its power through his muscles and bones, giving him what he needed to keep going.

It had never been this bad before, had always at least let him sleep through some part of each night, allowed him to stop to hunt and eat. 'Why the urgency?'

'You must get there before it's too late.'

He blinked. It had answered him again. 'What is too late?'

It simply nudged him forward along the trail. A trail that told him others had travelled this way with reasonable regularity before him. Too narrow and steep for a caravan of goods, it was nevertheless a well-trod route. It gave him hope that he might find some form of civilisation on the other side of the mountain and that it would be the end of his journey. For if it wasn't, he'd have to find work somewhere to replenish his empty coin pouch.

He crested through a narrow pass.

And gasped at the view that lay before him.

Another loch lay in the valley below, glistening in the sun. A large village nestled near the shores of the loch—the civilisation he'd speculated would be here. Manicured fields of what looked like mostly lavender spread away from the loch on one side of the village towards the moors that lay in the distance. There were other fields, obviously farmed, that probably supplied vegetables for the village, with an orchard between the fields and the gentle forest that skirted the mountain he stood on.

A perfect idyll.

Was he headed there?

'Towards the forest.'

A surge of energy shoved through his body, lengthening his stride, making him hurry towards his objective. It was here. He was certain of it now. But if not the village, then where? How could the forest be his goal?

Then he felt it; the power of the old place the farmer had mentioned. It was an ache in his bones, setting his teeth on edge. It was a thrum in the air, urging his magic to prickle at his fingertips. He curled his fingers into his palms, dampening the spark threatening to shoot from his hands. He'd never lost control like that.

The power of this old place was nothing he'd ever felt before. It was not just old; it was ancient.

His destination? Yes. He was most definitely headed that way.

So this *was* about his magic. The flutter of hope he'd tried to ignore, that he was perhaps headed towards his dream woman, stilled. He rubbed his chest at the ache of its loss even though he'd never believed it true. His wolf howled at his sadness but did not try to break free of its cage.

He sighed his relief. 'If you behave yourself, I will remove the shield.'

His wolf whimpered its acquiescence, and as soon as he withdrew the internal shield, it rubbed against his skin, as if to soothe him. He almost stumbled, startled by its unfamiliar gentleness.

He blinked rapidly and focused on the forest that was his destination.

It was unlike any forest he'd walked through before. Lighter somehow, as if touched by eternal spring or summer, with trees showing leaves in colours ranging from spring green to autumnal fire of deepest red and vibrant orange. And those leaves, their rustling was almost musical as they swayed in a non-existent breeze.

Strange.

But not the only strangeness.

The scent of wildness he had sensed on the other side of the mountain was stronger here. Much stronger—it seemed to be lifting from the loch-side of the woods and also came from the village. There were Were in that village! It was never something he'd come across before. His mother's pack had lived in caves, as had the other packs he'd managed to evade over the years. How had these Were come to live in what looked to be a moderate sized and prosperous village?

Even stranger was the electric tingle of magic all around him. He'd thought its source the old place, but while the power from there still sang through the air, a different kind of magic flowed alongside it; a living, moving flow that he had only sensed when near his father's people.

Witches and warlocks lived nearby.

Mingled along with the Were if he was to trust his senses.

By the Gods, maybe there was something wrong with him and his senses because this was impossible. Covens and Were didn't mix. If he knew anything from what he'd gleaned from his parents' relationship and what had happened to him and his siblings after his parents were murdered, it was that the covens and the Were, while not exactly enemies, certainly did not like or trust each other. It was why he and his brother and sisters had never found a safe place to stay; were never taken in by either their father's people or their mother's.

So how was it that he could sense both here now? Living side-by-side?

'You have so much to learn. But not yet. First you must go to the meeting place.'

'What meeting place?'

The voice didn't answer, just pushed him on in a direction that was not down towards the village or across the mountain towards the forest that skirted it where the old place lay.

For the first time, he was thankful that the urge did not seem to want him to head that way. Whatever was down there to discover, he was certain of one thing: he would never be accepted there.

He was a one-off. An aberration. An abomination. And after what had happened to dearest Sophie—he swallowed hard at the memory of what his youngest sibling had become, what she'd tried to do to Frederique and Amandine—he couldn't blame either the Were or the covens for thinking such.

He lost sight of the village as he walked through a cleft that led him towards the hills at the base of the mountain and the forest that covered them.

Wherever the urge was leading him, he was close. So close. Energy surged through him and he began to run as he reached the end of the cleft, his boots slipping and sliding on the shale and moss-covered rocks, his wolf-nature the only thing enabling him to keep his balance and not fall.

The sound of running water tinkled on the air, an inviting song. The urge drew him towards it. A sense of something magical trembled over his skin, making his wolf whimper again inside him. He braced to fight it, but it did nothing more than brush gently against his skin and settle, as if content to wait.

Wait for what?

Then he came upon an open space where the source of the running water was made clear.

Two springs; one set higher, its waters tumbling into the other just below. Hot springs by the feel and scent of them, the minerals in the water lifting heavily all around him, covering his ability to smell much of anything else.

The compulsion surged, pushing him towards the lower spring. He stopped on the rocks on the near side. His wolf whimpered in his chest.

It wanted to go for a swim.

So did he. He was filthy and sweat-covered and his bones still held the chill of walking through the storm yesterday and into the night. And he was so exhausted, the energy shoved into him by the voice gone.

He drew to a stop, bracing for the pain he knew would come.

It didn't.

Instead, a buzzing under his skin replaced the compulsion to move, the power sinking down, as if anchoring him in this place.

'Here. This is where you need to be. Stay here until ...'

'Until what?'

'You will see.'

He stared around him. This is where the voice had forced him? To hot springs in the middle of the Scottish Highlands? What of the old place? Was he wrong to think this was about his magic?

His wolf grumbled.

It was right. Pointless to question why when right now, he had a moment of freedom to do the thing they both needed. Maybe the voice had finally accepted he did actually need to rest and revive; that its boosts of power were not enough.

He dropped his pack and stripped off his clothes, leaving them in a pile on the stones on the edge of the spring—he would wash them and lay them out on the grass to dry, but first, he wanted to rid himself of the chill of yesterday and wash the dirt of travel from his tired body.

He took a breath and dove into the spring, glorying in the warmth of the water as it engulfed him.

MORGHANNA TRIED CALLING to her sister for the fiftieth time since Morrigan had flown off, but to no avail. She'd never been much good at mind-speech, even with a familial link to help her, so it was doubtful that she could reach her sister over the distance she must have flown by now.

She clenched her fingers in the rough material of her work apron. What was she going to do? Without the Pact, Morrigan wasn't safe. A powerful witch with more than the couple of gifts that most of their kind were given by their Goddess—a sign of just how blessed by the Goddess she was—Morrigan had helped so many people with her magic; magic that, if not tied into the packs, might one day explode out of her, not only killing her, but those she was trying to save. Just like St John's power had destroyed their home, like their parents and their cousins and Morrigan's childhood friend had been destroyed, each violent explosion of power forcing them to move once again to keep them safe from those who were afraid of them and their magics —so afraid, they burned those they thought witches at the stake whether they were or not.

She and Morrigan and Bridgette had led the covens to ever-more isolated places even in the midst of their grief, until the catalyst that had been Bridgette's husband had changed everything.

He'd taken his life and the lives of every one of their Council of Elders with him when he'd lost control of his magics. But rather than simply being a profound tragedy, it had signalled the end of their acceptance of the hand the Fates had woven for them. It had spurred Bridgette, Morrigan and herself to find a solution, to make sure such senseless loss of life never occurred again.

How had Morrigan gone from being the greatest advocate of change to this? Maybe if she'd been the one to stumble upon the injured Alpha of Pack McVale as Bridgette had done, then things would be different.

Morghanna shook her head. No, they wouldn't. It was a stupid, useless thought. Only Bridgette would have looked at Ioan McVale and seen what must be done. Only Bridgette was strong enough to doggedly keep going despite the many and various difficulties and dangers until it was accomplished.

Accepting the Pact and what it gave them had not been easy for either side. So much mistrust, so many misunderstandings, had lain between their two peoples. But after years of negotiation and struggle —and the luck of having Ioan McVale's strength and support behind them—it was done and now the Pact smoothed the way between them; a way to share power and save them both.

Despite what Morrigan thought, it was good. For both Were and coven. It had created a conduit of understanding and a way to heal the rifts time and misunderstanding had created. Things were by no means perfect, but she and Bridgette and the other leaders of the covens were working with the Alphas and their lieutenants to sort through the issues, to set rules and new laws to be passed down and obeyed by all. Her gifts had been truly helpful in this process at least, allowing her to commune with the spirits, to cross boundaries of language, to discover shared experiences and find ways forward. But there was so much more she needed to do to make sure those new laws would be obeyed.

She wasn't sure how she'd become Coven Leader to the second largest pack in Scotland and the British Isles after Pack McVale—but she was and she needed to learn how to cope and do a good job. It did not matter to those who looked to her for leadership and guidance that she had so many doubts; that the job was meant for one who had more than her limited talents.

She sighed. Morrigan was wrong about her strengths and ability to do this job, but she wasn't wrong about their struggles. The problem was, she just didn't know how to fix the issues. They seemed beyond her right now. She needed help.

Perhaps it was time she spoke to Bridgette about her troubles here. She'd put off bothering her friend with this—Bridgette had enough worry on her shoulders right now, with every coven and pack looking to her for strength, leadership and guidance. But after this blow-up with Morrigan, she really couldn't put it off any longer.

Besides, maybe she wasn't the only Coven Leader coming up against these issues of sexually aggressive young Were. Not to mention the issues of blending multiple covens such as the one she was now leader of. It had proven a task in itself, with so many of their people mistrustful of outsiders and grieving the losses which had decimated their numbers. That on top of dealing with the bonding with the packs had to be giving others trouble as well, surely?

But then again, she'd hate to find out she was the only one unable to deal with these issues and misunderstandings. She knew for a fact that Bridgette's relationship with the Alpha of Pack McVale was a much closer one than what she herself shared with Iain MacCrae. Possibly helped by the fact Bridgette had mated with her Malcolm, a Pack McVale Healer. That would certainly go a long way to bridging gaps.

She sighed deeply. But finding a mate at all wasn't an avenue open to her. Not with her powers being what they were.

Also, Iain was a very different Alpha to Ioan McVale. Iain could be strangely reticent and prickly. Understandable given his past. He'd lost all of his family except his son. Even his mate. If Morghanna understood the mating process right, it took an incredible strength to outlive one's mate. Usually Were did so because others were counting on them. Which meant Iain had to have a deep commitment to his people and their needs.

Why hadn't she thought of that before? It gave her something to appeal to, despite his prickliness, to help make matters better. Yes. She wouldn't bother Bridgette with this yet. First she would work on forming trust with him through their shared need to do best by their people.

She only hoped he would listen. No. She had to make him listen.

'Morghanna, are you okay?'

4

Morghanna looked up to see Dougal, the Alpha's second, standing at the edge of the field, a hunting party behind him. They were back already? They were usually gone for at least half a day. How long had she been standing there calling to her sister uselessly?

Shadows of late afternoon marched across the land so she'd been standing there for at least an hour. Damn.

'I'm fine,' she said, smiling brightly as she walked towards Dougal. 'I see your hunting went well.' She nodded at the stag slung over his shoulder and the game the other Were carried.

He smiled his easy, generous smile, deep dimples creasing his cheeks. 'It did. We have enough to feed our people for the next week.'

Our people. The way he said it so easily—it made her smile. Here was at least one other person who didn't think the Pact a massive mistake.

If only he were the Alpha and she got to work with him. She had a feeling none of these issues would be happening if he was in charge.

But no, that wasn't fair. Iain had his own set of pressures that

Dougal did not. Shoving her useless wishes aside, she said, 'I look forward to eating fresh meat for a few days.'

'As do we all.' He brushed his slightly too long mop of dark auburn curls back from his high brow with his free hand then gestured at her. 'You should come out of the sun and have a rest. You look hot and dusty.'

She glanced down at her torn skirts and lavender- and dust-flecked apron. 'Actually, I might go up to the springs and bathe.'

'I will tell Iain and the Council.'

She wanted to tell him not to but saved her breath. The Were were insanely protective of what they thought of as theirs. It was both comforting and incredibly frustrating. Just one more mountain for her to climb with the changes that needed to be made if this was to work for them all.

Instead of arguing, she simply nodded.

'Enjoy your bathing,' he said before turning to his men. 'Time to get this lot to the butcher hut. If we're to feast tonight, these stags and rabbits will need to be dressed and prepared for roasting.'

His words made her stomach grumble a little. Perhaps she should go and get something to eat first, and a clean change of clothing?

But instead of following the males to the village, something compelled her to turn around and head in the opposite direction, back through the field towards the hills where the springs lay.

She tried not to wince at the damage she and Morrigan had created when they'd raced through the lavender. If she were Annabella, she'd be able to heal the plants as she walked past, but there was no way she could do that with her talents, such as they were. She'd have to get the witch with her plant magic out here to heal the damage. Not a great use of Annabella's talent, but necessary if she was to stop the farming cohort from popping a vein when they saw it.

She sighed; the weight of all that her role entailed a heavy stone around her neck. The scents of hay and lavender and heather wafted around her but didn't calm her as they usually did. She wished Bridgette was back from her travels. Not that she could talk sense into Morrigan—the only person who'd ever talked Morrigan down was Abigail and she was unwell. Morghanna wouldn't put that pressure on the old witch.

Thirsty, she stopped at the well—there was no water she could drink at the hot springs. As she pulled on the rope to bring up the bucket, her mind spun over her confrontation with her sister. The real tragedy was that she'd thought Morrigan had started to listen. Then the young pushy male had begun his campaign and hadn't taken the hint quickly enough.

'Damn the devil and his crows.' And all too horny and pushy Were-males.

An image of Lachlan came to the fore.

She banished the thought of him, but not quickly enough. Her fingers tingled as her anger rose, inciting her power, spirits rustling and moaning around her, eager to help. Her fingers tightened on the rope. She could make them haunt him, to pay him back for his actions.

But no, she couldn't do that. Even though this had started with him. If only he'd taken the hint that she wasn't interested, maybe Morrigan wouldn't have ended up so tied in knots when any Were so much as looked at them—or any of the coven's female members.

An ugly sensation skittered over her skin as she thought of the last time she'd been caught alone with Lachlan. If not for Morrigan coming along when she had, Morghanna hated to think what would have happened next. He'd been so close, staring at her lips, looking for all the world like he might just grab her and kiss her and who knows what else. Morrigan had been furious, but Morghanna refused to let her sister say or do anything about it. It was her problem to deal with.

Of course, too much else had landed in her lap—an illness that struck the elderly; a fight among the Were and coven members in the farming cohort about whose harvesting processes were best; and multiple meetings with the Council to sort out the new laws to help rule them into the future—and she hadn't got around to talking to either Dougal or Iain about Lachlan's behaviour.

Now Morrigan was gone and it was too late to talk it over with their Alpha. Not that talking with him would change behaviours overnight. Especially given he was part of the problem with his 'boys will be boys' attitude.

Still, she should have done more.

She would do more.

But how could she let Morrigan know if her sister didn't want to be found?

Purple and orange sparks flickered over her hands, the sharp tingle of them pleasure and pain, making her let go of the rope. The bucket fell, the splash a moment later distant and echoing.

Not so long ago, a surge of magic like that would have sent her into a fluster, but since the Pact had come into effect, there was no need to panic—although the memory of it pulsed through her veins, making her heart pound a little harder. Taking herself in hand, she took a few deep breaths and sank inside her mind. Even angry with herself and Iain, she would use the bond to channel her power into him, giving them both freedoms long denied.

The new link, their saviour, glimmered like a pulsing rainbow inside her mind. Pouring the excess power into it, she felt the buzz of thanks that came from the Alpha she was joined with through the Pact, sensing as the power distributed from him to his pack.

Morrigan might call it a chain, but the bond created by the Pact was freedom. Freedom for the covens and freedom for the Were. Bridgette had been so clever, creating this beautiful symbiosis that allowed excess power to be passed from witches and warlocks to the pack they were bonded to. They no longer had to be afraid of their power building and building until it was out of control, and the power they channelled into the pack gave the Were control over their change. Control they'd not had since the Darkness—an evil parasitical being they still knew so little about—had infested them long ago beyond any remembering, blocking them from the true symbiosis they'd once shared with their wolves.

The Pact had driven out the Darkness with the power of Bridgette and their Goddess combined, saving Were-wolf-kind and the powered from the unjust fates that had been mistakenly woven for them.

Free. They were free. And here was the proof, in this moment of sharing, of release and relief. If only she could make Morrigan take part, she'd see for herself. But she may as well wish for a forever love for herself for all the chance that would have of occurring.

She sighed in relief as the dangerous build of power gave one final tingle before being sucked into the link and sent to those who could use it positively. A howl lifted in the distance. She smiled. The joy in the sound and the pleasure in the giving gifted a clarity that had escaped her moments before.

She would give Morrigan a week or so to cool down and then she would track her. She was certain one of her coven mates, gifted in ways she was not, would help. Leanna was proving to excel in scrying, using both water and crystal as a medium. She was certain, if she found her sister, she could talk Morrigan into coming home—as long as she'd sorted the issue with the pushy Were-males. But she would; she had a plan now.

And after ... well, she'd just keep persevering with her sister, trying to get her to accept the Pact within herself and bond to the Were. If she did that, Morrigan would immediately see how wrong she was.

The joy of the power-sharing left her, warmth sliding away with it, leaving a prickling cold on her skin despite the warmth of the late-summer sun.

Sad and suddenly tired, she pulled the bucket up, slaked her thirst then continued on to the springs.

She made her way back towards the forest where the path led past the Dance and up to the springs, walking alongside the cooling stream as it wound through the copse of ancient rowan and wild cherry trees, the colours of their leaves even more vibrant after the rains that had come through last night. She picked some cherries and ate them to take care of the hunger pangs in her stomach that the water hadn't taken care of. Their delicious, slightly tart flesh filled her mouth, the juice dripping down her throat as she chewed. Her stomach grumbled its pleasure.

When she'd had enough, she continued on.

It was cooler under the trees, a gentle breeze whispering through her hair, drying the sweat on her skin as she made her way through the forest and up the rise of the hill to the hot springs. She took long, deep breaths as she walked, enjoying the peace and quiet and sense of freedom being there brought.

Her coven had made a haven of these woods since coming to MacCrae Packlands. She'd insisted the village be built near them— Iain and his people had thought to stay in the caves they'd lived in nearby, but it was one thing she'd been firm on. They needed to build a new life together and building a village with houses and shared spaces for them to use was essential to that. It had been remarkable how quickly the cottages and other buildings went up when the pack had accepted the idea. The Were were a resourceful and self-reliant people, utilising the local timber, slate and stone, to create a lovely village for them all to call home. Her people had helped where they could with their magics and it had all come together in a matter of months.

It was one thing she was proud of in what she'd accomplished so far.

That and her insistence her people needed their own spaces on the land the pack had claimed as theirs centuries ago. There had been little to no argument when she suggested the coven have free and unfettered access to the woods, stream and springs that lay behind the coven's side of the village, which had surprised her until she realised that was where the Dance lay. The Were were superstitious about the ring of stones and the magics that lay there and tended to avoid it at all costs unless they had to go there—which they'd had to when the spells of the Pact were canted and the bond created between her coven and Pack MacCrae.

She really should try to allay the Were's edginess in regard to the stone ring, as there were times they would have to come and be a part of various festivals and worships there if they were to truly build a strong connection. However, right now, she was reluctant to do so. The coven needed places to go that were theirs alone if they were ever to feel at one with this new life. It was just wonderful that the warm springs lay in the rocky hill beyond the Dance. It gave the coven a place to bathe and melt away the stresses of the day and find their centre in a place that felt so very close to the Goddess.

She needed a bit of that now to help shore up her determination to confront Iain with the problem of his over-sexed Were.

She made the climb up the last of the slope, through the narrow, steep defile cut into the stone by thousands of years of rains and wind, determining to think no more on her problems. The hot springs should help soak away her concerns at least for a little while.

She pushed through the last of the bushes, hands raised to undo the fastening of her dress at the back of her neck. She was so looking forward to ridding herself of the day's dust, grime and sweat. Nobody else would be up here at this time, so she would have the place to herself. A rare treat indeed.

She broke through the bushes edging the springs and came to a shocked halt.

The springs weren't empty. A man was in them. A strange man she'd never seen before.

He stood under the fall of water that fed from the hotter spring a few metres from where she stood. His torso was bare and glistening in the sunshine, strong sun-browned hands lifted to scrub hair the colour of the night sky touched by dawn. She must have gasped or made some sound because he swung around.

If she hadn't been pinned to the spot already, she would have been as his gaze collided with hers.

Holy Goddess, those eyes! They were like fractured bits of the sky seen through a green canopy of spring leaves, a combination of vibrantly light blue and green that seemed to glow as if lit from within. Her breath caught as she drank in the sight of him, his chest, his remarkable eyes set in a face of slashing lines, bracketed by the darkest of dark brows fringed by thick dark lashes. The lashes were pretty, but the eyes and the face were not. Wild, untamed, brimming with a sense that he was only moments from violence.

She stared at him.

He stared at her.

Neither moved.

Everything faded to nothing—the rushing drum of the water as it hit the pool around him; the chirping of the birds; the dappled sunlight that shifted in time to the dancing breeze around her; the scents of grass and mud and heather—as if the world held its breath, waiting, waiting, while something of the utmost importance came to realisation.

Him.

It was him.

A sound left her throat as she let her arms drop to her sides.

At the same moment, he began to stride through the water towards her, his gaze never leaving hers.

'*C'est toi.*'

The words, said in a low, slightly husky voice, caressed her, making her shiver, touching something deep inside her that ached and lurched towards him. Her eyes flickered down to his full lips, a delicious blush pink against the darkness of his close-cut beard.

Muscles rippled across his chest and arms as he hoisted himself onto the rocky ledge that bounded the pool on this side. Her gaze flickered down his length as he straightened, his naked skin shining in the late afternoon sun with the kind of healthy glow that suggested he was not averse to going sky-clad.

Power radiated from him, edged with something else she didn't recognise. He was a warlock, but that wasn't the entire story. She couldn't pin it down, could only see the flare in his aura that suggested there was something untapped, something hidden.

He stopped an arm's reach away, waiting.

Her skin tingled at his close proximity. She ached with need.

She lifted her hand to touch his face, stopped a breath away from his skin. He stared at her, nodded. Her fingers brushed over the stubble of his beard. Breath punched out of his parted lips, tangling in her hair, warming her skin despite its coolness. But it wasn't the only marvel. The tingle on her skin turned to a delicious prickle that raced over her as she traced the strength of his jaw, the warmth of his skin. 'Oh.'

He raised his hands to touch her face, paused. She nodded.

Breath exploded out of her as his hands covered her cheeks, fingers pushing into her hair.

Heat and dizziness rose through her as she stared up into his astonishing eyes, as if the world had just turned inside out before falling into place.

'Who are you?'

He spoke in French, her gift allowing her to understand him perfectly. And yet, she was captured by his deep voice, closed her eyes to savour the shivering rightness of the sound.

'Who are you?' he asked again, this time in heavily accented English.

She opened her eyes, smiled. '*Je m'appelle* Morghanna Cantrae,' she replied in fluid French. '*Et toi?*'

'Alistair Sinoir.'

'Why are you here?'

'For you.'

'Of course.'

They were both speaking in French now, and he didn't seem surprised that she had slipped into his dialect. Just as she was not surprised that he had come here for her. Because she suddenly knew —this had always been meant to happen.

She had dreamed of him for years, coming to her, binding with her, loving her, making her feel strong and safe combined. It was a dream she'd always held onto for a few glorious minutes upon waking before reality crashed down on her, making her put aside the sense of belonging, of oneness she felt in the dream, knowing it a foolish fantasy. It had been drilled into her that finding that kind of love was unlikely to be her path. Those with powers like hers rarely partnered. The ability to see and converse with the spirits often led to madness or to a kind of instability that meant practitioners of spirit magic couldn't let go of their emotions long enough to let another in. And so, she had never expected something like this. Had tried to make herself believe she did not long for it.

Yet the dreams were true. Here he was. Looking at her with a sense of recognition that suggested he too had seen her in his dreams.

His thumb stroked over her lip.

She trembled, closing her eyes momentarily, hoping when she opened them, he wouldn't evaporate as the dream image always did.

'I am here,' he said, his deep, husky voice a soft caressing rumble.

She opened her eyes.

He wasn't a dream. The shear physical impact of him had never fully come through in the dreams, nor the jolt of sensation his touch sent trembling through her, the heat of him, the fresh, manly scent of him. She'd never dreamed those things.

He *was* here. In the flesh. And she had nothing to fear. Not with him. This, what she felt now, was right. It was good. She could trust her emotions to him. Because he was everything.

She tried to imbue that trust, that belief, into her touch as she traced his cheekbones, his brow, but it wasn't enough. So she slipped her fingers through his hair and pulled him down to her.

Their lips met.

Everything exploded inside her, surging up and out, a riot of heat and sensation that stripped her to her core and laid her bare for him.

Only him.

She pulled back and stared into his amazing eyes.

'It *is* you,' he said.

'Yes.'

Their lips met again and the world around them ceased to matter; the only feeling, his touch; the only scent, his masculine, earthy one; the only warmth, the one he created in her.

She'd never been a person comfortable with touch, except with those she loved and trusted. She'd thought that love, that passion, was not for her, afraid to risk losing what so many she cared for had lost. But in this moment, as Alistair stripped her dress from her and laid her down on the soft moss-laden grass, their clothes a cushion under them, she realised she'd been waiting for this, for him, all her life.

Alistair.

The only man she could ever be with because his love was strength, not insanity.

5

Alistair's mind was still in a whirl as he ran his hands over Morghanna's slender form, her skin a soft, silky warmth under the roughness of his fingers.

Her. It was her.

The woman from his dreams.

Was she what the voice had been leading him to? It seemed impossible. Every time he'd thought it on the journey here, he'd pushed it aside—a hope he'd never truly let himself hold.

More likely he was dreaming now. It was possible given how exhausted he was.

But ...

He could smell her, hear her breath, the beat of her heart, feel the warmth of her slender fingers as they stroked across his face, the swell of her hips under his palms. She was here in front of him. Telling him her name. She'd never done that before.

He cupped her face. 'Morghanna.' Her name on his lips felt right, felt true. As true as her smile as she stared up at him.

She wasn't a dream but a reality. Even the ethereal quality, an air of the otherworldly about her that he'd always thought proved she was but a fantasy, was present in her as she looked at him with such longing that it punched the air from his lungs.

Even while gasping for air, everything fell into place. His entire life made sense. The voice had been right. The compulsion that had made him keep going. The dreams. They had all led him here.

To now.

To her.

To this: her in his arms. Touching him. Kissing him. Driving him through madness to a kind of clarity that had never been his before. He should be afraid to touch her—was afraid of hurting her if he lost control of his wolf's animal violence—but he couldn't stop himself. The need was greater than the fear. Besides which, his wolf suddenly seemed strangely content to just be.

He didn't have time to think about the strangeness of that as she nipped then kissed his neck where his pulse ran riot, the sensation of her mouth on his skin causing every thought to skitter from his mind. He groaned as she kissed up to his chin, her hands a fever over his back, her little sounds of pleasure driving his passion higher. His cock flexed against her moistness, harder and larger than it had ever been before.

Holy Goddess, if he didn't join with her soon, he was going to explode.

But she was not ready. He could feel it in her touch, in the untried press of her lips against his. So innocent.

But no more innocent than he when it came to this. Many a man would laugh at him for that fact, but how could he have chosen other than he had? How could he have trusted himself and his wolf with this kind of raw passion? He couldn't.

And yet, he realised suddenly that with her, he didn't need to worry. It was an impossibility he couldn't quite encompass, but he couldn't deny the gentleness with which his wolf looked upon their Anna. His wolf hummed inside him, the need to care for, and be careful with her, a song in the wolf heart of him.

He could even wait if she thought it necessary.

Pulling back, he took her face in his hands once more, looking deep into her eyes. 'We do not have to do this now, my treasure. We have time.'

'I do not want time. I want you. Now.'

'You are untouched. I do not want to hurt you with my passion.'

She laughed, snorted actually, then brushed his face with her fingertips, her thumb caressing his lip. 'You too are untouched if I am correct.' He dipped his head, embarrassed, despite his previous thoughts, to hear the truth of it on her lips.

But her hands firmed on his cheeks as she angled to look into his eyes. 'It matters not to me. In fact, it feels right that it is so. Does it not for you?'

'It does.' She was right. There was no need to be embarrassed. It was a special treasure he would hold to his heart that she would be the only female he would ever share this intimacy with. Yet ... 'What of the pain this first time? There will be none for me but there will be for you.'

Her smile softened. 'There will always be pain the first time. You cannot change that.'

'It will be better if you are ready.'

Laughter again in her eyes. 'Oh, I am ready.' Another stroke, across his chin, down his throat. 'But I am certain you can make me even more so. Just as you did in our dreams.'

'Really?' He arched his brow, enjoying her playfulness. Surprised by his enjoyment of it—he'd never been the playful type—but wanting more. Much more. He ran his hand down her body, brushing over pebbled nipples, across the soft skin of her stomach and into the curls that hid the treasure at her core. Warm and oh so wet. His lips twitched in satisfaction when she arched, rising against his stroke, a moan escaping her full lips. 'You may be right.'

She opened her eyes, a smile once again lighting in them alongside the fire of passion and desire. 'Oh, I am.' Her hand was suddenly on his cock; he twitched against her, a deep moan rumbling in his chest, his throat. 'It appears you need no help yourself.'

Her grip tightened and he thought he might explode then and

there. 'Hell, treasure, you have to let go or this will end faster than either of us wishes.'

'You would take care of me none-the-less.'

'Yes.' He would. He wanted to taste every inch of her and he would. But he also did not want their first time together outside of the dream to be restricted to hands and mouths. He wanted to meld his flesh with hers, to be one. He wanted to take care of her needs first, before claiming his own.

She moved her hand and he thought he was going to have to pry her fingers from his throbbing length, but he stilled as she guided him to her wet entrance, tipping her hips so he slipped a little inside. 'I do not want you to take care of me, though. I want us to take care of each other.'

'Yes.'

'Join with me, my Ali.'

Her Ali. He liked that.

'Be one with me. Show me what I thought never to have.'

He frowned—why would she also think love was never to be hers?—but she moved again before he could voice the thought and he slipped further inside her. The hot, wet tightness of her stole his questions; threatened to sunder his control. A control he'd always prided himself on. A control that had helped him to keep his siblings fed and sheltered and as safe as they could be. He'd never let go of that control before today.

He didn't want to let go of it now. 'Stop. Slow down.'

'How can I do that when it is you?' She shifted, frowned. 'Do you not want me?'

Oh, she was the devil's handmaiden sent to torture him. Such delicious torture though. Smiling, he said, 'You know I do. More than my next breath.'

'I want you too. I never knew I could want so much. It hurts.' She sounded bewildered.

Merde. His control slipped once again. He grasped at it, even knowing it was too late. 'I do not want you to hurt, treasure.'

'Then put me out of my misery, Ali. Make me yours so I can make you mine.'

'Anna,' he breathed. 'You undo me.'

'I am already undone.' She moved again and he slipped further inside.

A delirious, extraordinary sensation of rightness overcame him and he could hold back no longer. And while neither of them had done this before in the flesh, they'd been together many times in their dreams. He knew her, what pleased her, what would make her moan and sigh. She knew the same about him.

Slowly, gently, trembling, he pushed forward, sipping her moan from her lips. Somehow, incredibly, it was so much better than in his dreams.

She stiffened as he reached her barrier. He halted, every muscle straining for completion, afraid to cause her pain.

Instead of crying out, instead of pushing him away, she gripped his buttocks and met him, eyes aflame with need, a need that caught him in its snare, that doused the rage that had been inside him from the moment his mother and father had given their lives to save him and his siblings from his uncle's fatal power surge. Suddenly set adrift from his rage, from his purpose, he was lost, not knowing where his next breath came from, let alone where he was supposed to go from here.

'Here, lover. I am your safe harbour. You need hide nothing from me. You need not always be strong with me. Give me your burdens and I will give you mine. Together we will be stronger than either could be alone.'

She was right. He knew it in his heart, his soul, her words a kind of prophecy shining through him, lighting him up, setting him free. Oh, but he did not want to be free. He wanted to tie himself in every possible way to this witch, to her bright light. 'Anna. Treasure. You are mine.'

'As you are mine.'

She pushed up and he sank deep inside her. She let out a hiss of breath, stiffening. He didn't move. 'Anna, treasure,' he breathed out, the words fluttering in her hair. 'Did I hurt you?'

Pulling back, she stared into his eyes. 'Nothing to signify, my love. It will pass.' Then she clenched around him, so tight.

He did not dare move for fear of hurting her further. 'I am in your power.'

'As I am in yours, Alistair-mine. Kiss me.' She pulled him down until their lips met.

As they kissed, she softened around him and he sank in deeper.

And as he did, revelling in the joy, he felt a separate joy—one that had burst into being the moment he clapped eyes on her. But he couldn't let his wolf have a voice right now. He couldn't let it take over. Despite the fact it wanted this, that it loved her in a way he'd never experienced in the animal heart of him before, not even for his siblings, he was still afraid it might hurt her. It wouldn't mean to—he knew that. It never meant to. But he couldn't take the chance it too would not be overcome in the moment. He pushed that thought at it and it retreated slightly, enough for him to know it was under control.

He really needed to hold onto his control. He did not know what could happen if he didn't, despite the fact his wolf was currently behaving as it never had before.

She moved her hips. He hissed with the pleasure and his wolf's joy pushed forward once more. 'No,' he ground out as the wolf quivered inside him, begging to be released.

'No?' Anna asked him.

Mon Dieu. He couldn't let her see that side of him. Not now. Not so soon. If ever. It was a miracle she hadn't already balked from him as most others did when they sensed the wild violence at his core. Although, the only violence in his wolf now was the violence of its joy. Maybe that was why she hadn't yet balked from him or shown fear. But she would. It would come and he must delay that time for as long as possible. So instead of explaining the duality of his nature and that his 'no' had not been for her, he asked, 'Are you certain you are ready for more, treasure?'

'I am certain. Can you not feel how certain?'

He could. Her smile against his lips told him as much; as did her internal muscles clenching around him, pulling him in further. He couldn't help it, he moved, sliding in, then out, making her hiss and hum with the pleasure of their joining. And as he moved, melding with her in the physical, their powers began to play, dancing, shivering over their skin as he surged in and out of her.

Her legs and arms twined around him, pulling him in, holding him close and secure. Their lips met, breaths mingling as they gave the other the essence of their soul.

He cried out as her orgasm surged, his control gossamer threads around him. He tried to grasp at them but it was too late. She'd caught them. Caught him. It was there, deep inside, the link that had drawn him here solidifying, strands that were the broken parts of him melding with the broken parts that were her, becoming one strand, as strong as any metal ever forged.

A remarkable light glowed from that strand inside him, inside her, pulsing from one to the other, feeding their orgasms.

Strangely, he did not feel depleted by it but energised. More energised than he'd ever been. He lifted his head to the sky and let out a howl of pure joy—his wolf surged forward to add its voice.

No, no. He couldn't let it out! He withdrew from her, the suddenness of his action causing her to moan in protest. There was a stab of pain in his chest, as if he'd torn something inside.

'Shh, shh, Ali. All is fine. I should have realised when I first saw you. It is so plain to see now. I love you. All of you.'

'You do not understand,' he ground out, knowing he should instead be returning her words of love.

'Of course I do. Let me see him. I can feel he wants me to.' She stroked his face, his neck, his chest, settling him, sending the panic scuttling away.

Confused denial caught in his throat. She knew?

Of course she did. She lived with Were. He'd not noticed it in the shock of seeing her, of holding her, of being with her, but the scent of them was all around her.

However, it didn't matter that she lived with the Were in that village. She didn't understand. Couldn't. His wolf was different. Once she saw, once she understood the truth, she would never look at him the same. Not when faced with the wildness in his eyes, the violence that lived in his heart. Nobody but his mother and father and his siblings had ever been able to see his wolf without fear. And even Amandine and Frederique had at times been scared after what happened to Sophie.

But before he could say any of that, his wolf pushed forward, slamming against his control. A rainbow light shimmered around him.

Merde! Not now. This couldn't be happening. It would hurt her. It was too excited, its joy too violent a thing to control.

He scrambled to gain back his dominance over his wolf but it was a lost cause. No matter how he tried to use his power to push the animal back down, to build the shield to cage it as he'd done before, it was no use. His shield was but threads, washed aside with the greater need of his wolf; it wanted to be seen.

No. Don't hurt her. Please don't hurt her.

The pain of the denial was hot spikes through his bones, pushing out of his skin. He couldn't stop the half-howl, half-scream erupting from his lips, echoing into the sky.

He had to get away. Had to leave her before she saw. Before she ran screaming from him.

He moved to pull away. She caught his face, knowledge and understanding shining in her eyes. 'Do not hurt yourself so, *le sang de mon coeur*. Let me see him. He is an essential part of you and I love him too.'

Her words! *Mon Dieu*, her words; they knitted the torn thing inside him back together.

His fight was lost. The rainbow glow expanded and took him over, a wave he could no longer stand against. For a moment, he could see nothing but the glitter of colours across the spectrum, and then he saw the world through his other eyes. Saw her through his other eyes.

Intense hunger surged through him. Fear skittered across his nerves. He knew she could feel it—the bond between them vibrated almost painfully with his hunger—but instead of running away, she simply sank her hands into the fur on either side of his face and rubbed her cheek against him. 'Beautiful,' she whispered. 'So beautiful.'

Her acceptance and love rushed over him, making him tremble. And as he trembled, the reason for the hunger became heart-achingly clear.

His wolf, that part he had denied space to unless useful—because it reminded him of what little Sophie had become, not to mention those who had caused her violent, tragic death to play out as it had—was starving for love, starving for affection, starving to belong. Its violence, its wildness was a product of *his* behaviour, not part of its true nature.

Mon Dieu. What had he done? He'd hurt his wolf and hurt himself in keeping it under lock and key. A hurt that would have continued, would have driven them both insane, if not for her.

Morghanna.

She had repaired that which he hadn't even known was broken. With the bonds of her love, she had set him free.

He lifted his head and howled into the sky, the sound of joy joined by her laughter as she wrapped her arms around him and made him—all of him—feel loved and alive and accepted.

He was home. Home.

6

Morghanna laughed as her lover, her mate, leaped and danced around the edge of the water. Her heart was full of his joy. She laughed again when he came over and nuzzled her neck, sinking her hand into the softness of his fur, tugging him closer so she could bury her face in his neck and breathe him in.

Pine and sunshine and mountain air. That's how he smelled. She would always recognise him by his scent—so intrinsically him, now a part of her. If she sniffed her skin, his scent would be mingled with hers. As it should be. As it always would be.

She pulled back from him, holding his large wolfy head in her hands and stared into the glory of his incredible eyes, wolf and man so indelibly intertwined that they didn't change regardless of his form. How had she not realised what he was when she'd first laid eyes on him and looked into those spectacular eyes?

So incredibly rare and precious.

Just like him.

She smiled and stroked her hands over his head again and again until he made a huffing sound. One full of contentment and happiness. She leaned her forehead against his. 'I thought I would never have this joy as mine. Why did you take so long to find me?'

She did not expect a response, but in her mind, she heard, *'I did not know you were real. I thought you a figment of my imagination.'*

She sat back with a jerk, frowning at him.

'What is it, my treasure?'

That voice in her mind again—his voice. 'You can talk to me.'

'What do you mean?'

'Apart from the fact I've never been good at mind-speech, the few other witches and warlocks I know who are mated to a Were say they can understand the feelings of their mates, but they cannot hear what they think when their mate is in their wolf form. Why can I hear you?'

'I do not know. I did not know I could be like this.'

She blinked at him. 'You did not know you were Were?'

He snorted, what might be laughter but was filled with little amusement. *'I knew. What I mean is, I did not know my wolf could be gentle in this way. It's always been wildness and violence. To be let out only to hunt or for protection.'*

Morghanna sat completely upright, a gasp in her throat. 'You denied your change?'

'Of course. You would too if you'd seen the monsters who came after us. Those who share my blood. They were killers. I thought I was one too.'

'No, that's not what I meant.' She shook her head, wonderingly. 'You controlled your change. Before the Pact. How is that possible?'

'The Pact?'

She stared at him again. 'You do not know of the Pact? Then what drew you here?'

'A voice came to me. It brought me here. To you.'

'A voice?'

He rubbed his head against her cheek. *'I have dreamed of you for years, but never thought you real. Then, about six months ago ... everything changed. The voice came. It spoke to me, compelling me to travel. I tried to ignore it—I had found my brother and sister a new home, a new family, and wanted to ensure they were happy and settled, but the voice would not let me. It forced me to move on and keep moving until I found myself here.'*

'Six months ago?' He nodded. 'That is when I used the Pact to tie myself to this pack.'

'I know nothing of this Pact of which you speak, only that I could not ignore the voice and its compulsion. I hated it for much of that time, fought it when I could, but now, I am so grateful it came to me. If it had not, I would never have found you.'

'I am glad it brought you here, whatever it was.' And she was, wanted to glory in it except his lack of knowledge of the Pact was disturbing. 'Your pack did not know of the Pact? I was certain we had reached all the packs when we put out the call. How could we have missed one?'

His shoulders moved in what could only be described as a shrug. *'I do not know if my mother's pack knew about it, nor do I care. They denied my siblings and me a home when we needed their protection most. Especially my youngest sister, little Sophie. My mother's pack can go to the devil for all I care.'*

'You are packless?'

He nodded. *'I do not need a pack.'*

'Even a Lone Wolf needs a pack.'

'I had my brother and my sister. They were all I ever needed. Until you.'

She looked deep into his eyes, saw the conviction there, the truth in what he was saying. She searched for the Packbond, expecting to find it alongside the mating bond where it should be. There was nothing there.

Stunned breathless, she searched deeper for it, but it really wasn't there.

How? It was inherent in Were law—they only survived when they had a pack. There was some kind of symbiotic connection that each and every one of them needed to live. Without it, they would wither and die, or become savage animals who hunted and killed those they'd once loved until they were killed by a Pack Hunter.

They surmised it was this connection that the Darkness had used to gain access to the first pack it came across; and it used that link to infest all packs the world over. It was that very connection that Bridgette had used to bind all covens to the Were and oust the Darkness into the nether.

How could Alistair have no Packbond? It was not possible. Unless ... 'Your family. They must have acted as your pack.' Although, generally, a single family wasn't large enough a source to act as a pack, and there was no visible link she could see within him to any outside person or people.

Slowly, he shook his head, his fur rubbing against her hand. *'Only my youngest sister was full Were like my mother. Frederique and Amandine took after my father, although their magics were nowhere near as strong as his. Or mine.'*

She gaped at him as the impact of his words hit her fully. When she'd dreamed of him, there was no sign of either his power or his wolf, just as there had never been any sign of her magics—it had been only him and her. Despite that, the fact he was so obviously a warlock the moment she'd clapped eyes on him had not been a shock. Nor had it been a shock when it became clear that strangeness she'd felt in him was his wolf.

But somehow, her mind hadn't put the two together until now.

He was warlock.

He was Were.

'How is this possible?' As far as she was aware, there had been no matings between the Were and the covens until the Pact was made. Bridgette's mating with her Malcolm was the first interspecies union she had ever heard of. Since then, others had mated, but it wasn't common.

Witches and warlocks mostly paired up with their own kind, very rarely marrying outside with humans, but mixed matches did occur.

The Were were different.

Were had always mated Were. It had been that way for centuries. They were now aware this had to do with the infiltration of the Darkness within them. As the wildness and violence of their animals grew more and more unpredictable, they had withdrawn from the rest of the world. Unwilling to hurt those far more fragile than themselves, they had shunned outsiders, humans and the powered alike. As the years passed and the symbiotic connection with their wolves became even more tenuous due to the Darkness' influence, the avoidance turned into a kind of hateful mistrust—especially of the covens who wielded powers to be afraid of.

So how had a Were and a witch mated before the Pact was created?

The Pact ... it had rid them of the Darkness.

The Darkness that was nowhere in evidence in Alistair.

Another stunning truth that held her motionless as her mind struggled to understand.

All Were had been touched and affected by the Darkness before the Pact.

Without exception.

Except, as far as she could tell, Alistair. For, despite the fact he'd kept his wolf locked inside him much of the time, it had been his choice. A choice he would never have had if under the control of the Darkness.

'Holy Mother Goddess and all her children,' she said, hands fisting in the fur on either side of his head as she stared into his eyes. 'Are you the ultimate cure to the Darkness?'

The rainbow glow surrounded him again and she stilled in wonder at its beauty, and then suddenly, she no longer held the wolf's head between her hands, but his human one. The bristles of his beard rubbed against her palms in a delightfully erotic way as he tipped his head to the side, his remarkable eyes glowing with all the power he held within.

She was so lost in his gaze, in the astonishing beauty of him, that she didn't at first hear what he asked her.

'Morghanna?'

'Yes? Sorry. What did you ask of me?'

He tipped his head to the side just like his wolf had. 'You have mentioned this Darkness a number of times. What is it?'

She told him briefly about the entity that had secreted itself inside all Were, had bound their change to the moon, creating a schism between human and wolf that had turned their wolf-nature violent and created fear of the wolf in the human side. She told him about the Pact and how it had brought the Were and their wolves freedom, as it had brought the covens a sense of safety and control they'd not experienced for a thousand years.

As she spoke, part of her mind worked over the miracle of the male in front of her and what that meant. Had that evil entity falsified all that mistrust between the powered and the Were because it had known the danger that one of mixed race—Were and powered —was to it? That a bond—a close, unchanging bond—could restore the true symbiosis of man and creature within them, creating a place of love and acceptance where its evil could no longer survive?

And if it had engendered such a mistrust between their peoples to make certain such a bond would not come to be, did that mean that it had occurred before? Was that why the entity they called the Darkness had fought against the Pact like it had? So hard it had almost killed Bridgette despite her incredible power and strength. If the Goddess hadn't come and imbued her with the power to thrust the threads of it out each and every time the bonding ceremony was performed, it might have succeeded.

Or had the Darkness only suspected what was possible in such a bond until this male in front of her, the first of his kind, the only proof of such a union and what a boon it could bring, came into existence?

'Your mother? Was she able to change at will?'

His head dipped. 'Umm ... *mais bien sûr.*'

His hesitation, and the fact he'd dipped back into French when they'd been speaking English since his change to wolf and back again, made her ask, 'Was she always able to change at will?'

He stilled for breathless seconds and then said slowly, 'Not until she mated with my father. She told me the mating enabled her to stop the change when the moon was full. Although, after a time, she stopped fighting that change because she noted her wolf was more settled when she let it out, showing a desire to protect rather than the insanity-driven violence it had shown before.'

'And after she became pregnant and had you?'

'She was no longer bound by the moon. She changed at will. And often did when we were at home.' He bared his glinting canines in what she interpreted as a smile. 'She loved her wolf so deeply. We often ran together.'

She stared at Alistair, eyes widening at the preciousness of this male she'd mated to only moments ago.

It was him. Her Ali was the very embodiment of the Pact.

His mother had found peace with her duality after his birth. The mating had helped, but his birth must have truly ousted the Darkness from her. His warlock and Were natures, in symbiosis from birth, gave the Darkness no foothold in him or anyone he was bonded to. It was probably what enabled him to survive without a pack as well. And also why he'd not been driven insane by the build of uncontrollable magics inherent in someone as powerful as he— and he was powerful. His power sang through their bond.

The enormity of what all this meant threaded through her, chasing frissons of excitement over her skin, through her nerves.

He hadn't needed the Pact because he *was* the Pact.

She couldn't wait to tell Morrigan—her sister couldn't deny the Pact after meeting Alistair. She sent a silent thank you to the heavens —the voice he'd heard must have been the Goddess bringing him to her, not only a gift of love for her, but the answer to all the problems she'd struggled against since being bonded to Pack MacCrae.

A gift. He was a gift. One she was never going to stop thanking the Goddess for bringing into her life.

ALISTAIR STARED down at his mate—such a wonderful word he never thought to use for himself—bewildered by the wonder in her eyes. But before he could ask her about it, a tingling sensation, a warning, had him spinning around into a protective crouch in front of Morghanna's naked form.

'Ali, what is it?'

She shifted as if to move forward, but he held his arms out as a snarl sounded in his throat. Skin zipping and snapping with the energy of the change that he just managed to hold back, his gaze collided with the shocked stare of the male standing across the other side of the pool. 'Who are you?'

The male's gaze roamed over him. Alistair's clothes were on the bush two paces away where he'd placed them to dry after washing them but he didn't move to cover himself. His nakedness didn't matter. Only protecting Morghanna from this man's prying eyes did.

But those eyes had already spied the form on the grass behind him. Something in the male's gaze shifted, became predatory, avaricious. Alistair's wolf bristled. He agreed. They didn't like this male and how he looked at their mate.

He took a threatening step forward so that the male's attention came back to him, the snarl turning into a growl as his wolf pushed forward into his throat, intent on protecting their mate from the gaze of this intruder.

'Lachlan? What are you doing here?'

His Anna knew who this was, but still, he didn't rise from his protective crouch. There was something about this male, and the sound in Anna's voice, that had his hackles rising.

Lachlan didn't answer Anna's question, instead just said, 'What have ye done to my bonnie lass, ya scrote?' His gaze lingered on Anna.

Alistair took another step forward, blocking the stranger's view, teeth bared, growl ripping from his throat. 'Do not look at my mate.'

Lachlan staggered back a step, as if struck. 'Yer mate?'

'*Oui.* My mate.'

The other male's teeth bared as a growl ripped from his throat.

The hackles on Alistair's neck rose further.

He was a Were. The first Were Alistair had seen since he'd been forced to kill his beloved Sophie. He must be from the village Alistair had seen in the valley—the one that had the scent of both Were and coven.

From what Anna had already told him, the Pact must be responsible for them living together. So, given she knew this Were, he must be from the pack she was bonded to. And while there was something about this Lachlan that set both his wolf and his nerves on edge, for her sake, he needed to step carefully.

He raised his hands and forced himself to stand upright from his fighting stance. 'Friend. Let me and my mate dress. Then we can come down to your pack and you can all see for yourselves the truth of my words.'

The male glared at Alistair, his growl becoming a snarl.

Alistair sensed Anna moving behind him but didn't want to take his eyes from the Were in front of him. He didn't need his wolf to warn him of the danger of such a move. 'Anna, get dressed, my love.'

She didn't reach for her clothes, just said, 'You are not supposed to be here, Lachlan. It is agreed this space is for the coven alone. You Were still have your own spaces in which to roam. So why are you here?'

'Ye werena in yer cottage this afternoon when I came back from my patrol. I worried and so followed yer scent.'

'Dougal knew where I was.'

He sneered. 'Ye are not Dougal's to look after. Ye are mine.'

A hissing sound escaped Anna. 'For the last time, I am nothing to you.'

He didn't answer, didn't even acknowledge her fury. Instead, his hate-filled gaze returned to Alistair before flicking back to her. 'Ye shouldna be fucking some doaty bassa. Ye belong to me. I laid claim first.'

Alistair stiffened, but then had to move to shield Anna's nakedness as she stood. She put her hand on his arm as she said quietly to him, 'I am not afraid of being seen sky-clad. Neither should you be.'

'I do not wish for him to see you this way.' Naked. Vulnerable.

She tangled her fingers with his. 'He has seen me such before, during the coven rituals. We are not afraid of our nudity.'

Alistair swallowed hard. His father had taught him the sacredness of going sky-clad for certain rituals—although he hadn't followed any of them, sky-clad or not, since Sophie had died. He had never felt like losing himself to the sacred gravity of celebration that was their nudity before nature and the Goddess. Not when that Being had so abandoned him and his family. That aside, it was a fight to stop the animal instinct screaming in his head that she was his to protect; his alone to see like this. 'You are my mate,' he managed.

'Shut ye geggie. Morry isna yer mate. She canna be.'

'But he is. What Alistair says is true.' Anna moved to stand beside Alistair, threading her fingers through his.

The other Were's nostrils flared, his lips thinning as he said, 'Fucking some bawbag Were who turns up unwelcomed and unannounced doesna mean he's yer mate.'

'But he is not unwelcomed,' she said, chin rising, shoulders squaring, a leader whose power was more than simply from the magics he'd sensed in her. 'I welcome him. I accept him into Pack MacCrae.'

Accepted into the pack? His wolf whimpered longingly at the idea, but he wasn't sure if he liked the sound of it. His mother's pack had denounced him and his siblings, had come after them threatening to tear them apart if they ever saw them again. And even if he could trust this pack with their coven attached and Anna at their head, how would he possibly fit into the structure and strictures of pack life? He'd lived too long the leader of his small family; the one who made all the rules and enforced them. The burden of responsibility and decisions for their little family squarely on his shoulders and his shoulders alone. Did he want to bow down before the Alpha of this pack when he was used to holding that position?

It seemed impossible he could ever be happy with that. And yet, the moment Lachlan said, 'Tha' isna yer right,' he suddenly wanted it more than he'd wanted anything—except Anna—if for no other reason than to prove her right and this bastard wrong.

'Of course it is my right,' Anna stated, head held proud, eyes flashing. 'You will welcome Alistair into our pack as a fully-fledged pack member and as my mate.'

'Nah, nah,' Lachlan said, his voice rising, face reddening. 'My father, Alpha of Pack MacCrae, is the only one who can welcome Were from another pack and accept yer mating into tha pack.'

'It is fine, Anna,' Alistair said, touching her arm, trying to lessen the rising tension in the air. 'I do not need for them to welcome me. All I need is to be with you.'

'No, it is not fine. I am Coven Leader of Pack MacCrae. If I say you are welcome, then you are welcome.'

'Ye canna—'

'I have the same rights as your father.'

'Niver. Yer meant for me!' With a howl, Lachlan leaped across the spring, the rainbow glow of his change glistening on the water as man became wolf.

'Lachlan, no!' Anna's magics surged forward—astonishingly strong Healer ones of empathy and calm. They struck the changing Were but they were not enough to stop the claws already stretched to tear at Alistair's throat.

No. Not his throat. Anna suddenly was in their path.

Power channelled through Alistair and he raised his hands. Warlock lightning flew from his fingers—almost completely opposite to the waves of golden warmth emanating from Anna. Bolts of blue slashed through the air to strike the wolf diving at them, hitting him in his chest with a deep, resonating thwack.

The wolf yelped as he was thrown backward by the blast. It didn't stop him though—he got back up almost immediately, and snarling, teeth bared, leaped back towards Alistair, killing intent in his eyes.

'Lachlan, no!' Anna cried again, her hands going up to grab Alistair's arm, trying to pull him out of the way.

He didn't budge, just curled his arm protectively around her, his other arm stretched out, palm raised, as he sent power forth in a way he'd never used before; all he knew was that it was instinctual in this moment to do so.

Silver and green bolts joined the blue.

Anna gasped as the attacking wolf stopped in mid-air, hanging there, his legs moving frantically as if trying to gain purchase, eyes rolling in fear as silver, blue and green energies cascaded around him.

Alistair wanted to laugh—the image was so comical. But Anna ducked under his outstretched arm to stand in front of him. Her cool fingers cupped his face, forcing him to look at her.

'Ali. You cannot hurt him.'

'He intended to hurt you.'

'The pack will never allow you to stay if you hurt him.'

'You think that worries me?'

'It worries me. I want you to stay. I need you to stay. Because I cannot leave.'

He clenched his jaw, staring at the Were fighting in the grip of magics Alistair hadn't known himself capable of wielding until this moment. Was it this place that had unlocked this power inside him, or his mating with Anna? Not that it mattered right now. All that mattered was his Anna and that he didn't want to upset her.

So, even though it rubbed him and his wolf the wrong way to let this donkey's arsehole go unpunished, with a flex of his fingers, he sent the wolf flying through the air to land in the deep end of the spring.

Water sprayed up over the embankment and waves lapped at the banks. Lachlan surfaced, scrabbling through the water, his bark-brown eyes wide with fear, breath puffing out loudly as he paddled to the edge and scrabbled out. He stood on the muddy bank, chest blowing heavily as he coughed out water, his dull grey coat dripping. He shook, then made a half-hearted attempt at a snarl, but when Alistair lifted his hand once again, he yelped and took off down the slope back towards the village.

7

Morghanna stared after the fleeing Were, her mind a shocked blank for a breathless few seconds. 'That was—' She burst out laughing.

'I thought you would be angry.' Ali stared at her in consternation. His expression only made her laugh harder.

'Are you okay?' he asked as she bent double.

She waved her hand at him. 'I am. Fine. It is. Just. That. Was. The funniest,' she gasped through her laughter, 'Thing. I have witnessed. For an. Age.' She plopped down on the ground, holding onto her stomach, the peel of her laughter ringing in the air around them.

Ali chuckled as he knelt beside her. 'I did not think it that funny.'

'Oh, believe me, it was,' she said through shuddering breaths. 'I should not ... be laughing ... but oh ... he had that coming.' The laughter left her as suddenly as it came and she frowned at where water still lapped at the embankment from Lachlan's recent struggles. 'You do not know how much he had that coming.'

'He will not cause trouble?'

She waved her hand. 'No more than usual.'

His brow furrowed as he looked deep into her eyes. 'He has caused you trouble?'

Her mouth cocked as she tried to find the funny again. 'You heard him. He fancies himself in love with me.' She made a face. 'He is a fool to think I would ever return his so-called love.'

'He seems a spoiled child.'

Her frown deepened. 'It is not even that. There is something ... missing in him.'

'Missing?'

'I do not know how else to explain it. There is just something ... not right.'

'That does not excuse his behaviour or why he gets away with it.'

She sighed. 'As he is so fond of reminding everyone, his father is Alpha of Pack MacCrae. Also, the females of the pack who are of an age have apparently been vying for his attention since he came of age —probably more to do with who his father is than anything particularly special about him. But the end result is the same: he is used to thinking himself irresistible.'

'Then why does he bother you with his attentions?'

She shrugged, as bewildered by it as she'd ever been. 'After the Pact was created and I was assigned to bond my coven to this pack, he decided he wanted me. It did not matter the feeling was not returned. He has made a pest of himself ever since.'

His brow raised. 'From his reaction, I think perhaps you understate the matter.'

She twisted her mouth, looking into his astonishing eyes. The bits of blue and golden-brown in the green, like fractured mirrors of the forest floor under speckled sunlight, still sparked with the power he'd just unleashed. 'You sound like Morrigan.'

'Morrigan?'

'My sister. We argued just before I came up here about the fact some of the younger male Were do not seem to be able to take no for an answer. She was always begging me to allow her to put Lachlan in his place, but I would not let her.'

'Why could you not use your magics to stop him? A quick slap of witch lightning would have stopped him in his tracks long ago.'

She looked down at her hands. 'My magics are strong for what they are—if I had not been so annoyed with his behaviour, I would have been able to calm him and send him on his way just now. But as for witch lightning ...' She shrugged. 'I do not have access to offensive-capable powers without the Goddess' aid.'

'But you used witch lightning now. I saw the colour of your power as it flew towards the bastard.'

'Did you?' Her gaze darted to his to find only truth in their depths. 'That is ... interesting.' Her gaze returned to where Lachlan had stood, as if she could still see the colours dancing in the air there. 'I was not aware my power, when used like that, had a colour. At least, nobody has ever noticed it has before. I wonder if you seeing it has something to do with the mating bond?'

'I think it more to do with the strength of your power.' She would have scoffed at that observation, except before she could he asked, 'What is your power? I felt Healer abilities, but there was something else.'

'Yes. Something else.' She screwed her mouth to the side. 'I am a Spirit-talker with a minor power as a Healer.'

'Spirit-talker?'

'Sounds fancier than it is. I can commune with and call on the dead; it helps me keep our coven connected to our past, as well as helping me to pick up other languages like I was born to them.' She let a smile flicker to her face. 'Hardly the sort of energies that could put the fright in anyone. Not like the astonishing power you wield.'

'Not so astonishing,' he said.

'I think Lachlan would beg to differ.' She snorted a little laugh and shook her head. 'By the Goddess, Morrigan would have loved to be here today and see you put him in the water like that.'

'Could you not have enlisted the aid of others in your coven with more offensive capabilities to stop him from bothering you?'

She sighed. 'Morrigan talked about doing just that, but I did not want her making trouble in the pack. The laws we are creating forbid us from using magic and spells on the Were; and they forbid the Were to use claws, teeth and Were-strength against us. Unless of course it is to help in some way. Or for defence.'

'Is that not what we did here?'

'Yes. But it would be a difficult argument to make at this point that a Were making advances they think perfectly reasonable on one of us is an excuse for us to use magic as a defence.'

'It sounds like you need to change those laws to cover pests like Lachlan.'

She shrugged. 'You and Morrigan agree there.'

'You do not?'

She paused before saying, 'Up until recently, no.'

'What did he do?'

She bit the edge of her mouth, unwilling to share the words that had hurt her at a deeper level than she'd ever admitted.

'My Anna. Treasure. I feel your distress despite your laughter over Lachlan's dunking. You cannot hide it from me.'

She made a cutting movement with her hand; she really did not want to tell him.

'Anna. Please.'

'It no longer matters now we are mated.'

'It matters to you.' He tucked her hair behind her ear, and gripped her chin in his large hand, tipping her face up so that she met his gaze. 'Tell me.'

'You cannot go after him. I did not want Morrigan causing trouble within the pack and I do not want you to either. Promise.'

'I promise.'

She swallowed hard, let out a deep breath. 'Very well.' Another breath to swallow down the bile that memory of Lachlan's words, the nastiness of them, always brought. 'He said innocent prisses like me always played hard to get. He called me a tease. Said he knew I wanted him because he could smell my attraction.'

What he'd actually said was something far more vulgar that still made her shudder every time she thought of it. She'd never been talked to in such a way before Lachlan.

'That was not all, was it?'

She bit her lip. 'No. He ... said what he said and then he grabbed me and would have kissed me, if not for Morrigan arriving home.'

A growl deep in his chest as he said, 'I think a kiss was not all he was after.'

She shrugged. He was probably right, but she didn't want to voice the thought. 'Whatever he intended, it does not matter. Morrigan's arrival stopped him.'

'I need to thank this sister of yours.'

'She is not here. She left just before I came to the springs. A small disagreement,' she said when his brows rose. 'But I hope, now that you are here, I will be able to talk her into coming back. She was angry with me for not putting my foot down and making our Alpha do something about Lachlan and the others who were becoming pushy with some of our women.'

'I can understand. I barely know the bastard and I want to kill him.'

Despite the violence of his words, his beautiful deep voice and beguiling accent filled her with a sense of love and longing she'd never experienced until him. But she couldn't let it carry her away, no matter how she longed to feel him inside her again.

Taking a calming breath, she said, 'No. Please. Do not make more of this than needs to be. We are mated now and with you by my side, I will be able to make Iain understand the impact some of his males' behaviours are having on my coven. So, you must promise not to take things into your own hands. You cannot use your magic on him again as you did today.'

'What about punching him in the face?' He growled low in his throat.

'Alistair. You promised.'

He stopped growling and bent to kiss her. 'I promised not to go after him for today's, or past, infractions, but if there are any other towards you, I may not be able to stop myself from doing what I did today.'

She smiled up at him. 'I doubt that will be a problem. After the mating has been accepted by the pack, he will no longer be able to think there is something between him and me.' She shivered. At least, she hoped he would see reason.

There was a tension in Ali's muscles as he wrapped his arms around her, tucking her under his chin. 'I was not brought up in a pack, so perhaps I am wrong, or perhaps it is different here, but my mother told me that a mating cannot be denied. Even her family could do nothing to her or my father once they were mated.'

'They did not let her and your father live with them?' She looked up at him, stroked his face, his distress at the memory a frisson deep in her bones.

'No. When I was growing up, I assumed they chose not to live with her pack and chose to live instead near my father's family and his coven. I never imagined it was because they did not accept us—their offspring.' His gaze turned brooding as he looked past her and into the distance. 'Not until they refused us.'

She stroked his back and kissed his chest, happy when his muscles relaxed under her touch. 'I promise, you will be accepted here.'

That sudden tension again and a cautiously asked, 'How can you be so certain? Especially after what just happened. What would make your pack take my word over his? He is most likely poisoning them against me right now.'

She looked deeply into his eyes, sensing hurt based in a deep sense of ... betrayal and rejection? She needed to get to the bottom of it—but not now. Now, she needed to allay his fears about joining the pack.

It wasn't easy to know the best way forward though.

If only the mating bond allowed her to read his mind. However it only allowed her to sense his emotions.

Oh well. She would just have to use what lay to hand.

Greedily watching his every expression to try to figure out if he believed her, she said, 'Your mother was right. A mating cannot be denied. Even Lachlan will have to accept it.'

A slight lessening in his tension. Perhaps she was wrong. Perhaps his worry over being accepted was all this was. She took his hands in hers. '*You* are my mate. There is no doubting it. The pack must accept you if they want me to stay. Mates cannot be separated. It is forbidden.'

'That may be the case, but that does not mean they will accept me into the pack. A part of me may be like them, but I am also different. I have seen and experienced too often how those who are different are treated, how they are rejected and abhorred. I will not live somewhere I am not fully accepted. I cannot.'

Ah, so she was right—betrayal and rejection were at the heart of the issue. Those were things she couldn't fix now, but she could at least allay one of his fears.

'I would never ask you to do such a thing. If the pack do not accept you, we will live away from them. It will have to be close-by to begin with—I cannot leave my coven without a leader. But when I have trained someone up and given over my direct bond with the Alpha to them, we can leave the area and not look back of that is what you need.'

'I could not ask you to leave your home and all you love for me.'

'You do not have to. The choice is simple: you are mine and I am yours. Wherever you are, so too will I be. All right?'

'But your coven? Even if you are not their leader, could you truly leave them?'

'If they do not accept my mate and see the beauty and gift that is at the heart of you, a gift to both our peoples, then yes, I could.'

His lips thinned. 'I do not wish to be the reason you separate from your people.'

She ran her hands back up his arms to hold his face and his gaze. 'You will not be. I only bring up these last resort solutions to help you to relax about what is ahead. But I say them knowing you will be accepted. We will never have to resort to leaving or even living slightly apart.' She held firm under his searching gaze.

'You are so certain.'

'I am.' She smiled as she brushed her thumb over his jaw. 'For you are the proof that what we have done and are trying to build is right. Your very existence is a blessing. I see it; so will they. And then, so will you.'

They stared into each other's eyes for long moments, then, at some unspoken agreement, hands caressed, lips found lips, taking the solace and comfort only they could offer each other, fuelling passion, deepening commitment.

8

The bond thrummed inside Alistair, strengthened by each touch, each kiss as he laid her back down on the soft grass. She didn't stay under him for long. In a swift movement, she rolled on top of him and took him inside her; one long, slow stroke.

The bond vibrated between them, growing even stronger as she began to ride him.

He stroked her breasts and rose up to meet her, the wonder of it, of her, striking him anew. This was more than he'd ever dreamed possible. But unlike any dream he'd ever had about family, about belonging, about her, this was real. And despite his reservations in regard to joining her pack, he would do so if it meant being with her; if it meant keeping her happy, and never letting this feeling go.

Somehow, he would make it work.

They reached their peak as one. Their magic twined together, releasing into the sky in a burst of colour and light that shimmered and rained down over them. Each thread and droplet of power increased the strength and length of the orgasm until trembling, sated, complete, they collapsed in the embrace of grass that had grown to pillow under them.

He wound his arms around her as she lay on top of him and they remained that way until twilight fell and cooled her skin. 'You need to dress.'

'Not yet.' She kissed his chest and ran her hands up his sides.

He gasped and shivered, his cock rising inside her. 'Are you not a little concerned that someone else will come looking for you, especially after hearing the tale Lachlan has undoubtedly spread.'

'None of the Were will venture here and my coven will know that I am not in trouble. Because of the Packbond, the entire pack cannot help but feel part of my joy, and while they will undoubtedly be curious to meet the source of that joy, both Were and coven will wait for us to come to them.'

'Are you certain?'

She laughed up at him, the sound a burble of joy that caressed him, making his wolf preen against his skin. 'Of course. It is mating law. The mated couple cannot be disturbed.'

'How will they know of the mating? I am certain Lachlan will not share that side of the story.'

Her smile softened as she tangled her fingers in his hair, before letting them wander down his neck to his chest. 'He will not have to. The Alpha will have felt our mating, as would many other strong members of the pack. As per mating law, now they must wait for us to complete our part of the bond before we go to them to be accepted as a mated pair.'

'Then why did Lachlan come here? Why did he doubt what we are to each other?'

She frowned, stopping her exploration of his chest to look up at him. 'I do not know nor care why Lachlan disobeyed pack law. If this were another pack, he would be punished for it but ...' She sighed. 'Iain has a weakness where his son is concerned.'

'Do we need to be concerned that Lachlan will return?'

She shook her head. 'Regardless of what Lachlan did or did not do in coming here, I am certain Iain will not allow him to do so again. We will be left alone here until we decide to go down to the village.' She brushed her fingers over the frown lines between his eyes. 'Do you not trust me?'

'Of course I do.'

'Good.' Her lips curled into a smile that had his cock flexing inside her once more. 'For I am not done exploring you.' Then she bent her head and pressed a hot kiss to his nipple, making him in a few quick licks and sucks forget all about the Were and coven in the village not so far away.

The purple of twilight faded into darkness around them. The air was cool but it did not matter. They were warmed by their loving and when that was not enough, warmed themselves in the pool. He explored every part of her body, discovering the way she writhed and arched and gasped as he licked her to orgasm, the way she wriggled and laughed when he sucked her toes, the little noises she made when he spent time loving her beautiful breasts, the way she met him, open-mouthed and hungry, when their lips met again and again, learning the secret taste of her, of him.

She explored him too, hands and lips and teeth and tongue tracing over every inch of him. And when she took him in her mouth and sucked him in deep, her tongue stroking up the side of his thick length, he couldn't help but howl to the rising crescent moon above them before spilling his seed into her mouth.

When he was done, he pulled her up to take her lips with his, tasting himself on her tongue. And with lips and hands and body, he thanked her for all she'd given him this day, this night, by worshipping her anew.

The stars had made their journey three-quarters across the sky as they fell asleep in each other's arms, the blanket from his pack pulled over them, replete, satisfied—for now—their bonding almost complete.

MORGHANNA STRETCHED, snuggling into the warmth along her front as light filtered through her closed eyelids.

It was morning. The realisation made her sigh.

'What is it, my love?'

She moved her head and met Ali's eyes. Eyes that shone in the early morning light. How could she not have realised he was Were when she saw him yesterday? It was inconceivable to her now that she'd missed it because it was a force that pushed out of him. It had probably led others to shy away from him, especially as it added to the sense of 'otherness' gathered around him by the enormous power settled deep in his skin. Both were so forceful but drew her to him in ways she could not yet explain. It was as if his power and his wolf were the missing parts of her. Parts she needed if she was to—

'Morghanna?'

'Hmm?' Oh right—his question. She smoothed her hand over his chest and sighed again. 'I was wondering how long we can stay here.'

'I thought you said they would wait for us.'

'They will. But I have duties to perform. There is a new baby who is due for a check-up and another mother due any day now.'

'Are there not others in your coven to take care of those duties?'

'Not now my sister has run off and our main Healer has been unwell. I am all they have. Well, not all they have, but our Healer apprentice, Leanna, is not confident enough in her powers yet to deal with either by herself, even though her Healer abilities outstrip mine by a mile.'

'How is it that you have so few Healers? I remember my father's coven had several major Healers and others with more minor Healer abilities.'

'We have a few like that as well, but nobody who could take over Leanna's training. And even if they could, she is very shy and reticent to use her powers, and so far, has only done so under my tutelage and Abigail's—but as I said, Abigail is unwell.' She really had to do something to encourage Leanna, but that was a worry for another time. 'That is not the only reason I need to get back. Today is the day our lavender harvest is to be bundled and sent to market and I must be there for the Council meeting to decide how much we wish to sell for and what is to be done with the funds. And there are other matters regarding the laws we are trying to put in place that we planned to go over today.'

She rubbed her forehead, frowning a little. 'Also, I have a class to teach later this afternoon. It was Morrigan's duty but since she has gone, I must take her place until I manage to allocate someone else to the task of teaching our young the basic cantrips and spell work to help them tap safely into their powers.' She tipped her head. 'Perhaps you will be able to help me with that.'

'I would like to, but I probably know less than your students.'

'Your father did not teach you how to tap into and use your powers?' Ali pressed his lips together, frowning. 'Oh, I am sorry. I do not wish to bring up bad memories.'

He grasped her hands. 'It is not a bad memory. It is just ... I have spent much of my time hiding my powers. Under Catholic rule, the people of my homeland have become increasingly suspicious of anyone with even a modicum of power. Besides, I had little time to practice what my father taught me. I have to admit that, before yesterday, I had not used my powers for some time. I am surprised they came so quickly to my bidding.'

'I am not,' Morghanna said. 'The power in you is immense and the way you used it ... I thought you well-practiced. But you tell me what you did was on instinct alone?' She shook her head. 'I cannot wait to spend time with you as you learn from the stronger practitioners in our coven.'

'You will not teach me?'

'I will teach you what I can, but without using the Goddess' powers at the Dance, I will not be able to instruct you on how to fully control and utilise your power—especially the offensive magics.'

'But do you not teach the children?'

'I do, but only the beginner spells and cantrips, and our histories of course. I would be able to teach you about the latter, but I think you are probably well beyond the former given what you did yesterday.'

'Oh.'

His disappointment in her lack cut at her heart. 'I am sorry I cannot help you like you wish.' She shrugged helplessly. 'I am what I am.'

He tucked his finger under her chin, lifting her face to his. 'I am not disappointed because I think your magic weak or whatever is in your head. I am disappointed because if you are not to teach all to me, it means I will not spend every moment with you.'

'Really?'

'Really.' He kissed her nose.

She blushed—why that made her blush after everything they'd done together, she had no idea—and said hurriedly, 'Well, I am certain, despite what you say, you can help me in the classes with our young. Your instinctual use of magic might be something that could help a few of them who have had difficulties tapping into their powers since the Pact. The usual cantrips and spells have not worked for them and Morrigan and the other teachers and I have been wracking our brains trying to figure out how to help them.' She clapped her hands and laughed. 'Oh, the Goddess knew what she was about when she sent you my way so that we could mate.'

'You think the Goddess sent me here?'

'Who else?'

He made a face. 'She has never done me and mine any favours before.'

She reached up to lay her hand on his cheek. 'The Goddess does not rule all, my love—she can only do so much.'

'In my opinion what she does do is not enough.'

His lowly uttered words, so full of vehemence, had her grip his arm tightly until he met her gaze once more. Softly, she said, 'Do not blame her for what befell your family. She cannot change the Fates' weavings any more than she can create them. What happened to your family, as what happened to many a family, is a tragedy that cannot be reasoned away by blaming She who is Mother to us all.'

'I am certain that is what she and those like her wish us to believe.'

'Shh, shh, do not speak so.' She put her fingers over his lips. 'You were not brought up in the Goddess' grace as we were, and given your history, I can understand your vehemence, but please, my beloved, can you trust me when I say the Goddess is not like that? You will see when you become a part of Coven MacCrae and learn what we have to teach. Especially when you visit the Dance with me at the next full moon.'

His gaze was fierce on hers for long, breathless seconds—was he going to deny the Goddess here and now and never try to understand their beliefs and take them on as his? She had no idea what she would do if he did—but then he nodded and she took in a deep breath, letting it out shakily.

'I look forward to learning what you and the coven wish to teach me. But as to your Goddess ... If it was She who brought me here, I am eternally grateful, but I will not forgive the cruelty in how it was done.'

'I am sor—'

It was his turn to put his hand over her lips. 'No. It is not you who should apologise.' He kissed her gently before pulling away. 'I may not trust your Goddess, but I do trust you. With my heart, my soul, my life. Is that enough for now?'

'Yes,' she said on a breathy sigh and lost herself to his kiss once more.

A crow cawed in the distance, bringing her back before she was lost once more to her desire for her mate. 'We should head back. There is much to do and we will lose much of this day in the mating ceremony.'

'Ceremony?'

'Uh-huh.' She smiled at the horror on his face. 'It is actually quite beautiful. Your mother never talked about it?'

'No. I expect she never thought it was something that I would experience.'

'Hmm.' If that was the case, she had grossly misunderstood her son. 'The Alpha welcomes us as a newly mated pair, bonding us anew to the pack and then there is a big party. He will also do the ceremony to formally accept you into the pack.'

'What if he does not accept me?'

'He will.' She rose up on her toes to kiss his lips, softly, lingering, finishing by whispering against them, 'Although, as far as I am concerned, you are already one of the coven so it matters little what Iain MacCrae does or does not do.' He stiffened for a moment and she pulled away. 'What is it?'

'I do not know if I can submit to another Were. Not even your Alpha.'

She closed her eyes, swearing at herself for being such a dummy. Of course! That was the other side of his issue about becoming one with the pack. 'I do not know what your mother told you, or the mistaken idea you had from your encounter with her pack, but while there is an Alpha, there is no submission. Everyone has a place and is an important part.'

'But what if I am stronger than this Alpha?'

'Then, in time, you will become Alpha. It is the way of things.'

'I do not wish to kill to become Alpha.'

She stroked down his chest. 'That is the old way. We are forging new ways. And you will be part of that movement into a more enlightened way of choosing leaders for both the pack and the coven. Your strengths will add to our strengths and will enliven us. I will have to take you to the Dance to figure out the exact nature of your magics, but even before we discover the full depth of your abilities, I know your power will be an incredible boon to our already-strong coven. Iain will not be able to deny that they will make our pack even stronger.'

'Even though I am untrained?'

'That is no matter. Others can train you where you feel you need training if I am unable. And, as I said, from what I saw yesterday, you have much to teach us about your power and how you use it. I have never seen power wielded in such a way before. You have more to give than I.'

He reached for her before she could turn away, staring deeply into her eyes. 'You cannot believe that is true.'

'I know my own weaknesses. My own failures.'

He shook his head, his fingers smoothing along her cheeks. 'When I look at you, all I see is a kind of gentle strength stronger than the strongest steel. I think you do not see yourself clearly.'

'I see myself as I am.'

He clasped both her hands in his. 'Then that will be my task.'

'What will?'

'To hold up a mirror and help you to see what I see. Because that woman should never doubt the incredible person she is.'

A breath shivered out of her at his words, at the strength of his belief in them that she could feel through the bond and into the heart of her. She could almost believe they were true. Almost. If she didn't know better. 'We need to go.'

'Do we truly have to go down now? Can it not wait a few more hours?'

Oh she wanted to give into him ... but she couldn't. 'It is not what I want but what I must do.' She pulled her tunic over her head. 'Even if others could take over my other tasks, as I said, the Council is due to meet this morning. I cannot miss the session. We are to talk over some nuances and changes to the laws we are creating so our peoples can learn to live together in a harmonious society.'

'The Pact does not make that happen?' he asked, pulling his breeches over his long legs.

'In part. But it is a huge undertaking to mesh two distinct groups of people together; people who, up until recently, did not have to answer to anyone but their own leaders. Now there are leaders from each group needing to work together as well as the leaders of each cohort under them not to mention the rest of our peoples who take their lead from us. It is essential we get it right.'

'What of the mating ceremony and my bonding ceremony to the pack? Won't they supersede anything else that is meant to occur today?'

'Yes. But unless we get down there in time, the meeting will go ahead without me, and I do not want Iain to bully my people into concessions they are not happy with.'

She moved past him to pick up her shoes from where they lay in the grass, but before she got to them, he caught her arm and pulled her around to face him.

She let out a little sigh at the look on his face; such love, such pride in her.

That pride showed in the smile that spread on his lips and reached into his eyes. 'So strong, my mate. They cannot do without you.'

She snorted. 'I would not go so far as that. I am simply good at reading our Alpha and when he is full of stubborn, Alpha-machinations. I might not be one of the most powerful, but those who know me call me all kinds of stubborn.'

That stubbornness was due to too many years of leading her people when they began to look to her after her parents died. She still hadn't figured out why they'd trusted her to find them safe places to stay and organised them into groups so they always had food to eat, material to clothe them and made certain the young were taught what they needed to keep their powers under some semblance of control. But they had and she'd fallen in to the task, doing what her mother and father had taught her to do ever since she was young to ensure the health and wellbeing of her people. She had stubbornness aplenty when it came to looking after her people.

Pity that stubbornness flew away when it came to standing up for herself. And in managing her powers in the way she should be able to after all this time. She let out a sharp breath as she glanced to the side at the spirits who had appeared without her bidding, gesturing for her to hurry up. 'And I also get some help.'

He glanced around. 'The spirits? Are they here now?'

'Yes. And they're telling us to hurry up.'

They finished dressing and headed down the hill towards the village. The springs were only a fifteen-minute walk from the coven's side of the village. As they walked, they were unable to stop touching, fingers linked, his lips finding her shoulder, her knuckles, her fingers brushing over his jaw, his hair, finding the corded muscles of his arms as she fitted herself against his side, his arm slung around her. Their strides matched, as if they'd been walking alongside each other forever. Every breath was filled with the scent of the other, their loving, the freshness of the morning air and something that was new, but she thought might be a scent that was of them. One that had come into existence only for them.

She wondered if that was what the pack smelled to confirm a mating. They could not see the link like she saw it, in her mind, strong and vibrant and golden and warm, a thick cord, threads of strongest silk wound together, stronger than the strongest metals. A bond that would grow in strength with each passing year—a thing unbroken by anything other than death. Lachlan might not like what had happened but there was nothing he nor anyone else could do about it.

She was mated.

They must accept Alistair.

It was law.

She glanced up at her Ali. He would come to know the Goddess as she did, to trust in Her, to know his importance in the greater scheme of things. And he would finally have a pack, a place to belong. The thought made her smile.

He must have felt it—he looked down at her and kissed her as if to sip the smile from her lips. She wanted to stop and sink into the kiss, to give in to the need to share her body with him again, to strengthen the bond that was already so strong.

'Ali.'

'Anna.'

She smiled. She loved the way he shortened her name, the sound of it in his slightly husky baritone warming her deep inside. She stood on her tiptoes to kiss the sound of it off his lips.

'Who the hell are ye, yer bassa, and what are ye doin' with yer hands on our pack's Head Witch?'

9

Morghanna spun around to face the disapproving scowl of the pack's Alpha. 'Iain.' She forced herself to smile brilliantly. 'I am pleased to introduce Alistair Sinoir. The newest member of Pack MacCrae.'

'The fuck he is!'

'Iain.' Morghanna moved in front of Ali, aware of the low growl emanating from him; a completely justified reaction given how Pack MacCrae's Alpha was growling at him—a fact she couldn't understand given Iain had to have felt the mating. 'Iain. You are being rude.'

'Growling at an unwelcome bawbag trespassing on my land isna rude.'

'Alistair is hardly an unwelcome interloper, nor is he trespassing.'

'Ye ken he was not welcomed here by me.'

'No, he was not. He is, however, welcomed by me.'

Iain turned his glower on her. 'Lachlan said ye'd given yerself to a stranger, but I didna believe it to be true.'

She stiffened. 'You trust what Lachlan says rather than what you feel to be true?' She took Ali's hand in hers and tugged him to stand beside her. 'Alistair is my mate, as you must well know. You could not have failed to feel it affect the Packbond.'

'Yer aff yer heid.' Iain sniffed deeply, eyes flaring as they flickered from her to Ali. 'It didna feel like any mating bond I've iver come across. It felt ...' He shook his head.

She didn't know what he was talking about. Although, maybe it was different because of Alistair's dual nature. Regardless, they were mated and she would not have anyone question the depth or truth of the bond. 'The mating is true. It is simply different because Alistair is not just Were; he is warlock too.'

'Impossible.'

'You know that is no longer true. What is true is that we have much to share with you and the other Council members. Which we will do after you have welcomed Alistair into the pack as my mate.'

'Tha' is no' how it works when the mate is from a different pack.'

'Alistair has no pack, so those laws do not apply even if they mattered anymore. The Pact overrides all laws that would ostracise any Were, witch or warlock who wish to join with a pack. The Pact seeks to strengthen us all. This means accepting more into the fold. You know this to be true. We are all connected by the need to survive, so Alistair is not an outsider.'

'He's no' a true Were. I dinna like it.'

'He is simply the first of a strong line of mixed blood—the powered and the Were—that is going to appear through the mixed matings that are already happening. He is proof that what we have done is right. That it will save us all. Iain ...' She stepped forward, gaze intent on his. 'He has never known the Darkness.'

His electric blue eyes—the eyes of an alpha—darted to Alistair then back to her. 'Tha' be true?'

'I would not speak it if it were not. So, you see the gift he brings us.'

Iain's mouth worked as he thought this over.

She wanted to shout at him. To shake him or hit him until he saw he was being rude and stupid and incompetent. Lachlan was to blame for this. She was sure of it. Although, not all blame could be lain at Lachlan's feet. Iain had never been able to say nay where his son was concerned. It had always frustrated her but now it made her furious. But this was too important for her to ruin with inopportune words or actions at this point. So she took a breath and kept her mouth shut until he'd had a chance to think things through.

Waiting killed her though.

Ali's hand tightened around hers—hells, he could obviously sense her anger—and she glanced at him, taking strength from the fact that even though this was not going the way she'd promised it would, he had done nothing more than growl. He trusted her to make this right. And she would.

She opened her mouth to start again but ...

'Yer our Head Pack Witch,' Iain blurted out. 'Ye belong to us.'

Oh good grief. Of all the possessive ridiculous things to say. But it was all she had to work with, so she took another, calming breath and said gently, 'I do. As you belong to me. Nothing can change that, thanks to the Pact—you know this to be true. You have seen it with Bridgette and Malcolm's mating.'

'She joined Malcolm's pack.'

'Which is what is occurring here. Alistair does not wish to take me from this pack. He wishes to join it. So the only change to our situation is that you get both a strong Were and a warlock in the pack and I now belong to Alistair, as he belongs to me. But that belonging, like any mating, takes nothing away from my bond to the pack. You know this to be true.'

'Hmph.'

She leaned into Ali, needing to feel him more securely by her side as she faced up to this stubborn Were so full of mistrust and fear—a not-unwarranted mistrust and fear given what the Were had been through at the hands of the Darkness. But they had all been through horrors and now must start anew. 'He is one of us, Iain. Welcome him to Pack MacCrae. Let him know he is home.'

'He is so strong.'

'A bonus to us all. His strength will strengthen us all.'

'No' if he's too strong. He has the smell o' Alpha about him.'

'I will not challenge you,' Alistair said solemnly. 'Not unless you give me reason.'

'Is tha' a threat?'

'No. Simply a part of my nature.'

'As it is for any Alpha,' Morghanna quickly butted in. 'Alistair only wishes the best for those he considers his. I am certain you understand that.'

'Is tha' what you meant?'

'Of course. I wish only to be with my Anna.'

'See,' Morghanna said brightly. 'Besides, his eyes have not turned blue, so there will be no problem.'

'I'm no' so certain abou' tha. Who knows what being of mixed blood does in tha' regard?'

'These are things we are all going to find out together. All I can assure you now is that Alistair's only interest is to be with me.' She glanced at her mate.

He nodded solemnly and kissed her knuckles. 'Very true.' He looked up at Iain. 'Besides, I do not wish the burdens you must carry. I have had enough of those kinds of burdens to last me a lifetime.'

Iain's mouth worked and he sniffed again, a resigned look coming into his eyes as his gaze returned to Morghanna. 'Lachie was so sure ye were meant for him, lassie.'

Ali stiffened. She stroked his arm, hoping he would take her cue to remain calm. 'I was never meant for Lachlan. There was never anything there.'

'Some matings take time to develop.'

'In rare cases, yes, but there is always a sign. A friendship or a deep abiding kinship. There was nothing like that with Lachlan. Not even friendship.'

Iain snorted. 'Lachie believes ought.'

'I do not know why. I have told him often enough. He is too stubborn to listen.'

'Aye, he is at that.' Iain's gaze roved over her face and up to Ali, his eyes narrowing a little. 'There is no denying what I smell e'en though the feel of it is no' what I am used to. Ye are mated.'

'So, you will welcome Alistair.'

Iain made a noise in the back of his throat, almost like a growl, but then he nodded. 'He is welcome.'

'Then welcome him.'

The muscles in Iain's jaw worked for a moment and then he wiped the sweat off his brow with his palm and held out his hand to her mate.

She had to nudge Ali forward to take Iain's proffered hand, but he did so, never letting go of her.

'With my scent I mark thee.' Iain pulled his hand away slowly, then spat on his palm and cupped the side of Alistair's neck. 'With my waters I mark thee.' He lifted his hand one more time, took the knife from his belt, bared his chest and made a shallow cut above his heart. He took Alistair's hand—she thought for a horrible moment that Ali would pull away, but thankfully, he let Iain make a shallow cut across his palm. Iain indicated Ali was to place that bloody hand over the cut on his chest. 'With our blood bound, I mark thee.' He lifted his other hand and pulled Alistair's head forward until their foreheads touched. 'With scent and water and blood, the holy three, I claim thee to Pack MacCrae. Ye are ours. Yer strength will be added to ours as ours will be added to yers. No longer Alistair of somat else, ye are Alistair of Pack MacCrae. Yer sweat our sweat. Yer waters our waters. Yer blood our blood. From now and forever more. *Fàilte.*'

'From now and forever more,' Alistair intoned, somehow knowing he was meant to—perhaps his wolf had guided him. Or perhaps her death-grip on his hand had told him what he must do.

There was a prickling in the air all around them, a surge of energy that wove around Morghanna and drove through her, making her powers spark in her fingertips, his powers sparking alongside hers. She smiled up at Ali. 'From now and forever more.'

Iain stared at them, eyes wide with shock. 'What the ever-loving-hells was tha?'

'The Goddess' benediction,' Morghanna guessed—for what else could it have been? 'There is no doubt this is meant to be. *Fàilte.*' She reached up and pulled Ali's head down to hers in a short, hard kiss that stole her breath despite the fact she was the one doing the kissing. Ali's incredible eyes were sparkling when she pulled away, and then, on a shout filled with pure jubilation, he picked her up and swung her around, their laughter weaving around them, a benediction of their happiness.

But he was forced to put her down as wolves and pack members in their human forms began to descend upon them, drawn to the power and mating they couldn't have helped but sense through the Packbond. The barrage of questions was overwhelming, but Iain soon calmed them as only an Alpha could, and Alistair and Morghanna were smothered in hugs and touches. Cries of *fàilte* lit the air to welcome their newest member and a miraculous mating.

Morghanna laughed and accepted their joy; however, she couldn't help but be aware that Ali didn't seem to be as caught up in it as she'd hoped.

It was going to take a little more time for him to truly feel accepted, but she would do everything she could to work to that end as quickly as possible.

ALISTAIR WASN'T certain what to feel as he was led to the centre of the village where tables were already being made ready. Some of the Pack wanted to start celebrating immediately, but Morghanna insisted they still go ahead with the Council meeting to discuss the issues they'd planned to talk through today.

'I suppose we can,' Iain said. 'It'll take an hour or more fer the pack to ready a celebration they deem worthy of our Head Pack Witch and newest packmate. Mayhap yer mate will want to stay an' help. It will allow him to get to know some o' the other males.'

'No. I want him to join me. It is his right as my mate.'

Iain's jaw clenched but he nodded and they both turned to Alistair.

He nodded and followed them to the Alpha Hall where all meetings were held, but he was torn. He wanted to do what pleased Anna, but despite the fact she said he would be accepted—he had evidence now that she had indeed spoken the truth on this matter, strange though it may seem. The pack and its coven had been excited and eager to welcome him earlier—however it was obvious Iain still struggled with how dominant he was. Not to mention the fact that the bond to the pack—which he was certain should have snapped into place, strong and sure, the moment he shared the blood vow with the Alpha, was not what he had expected. Certainly not what he sensed between his mate and the other members of the pack.

But what did he really know? He had no true experience of such things. He just thought it would be something similar to his bond with his Anna—maybe not quite as bright and vibrantly powerful, but still, a light of strength inside him all the same, especially given the sign that Morghanna's Goddess had approved the bonding.

Maybe his Packbond would strengthen over time. Perhaps that was one of the things he could research in the weeks ahead. It certainly wasn't something he would mention to his Anna now. He did not want her to worry that he didn't feel as connected as she wished him to be to this pack she'd bound herself to.

The other Council members greeted him warmly and offered him a place at the table given his status as Anna's mate, but he declined. He really didn't want Anna and the others to notice the looks Iain shot him when he thought nobody was looking. Not only that, he wanted to watch Anna as she handled this eclectic group of witches, warlocks and Were.

So, he stood in a corner to the side where he could see her clearly and watched. The discussions almost turned to argument on two occasions when trying to settle on the wordings of two of the new laws meant to guide them all into the future, but somehow Anna managed to defuse the sparks of disagreement before they could blaze to anger. He couldn't quite see how she did it. He did not feel the influence of magic, and yet, with a calm, steady voice, and a deft handling of the vastly different temperaments involved, she managed to bring them to agreement.

She was remarkable. A born leader.

He couldn't understand why she thought she wasn't strong enough for the role or necessary to the pack? From his observation, she was not only necessary, she was essential.

Anna had just said, 'Now, to the last point of business for today,' when a few female Were, made up of those who'd been the first to hug and congratulate him and Anna earlier, broke into the hall and announced the mating celebration was ready.

Two of the older Were females rushed forward and, grabbing his and Anna's hands, led them outside before anyone could gainsay them.

Rather than be annoyed her meeting was interrupted, Anna laughed, her joy a warmth in his soul he wanted to experience over and over.

A remarkable transformation had taken over the square, with tables set around it full of platters of food and tankards of drink. Bunting and floral arrangements had been hung from the eaves of the buildings that surrounded the square with strings of lanterns crisscrossing the space, ready to be lit when darkness fell. A fire-pit had been revealed in the centre of the square and a large bonfire was already lit, sending sparks into the air.

A mighty cheer thundered through the square as they appeared, hundreds of people gathered to wish them well—more than he'd seen in one place in some time. He had underestimated the size of the village; there must be homes hidden in the forest to accommodate all these Were and their coven.

They were led to a table at the bottom of the stairs that led into the Alpha Hall and seated in the place of honour at the centre of the table.

Soon after, with mugs and skins overflowing and platters of food making the tables groan, cries of *sláinte mhath* and *do dheagh sláinte* filled the air with their good cheer and with an acceptance he never thought would be his due.

And despite the fact there was still something odd about the mating bond, despite the fact he still didn't feel the connection to the Alpha he thought he would feel, at this welcoming—this acceptance of him into pack by not only the majority of the pack, but also by the coven who were bonded to them—the link firmed. It might have been a link made through sweat, spit, blood and vow to the Alpha, but now it was welded through willing acceptance, the strength of it wrapping around the mating bond, securing it further.

And as it did, he realised just how much he'd been missing. There'd been a hole there, one he'd managed to ignore, but now it was filling, he didn't think he could ever do without it. His wolf was overjoyed at the acceptance that was finally his.

For a moment, shame at how he'd treated his wolf slashed through him. But then Anna turned to smile up at him, squeezing his hand in hers, and the shame fell away and only happiness and contentment remained.

He turned to accept another greeting and couldn't help see Iain MacCrae standing just outside the circle of well-wishers. He wasn't frowning, but neither was he smiling as everyone else was. In fact, there was something entirely odd about the way the Alpha stood where he was, not part of the festivities he should be virtually at the centre of.

So, he still wasn't certain about welcoming Alistair into the pack.

Maybe it was simply because his son wasn't here. Alistair quickly scanned the crowd and couldn't see hide nor hair of him. Perhaps that was all this was. The Alpha didn't have a problem with him necessarily, just with how his presence upset his beloved son.

It was understandable, but quite frankly, both of them needed to get over it, because he wasn't going anywhere. And from the feelings he was getting through the Packbond, everyone else accepted him wholeheartedly and no Alpha worth his position would gainsay his pack's joyous approval. At least, he was certain that was how it must be, because given how the Alpha's aura was pulsing stronger with the joy of his pack, he needed their support in a way that was far more essential than simply a leader needing his people's approval.

As the celebration and joyful welcomings continued, the sensation of belonging grew inside him; and as it did the mating bond intensified and the joy inside him grew—his and his wolf's.

It was a bewildering sensation, his own happiness alongside his wolf's. He hadn't felt happy in so long, but to feel it on two fronts was dizzying. He didn't have time to parse over it though, because people —Were and coven—kept coming to the table to welcome him and wish him good health, offering him and Anna gifts to help them in their new home.

Home?

He looked at Morghanna and she nodded in answer to his unspoken question. 'Every newly mated couple are given a cottage of their own. Later this evening, they will lead us to ours.'

'It is already built? How did they know?'

She laughed. 'There are always a few cottages built in preparation for matings. When we take ours, another will be built for the next couple who are mated. You will be invited to help build it—it is a beautiful way to work with the pack and solidify the bonding. It is a tradition we discovered in a few of the old Pack Lore Keeper diaries, from before the Were began to live in caves. It is one of the things they were keen to embrace again, as were all the covens. Despite the hardships and horror all our peoples have endured, it is a reminder that not everything about our lives was bleak. That at one time, they lived openly and as a community, as did we.'

'It is a beautiful tradition.'

'It is.'

The impromptu celebration raged through the day and deep into the night. It was overwhelming at times, but his wolf helped him through it, seeming to be in its element, especially when he was invited to change with the pack's elders and lieutenants to howl at the recently risen moon before taking a lap around the village to discover its scents. He didn't want to leave his Anna, but she laughingly urged him on.

Just as later, when he was back in human form, she urged him to dance with her and with many of the other coven and Were females she introduced him to. He tried to keep their names straight but there were too many and when he mentioned to Anna he wished there was a way he could remember them all, she laughed and said it took her a month before she had all the Were's names memorised and he had twice that number to remember.

'Nobody will expect you to remember their names tonight. But tomorrow, we will start our visits and I am certain it will give you a chance to learn them in a less confusing way.'

'I hope so,' he said.

They ate and danced and drank and listened to speeches. Given he had nobody to speak for him, he was encouraged to get up and share some of his life with them all, which he did reluctantly, only sharing the broad brushstrokes. But what he did share led to many of the maternal Were females coming to hug him once more and offer their help and guidance through his transition into being a member of Pack MacCrae.

Then at some unseen signal, they were escorted through an honour guard of Were and coven to a cottage on the outskirts of the coven's side of the village—a two-story structure of wood and stone with flower boxes at the windows that sat either side of the red-timber front door and dormer windows peeping out from under the roof's thatched peak. A path ran up to the front door between garden beds that included flowering plants and herbs, and he spied a wood shed to the side at the back of the cottage and another building that could be a stable.

It was larger than the cottage he'd lived in the first eighteen years of his life, with room for the family he never thought to have.

Home.

Their home.

The first he'd had since a boy. He blinked away the moisture in his eyes. He wished Frederique and Amandine were here to share in this joy.

As the pack left them standing at the gate into their home, Morghanna turned to him. 'We *should* write to your brother and siblings and invite them to at least visit as soon as possible.' Once again, reading his mind, his emotions.

'I do not wish to disrupt the life they have built for themselves, nor take them from the baker and his wife. The older couple were so happy to claim my siblings as son and daughter and they cannot manage their business without Frederique and Amandine to help them.'

'Then perhaps, after you are settled within the pack and the coven is strong and sure enough to do without me for a time, we can journey to them.'

'You would do that for me?'

Her smile was of the sun, his sun. 'Of course. As you would do the same for me. But in the meantime, you can write to them. And I can write to Bridgette and ask her to check in on them when she is nearby.'

'Bridgette?'

'The powerful witch I spoke of earlier; the creator of the Pact. She is my dearest friend and the leader of our people. It is through her the Goddess channelled the power to defeat the Darkness and helped us all to survive.'

'Like you did.'

'No. I do not have her powers. She is the only one the Goddess has spoken with.'

'I thought you said you communicate with your Goddess.'

She tipped her head to the side. 'It is more communing with. Impressions she gives me, feelings that help to give me direction when I fail to find it myself. Which is often.'

'I doubt that.'

She pressed her lips together as she led him through the garden to the front door. 'You see me through the tint of the mating bond. That tint lacks the clarity to see my faults.'

He looked at her. 'Oh, I see them, but I do not think they are the failings you seem to believe them. My father used to say there was strength in every weakness, a light to brighten the darkest or dullest power.'

'Bridgette says something similar.'

'Then you should listen to her. She sounds like a remarkable and insightful woman.'

'She is.' Her eyes dulled for a moment, but before he could, through the mating bond, grasp a hold of those emotions causing that dullness, she had shoved them aside, or deep down where he could not access them, and smiled up at him again, a wicked delight in her eyes. 'She was the first of us to mate a Were. Though they have not had any children, so we did not know *you* were possible.'

He stared at her for a moment—how did she do that? Push aside her feelings as if they didn't matter? And do it in such a way that he could no longer sense the sadness in her; the longing for something more. No, not for something more. It wasn't that avaricious.

But because the feeling was gone, he could no longer figure out what he'd sensed in that moment. And, given what he did know about her, about the stubbornness she'd exhibited in getting him down here and bonded to the pack, then how she managed the Council in the meeting, there was no point in pushing her on it now. She would only deny and hide it further.

She seemed adept at that—was that another part of her power?

There was much to discover about his astonishing mate. Much to help her with in the burdens she carried. Much to do to help her see herself as others saw her—a powerful witch who was exactly the right person to lead their people forward.

Their people. He was starting to believe that might be true. Who knew, he might even win over Iain MacCrae one of these days.

'What is it, my love?'

He brushed his nose against hers before kissing the tip, then pulled back a little. 'I was thinking of what you offered. Where is this Bridgette of yours that she could contact my siblings?'

She pushed open the door and, taking his hand in hers, led him through the room that was kitchen and sitting room towards the stairs. 'She is travelling through Europe to meet all the packs and covens I brought into the Pact at her behest. She and her mate want to make certain they are settled and work through any issues personally. It is a difficult transition for many.'

'A fact I can understand. My mother's pack tended to kill first ask questions later of any strangers. Being bonded to an entire coven of them would be a challenge, even with their wolves no longer violent.

'Yes.' She guided him up the stairs. 'That is her worry, which is why she is travelling as she is. She is also making notes so that we can continue to expand on the new laws for all packs and covens to follow now and into the future.'

He shook his head. 'I cannot ask her to stop such important work to check on my brother and sister.'

'Of course you can. And she will be delighted to meet the family of the man I love. In fact, it will help her to stay where she is doing the work that is hers to do and not come racing back here to check you out and make certain you are indeed the one meant for me.'

'Protective, is she?'

'As I am of her. I was most uncertain of her mate at first. Before the Pact, contact between Were and the covens was … strained.' She made a rueful expression. 'But I need not explain that to you. However, I could not have been more wrong to be so suspicious. Malcolm is the most loving, caring male I have ever met—until you. He is a Healer, a true match for her. As you are for me.'

She turned to him, her hands going to the tie on his shirt, her deft fingers undoing the knot then finding the skin at the base of his neck, caressing. 'Be with me now,' she breathed against his skin as she pressed a kiss to his heated flesh.

A large bed lay behind her, twice the size of any he had seen before and covered with furs. He had never slept in such a sumptuous-looking bed in his entire life. Even before his life became one of sleeping on hard ground or the softer but prickling clumps of pine needles and ferns he made beds out of for his siblings, his bed had been canvas slung between hooks that could be easily packed away in his parents' small cottage. He couldn't help but stare at the wonder of the bed in front of him.

She turned to look where he was staring and then back at him with a sensuous, mischievous smile. 'Want to try it out with me?'

He tore his gaze away from the bed, his smile meeting hers. 'Yes.'

He picked her up, and in a couple of strides, fell onto the bed with her.

Her laugher lit the air around them as they bounced. 'Slow

down,' she said around her laughter. 'There is no need for such haste. We have all night.'

He pushed her hair back from her face and stared into her glorious eyes. 'We have all our lives.'

'Yes. Show me how much you love me.'

He proceeded to do just that.

10

Alistair knew it was a nightmare but he couldn't wake from it. Images of people burning and screaming, a mob howling for pain, for death—scenes seen all over Europe and the British Isles as witches and non-witches alike were burned at the stake—seared into his mind, making him shake and sweat. Smoke rose all around him, choking him. He coughed, darkness descending ...

The nightmare images moved, shifted, flashing to him and his Anna, to them locked in the grips of a desperate fight against a terrible foe he could not see.

Despair hung in the air like a heavy miasma. Bodies lay all around them; the building they stood in was but a ruin, dust and ash still rising into the air from its destruction.

Above them, something black and roiling and evil spread like a fog, its tendrils reaching out to touch him. To touch his Anna. Those tendrils, they wrapped around him, squeezing. Burning. Suffocating him.

He couldn't breathe.

He couldn't breathe!

He sat up, yelling, scrabbling at his throat, lungs ready to burst, his skin hot—flaming hot.

'Ali. My love. You are safe. It is but a nightmare.'

Cool hands stroked his hair back from his face, down his neck, over his shoulders and back to his face. Butterfly-soft kisses on his brow, his cheeks, his lips, brought him to an awareness of where he was. Who he was with.

Home. He was home.

'Anna.' He grabbed her, even as he shook, holding on tight, the nightmares still gripping him.

'Ali. Ali. I am here. Come back to me.'

Safety. She was safety.

Yet, the nightmare showed him they weren't safe. Hadn't it?

It had felt so true, and yet, they were surrounded by packmates, by coven, in the heart of one of the strongest packs in Scotland. How could they not be safe?

Maybe this dream was born of his uncertainty over joining the pack. Or maybe it was because his journey was finally over and he still didn't believe the voice had brought him here solely to mate with Anna.

Why would it do that? Why was their mating so important?

He wanted to ask but the voice had disappeared, along with its compulsion, the moment he'd seen Anna. Maybe he was being stupid—questioning where there was no need to question. Perhaps it came of a life filled with never being safe, never being able to trust. Was that it? Was he simply unable to trust this gift he'd been given: a mate and a place to finally belong.

'Ali? You are still shaking.'

He was? He was. The nightmare had been that bad.

'Do you want to tell me about it?'

No. He didn't. He truly didn't. She didn't need the dark and evil images that even now lurked in his mind. He was aware she could sense his fear through the bond, feel the loss he'd experienced, the panic as the dark, oily thing had struck out, burning and choking, but he didn't need to let those feelings sink their claws in her too.

She was his sun. His moon. The thing that warmed his day and lit his night. She deserved nothing but love and joy; she certainly did not deserve a partner burdened by dark dreams he could make no sense of.

'They are not simply dreams. You know they aren't.'

'No,' he said out loud, sitting up abruptly as the voice sounded in his mind suddenly. Why had he wished it back? It never told him what he wanted to know. Only ever brought misery. He gripped his head, shook it. 'No.' The voice was wrong. They were just dreams. It was all they could be.

'Ali?' He was vaguely aware that Anna held him, her voice reaching out to him as if from far away, but not enough to stop the voice in his head.

'Your dreams showed you what would happen to your parents. To dearest Sophie. They led you to find a home for Frederique and Amandine. They led you here.'

'No.' The voice had done the last with its cruelty-laden compulsion. As for the others ... 'No,' he said again, his entire body shaking with his vehement denial. It could not be. He would not let it be. He was no fortune teller. He was no doomsday speaker.

'No, you are not. She is. You see what she sees.'

No. The voice lied. Anna was no seer.

'Your Anna does not know what she is.'

'You. It is you,' he said to the voice in his mind. *'You are doing this. You put these nightmares in my head. You want me to do something.'*

'I want nothing more than what you have already done. What you will do.'

'Why? I am not important.'

'Important? You are so much more than that, my friend.'

'You are no friend to me.'

Sadness drenched him with a suddenness that made him cry out.

Anna's arms tightened around him. 'Ali. Wake up. I fear you are still asleep. Wake up.'

Was he? It seemed like a nightmare. The voice in his head telling him things he didn't want to know. Didn't want to understand. Because it couldn't be true. What he saw couldn't be true.

For it was the end of all things.

'Ali. Ali, come back to me, my love. I am here. Feel me.' Hands on his face, kisses across his forehead, his closed eyelids, his cheeks. 'Do you feel me? Come back to me now. The nightmare does not have you. I do. You are mine. Forever mine.'

Yes. Yes. He was. Hers. Always and only hers.

He opened his eyes and stared into the wonder of hers. It was dark, but even so, the violet blue of them shone, like a light showing him the way. 'Anna,' he breathed.

'I have got you.'

Her hands moved over his face, into his hair as she made murmuring sounds, comforting sounds. He nestled into her, his head buried against the soft warmth of her breasts, letting her voice soothe the ache, the fear, the taint of something awful that lay sour in the back of his throat. She rocked him a little as she spoke words of nonsense and love, telling him as her hands and body told him, that he was safe.

Safe with her. As she would always be safe with him, the nightmares be damned.

'Talk to me,' he said, his voice raw like he'd been yelling for hours. 'Tell me about your stubborn sister.'

She smiled against his temple and spoke, her voice calm, husky with emotion as she told him the specifics about the argument they'd had before Morrigan had left.

'I think I would like your sister.'

She kissed his brow. 'I think she would like you too, if only she would get over her prejudices.' She moved, tipped his face until their gazes met. 'I just need to find a way to let her know about the miracle that is you.'

He smiled softly up at her. 'I hope somehow I can help.'

'You will. You will.' She kissed him lightly on the lips. He wanted more; wanted to drown in her. But she pulled back, stroked her thumb over his bottom lip and asked, 'You have siblings, so you know a little of how stubborn they can be I am sure. Which one is worse?'

'Amandine is by far the more stubborn. It was she who demanded I find them a home to live in, a livelihood to learn. Frederique is far softer and would have a real talent for cooking if he didn't drift off daydreaming all the time. That boy was born with his head in the clouds.'

She smiled. 'I love the sound of them already. And what of your other sister? The full Were ... Sophie I think you called her?'

All the joy he'd begun to feel at talk of his siblings fled. He said flatly, 'Sophie ... she is ... gone.'

'Gone?'

His grief was a sudden weight she could feel through their bond. Oh Goddess, it hurt. A part of her didn't want to hear this story, but the Healer in her knew he needed to tell it. And if he could have born the fact of it, she could certainly bear the telling of it. Although to tell a tale of such sadness so soon after his nightmare might not be the best thing for him.

She touched his face, met his gaze. 'Only tell me if you want to.'

He nodded. Kissed her softly, then held her close. It was a moment longer before he began to talk, his voice a low rumble in her ear.

'Sophie was ... our light. A surprise addition to our family, born only a few years after Frederique and Amandine.'

She nodded her understanding—Were did not usually have babies with such regularity. 'How much older were you?'

'She was twelve years my junior. She was fun and laughter with a curious spirit that delighted us all. She was only six when our parents died.' He sucked in a deep, shuddering breath. 'My father's coven had suffered losses too from the explosion of power that had killed my parents and were unable, and unwilling, to take us in. My mother had often spoken of her pack, although we had never met any of them. So, thinking they might take us in, we journeyed to their village.'

He paused, his muscles so tense she thought they might snap.

'I took Sophie with me, thinking they might be more ready to accept us if they saw we were like them. They took one look at us and chased us away. They called us abominations and threatened to kill us should we come anywhere close to their lands again. Something inside little Sophie died that day. It took months, but her wolf drove her insane with its grief and I ...' His voice hitched.

Oh Goddess. She knew what he was going to say. He was but eighteen when he took responsibility for his siblings, then was forced to take on the responsibility of a Hunter—one of the most horrible pack designations as far as she was concerned, for it was their job to hunt and kill rabid Were.

She wrapped her arms more tightly around him and met grief-filled gaze. 'You do not have to say the words. I know what happens to a Were who is packless. What they can do. What you were forced to do.'

His guilt was like knife slashes inside him—reverberating through the bond into her. He obviously thought he'd betrayed his baby sister, the one who perhaps relied on him more than the others combined for everything; the pain of it was extraordinary, stabbing at her heart. She almost let go of him to clutch her chest, but he needed her, needed her understanding more than he needed proof she now shared his pain.

She took his face in her hands. 'You know, there was nothing you could have done to save her.'

'I had kept her alive until then.'

'Yes, but she was fully Were. Even without the Darkness, she still needed a pack. And despite your strengths and the power you could share with her to help her live in harmony with her wolf, two Were alone cannot make a pack.'

'My mother was alone with my father for a year before she had me.'

Morghanna shrugged helplessly, only able to speak in supposition. 'Maybe your mother was still attached in some way to her Pack. Maybe she stole back there to spend just the right amount of time with them to stop the madness from taking her over. And maybe your birth was enough for her, given she was an adult wolf. I do not know.

It is a puzzle though, given your Sophie was young when your mother died, too young to have linked to anyone other than you and her.'

'There was nobody else.'

'The two of you should not have been enough unless ...' Her mouth dropped open a little. 'She was probably attached to the pack through your mother and when she died, the bond went with it. She needed more than you could give. If Frederique or Amandine had been Were too, with how strong your wolf is, she would most probably have been fine. But with only one to bond with ...' She stroked her fingers through his hair as she stared into his eyes, trying to make him feel the comfort of her love to assuage the sorrowful memories her questions brought up. She wished she didn't have to ask, but she did. She had to know everything there was to know to have the proof she needed to keep Morrigan, and any others like her, in the fold. 'Did she complain of an ache in her head after your mother died?'

He nodded. 'After that first week she never complained, but I knew she suffered.' His eyes filled with a sadness that made her heart ache. 'She was such a sweet little wolf. With golden-brown fur and the deepest amber eyes. Beautiful. So beautiful.'

His sadness made her want to weep, but she had to press further. 'Frederique and Amandine? You said they are not as powerful as you or your father?'

'They carry only a touch of power—enough to make them outcasts to the Were and not enough to be accepted by my father's coven. We were turned away at every step.'

Never accepted. Always alone. He did not need to say the words; she heard them in her heart and wept for him and his siblings. The Pact had been too late to save them from their grief. Too late to save his sister from her horrifying drift into madness when she was shunned by pack who were still driven to hostility by the Darkness. 'You looked after your brother and sister, though.'

'I did what I could for ten years. It was only luck that brought us to the baker and his wife. They were childless and more than happy to take Frederique and Amandine as their own.'

'What about you?'

'I was too old.'

She stroked his face again, tears pouring down her cheeks. 'It does not need to be like that. It is not like that anymore. You are no longer an outsider. None of you are. You are welcome here. All of you. I should have said this before when I mentioned writing to them and visiting them, but I didn't want to speak out of hand given I knew so little.' She grasped his hands in hers. 'You would be welcome anywhere now the Pact has been made. Your siblings and you do not need to be alone again.'

'But, they have no true power. How will they fit in?'

'We will find a place for them. I promise. Frederique can pursue his cooking talents here and Amandine ... well, stubborn women with a need for a purpose will always find a place within the pack. Write to them. Ask them to come. I want all my family here with us. Write to them tomorrow. I don't want to have to wait months and months before we can travel to meet them. The invitation needs to get to them as soon as possible. And I will contact Bridgette as soon as possible too. I'm sure she will help to bring them home.'

Joy, so much joy, sang along the mating bond at her words. But mistrust thrummed there too, almost hidden by the joy that sparkled and sang. Not mistrust of her—he believed she believed in what she was saying—but mistrust driven by years of being outcast. Neither truly Were nor truly coven, he was lost in a nether world of in-between. He, more than his siblings with their small amount of power, who were most likely passing for human. He never could. He was too ... everything.

She searched his eyes, hands tightening on his. 'Am I speaking out of turn? Do you not want them to come here?'

'No! Of course I want them with me.'

Then why ... oh! Had she misread his story entirely? She didn't wish to cause him more pain, but she had to get to the bottom of why he wasn't jumping at the chance to have his brother and sister come to live with them. She took a deep breath and asked carefully, 'Frederique and Amandine? Did they ask you to leave them?'

Sadness filled his eyes as he stared at her. 'No. My brother and sister did not wish me to go. But I could not ruin their chance at a normal life. They know the rules about their powers. Know how to hide them.'

'Would you have stayed with them if not for the voice compelling you to come here?'

He looked away. 'Once they were with the baker and his wife, they did not need me to hunt for them or to protect them in the forest against things that might harm them. They can pass. I could not. I wanted to stay to make certain they were happy and settled, but once I was certain of that, I intended to move on. I was a danger to them. They do not need me in their lives anymore.'

'But you are their brother.'

'I am a monster who has the power to hurt them.'

11

The words hung between them, vibrating with tension. Morghanna clenched his hands in hers and said with certainty, 'But you never did hurt them, did you?' He didn't answer. 'Did they say they feared you would?'

'No. Never,' he said abruptly before his agonised gaze met hers. 'Although I saw the fear in their eyes at times when I returned from the hunt in my wolf form. They had a right to be afraid.'

'No, they did not.' She tipped her head to the side, thumbs stroking bristly chin, thinking about all he'd said. His idea that he was a monster hadn't come from his mother and father. It had begun when he'd tried to find a home for him and his siblings.

His mother's pack. They had made him feel monstrous. But because of what had happened to Sophie, he couldn't see their fear for what it was.

To get him to believe, she had to lead him to it very carefully.

Slowly, she began to stroke the back of his hands with her thumbs. And carefully, so carefully, she said, 'When you went to your mother's pack, did you go in your wolf form?' He nodded. 'Was it a full moon?'

He shook his head. 'No. Why is that important?'

'Because until Bridgette created the Pact, the Were's ability to change had been bound to the moon for as far back as they can remember.'

A light dawned in his eyes. 'I thought my mother's pack were following some absurd custom.' He shook his head slowly. 'They turned on Sophie and me immediately, calling us abominations, shouting about changing with the moon and only the moon. I did not understand.'

She pulled him down, held his head to her chest and stroked his hair. 'You could not have known. Your mother was not like them because of your father and then you. She had power over her change. As did your little Sophie ... up until she was driven rabid by the loss of your parents and her Packbond.'

He nodded against her chest, his arms going around her to hold her to him, tight. 'I always wondered why our mother acted like changing into her wolf was such a gift. I did not know a time when we all could not change at will.' He nuzzled against her neck. 'When she was gone, I thought she had lied. Or there was something wrong with me. My wolf was the reason we were turned away from everyone who was supposed to take us in. I blamed it, especially after my mother's pack turned on us. I was afraid, so afraid, that they were right. And after Sophie went insane and attacked Frederique and Amandine, I thought that was in my nature as well. I only ever let it out to hunt, to protect. I thought I could trust it for little else. It came to feel the same.'

She pulled away, slowly, holding his face in her hands once more, so that he would know she didn't pull away from him, not as others had done, but just so she could see his face. 'You and your wolf are a pair. You live in symbiosis. There must be a harmony, an acceptance. The moment you began to distrust your wolf, only letting him out to kill and never to play, to enjoy, you hurt him horribly. It is only a miracle he never turned inward, retreating into the part that is only animal. Like your mother's pack had, bound by the moon as they were because the Darkness had infected them.'

He shook his head, his eyes filling with horror, with sadness. 'You are saying it is my fault?'

'No.' She leaned in and kissed him, his mouth, his cheeks, his forehead, his nose, then back to his mouth, each kiss punctuated by a 'No'. She pushed her fingers into his long hair, the strong, dark silky waves glinting with hidden fire in the afternoon sun and held him so that he must look at her. 'None of us understood until Bridgette was sent by the Goddess to heal the Alpha of Pack McVale and discovered the nature of the Were and how they were locked to the moon. The power she used to heal him gave him control for that month over his wolf, and in that discovery, the Pact was born and the Darkness was ousted.'

He sat back, his extraordinary eyes wide. 'That is a similar story to how my parents met. One day, a day he should have been seeing to his duties in the coven's library, my father had an overwhelming urge to go into the forest that bounded the coven's village. He wandered far deeper than was considered safe because of the wild animals reported to live there. It was there he found my mother.' He swallowed hard, the memory obviously difficult.

'You do not have to tell me.'

He nodded. 'I want to.' He took a deep breath. 'My mother was returning from visiting her sister—who had mated into another pack across the mountains—when she was set on by thieves. They would have robbed her and raped her had she not been almost as fast as her wolf, but in her haste to get away from them, she slipped and fell down an embankment, breaking her leg. It was not a full moon so she could not shift to heal the break and had been lying there for two days, fearing the gang would find her any moment and kill her. She knew she should have been wary of a magic user, and yet, from the first moment our father appeared out of the trees, she knew she was safe with him—it was her favourite stormy day story to regale us with.' He smiled softly then sighed. 'My father took her back to his village and they married soon after—although, now I realise they must have mated. His coven were mistrustful of her to begin with, so they lived in the forest a short distance from his village, but they were happy. We were all happy.'

'Did her pack know where she was?'

'Possibly. As you say, she must have returned to them often enough to keep her Packbond intact. Although, given how surprised they were to see my siblings and myself and sense our mixed blood, she must not have told them about her children.'

Morghanna shook her head, astonished anew at what had gone unknown for so long—a truth his very existence made clear in ways it had never been before. Oh, they'd hoped, but they'd never truly known if what they did was right.

'If only we had known what was possible in the mixing of our two races, so much suffering would have been averted.' She stared at him, unable to hide her smile of joy as she stared at this male who was a revelation to her in so many ways. 'You are a miracle. Everyone will come to see this to be true as they get to know you and hear your story.'

'I do not care what others think of me. I only care about your thoughts. And the fact you are my miracle.'

'We are each other's miracle.'

'Yes.' She cupped his face, kissed him slowly, reverently, but before she could lose herself in the kiss, pulled back. She needed to finish her point. 'So, given all that, given your wolf is not a danger and you are not a monster and never were, do you concede that maybe your brother and sister would much rather be here with you than across the sea with a couple who, no matter how they care, will never truly be their family. Not like we are.'

'Yes. I concede. Amandine and Frederique should come live with us.' His brow furrowed a little. 'Although, I will not demand it. I will ask them. It must be their decision.'

'Of course. But I know they will come. I have a happy feeling in my heart about it.'

He smiled up at her, his tension gone. 'You are truly my treasure, Anna-mine.'

His arms tightened around her and she held him to her, stroking his hair back from his brow.

His eyes closed, his limbs loosened and quiet surrounded them once more. She thought maybe he'd fallen back to sleep; was almost there herself.

Then on a shout, her mate shot upright.

'Ali? What is it?'

A susurrus filled Alistair's ears; the sound of leaves rustling in the wind. Something brushed against his foot as it had done just as he was falling back to sleep, but when he turned to see what it was, there was nothing there.

Except, there was. He could feel it. Feel them.

'Anna?' he asked, his voice hoarse. 'There is something in the room with us.'

She let out a little chuckle. 'It is but the spirits. They were disturbed by your nightmare. They are simply showing their concern.'

'For me?'

She kneeled beside him and brushed his hair back from his face, smiling. 'Of course. You are theirs to protect now, as they protect me.'

Protected by spirits? How could they possibly protect anyone? And if they could, why hadn't his parents protected him and Frederique and Amandine and little Sophie?

Another touch to his foot, his shoulder. He shivered again.

'Stop that,' Anna said to the air at the end of the bed. 'You know you should never touch those who do not invite it.' Wind blew her hair back from her face in answer. She shivered.

He leapt to a crouch in front of her, arms out. 'She said, do not touch.'

Her hands on his back, stroking, urging him back to her side as she said, 'It is fine. They know better than to touch me without asking.'

'Then why did you shiver?'

'There are a quite a few of them here right now. It is ... a lot.'

'Then they are not here all the time?'

'No. Usually only when I call them, and even then, only one or two.'

'Then why are there so many here now? Did you call them?'

'No. They felt your need. And they do not always do as I wish,' she said with a twist of her lips. 'There are spirits here I have never seen before, both Were and the powered. I think maybe some might be ancestors of yours. They probably followed you here to make certain you arrived safely.'

'My mama and papa? Are they here?' The ache in his chest pulsed with equal amounts of pain and pleasure at the thought that maybe they had been looking over him.

She tipped her head to the side as if listening, but then shook her head. 'No. According to the spirits here, they stayed to look after your brother and sister. But they have sent others to ensure you are well.'

'Oh.' He took a breath against the pang—although, it was right his parents chose to look out for Frederique and Amandine rather than him.

'Are you okay? It is a lot to take in.'

Yes, it was. He didn't know what to think about the fact he had ancestors looking out for him, let alone that his mate could see and talk to them. But, it wasn't an awful thought. 'I am well.' He looked around the room then back at his mate as a thought struck him. 'The voice that brought me here—perhaps it was not your Goddess at all. Perhaps it was one of them?'

She frowned for a moment as if deep in thought. 'It has occurred that strong spirits have broken through and spoken to those without Spirit-talker magics. However, given how powerful you are, I do not think it possible.'

'Why?'

'From what I saw at the hot springs and the different colours that made up your warlock lightning, I rather think your magics encompass many disciplines and are on the immensely strong side. I do not think a spirit could compel you like you were compelled. That is something only a being of great power could do.'

'That does not sound good.'

Her face warmed into a smile. 'Do not look at it that way. If I am right, the Goddess spoke to you and brought you here. It is just another reason you are a treasure to our people.'

'Is it why I am a treasure to you?'

'No, my Ali. You are a treasure to me for an entirely different reason.' The look in her eyes—it warmed him despite the cold of the ghostly touch still shuddering through his body. He brushed his fingers across her cheeks and into her hair, loving the silky warmth, the way she moved with him until her breasts brushed against his chest.

Heat flared in her eyes. He brushed his thumb over her lips, loving the little sound that escaped her. Her tongue dipped out to wet where he had just touched.

He took an unsteady breath. He wanted to kiss her, to take her, but not in front of an audience of spirits. Had any of them been there the other times he and Anna had joined? Hells, he hoped not. 'Do they have to stay?'

'Not if you do not want them here.'

'I prefer privacy when I do this.' He bent down and took her lips with his in a kiss of heated promise.

'So do I,' she said a moment later as they came up to breathe.

'Then they are gone?'

She waved her hand and his skin prickled with awareness that magic, strong and sure, had been used. 'There. Gone.'

'Will they stay away?'

'Goddess, I hope so.'

She pulled him down to her this time and he sank into her kiss, holding her precious face, settling on the bed so she could straddle his thighs, where she paused over his already turgid length.

'Anna. I ache.'

'Find your comfort in me,' she said as she sank down onto him, surrounding him in tight, wet heat. He took her hips, holding her still for a moment as, eyes closed, he tried to find his breath, his control. He'd already lost control in his nightmares; he didn't want to lose it again.

She held his face, kissed him, his brow, his cheeks, his eyelids, his nose and finally, his lips. Then she pulled back and said, 'Ali. My mate. Open your eyes. I want to see your eyes as I ride you.'

He shook his head. If he looked at her now, he'd be lost.

She kissed him again, her smile playing against his lips. 'Let me move.'

He shook his head again.

She kissed him once more, long, lingering and yet gently persuading. 'There is no need for control, my Ali. Only sharing.'

She stroked her hands down his back, then up, making him shiver with agonised pleasure. She leaned into him, as much as she could with his hands holding her hips in place. Her breasts brushed up against him. He groaned.

'Feel my heart.'

He let go of one hip as she touched his hand, letting her guide his palm to her breast. Through the soft flesh he felt her heart beat in time to the wild pulsing of her internal muscles as they wrapped around him.

'Feel my soul.'

Through the ethereal cord that bound them together, the mating bond, he sensed her scent, her taste and something more, something eternally hers that was only for him.

'You are safe,' she whispered against his lips. 'I will always catch you when you lose control.'

He opened his eyes to see the glory of the woman in front of him, the woman that was wholly and utterly his.

'Take me, my Ali; my love. Find your comfort in me.'

Holding his gaze, she moved as his hands loosened their grip. His eyes flickered, wanting to close, the pleasure so intense, but she gripped his face and said, 'Stay with me. Lose control with me.'

And he did. He pushed up and into her as she bore down on him, desperate to feel the connection he'd only ever felt with her, to exorcise the vision that had threatened to bring him undone and the pain-joy of discovering his parents had sent ancestor spirits to look after him. But he didn't want to think of any of that now, or what the voice, whoever it was, had said. He just wanted to hold on to the joy of his mating, to the joy that was her. He was happy. Finally happy. Surely, he could give himself up to that for now? He didn't want to think of anything other than his treasure. His Anna. And the way she made him whole.

The needy animal part of him agreed, urging him to take more. To give more.

He ran his hands up her sides, over her breasts, her shoulders, held her chin and brought her lips back to his, losing himself to the sweet depths of her mouth as his cock plundered the sweet depths of her feminine core. She openly welcomed his possession, nails digging into his skin, kiss deepening as she moved on him, riding him, taking him deeper, moaning her pleasure. Around the kisses she spoke words of love, acceptance, comfort. 'I am here. I am always here. I will always be here.'

'Yes. Yes.' He knew she meant it; so desperately wanted it to be true.

'It is true, my love. Nothing can tear what we have apart. Not even death. Do not fear the future, my love. Always, forever. That is what we promised. It is the benediction the Goddess gave to us. That is what is true.'

'Always, forever.'

She moved over him, faster, working them both into a frenzy, until she threw her head back, crying out as she pulsed around him, driving him up and over, his seed spurting inside her so hard the pleasure of it almost hurt. His cry met hers, the wolf howling his ecstasy inside his mind. The pulsing—his, hers—went on and on, the sensation of shared pleasure creating more and more. He felt so much of her inside him, it was like they were one.

'We *are* one, my love.' Her voice trembled, exhausted, her breath a puff against his face, cooling the sweat on his skin.

Finally, the last tremors faded and they collapsed onto the bed, her on top of him, her limbs draped around and over him, his cock still inside her, and together, they fell into the sleep of oblivion only sweet exhaustion could bring.

Even so, he woke a few hours later, the threads of nightmare images whispering in his mind once more. He stilled, wondering if they were his—or Anna's, as the voice had said.

But Anna did not move from where she now lay at his side, her arm and leg lying heavily over his chest and stomach.

So, it had lied. The images were in his mind alone.

Unable to sleep with the nasty sludge of them a bitter taste in the back of his throat and a crawling under his skin, he wished he could get up and go for a run. However, he stayed still, not wanting to disturb his Anna—she needed her sleep. So, he lay there and tried to figure out what the images meant, and why the voice would lie about where they came from.

But the more he poked and prodded, the more gossamer-like they became until what was once a tapestry of images became nothing but threads blowing on the wind.

Surely if they were visions, if they were important, they would not blow away like that?

A shudder chased over him.

And if they were visions, how could he go about finding out what it all meant before it was too late?

12

The next few days flew by, but not in the way Morghanna expected. She hadn't truly hoped to get the honeymoon period that mates were usually gifted by the pack where they were left to their own devices for a month as they settled into their mating. Her leadership role would never allow for that. But she had expected at least a few days reprieve. And she was especially keen to take Alistair to the Dance to test his powers with the trial so they could start organising his training.

However, it wasn't to be. The very next day, as they were about to head back to the springs, she was called into Council and then off to a difficult birthing then to the coven's school where one of the younger witches was having trouble limiting the flow of her magic through the bond with the pack. Ali accompanied her, listening closely at Council, helping where he could with the birthing and sitting with the students at the school—although he couldn't learn much yet; not until she'd taken him to the Dance to figure out his natural magical proclivities and she found him the appropriate coven members to teach him.

And then there was the pressing need to contact Morrigan. At least that was something she could do in their home with him at her side.

So at the first chance a few days after the celebration of their mating, in a lull between the chaos, she sat down to try and scry for Morrigan.

Alistair stopped his preparations for their dinner—she's been delighted to discover he was a talented cook—and sat opposite her, watching with interest.

'How does the water help?' he asked when she'd positioned the scrying bowl in front of her.

She looked at him curiously. 'Your father did not teach you to scry?'

He shrugged. 'There was no reason. We lived near his coven so he could just walk there if he needed to talk to any of them.'

'They did not communicate with other covens?'

A wry smile. 'If they did, they did not share that with us. Our presence was tolerated but we were not included in coven business or even their festivals.'

'You have never gone sky clad before the Goddess?'

'Not at special coven festivals. But my father did take me to the local Dance and we did a ceremony there when each of my siblings were born.'

She reached across the table and squeezed his hand. 'I am sorry you never had a chance to explore either sides of your heritage. But that is not the case now. Here, you are one of us and you will share in everything both Were and coven do.'

He smiled softly at her. 'I look forward to it.' He gestured at the bowl of water. 'So, show me how to scry.'

She screwed her mouth to the side. 'I am perhaps not the best one to teach you. I am not very good at it. Although, I do have more chance of reaching someone I am related to or strongly attached to emotionally.'

'So you should be able to reach Morrigan.'

'If she is open to receiving my message, yes. If not, I should still be able to see where she is and what she is up to. If it works.'

'Why would it not work?'

She looked down at the bowl and muttered, 'Well, as I said, it is not a skill I am very proficient with.'

'If it worries you so much, can you not ask someone else to do it who is?'

'I could. Brionne is our best scryer and can astral travel with an ease I have not seen in anyone but Bridgette. But I do not wish to bother her with this. She and Morrigan never got along.'

'Is there not anyone else?'

'There is, but I do not want to ask any of them yet. Not until I have tried first.'

He gestured at the bowl again. 'Could I do it?'

She smiled wryly once more. 'I imagine you could. But probably not with me as a teacher. I will ask Brionne to take over that part of your education. She can teach you things I could never dream of doing.'

'I look forward to it.'

She closed her eyes with his smile warming her heart then placed her hands on either side of the water, pointer finger touching the surface ever so slightly. They had discovered it helped her to build the link with a blood relative or someone she was close to—something a true scryer would never have to bother with.

She filled her mind with the image of Morrigan's face: her pert nose with the scattering of freckles across the bridge and cheeks; the creaminess of her sun-kissed skin; the curve of her dark lashes that framed eyes the colour of the sea on a stormy day—a curious greyish green that seemed lit from within; the thick dark brows slashing across her forehead, a match in colour to her long wavy black hair, that always gave her the air of someone who took life too seriously even when she laughed; the pointed chin which gave her face a slightly heart-shaped look; the wide breadth of a mouth Morrigan had always thought too large but simply reminded Morghanna of their mother and her never-ending smile; and finally, the determination and energy that made Morrigan a force to be reckoned with even when she was in the best of moods.

The image lived large and clear in her mind, as solid as if Morrigan stood before her. She longed to reach out and touch her sister's cheek, to brush back her wayward curls, but this was just an image. Sadness flooded through her but she pushed it aside and opened her eyes, and with a burst of her magic, pushed the image at the bowl of water as she said the cantrip.

The water swirled anti-clockwise, slowly at first then faster and faster. A fog appeared in the centre of the whirlpool, spreading outwards. Images flashed on its surface then Morrigan's face appeared.

'Morrigan,' Morghanna said quickly. But as the name left her lips, the image flickered, the fog disappeared and the water stopped swirling so suddenly it sloshed up the sides of the bowl and onto the table.

'Damn it!'

'What happened?'

She waved at the bowl and the mess of water on the table. 'It did not work.'

'But you saw her. I saw her.'

'That may be, but the connection did not take. Either she refused it, or it just was not strong enough to begin with.'

'Do you wish to try again?'

She sighed heavily, waving her hands at the bowl of water in front of her. 'I need more water.'

'I will go fetch it.'

He was back a few minutes later, in which time she'd composed herself, pushing aside her disappointment. He placed the bowl in front of her and sat opposite, watching as she tried again.

She didn't even get to the fog stage the second time.

The third try, the water swirled slightly, but then fell still.

'What happened?'

'Nothing. Absolutely nothing.' Trying not to let the bitterness of her disappointment take over, she stood, picked up the bowl and tipped it on the herbs growing on the windowsill. She turned back to see Alistair watching her carefully.

'You are giving up?'

'Three tries is enough to tell me I am unable to do it. I am unable to even get an image of where she is let alone link to her. There is no point flogging a dead horse.'

He pursed his lips slightly, a small frown furrowing his brow. 'You and your gifts are hardly a dead horse.'

She snorted.

His frown deepened but he didn't argue further. 'What happens next?'

'It seems I have no choice. I will have to ask Brionne or one of the others to scry for me.'

'But if Morrigan is blocking the scry because she does not want to be found, then will their attempts be any more successful than yours?'

'I think it more likely it is my lack of skill that is the problem. Morrigan would not keep blocking me. She would know I would only keep trying to contact her if it was important.'

He tipped his head, his eyes assessing. 'From what you have said of your sister, I think she is stubborn enough to block the scry repeatedly if she is still angry with you and the pack.'

She bit the corner of her lip as she considered his words. 'Maybe. Either way, I am not strong enough to break through. Brionne could break through all but the strongest of blocking spells.'

'Do you wish to go to her now?'

She was about to say that it could keep for later, but he stood and joined her, taking her hands in his. 'This is important to you. Do not put it off. Not for me. Not for anyone.'

She took in a shuddering breath and then, cupping his face, pulled him down for a kiss.

After a minute he pulled back a little, enough to say, 'Morghanna Cantrae, are you trying to distract me from my purpose?'

'Not if your purpose is to make love to me.'

'What of scrying for Morrigan?' It was a half-hearted argument— his fingers were already working on the fastenings of her dress.

She waved a hand and said a little breathlessly, 'That can wait for a little while. I will ask Brionne when I see her at Council later today. For now, I much prefer to do this.'

Later—much later—they emerged from the cottage and hurried to the Council meeting. After business was concluded, she pulled Brionne aside and asked her to scry. Thankfully, even though she didn't like Morrigan, the skilful witch immediately agreed.

She invited them to her cottage and set to scrying as they watched. But she was as unsuccessful as Morghanna. Finally, after her fourth try, she sat back and blew out a breath. 'She really does not want you or any of us to contact her. That blocking spell is the strongest I have ever come across. It is going to take some time to figure out how to break through. But I promise you, I will figure out how to do it.'

'I do not want you wasting all your energy and time on this, Brionne. You have far more important things to do, what with the work you are doing in helping Bridgette contact the European packs and covens.'

Brionne's lips set in a stubborn line. 'I can do that and still do this. Besides, it is not a waste. It is a matter of pride, now. I cannot have Morrigan besting me.' She winked at Morghanna. 'But I promise I will rope some others in to help me. We can take it in shifts so she has no quarter. One of us will eventually break through. She cannot keep that blocking spell fuelled for all hours of the day or night for long.'

'I do not know how to thank you.'

Brionne stood then and took Morghanna's hands in hers, looking her firmly in the eyes. 'You never have to thank us for anything. You are our dearest leader and friend; the one who took care of us when we thought all was lost and led us here to this place of peace and plenty. We will never be able to pay you back for all you have done for us or all that you continue to do.'

Morghanna didn't quite know where to look or what to say to that. So she simply brought up the subject of Brionne teaching Alistair what she knew about scrying and astral travel.

'I would love to teach your mate. When would you like to start.'

Before either of them could answer, there was a knock on the door and a voice called out, 'Brionne, is Morghanna in there with you? She is needed by the fields. There has been an accident.'

Brionne opened the door and Morghanna moved forward to see Stephen Samuel, the coven representative of the Harvest Co-op. He stood there, shifting from one foot to the other, a worried frown on his face, hands wringing a cloth that looked to have blood on it.

'What happened?'

'It's young Claud. He got into an argument with one of the young Were in our co-op, Alexander MacPherson, about who could till the field the fastest; him using his magic and Alex using his Were strength. When Claud realised that he was going to lose, he made a grab for the Packbond to give himself more magic and accidentally pushed the last of his energy into it rather than taking what he needed to keep him going. He flared out, but that's not the worst of it. Because of the push of power into the bond, all the Were who were close by changed. Alex changed in mid swing of his hoe and cut his leg. I felt Claud go and ran from the potato field to see what happened. Young Alex's leg is almost severed. I tried to staunch the blood,' he waved the blood-soaked rag—she saw now it was his tunic —but other Were arrived to help, so I ran to come and get you.'

'You should have gone to Abigail and Leanna.'

'I did. They're not in Abigail's cottage and nobody knows where they are.'

Morghanna cursed under her breath. 'Abigail was muttering the other day about needing to collect more Healing herbs from the forest. She probably made Leanna take her out there even though she knows she shouldn't exert herself like that.'

'Can I help?' Alistair asked at the same time Brionne did.

'Yes.' She turned to Alistair. 'Can you and your wolf find Abigail and Leanna. If the injury is as bad as Stephen says, then we are going to need them both.' He gave her a swift kiss then ran out the door. She turned to Brionne. 'Grab bandages and the poultice to stop blood flow and come to the fields. Stephen, take me to them.'

It was hectic when she got to the fields, with coven members gathered around the unconscious Claud and Alex's mother, Sally, holding her boy in his wolf form as he writhed and screamed in pain, her face pale and tear-streaked. Other Were gathered around, trying to help calm her and him but doing nothing else. Not that they could do much. The MacCrae's Healer had died some years before of old age and they hadn't had another true-born Healer born to the pack. Some of them had learned the basics and knew their way around simple medicinal herbs and bandaging but were not up to dealing with a leg that had almost been severed in two.

She said to the coven members there, 'Take Claud back to his mother.' She could tell from her link through the Packbond to her coven-mates that he was not in any danger. He had exhausted his power but there was nothing to be done for that other than making him comfortable and allowing him to sleep.

His mother, Susanna, would know how best to care for him until he woke in a day or so. He'd be exhausted for a while and ravenously hungry. His powers would be weaker for a while as well until they'd had time to fully replenish.

A suitable punishment for an act of stupidity and thoughtlessness. Although it would not be his only punishment. She'd make certain of that.

The state Alex was in was another matter.

She rushed over to him.

It was a terrible injury. She had no idea if they could Heal it properly, but if she didn't get started quickly, they wouldn't have that to worry about. The boy would be dead.

She would have liked to move him but didn't dare try for fear of making his injury worse. So she set to trying to stop the bleeding, first using a spell of sleep to stop his thrashing and then using a spell of stasis on the injury. She wasn't strong enough to completely stop the bleeding, but she slowed it enough so that when Brionne arrived with the supplies, it was not quite as dire as when she arrived and with Brionne's help, she stabilised the limb. They decided though it was best not to do more than put the poultice on it until Abigail had a look at it.

She was very grateful when twenty minutes later, Alistair arrived with Abigail and Leanna in tow, ready to do the true work.

Abigail asked her and Brionne to keep their spells going while they began the work of Healing; stitching flesh and sinew back together was always a difficult task, but more so with an injury this severe. They needed all the help they could get, so Morghanna called on other members of the coven to come and give of their powers to keep the Healers going.

The two of them worked in the dusty field for hours, although it was mostly Leanna using her powers with Abigail instructing her, the older witch still being too unwell to spend much of her own energies despite the added power boost they got from the others. Morghanna was glad she didn't have to argue with her old mentor about that at least.

Finally the leg was stable enough for them to be able to move the boy to the Healer's Hall. Alistair helped a few of the other male Were carry Alex, while Morghanna, Brionne and Stephen helped Leanna and Abigail. They were all exhausted, but there was still so much to do to ensure the young Were didn't lose his leg.

It took them the rest of the day and most of the night, but finally, they finished the Healing and saved the leg. Alex might walk with a limp for some time to come—even his natural Were healing abilities the change gave all Were couldn't help with that—but at least he was alive.

Morghanna made certain everyone else was fed and resting before, with Ali by her side, she staggered back to their cottage and, without even changing out of her blood-stained dress, collapsed on their bed.

Just before she fell asleep, she realised they hadn't as yet set any times for training Alistair or discussed taking him to the Dance to do the trials so they could find out just where his abilities lay and how strong he truly was. But the thought whispered away as sleep took her and she didn't wake until midday.

13

When Morghanna awoke, she vowed that today she would make time to get Alistair sorted. He would never feel a part of the pack or coven until he truly knew what his powers were and how to use them. But once again, she was stymied in her resolution.

The needs of the pack and coven kept pulling her away. And it didn't let up for the next few days. Alistair never complained and kept close to her side the entire time, watching and asking questions and helping where he could. And while it was the most amazing experience to have him there with her sharing in her burdens, it was not what she'd wished or hoped for at the start of their mating or the start of his life within the pack, learning who he truly was.

But it wasn't only about his training.

She needed to spend more time with him. She'd barely tapped the surface of who he was—who he would be to her and to their pack —and wanted to dive in, to learn all his stories, the good and the bad, to hear him talk more of his life with his family both before and after his mother and father's death. And to hear his memories of little Sophie so she could help turn them from a cause of pain to the happy ones they should be. It was tempting to talk to the spirits who persisted in hanging around, despite the shields she put up to give herself a break from their presence. They would undoubtedly know all about him. But he did not have the same ability to find out about her, so she didn't. She wanted them to be on equal footing at all times.

Her parents had had that kind of relationship before they'd been lost to their powers, and she'd always dreamed that, if she defied the odds and managed to fall in love and be loved, she would have a relationship like theirs.

Spending time finding out about her mate from him alone was part of that process.

So, on the fourth day after they mated, when they were once again interrupted to come deal with an emergency—a young Were had gone into the loch on a dare and almost drowned—she bit down on her impatience and went to deal with the boy and his parents. Leanna and Abigail were still too drained from their exertions with Healing Alex, so she had to deal with this herself.

It took much of her energy to heal the gash on his head and the damage done to his lungs from swallowing too much water, and by the time she was finished, she was too tired to take Alistair to the coven's Dance as she'd planned for today. 'I will take you tomorrow.'

He smiled as he cupped her face and kissed her gently. 'I am in no hurry.'

'But it is important we go there so that I can use the powers of the Dance to help figure out what your major and minor powers are. Once we know that, we can figure out the best way ahead in your education.'

'Which I am looking forward to, but it can wait until tomorrow, surely? When you are not so exhausted.'

'I suppose. Oh.' Her eyes widened. 'I feel so terrible. I completely forgot.'

'Forgot what?'

'We still haven't followed up on asking your brother and sister to come live with us. I need to compose then send the letter to Bridgette.

And you must do your drawings for them so they know she comes on your behalf.'

After their discussion about his siblings coming to live with them, he'd admitted, shame-faced, that his brother and sister were illiterate.

It was a shock to her how much he blamed himself for that fact. But how could he have taught them as his father had taught him? They were constantly on the run living in caves and forests with no access to learning materials or the tie or energy to spend on such a thing. It was not his fault they had been too young to learn when their parents were alive. But she didn't try to reason with him about his shame at that moment—she knew too well the impact of such tragedy on a life and that nothing she said could allay his feelings of guilt. That was something only time and love could conquer. At least, she hoped it was.

So, rather than the letter she thought he could write, she'd suggested he make some drawings. He had done a drawing of her one night when she slept; it was incredibly lifelike. She was certain he could come up with some drawings to send to his siblings so as to explain he was okay and that they were to trust Bridgette when she came to them and asked them to come and live with him. Morghanna planned to write to Bridgette as well, laying it all out so she could say what she needed to say to make the younger Sinoirs believe she was Alistair's representative.

'We can do that now,' he said, a fire in his eyes that warmed her through. 'Or we could do a far more important thing.'

'Like what?'

'Like this.' He stroked her breast, backing her towards their bed, the look in his eyes stealing all thought from her as he toppled her onto the soft mattress and set about showing her just what that important thing was.

The next day, nobody interrupted them—she had a small suspicion as they went to the market to get bread and butter and some cheese and meat, given the looks a few pack and coven members threw his way, that he had done something to encourage the lack of interruption. She should be a bit cross but ... she cuddled up to his arm then leaned up to kiss his jaw. 'Thank you.'

'What was that for?'

'For looking after me.'

He smiled down at her. 'I will always look after you. You do not have to thank me for it.'

'Did you not like my thanks?'

His eyes glowed and his smile became truly seductive, but all he said was, 'After market, what would you like to do?'

'Perhaps we could go to the hot springs again. Relive our mating.'

'I hoped you would suggest that. I could do with a good soak. You have been running me ragged.'

'Oh, have I? Perhaps I can run you ragged some more.'

'I hope so.'

Sexual tension thrummed between them as they went about gathering their provisions—enough to have not only the Were winking at her but making jokes about combustion—and by the time they'd finished putting away the provisions and headed up to the springs, they were practically running. She was breathless when they got there, and so was he. They didn't say a word as they tore off their clothing, then Ali swung her around, leaning her over a smooth rock and took her from behind. Their joining was hot and hard and rough and just what she needed.

When the desperate need was slaked, he lay her down on the grass and paid worship to her body, slowly driving them both back to the edge before entering her again, their hands entwined, staring into her eyes and slowly, rhythmically, flew them over the edge.

After, the bond a lovely, warm pulse inside her, she lay in his arms, the soft carpet of grass tickling her skin, and they talked as she'd wanted to do since that first day.

The afternoon shadows had started to lay long fingers around them when Morghanna sighed. 'This was perfect, but we need to return, my love.'

He rolled over, coming to hover over her, a wicked smile playing on his face. 'I would much prefer to stay here.'

'So would I, but I promised to take you to the Dance today—and we cannot continue to put it off. Who knows when I might be called away by duty again?'

'Duty be damned,' he growled.

She smiled, touched her fingers to his brow. 'You do not mean that. Besides, it is past time I took you to the Dance. But first, I must write my letter to Bridgette and you must do your drawing for your siblings. We will be able to send them from the Dance with the Goddess' powers as a boost so they get to Bridgette immediately.'

'If the transfer is that quick, surely we can do it tomorrow?'

'Bridgette might be travelling further from where Frederique and Amandine live and will have to backtrack further the longer we wait. I understand you are nervous about upsetting their lives, but do you not wish your brother and sister to know you are safe and well at the very least? You do not wish them to worry for longer than necessary, do you?'

'You do not play fair.'

Her lips twitched. 'If memory serves, neither do you. When I mentioned leaving two hours ago, I distinctly remember you distracting me.'

'Should I distract you again?'

She groaned as he slid his hand between her legs. 'I want to say yes, but ...'

'Duty calls.' He removed his hand.

She leaned up and kissed him. 'Only because you are that duty right now. If not, nothing could drag me away from here.'

'Promises, promises.'

She simply kissed him again, brief and hot. They both moaned as they pulled away, barely looking at each other as they dressed. But as they walked, he held her hand and it was as perfect as she could have dreamed.

She collected her writing equipment as soon as they got back to the cottage and sat at the table to compose the letter. She sat for a long time thinking about where to start and had barely written a greeting when Alistair finished. His drawing of their cottage with him and Morghanna standing outside it was astonishingly realistic. 'This is remarkable. I said it before but I will say it again. You have an amazing talent.'

'My mother was the true talent. We lived on the money my father earned by selling her work to wealthy landowners.' He looked down at the drawing. 'After they died, I made some money, when I could get my hands on materials, by selling portraits in village fairs to help buy what I needed to make Frederique and Amandine more comfortable as we travelled. Amandine is skilled as well—although her preferred medium is clay. Most of the caves we lived in had plenty of that for her to work with. I enjoy working in both.'

'You are an artist. I should have known.'

'How would you?'

'There is a way you watch the world. My father had that same look in his eyes before he took up coal to draw.'

'Your father was an artist?'

'Yes. Not as skilled as you, but his work brought joy to many before he died.' Sadness filled her, but when he touched her cheek with his large, warm palm, she smiled up at him. 'It is a skillset we have little of now. Perhaps you might consider teaching those with an interest.'

'I am not trained.'

She looked down at the drawing again. 'Training is not everything.' Her eyes were glowing when she looked up at him. 'And it is something I have been unable to invest any time or energy into for those who have a proclivity to creativity. But I can no longer overlook the need in the face of the talent you bring. Will you teach?'

'Of course. If you think there will be interest?'

'When our people see your work, I am certain there will be.'

'Then—gladly.'

The smile that broke out on his face stole her breath momentarily. But she pulled herself back, sucking in air before saying, 'I will put the word out and see who is interested, then we will set up a timetable. I will have to take into account whatever role you end up taking up within the pack hierarchy, but I am certain we will manage enough classes a week to ensure everyone with an interest can have lessons.' She leaned over and kissed him. 'Thank you.'

His brow furrowed in bewilderment. 'What are you thanking me for?'

'Everything.' He looked about to protest but her stomach gurgled. Laughing, she put her hand over her stomach as it talked again. 'I forgot we missed our luncheon.'

'Let me get you some bread and cheese while you finish that letter. Or start it at least.' He winked at her.

She laughed, then when he placed bread and cheese at her elbow, she kissed him in thanks. 'You are not eating?'

'I will eat as I prepare the stew for our supper. Eat.' He pointed at the food on the plate beside her and only turned when she picked it up and took a bite.

'Mmm.' He'd added some of the pickle that Jeremiah MacPherson, the pack's cook, made for special occasions. She had no idea when or how he'd managed to get his hands on a jar of it—Jeremiah horded it for celebratory use only—but she was glad he had.

As she ate her bread and cheese, she watched him cut and prepare the meat and vegetables they'd fetched that morning at the village markets. It was wonderful that one of them had a talent with food—her efforts were rudimentary at best.

'I have not cooked for years,' he'd told her the night before as he'd prepared her a meal rather than collect something from the communal kitchens as many in Pack MacCrae were wont to do. 'My mother taught me baking and we cooked stews and soups together. I always enjoyed it. But after they died, cooking was a necessity, usually rushed, to feed my brother and sisters. Then when Amandine and Frederique got more adept at living in the forests and mountains, they took care of the cooking while I took care of the hunting. I forgot I used to find joy in it.'

By the time she finished her repast, he'd thrown vegetables, herbs and spices into the pot and then the meat to brown—it smelled delicious. She took in a deep, satisfying breath and when he looked up at her, blew him a kiss then turned her thoughts to her letter.

She had much to cover. There was Council news, not to mention her mating and the fact that Morrigan had left and that she couldn't connect via scrying and despite trying constantly, Brionne and her team had been unsuccessful as well so far. She was actually quite annoyed with Morrigan about it. Didn't she care that Morghanna would be worried? She had to know she would try and contact her? It's what they'd always done.

Now, because of her sister's stubborn nature and the way she held onto a grudge, despite the happiness of the last few days, worry hung over her. Was Morrigan safe? Where was she? And how was she going to get her to come back and listen to reason so she could be shown the beauty and gift that was Ali if nobody could reach her?

All of this poured out onto the pages to Bridgette; she'd always been able to confide most things to her friend.

She was on her third page when she sensed her mate had moved from the hearth and now stood behind her, reading over her shoulder.

'No. Do not mention my wolf.'

'What?' She looked down at the words she'd just penned. 'But why? Bridgette will be fascinated to hear about your mixed heritage and what that means regarding the Pact. And she needs to know so she can help me find a way to reach Morrigan and talk her into coming back now we have proof that what we did was right.'

She reached for him but he evaded her touch, instead pacing across the room, his confusion and uncertainty roiling through their bond. With a sinking feeling, she realised he'd not changed into his wolf since their mating celebration. She should have realised. 'Ali. You do not need to keep your wolf contained now. There is no need to keep him secret.'

She rose to go to him. He met her halfway, sweeping her into his arms, covering her lips with his for a mind-spinning kiss before burying his head in the crook of her neck. 'I am sorry. It is difficult to be so open about him after all this time.'

She stroked his hair, holding him close. 'You love your wolf. You always have. Do not let fear continue to be a wall between you.'

He jerked back to stare at her. 'I do not want it to be a wall. But my wolf and I are both afraid we are about to waken from the dream.'

'Does this feel like a dream?' she asked, kissing him again, her hands stroking down his back.

'No.'

She stilled, stepping back a little to look up at him. A frisson of doubt still worried at the bond despite his words—why hadn't she seen this before now? It wasn't simply that he wasn't used to trusting his wolf. 'You are accepted. The whole of who you are.'

'Iain does not welcome me.'

'That is just because of his son and the worries that plague him there. Lachlan still has not returned.'

'I did not think I had seen him around.'

'No, thank the Goddess. He apparently ran off after Iain bonded you into the pack. Sulking no doubt that he did not get his way. He will be back. But until then, Iain's worry will have him keeping up walls where you are concerned. Once that is sorted, he will most likely come to ask you to be one of his lieutenants. You are too powerful not to be an integral part of the hierarchy.'

'I want to be by your side.'

'And you will be. But your magical studies and artistic teachings are not the only things of importance you must see to. You need to fully connect with your wolf and to do that, you must find your own place in the pack. Maybe being a lieutenant will not be that for you, but it is worth trying things and finding out. And the more you do that, the more you will come to feel a part of the life we have here within Pack MacCrae.'

'I would ... like that.'

He sounded so uncertain. She placed her hand over his heart and looked into his beautiful eyes, still shadowed with too many years of betrayals and mistrust. 'Is this what your nightmares are about?' He awoke to them every night, although he obviously thought she did not know by the look of surprise on his face.

'I ...' He swallowed hard, fists tensing at his side. 'I do not want to talk about my nightmares.'

She held up her hands; it was best not to push. 'You will tell me about them when you are ready. But for now, all I ask is that you trust what you felt at our mating ceremony and the pack's welcoming.'

He took in a shuddering breath. 'I want to,' he said, voice rough with emotion. 'But ... are you certain the other packs and covens will feel the same as you do about my mixed blood?'

She sighed, looking back towards her parchment. 'It is true that in the past there would have been great mistrust. But that prejudice died a quick death. The Pact has changed everything. Your parents are not the only Were and witch or warlock to mate. Look at us, for instance. You are no longer an outcast and oddity. And as more witches and warlocks mate with the Were, any prejudices held by those who struggle to let go of the past will be replaced by the beauty of the truth. Your mixed blood is a blessing. A blessing we will pass on to our children; children who will light the way for the years to come.'

'Children?' He stiffened.

'You do not want children?'

14

His Anna's smile flickered.

Ali's fingers tightened on her back and he pulled her to him, his face buried in her hair once more. Damn, he had not meant to make her sad. 'No, it is just, I never thought to have children.' But now she'd mentioned the blissful possibility ... it was like she'd cracked open another wall he'd built inside himself.

'I must admit, it is not something I ever thought to have for myself either, what with the curse my power usually brings to those like me.'

'Curse? There is nothing of the curse about you.'

She pulled back, her expression serious. 'Perhaps not but ... my kind rarely get the chance to fall in love let alone have children. Given what usually befalls Spirit-talkers ...' She shrugged. 'It is easy to think of my powers as a curse.'

'I understand. I too thought I was cursed. I never thought to have children because I did not want to pass that curse on.'

'There is nothing of the curse about you, either,' she said fiercely, returning his words. She captured his gaze with hers as she cupped his face. 'You are a gift. To me. To your family. To our pack and coven. To the world. Do you understand? A gift.'

'As are you.' His lips quirked as she opened her mouth to deny his statement. He put his finger against her lips. 'You are so strong. So sure.'

'About you, I am. Sure enough for both of us until you become sure within yourself. You are safe now. You are welcomed. More than that, you are wanted, needed. The secrets of our future lie within you and our leaders *should* know the blessing you bring.'

He hid the shiver that chased through him as the nightmare images flickered into his mind—images that had terrified him in sleep the last few nights and made him awaken, shaking and covered in sweat.

He'd said to her that he didn't want to talk about them; he most definitely didn't want to think about them either; didn't want to believe them a kind of prescient vision the voice intimated they were; didn't want to think about the fact they might be hers and not his—a lie, surely, given she showed no signs of being inflicted with them as he was. They were his nightmares and his alone. And he didn't want them to affect the joy growing inside from the first moment he'd seen his Anna. *Please, let me have this moment of pleasure. This moment of joy,* he begged of the voice, whatever or whoever it was.

'What is it?' she asked, worry shadowing her beautiful eyes.

He shook his head. He had to be wrong. But if he wasn't, if they were visions, he would make certain the things he saw never came to pass. And that began with not worrying Anna about them. 'Nothing.' He smiled. 'Other than wonder over how certain you are that my mixed heritage brings such hope.'

She beamed at him, the sunshine of it chasing the shadows of nightmare images away. 'I want to shout my certainty to the world. I am proud of who you are. You should be too.'

He cocked his head to the side, smile blooming in the face of her happiness. 'I will settle for all the good you bring to my world.'

She kissed him, longingly, leaving him in no doubt of her feelings.

He was about to deepen the kiss when a knock sounded at the door.

He sighed. He supposed being constantly interrupted was just part of his life now, mated as he was to such a powerful leader.

His mate was the centre of pack life and though there were moments he wished all those who interrupted them to the devil, the fact his mate was so loved and needed filled him with pride. He wished she felt the same. But that doubt wasn't something he'd help do away with overnight. It would take time to get over the way she saw herself. He understood that better than anyone else could, given his own struggles.

The knock came again, more insistent this time.

'I suppose we need to answer that,' she said, her finger sliding across his lips.

He let go of her, but as she turned to walk to the door, took her hand and accompanied her to greet whoever was there.

Dougal stood on their stoop. Alistair hadn't seen him since the night of the mating celebration when he'd run with him in wolf form.

The lieutenant exuded a strength and power that suggested he was Alpha-born, although there was a slight discordance in the other Were's power. He'd noticed it when running with him at the mating celebration but now noticed it even more, the discordancy more prevalent. He'd never sensed anything like it and he wished to investigate further, but now was not the time. Dougal's expression was a lowering cloud.

'Dougal? Is something wrong?'

'Sorry fer interrupting, Coven Leader, but I just wanted to make certain ye had no' been disturbed.'

Alistair barked out a laugh. 'You are disturbing us to make certain we have not been disturbed?'

Dougal shot him a quelling look but then returned his attention to Morghanna. 'Aye. It might seem a bit doolally, but I were simply concerned.'

Morghanna stiffened. Alistair frowned, not understanding what she heard in the lieutenant's words that he didn't. 'What is going on? Why are you checking on us?' No, not on both of them. On Morghanna.

Morghanna sighed. 'Lachlan. He is back?'

Dougal's lips thinned, a tick starting in his jaw. 'He came back agin' last night. Said he were here to do his duty. But when he didna show up for said duty this morn, we worried he might ha' got up to mischief.'

'We have not seen him,' Alistair said stiffly. 'If we had, you would have heard about it.'

'Ali,' Anna said, laying her hand on his arm. Just her touch, it settled him, soothing the anger that roiled through him. 'You should check the wine-maker's store,' she said to Dougal. 'It would not be the first time he has imbibed too much and not turned up for his share of the rostered duty. I imagine he's sleeping off a rotten head and stomach this morning. He will undoubtedly turn up later.'

'Aye, yer most probably right. I'll need to give him a right bollocking when he staggers back home, numpty scrote that he is.'

'I am sure he is fine.'

'Yer more than right. Nothing iver seems to affect the doaty boy but he's worried his *athair* agin more than I like to see. Somat's got to get through to him. Maybe now yer mated, he'll stop gagging after ye and settle into his duties as is proper fer the son of our Alpha.'

'I hope you are right—Alistair!'

Alistair had Dougal by the collar, pushing him up against the doorframe. 'You knew?'

'Ali, please, stop.'

Despite the fact his fury on her behalf was a violent howl inside him, he could not ignore her pleading as she pulled at his arm. He let go of Dougal with a shove. 'You knew! You knew what that bastard was doing to my Anna and did nothing to stop him?'

Dougal brushed at his shirt, pulling it straight, expression an exercise in patience as he met Alistair's furious gaze. 'I will forgive ye this once fer putting hands on a senior lieutenant in defence o' yer mate, but try ought agin, and I willna be so understanding.'

'Answer the question.'

Dougal's expression remained the same but that dissonance around him flared a little more as he said, 'Aye. The other lieutenants and I are aware of his interest. We ha' bin doin all we can to keep him away, but he's a determined lad.'

'You make it sound like it is all a bit of a jest.'

Dougal's calm turned icy. 'I dinna say it be a jest. And I have bin doin all I can to avert the lad's interest.'

'A lot of good that has done.'

'The mon hasna hurt the lass, has he?'

'I think the "lass" has a different interpretation of that. The Alpha told her "boys will be boys".'

'Alistair. Dougal.'

Both men ignored Morghanna's interruption, too busy glowering at each other.

'I admit tha' probably was no' the right thing to say. But all tha's truly needed here is giving the lad some time to grow up and a firmer hand.'

'I suggest you use that firmer hand. Or I will.'

Dougal stepped closer. 'Dinna let anyone else hear ye threaten the Alpha's son. It willna go o'er well.'

'Letting Anna and her people be harassed by the hooligans of your pack 'willna go o'er well' with me. If the Alpha is not strong enough to control his own son, someone else should do it.'

Dougal's cheeks flushed and he growled. 'I thought ye said ye were'na lookin' to overthrow our Alpha?'

'It is not something I wish for, but if he cannot do right by our people—'

'Alistair. Dougal. Stop this right now.'

Both his and Dougal's eyes snapped to Morghanna. He was momentarily surprised that she'd not used her magic to calm them, but when he looked at her, eyes aflame as she glared at both of them, he realised she was too angry to have used magic in such a way. 'Do not talk about me as if I am not here.'

'I was not—' Alistair began, but when she shot him a look—filled with anger and hurt—he wanted to drop to his knees and beg her forgiveness.

She must have felt his contrition through the bond because she put her hand on his arm, her touch gentle, forgiving. But her words were firm when she spoke. 'Dougal has helped to keep Lachlan busy, often giving him sentry duty far from the village at the boundaries of Packland to give me some respite. But he is in a difficult position and cannot act against his Alpha.'

Alistair couldn't fail to see the strange expression that passed over Dougal's face as Morghanna spoke, but it was gone before he could figure out what it might be.

Morghanna turned her ire on Dougal. 'And you. You know newly mated Were are more possessive and likely to lose their cool when other males came close to their mate.'

Dougal, looking thoroughly chagrined, backed off. 'I wasna thinkin' ...' He turned to Alistair. 'Yer power makes it easy to forget yer also a Were.' He made a bow, exposing his neck. 'I apologise fer letting me anger get the better o' me. And I promise to do better in regard to Lachie.'

Morghanna raised her brows at Alistair and he found himself saying, 'Your apology is accepted. I hope you accept mine.' He too bowed and exposed his neck, although he rose a little more quickly than Dougal—he'd never exposed his neck to anyone before. Aside from his Anna, of course. He met the other male's gaze. 'I do not mean to act like a ...' He searched his mind for an appropriate phrase from the many insults he'd heard the Were throw at each other in the last few days. 'A doaty bawbag. Is that the right phrase?' The words didn't sound the same in his accent, but at least he was trying.

Dougal snorted, his lips curling into a smile. 'It'll do. And I will endeavour to do the same.' He held out his hand.

Alistair took it and shook. A knowing passed through him; of years with this Were at his side. 'Friend.'

'Friend.' Dougal said, returning his smile with his own wide one.

'Men!' Morghanna rolled her eyes.

The two men laughed as she disappeared back inside.

'I hope I havena caused trouble with yer mate.'

'My Anna is nothing if not understanding. I am certain she will forgive me my overbearing behaviour—as long as I promise not to repeat it.'

'Aye. I will leave ye to yer pleading for forgiveness. Lucky bassa.'

He laughed the grinning Were lieutenant away.

But before Dougal got more than to the edge of the gardens, he turned back. 'Why don' ye come with me and a few o' the o'er lieutenants on our run a bit later? We run as our wolves and do a regular circuit of Packlands and then swim in the loch. It'll be good fer all of us to run wi' yer wolf agin. And good fer yer wolf too, I ken.'

'I do not want to leave Morghanna.'

'Dinna worry o'er Lachie botherin' her. I will set someone to watch o'er her if ye come. Not that I think he will come near her agin. She's probably right. He's at the mercy o' a mighty hangover.'

The invitation sounded ... interesting. And his wolf was certainly keen. But ... 'Morghanna means to take me to the Dance later.'

'The Dance?' Dougal's brows raised in utter surprise.

'Yes. The Dance. What is wrong with that?'

'It isna a place we Were like to go near unless we have to. I'm surprised yer so keen.'

'It is the only way to truly test my powers, so Morghanna says. And I have never had a problem being in or near a Dance. In fact, it has always felt welcoming.'

'Hmm. I canna say being at the Dance has iver made me feel welcomed. Mostly it makes me feel like running away. Mayhap it's yer warlock genes tha' allows ye to go there so freely.'

'Maybe.' Alistair paused then asked. 'Does it worry you. This difference in me?'

'Don't be daft. Ye being what ye are brings hope that we have taken the right path in this Pact. And if what's in yer blood is passed to others of our pack own through the years, then it will only make us stronger.' He tipped his head to the side, his gaze going off into the distance as a smile curled one corner of his mouth. 'Imagine a time when all Were are unafraid to go into the Dance and gain from it what the covens do. It will be remarkable.'

Alistair had never thought that far ahead, even though

Morghanna had been saying very much the same thing since they'd met. 'Yes. It will be remarkable.'

Dougal snapped back to the here and now and asked, 'So, will ye come fer a run with us?'

Alistair looked over his shoulder to where Morghanna had disappeared inside the cottage. 'I really should go to the Dance with Morghanna. She is keen to understand more of my powers so I can start properly training them.'

'I understand.' Dougal shrugged. 'But at the same time, the Dance isna goin' anywhere and we willna do another circuit fer the rest o' the week. Ye could wait until then, but old MacClaverly says the weather will turn in the next two days and there'll be storms fer our next circuit. Ye'll see more o' our lands this day as they're meant to be seen.'

'I will check with Morghanna.'

'No need to check,' Morghanna said, appearing at the door. 'He will be there.'

'*Miorbhuileach*. I shall see ye then as the sun touches the tip o' the crag. We meet at the hall.'

Alistair waved him off with Morghanna at his side. Excitement skittered through him at the idea of running as his wolf with some of the most senior wolves in the pack.

But as he accompanied Morghanna back into the cottage, doubt wavered over him. 'Are you certain it is fine? You wanted to go to the Dance.'

'It can wait until tomorrow.' She took a seat at the table and picked up her writing instrument.

'But what about the letter and my drawing?'

'I can take them myself when I am finished.'

'I do not wish you to go by yourself. Lachlan—'

'Will come nowhere near the Dance. The Were are suspicious of the stones.'

'So Dougal said.'

'Yes, well, it took Bridgette a lot to convince the Alphas of each pack to meet her at their local stone circles to do the magics for the

Pact. There is no need to worry he will bother me there, I assure you. Besides, this is more important. I am pleased Dougal asked you to go with them. It is a good sign.'

'But the stew—'

'Will improve with the waiting.'

He ran his hand over her hair, kneeling at her side. 'Thank you.'

She smiled at him, taking his hand. 'For what?'

'For forgiving my sorry behaviour outside. I do not wish to give the impression I think you are weak or in need of my protection.'

She held her hand out to him, eyes curiously blank as she said, 'You cannot help bowing to the truth of who you are, no more than I can.'

'Anna.' He wanted to plunge a knife into his chest for being such an idiot. He'd promised to help her understand how special she was and instead he'd gone about doing the opposite with his mulish behaviour. 'I am so sorry for adding to your doubt, but you know, there is nothing to be doubtful about.'

She tried to turn from him, to pull her hand from his, but he held it tight, turning her face gently to look at him. 'Nobody but you questions your authority or your strength. I am absolutely certain that you will always find the best way to deal with any situation.' His lips curled. 'See what you just did for Dougal and me. We could have been adversaries—hell, I was certainly headed that way. But you turned that around even while angry and now I think he will be a friend. A good friend. Without you, that would not have occurred.'

'You are being silly.'

'No. I am not. I am being truthful.' He took both her hands in his. 'Look at the bond and you will see there is no artifice in what I say. As much as you believe in me and my value to pack and coven alike, I believe in you as a leader and powerful witch who will see us to a bright future. I am sorry my behaviour made you think otherwise.'

'Ali.'

He loved the way she shortened his name, the way her lips moved over the breath of it. And as she freed her hands to cup his face, he couldn't help but lean in, taking her lips with his.

She melted into him. He gathered her into his arms and stood.

'Ali!' she protested. 'I must finish my letter to Bridgette. And you must meet with Dougal and the others.'

'We have an hour,' he said, capturing her lips again as he strode towards the stairs.

'An hour with you is never enough.' Mischief and knowing lit her eyes.

He laughed. 'One thing you will learn about me is that I love a challenge.'

She laughed as he carried her up the stairs. It was the most wonderful, magical, sexy sound he'd heard in his life and he wanted to make her laugh like that again and again.

But first, he wanted to make her shout his name to the heavens.

'Ali,' she sighed into his mouth as he lowered her to their bed.

'Anna.'

Then there were no more words, just the sound of their sighs and the creak of the bed as they moved together as one.

15

Morghanna stirred the delicious stew and moved it a little further away from the fire on the swing arm. As she turned from the hearth to get the vegetables he'd chopped earlier that he said he had to go in about now, a smile played about her mouth as memories of their bedroom interlude ran through her mind.

Ali had lived up to his promise to make the hour more than worthwhile.

She stirred in the vegetables and sank into the memories, reliving the way his hands and lips and tongue on her body made heat rush through her veins and prickle under her skin until the rushing sensation tightened and tightened and everything came together to explode in utter bliss. Long, sumptuous, rolling waves of it.

And that was before he'd even entered her and started the madness all over again.

She drifted off into the remembered bliss. But then the memories were interrupted by a burning sensation in her hand.

She jerked away from the hearth, blowing on the redness where steam from the stew had started to burn her. She chuckled at herself.

So silly to get lost in her sexy daydreams when in a few hours she would have the real thing.

Still, reliving the last hour had been well worth the steam-singed hand. Although, looking at how the sun came through the windows, she'd been at it for far too long. It was past time she went to the Dance.

She put down the spoon then ran upstairs to get changed into her ceremonial robe—a wrap-around robe all coven members owned, designed for easy removal for going sky-clad. Not that worshipping in the Dance required supplicants to go sky-clad for every prayer and binding, but for this particular incantation, anything not of her would be sent through the aether to Bridgette along with the package of letters.

She said the appropriate prayers over the robe as she got dressed, then once done, shoved her feet into her walking clogs. She rolled the letter she'd finished an hour after her mate went for his wolf-run, along with Ali's sketch, and bound them together with some string.

She walked to the door, but before stepping out, peered around at the area before the cottage and the edge of the woods she could see.

Despite what she'd said to Ali about being safe from Lachlan, she couldn't help but worry he might be lurking about.

There was no sign of him or anyone else.

Even so, as she walked, she kept a watch out. The Dance was only a fifteen-minute walk from their cottage; it was within shouting distance of any Were in the village if she needed their assistance. But still it didn't hurt to be vigilant.

Once she was there though, nothing and nobody should disturb her except for coven members, so she could drop her vigilance then. Not that she would even have to try. The Dance, any Dance, always felt like home. No matter where they'd wandered in the past or how hunted and worried she and her coven had felt, if there had been a Dance, just spending some time in or near it had always made them feel better.

She wondered if Ali felt the same. She would have to ask him tomorrow.

She rubbed her hands together as she walked, smiling to herself once more. She couldn't wait to find out what the Dance would tell her about his powers. She was certain it was going to be something remarkable.

Suddenly, joy sang through the bond. It became more present with every breath she took. Ali was obviously having a wonderful time on his wolf-run. His pleasure was a beautiful warmth inside, energising her, making her long for his return. Maybe she could talk him into a visit to the hot springs again tonight after they'd eaten.

Spirits clustered around her, some seen, some only heard or felt. She didn't engage with them—she needed all the energy she had for her sending, even with the Goddess power she would borrow for the task from the Dance. The spirits were persistent though, bumping up against her shields, echoes of voices sounding in her mind. She firmed her jaw and strengthened her shields, unwilling to give in to such rudeness. Still a few persistent spirits fluttered around her, trying to be seen and heard despite her efforts. Damn it. She thought she'd been getting better at blocking.

She began to hum to herself to drown out the echoing sound of them. They'd be gone soon enough—the spirits, like the Were, did not seem to like the power that emanated from the Dance. Or perhaps it was the spirits that lived around the Dance they did not like; spirits of ancient things, alien and powerful. A good thing, as they were nothing but a distraction she didn't need right now. Her mate's joy, thrumming more strongly through the bond with every breath, was distraction enough.

Maybe that's why she couldn't seem to completely block the spirits. Something to look into later, but for now, she really had to concentrate on what she was about to do if she didn't want it to go wrong. Castings of this sort were not her milieu.

She roped in her thoughts just as she reached the long grass that shot up between the thinning trees that marked the border of power that leaked from the Dance.

Changing her song to one of prayer and supplication, she began to undo the sash that held her robe together.

The prickle over her skin began as it always did as she approached the ring of stones that made up the Dance. The power emanating from them stroked her senses, both invigorating and welcoming, yet at the same time, slightly off-putting. It was a sensation she'd talked over with Bridgette when she'd first entered a Dance after her parents had died and their covens had joined.

'It is the power of the Goddess you feel,' her friend had said, in that way of hers that seemed to be coming from somewhere else. 'While it welcomes ones like us, it also repels because it reminds us of how small we are in the eyes of the heavenly beings who rule the skies and the stars within them. It is a constant reminder of how small we are, how inconsequential, how very little we actually know in comparison, but at the same time, how lucky we are that our Goddess shares her powers with us and loves us as she does.'

Since Bridgette had said that to her, they'd learned so much about the world they hadn't known before. She wondered how much more they had to discover in her life alone, let alone those that were to come after. The wonders that were to come. It was overwhelming. And exciting.

She wished she could live to see it all.

She sighed, knowing that wish was not to be, then placed all such thoughts aside. If she was to send to Bridgette successfully, her thoughts needed to be clear of all worldly concerns, wholly concentrating on the spell at hand.

She bowed to the stones of the Dance as she entered the clearing, muttering the appropriate blessing. Then she approached solemnly, placed the letter on the ground and disrobed, folding her dress to sit on top of the protection of her clogs. The late afternoon sun was warm, but there was a slight coolness in the air that hadn't been there a few weeks ago—autumn was just around the corner. She rubbed her hands over the goosepimples on her arms and ignored the prickle that ran over the back of her neck—the power of the stones washing over her, through her.

Picking up her letter, she took a breath and said the blessing asking for permission of the Goddess to enter the circle of stones.

Wind whispered through the trees surrounding the clearing; the voice of the Goddess in the way she always heard it, giving rights over entry to her.

Nodding her thanks, she stepped into the Dance.

Power sang over her skin, lifting her hair in a breeze that was not of this world. Whispers surrounded her, overlapping and echoing so she could not make out the words. One of the whispers was louder than the rest, insistent, pushing into her, making her jaw clench, its words, even unheard, disturbing her in some way.

'What are you trying to tell me?' she asked the spirits of the Dance, those ancient beings whose essence had been woven into the stones. But her ability to talk to them as she did with other spirits was limited and, as usual, she could not make out their words, only a sense of foreboding and urgency.

Then one whispered word reached her. 'Mate.'

She stared at the wisps of spirits as they surged around her, that one word ringing in her mind. Were they behaving like this because she hadn't brought Ali here yet to discover what kind of magics he should be trained in? The thought seemed to enliven them, their whispers growing louder yet still unintelligible. Okay. 'I will bring my mate here as soon as he returns from his run.' So much for going to the hot springs again tonight.

The noise didn't cease, but it didn't get any worse, so she continued forward, concentrating once more on the spellwork before her.

The press of the Dance's spirits faded as she walked to the centre of the circle and stood beside the altar stone. Lifting the rolled parchment high, she tipped her face up to the sky. Late afternoon sunlight streamed down, warming her skin. As she canted the words of the transportation spell, the sun's heat intensified, coating her in a flush that caressed and wound around her in soft, humming waves.

The humming became a reality as the power of the Dance rose around her, running through the earth, through the air, touching her, filling her, becoming one with her. Her hair danced around her shoulders in time to the beat of the humming. Then, as the sound reached its peak, she cried out the final words of the spell and let the letter go.

It hung in the air above her for a breath before a flash of light took it and it was gone.

She staggered, the power of the release more than she'd expected given the letter was not heavy. Bridgette must be at the furthest reaches of her sending ability.

She caught herself on the altar stone at the centre of the Dance and breathed in deeply, letting the dizziness and the extra spark of powered energy fall back through her body and into the ground from whence it came.

Finally, when the world stopped spinning and control of her limbs returned, she let go of the stone and stood straight so she could make the benediction to the Goddess, thanking her for allowing her loyal servant to borrow her powers. Once done, she reached out with her mind, entered the aether and tapped Bridgette to let her know something was coming for her.

Instantly, Bridgette opened to her, her power strengthening the weak connection.

'Morghanna. How delightful. I did not expect to hear from you this week.'

'I am sorry to interrupt you, my friend. Even sorrier that I do not have time to chat now. Read my missive and you will understand why.'

'Certainly. You seem happier. Is Morrigan behaving herself? What about the issue with Lachlan?'

She tried not to allow her worry over her sister into the connection—or her annoyance with that Were and his father—instead thinking only of Ali. Smiling softly, she said, 'It is all in my letter. I must go. I used too much energy sending it to you. I need to eat and replenish my energies.'

'Go, eat and rest. We will talk tomorrow or the day after. I will contact you so you can preserve your energy.'

'Thank you.'

'No need to thank me, my dearest friend. Take care of yourself.'

Bridgette sent hugs and love feelings with her words and then was gone.

Opening her eyes, Morghanna looked around her and noticed from the angle of the sun that she'd taken longer than intended. She'd have to run back to the cottage if she were to get there before Ali was due back.

She backed away from the centre of the Dance, surprised when the Dance's spirits rushed to her again as she did so. 'I will bring him,' she assured them as she backed to the opposite side from which she'd entered. She expected to feel them fade back into their stones, but they didn't. They kept hovering around her, their voices a maelstrom of sound heard at a distance.

Why were they behaving in such an odd manner?

She wished she had time to get to the bottom of it, but she really needed to leave if she was to have dinner and bring Ali back here for the testing. She didn't want it to take all night. She had plans for her and her beloved once they were done here.

Smiling to herself, she said the final words of blessings and thanks to the Goddess and the stones, then stepped out of their protection. As she passed through the ring, a sense of rightness and calm brushed over her—she always imagined it was the Goddess' caress. Normally she would take a moment to bask in that feeling, but not now.

Now, she needed to get dressed and hurry back home.

Home.

The word held new delight.

She turned and then stopped.

Hundreds of spirits in their manifest, ghostly forms, stood at the edges of the clearing, their frenetic energy buzzing her nerves even through the power emanating from the stones behind her.

She blinked, wondering if she was dreaming. But she wasn't. They were all there, waving their hands, shouting something she couldn't quite hear.

What in all the hells was going on? Had someone been hurt? Was that why they were all trying so desperately to get her attention? Had Ali been hurt?

No. She would have felt it if something had happened to him. Then what was it?

She hurried around the circle of stones to where she'd left her clothing, power prickling strangely over her back and neck, more intense than before. A few strong spirits broke through the boundary of the Dance's clearing, rushing to her. They flickered as if they had trouble holding their forms, their words a roar of sound she couldn't comprehend because the power here affected the source of theirs.

Goddess. Something terrible must have happened. 'I cannot hear. Come to me when I am away from the Dance and I will try to help you.'

The spirits became more insistent, spinning around her so that their movement created a breeze that lifted her hair. Her skin prickled and twitched as they moved around her, almost as if they wished her to go in the opposite direction. But she couldn't leave without dressing first.

She came upon the grass where she'd left her clothing.

Only her clogs were there. Her robe was gone.

Something rustled at the edge of the clearing. The prickles intensified and the spirits spun around her, as if trying to form a protective barrier.

She shuddered.

A twig snapped behind her in the trees nearest to the Dance. 'Alistair?' she asked, hoping desperately he'd returned from his run early, even while knowing that wasn't the case. Alistair would never create such unease to shift and slide through her. Nor would the spirits react like this to him. 'Who is there?'

'It is I, my bonnie lass.' Lachlan stepped out from behind a tree, her robe cradled in his arms.

16

'Lachlan.' Never when sky-clad had Morghanna felt like covering her nakedness as she did now with Lachlan's avaricious gaze on her; worse than any time before when he'd watched their ceremonies; even worse than when he'd spied on her and Ali up at the hot springs.

He must be the reason the spirits were behaving strangely. They had never liked him and were doing their best to crowd around her now, to protect her in some way, despite the fact the energies of the Dance made them nothing more than mere wisps in the air.

Fighting the shudders creeping up and down her spine, she forced her voice steady. 'Lachlan. How long have you been here?'

'I saw ye leave yer home. I followed ye. I wanted to make sure ye were safe given yer mate didna seem to think it were worth his while to protect ye.'

Unsaid was that he'd been watching her home. He must have come after Dougal had left or the senior lieutenant would have scented him. And he had to have made an effort to hide given neither Alistair, nor any of the other wolves who were looking for him, had seen or sensed him.

The spirits pressed so tightly against her now their presence made her stomach roil with nausea. Knowing she needed her wits about her to deal with Lachlan, she made a quick sign with her hand to send them away. It didn't work. Fear was a skittering presence playing her nerves, making it hard to think straight or use her magic.

And the spirits were making it worse, not helping.

She took a calming breath and tried again.

By some miracle, the spirits, screaming their protest, faded into the veil. Swallowing down her unease—she couldn't show a weakness in front of him—she made her expression neutral as she addressed his last statement. 'Surely nobody would be able to get past the sentinels to attack me at this most sacred of places.'

'Of course they couldna,' he said, stiffening.

Damn, she hadn't meant to insult him—the sentinels guarding Packlands in the woods and hills behind her were under his auspices, something Dougal had put in place to try to keep him busy and away from her. Also, she was certain, to see if giving him some authority could evince a change. So far it hadn't. 'Then why follow me? If I cannot be harmed with the sentinels doing their job, then am I not safe?'

The muscles in his jaw twitched as he stared at her, obviously trying to think of something that didn't sound like he was inferring he and his guards were inept. 'I didna know where ye were going. You didna tell the pack leadership ye were heading out today.'

This time her back stiffened. 'I was not aware I needed to announce my daily comings and goings to the pack leadership.'

'Tha' isna what I said. Ye can come and go on Packlands at will.'

'Then why follow me?'

'I was concerned.'

'About what?'

'Ye left without yer mate. I wouldna ha' let ye do the same if ye were mine.'

She refused to be pulled into that pointless argument all over again. 'Alistair knew where I was going and trusted I would be safe. However, he will worry if I do not return home soon—he is expecting me back for supper.' She kept her face neutral, hoping he didn't know Alistair was out for a wolf-run. 'Please return my clothing.'

'Aye.' He didn't move. 'But first, I ken that ye might owe me somat in return.' He smiled that smile she knew other females found charming but had always made her nauseated. His charm was less than skin deep, the light in the back of his eyes marred by a darkness that came with a male who thought females were property, only there for his pleasure and benefit, and not a breathing, thinking, feeling person with her own set of thoughts and rights.

His attitude made her anger flare. She knew she should control it —she really needed to keep the situation calm and controlled—but Morrigan's words before she left still stung and she couldn't help snapping, 'I am Head Pack Witch and Coven Leader. I should not have to barter with you, let alone for the things that are mine.'

He made a movement with his mouth that might have been his attempt at a little-boy-pout. 'Ye arena any fun, Morry. I were only teasin'.' He held out her robe, still making no move towards her, or indicating he would toss it to her. Typical manipulative Lachlan. It was a game, making it seem like she wanted to walk closer, to be near him, when it was the last thing in the world she wanted. Especially with his possessive gaze running over her naked form, halting on her breasts and the curls at the juncture of her thighs.

He licked his lips.

She wanted to smack him. Instead, she held out her hand and canted a simple spell of translocation. The robe disappeared from his grip, appearing in her hand a blink later. She staggered; her reserves of power nearly depleted after the magics she'd so recently used.

A different frisson of panic fluttered to life in her chest. She shouldn't have done the spell—she needed her magics to help keep him calm, especially now she was certain she'd angered him. A hard expression had replaced the genial one that had been on his face up until that moment.

Shit. Shit. She snapped out the robe with trembling hands, wrapping it around her quickly as she tried to think of some way of calming him without using her magic. Her fingers fumbled on the tie and she swore under her breath, hoping he didn't notice her weakness.

'Tha' wasna nice, Morry.'

His voice—hard, cold—made her shiver and she didn't even bother to correct him about calling her 'Morry'. Not that it mattered to him that she didn't like it—no matter how often she'd asked him to stop calling her that, he'd never listened.

He took a few sauntering steps towards her, a slick smile on his lips. 'Ye need to be nicer to me, Morry.'

She took a step back, the buzz of the Dance hot on her back. She couldn't retreat any further without saying the words of blessing, asking for permission to enter the Dance. To do that, she'd have to turn her back on him—and she wanted to turn her back on him as much as she wanted to turn her back on a rabid animal. 'I wanted my robe. I was cold.'

'I was gonna give it back. Ye just had to ask nicely.'

'I should not have to. You had no right to take it in the first place.' Damn, why was she arguing with him? She needed to placate him, not rile him up.

'Ye could ha' said pretty please,' he said, as if she hadn't spoken. 'Or begged a little. I like it when my females beg a little. And they usually do. They like to beg me fer many things.' He tipped his head as he let his gaze roam over her again. 'But not ye, ye wee bessum. Nae, ye've always been a bit too high and mighty, havena ye? As if yer too good for me. Me! The Alpha's son. The next Alpha of Pack MacCrae.'

She bit back a gasp—how could he not know he didn't have the scent of an Alpha on him? Nor any signs that he was to gain the electric blue eyes only an Alpha carried.

Dougal had both the scent and the sign of blue starting to show in his eyes, but Lachlan didn't. However, calling attention to that fact now wasn't a good move. He was in a mood and she was better served to let him get it out of his system, have his little rage. He was unlikely to hurt her. There would be consequences even he would not like to face if he did. Even so, it was hard to keep her fear from showing.

His lips curled into a sneer. 'Ye are'na being very friendly, Morry. I thought we were friends at least, even if we can no longer be mates.' His gaze raked over her again, possessive, the cruelty he took such pains to hide from the world as clear to her as it had been the first time she'd laid eyes on him. 'Now, I ken what ye can do to make up for bein' so unfriendly.'

She swallowed hard, trying desperately not to break covenant with the Goddess and step backward into the sacred stone circle— she just couldn't commit the double insult of not facing the Goddess and not asking her permission. Better to endure whatever Lachlan had in mind than giving such insult to the source of her power— probably no worse than a kiss, though even the thought of that had her stomach turning.

He stepped closer, reaching out to touch her. His finger slid down her cheek, his thumb running over her lip, pulling it down, the jagged edge of his fingernail digging into the tender flesh. She hid her wince, wishing more than anything in this moment that she had powers like Alistair's that could hold him in place and fling him away from her. Not that she could really use such power on him. It would only make things so much worse if she did. She had seen what happened to others who incurred his hateful wrath. It was already bad enough that wrath was aimed at Alistair.

She needed to try to sweet-talk Lachlan into forgetting about any repercussions he planned and use the dregs of magics that were still hers to use, even if doing so made her flame out.

Skin crawling at his closeness, at his touch, at the possessive insanity that lit his eyes, she stood still, and grasped at the dregs of power she still had access to, trying to smooth them over him, to touch him with some empathy and kindness.

Her powers stuttered, too sluggish still from her exertions in the Dance. She pushed harder.

His gaze caught hers, eyes narrowing. She stilled, pulled her powers back a little. Had he felt that? She hoped not. They weren't supposed to use their powers to manipulate Were, but surely this was an exception?

'Ye carry the bassa's scent.'

'Of course I do. With pride. Alistair is my mate.'

He leaned in and sniffed her. 'I preferred it when ye didna smell like a scabby bawbag.'

She slapped him.

For stunned seconds, they stared at each other.

Goddess, what had she done? It was like she had Morrigan inside her, making her do what she normally would not. She waited for his flare of anger, but only coldness showed in his eyes. Hells. 'I am so—'

He grabbed her, fingernails digging into the flesh of her arms through the material of her dress. Before she could move, he jerked her closer, his nose running along her neck. 'How about I make ye carry the scent of a true Were?'

The power of the Dance sparked at her back. Too many years of obeyance to the laws of the sacred rings of stones made it impossible for her to enter them without permission even now. Instead, she pushed at him, hoping to make him move back a few steps and give her room.

He didn't let go, his fingers tightening around her arms painfully. Then, moving more swiftly than she'd thought him capable, he grabbed both her hands. Jerking her forward a step, he forced her hands behind her back, where he manacled them in one of his.

She struggled against him, shocked he had gone so far, fearful he would go further than a kiss. 'Lachlan, stop. You do not want to do this. There will be repercussions if you hurt me.'

'I will only hurt ye if ye continue to struggle agin me. Come now, Morry. I ken ye want this. Ye've always wanted this.' His erection pressed against her stomach.

She shuddered. 'I am mated! Let me go.'

'It be a false mating. He be no true Were. And, I dinna wish to e'er let ye go.' He rubbed himself against her.

She wished now she had taken heed of the spirits and moved further away from the Dance so she could call them to help rather than send them away. If anyone deserved to be locked in never-ending terror and insanity as the spirits did their worst, it was him.

She couldn't even ask for the help of the Dance's spirits, given she was outside their domain.

Her fingertips tingled, but not with magic—he was cutting off the blood flow with the strength of his grip. She tried again to grab at the dregs of her powers and shove them at him, to calm him or maybe even make him sleepy, but they simply stuttered and did nothing more than stroke the edges of his anger, his insanity.

Panic threatened to overwhelm her, but she couldn't let it. She tipped up her chin. 'You will be punished for this insult. You are breaking the new laws.'

His mouth twisted into a smile and he trailed his free hand up her side, skating across her ribs, between her breasts to circle her throat. He squeezed slightly—a promise? A warning? —before he let go and began to stroke her hair. 'What care I o' the new laws when ye look at me wi' those come-fuck-me eyes, Morry?'

Before she could answer his insult, his mouth was on hers, mashing her lips against her teeth in a punishing, horrifying kiss.

17

Morghanna was so shocked she couldn't move. He didn't care that he was breaking all sorts of laws. Didn't care he would be punished.

She'd been such a fool.

Morrigan had been right. Lachlan wasn't a mere nuisance. She should have done more to stop this from ever coming to pass. How could she have expected Iain to take it seriously when she hadn't?

Not that why mattered right now. Only how she could get away from him.

She struggled against him, turning her face. The hand gripping her hair tightened, stopping the movement. She could barely feel her hands now but she could feel the Dance, its powers sparking close behind her. Maybe she should try to enter it—it would make him let go. And he couldn't enter the Dance; her more than any of the Were in Pack MacCrae had been afraid of it. It was surprising he had even drawn this close.

Surely the Goddess would forgive her now for breaking her covenant to keep herself safe from him?

She lurched back, taking a few, stumbling steps towards her goal.

He swung her around, away from the edges of the Dance and

down to the ground, her hands trapped behind her. Her cry was punched out of her and into his mouth as his weight pinned her to the hard ground. Sticks and sharp stones dug into her back. She tried to think of a spell to push him away but couldn't bring anything useful to mind—not that she had power left to use. Even so, she tried to send out empathy and calm through her aura.

As she did so, a tiny bit of power sparked inside her—possibly energised by her situation. *Thank you, my Goddess.* With that small gift, she tried to bind him with a spell of sleep she used on patients.

It simply slid off him.

Her hands were numb under her, the loss of blood a scream in her arms as his mouth ravaged hers, trying to force hers open as his hands and body held her in place. She clamped her lips together and firmed her jaw, fighting him with every part of her that wasn't her magic. She bucked, lifted her knee, aiming for his groin. He shifted just in time, her knee connecting with the inside of his thigh.

He grunted and pulled back, a glint in his eye. 'Ye do like the rough.'

She opened her mouth to scream, but he slapped her, hard enough to make her ears ring.

'Ye want to scream? I'll make ye scream.' He punched her in the jaw. Stars spun across her eyes, shock and pain robbing her of control over her limbs. She lost control of the barrier around her aura.

That was when she truly felt him, the secret, horrible heart of him. It was an emptiness inside him, a dark oily thing that clung to his soul—was this the reason her powers had slid right off him?

If it was, that made it even more terrifying.

As she lay there, frozen in shock at the reality of it—she'd always sensed some part of it, but not to this degree—tentacles of dark, oiliness moved out, poking at her, trying to find a way in.

Goddess, help me. She couldn't let it in. If she did, she knew with certainty that it would pull her under; drown her soul.

She struggled again, harder. And as she did, she suddenly knew what it was.

She'd never seen it before. Only Bridgette truly had. But from her descriptions, this was it.

Oh Goddess.

She really couldn't let it touch her, couldn't let it—

Her breath exploded out of her as he grabbed the collar of her dress, tearing it. She bucked and tried to strike him once more with her knee. He backhanded her again.

Multiple points of pain shot through her head. She couldn't think. Could hardly breathe past the pain, the nausea. He shifted, his hand moved down her leg, pushing her dress up.

Pain shot through her arms—they were no longer trapped beneath her. He'd lifted from her enough so that she rolled off them in her struggle.

He lifted his hand, a dark glint in his eyes, his erection pressed against her inner-thigh. She swung her arm and whacked him in the side of the face, gouging with her fingernails. She'd been aiming for his eyes, but her arm wasn't functioning properly, pins and needles shooting along its length, the limb ten times heavier than usual. But the hit was enough to make him lurch sideways.

She pushed with her hips, further unbalancing him, heaved again and managed to push him off her. She kicked out, connecting with his groin. Kicked again as he screamed his pain. He fell sideways, hands grasping where she'd landed two good kicks. She scrabbled sideways, away from him, trying to make it to her feet.

Her head swam and her ears rang. Her numb arms weren't working properly and she couldn't gain traction to push herself upright. She centred herself, remaining on her knees as she breathed in, trying to regain some calm, hands planted on the ground. But her head kept swimming and she couldn't see straight. Behind her, Lachlan moaned, but it wouldn't be long until he pulled himself together and came after her. Her feet were bare so her kicks hadn't packed the punch she needed to keep him down long.

She had to move. She had to.

She took a deep breath and pushed upright, groaning against the pain as her head throbbed. She thought she was going to manage it, but the world swung around her, nausea rising to coat her throat. She stumbled on the rough ground, falling with a thump to her knees. Her ears rang and she couldn't hear properly on the side where his blow had landed. It had affected her balance. What was she going to do?

Her fingers curled in the grass.

They began to tingle with power.

She gasped.

Power surged in the ground around her, rising, ready for her to pull on.

A gift from the Goddess to help her in her time of need? Or simply power that leaked from the Dance into the surrounds? Not that it mattered. She could use this power against him. It was allowable within the Pact to defend against rabid, unthinking, violent Were or coven members who used black magics.

However, could she use this power without the proper prayers? Using this residual power that came straight from the Goddess, without the proper spells to prepare herself, the proper respect paid to the source of such power, would bring untold consequences. She'd be punished. Perhaps her coven with her. But surely, to protect herself from this violent Were, she would be forgiven? Surely, by making it known this power was here, waiting for her to use, the Goddess was giving her permission?

But what if she was wrong?

Did it even matter right now?

Then another thought hit her. What if it was too much? If she was too weak to hold it? What if it burned through her?

As if in answer, the power flared, burning her fingertips. She cried out with pain, pulling them against her chest.

Hell. If it was that bad with just that little flare, it would be too much if she tried to take on more without asking for permission; with permission would come a certain amount of the Goddess' protection.

She made a sound of frustration, her anger and pain ringing through the air.

She had to think; had to think. She didn't have time to ask for permission, so what could she do?

She was closer now to the spirits who clamoured around the boundary of the clearing trying to get to her. But could they truly help? Lachlan was strong. And insane. Would the spirits rushing him even worry him at all? Especially given what she suspected was inside him, driving him to these acts of madness and violence.

Her gaze landed on the circle of stones across the other side of the clearing. She pushed to her feet. The blessings of permission to enter didn't take as much time as the rituals of gaining permission to borrow power. And once inside, the Goddess would surely help her. Give her access to magics she could use to stop this violent Were or call others who could.

Lachlan's screams of pain turned to screams of rage. She had to move or he'd be on her again in a moment. She pushed herself up.

She had to get to the Dance.

She stumbled a few steps before falling back down. The fall knocked the breath out of her. Her head span.

She tried to pull on her magics again, to clear her head, but her attempt sputtered, failed. She dug deeper. Then noticed the Pack-bond shining brightly within her.

Yes! Why hadn't she considered this before? Even though the covens mostly used the conduit to give excess power to the Were, they could also pull power the other way if need be, like Abigail and Leanna had done to heal Alex's broken leg.

She'd never thought to use it in this way though, but if there was a time to try it, surely it was now. It was her only hope to hold Lachlan off until she managed to get to the Dance.

She focused as best she could with panic and pain scattering her thoughts, grabbing at it inexpertly. Iain would no doubt wonder what the hell was going on, but she couldn't let that worry her now.

She braced herself for the rush of wild power to cascade through her.

Instead, she was shoved back.

What? Why would Iain resist her need like this?

She was about to try again when another bond throbbed in her mind, a far stronger bond, pulling her attention to its glow.

The mating bond.

Of course. She could use it. Why had she not thought of it before? She touched on it.

A roar of rage thrummed through the bond, vibrating through her, giving her strength. He was coming—he'd felt her terror, her pain when it started minutes ago—but was too far away to help her right now.

But she could use the strength she gained from their bond to take control of her power.

It began as a tingle and then with a rushing roar, surged through her, firing every synapse, every sense, clearing her head, pushing pain and fear away. She felt so strong, stronger than she'd ever felt. She snapped upright, suddenly on her feet with no memory of even trying to gain them.

Lachlan had pushed himself upright and was snarling at her. His claws were out, glistening like ebony, fangs elongating in his mouth. Rage pulsed from him; a rage that could not be reasoned with, could not be stopped by pleading or reminders of what he owed his pack, his coven's leader. Even the wolf was gone from his eyes, taken over by something else. Something darker and totally, utterly insane.

'Ye are mine!' he roared and then sprang towards her.

The Dance was still too far away. Without a second thought, she pulled on the mating bond and sent power spiralling out of her fingers—not her orange Healer power, or the purple of her Spirit-talker power, but one that was blue tinged with green.

It struck Lachlan square in the chest, the strike so strong it threw him across the other side of the clearing to smash into a young tree. The tree cracked then fell to the ground. She turned, thinking to make it to the safety of the Dance, but Lachlan sprang back up before she'd taken two steps—how had that not knocked him out? A snarl of rage filled the air.

He leaped towards her once again, claws lengthening.

She struck out with a stronger blast of the power—Ali was

purposefully fuelling the bond now, sending her too much, and yet, she couldn't refuse even though it would weaken him. She needed everything if she was to knock Lachlan out for long enough to get to safety.

The power slammed into Lachlan with a smack like thunder. He flew back, further this time, smashing through a tree, sheering it in two before colliding with another. It wasn't enough. He leaped up, bounding towards her, his hands half-changed, face the same. Long sharp teeth glistened as he howled to the sky.

A beast.

It wasn't a Were transformation. It was nothing she'd ever seen before.

She didn't have time to run, only had one more chance to stop him with a hit of Alistair-fuelled witch-lightning. Her mate was so strong, but she'd already pulled on too much power, and there was a limit. Always a limit.

She raised her hands. Lightning shot from them again, striking Lachlan as he came at her, murder in his eyes.

He flew across the clearing, taking down another two trees. He didn't move for one breath, two. Had she done it? Stopped him? Goddess, she hoped so. She turned to run to the Dance, the blessing of permission to enter forming in her mind.

A horrifying broken growl tore through the air. Morghanna glanced over her shoulder, stumbling to a halt as her eyes widened. She should run, keep running, but the sight of him ...

His shirt rent down his back as his body morphed into something half-man, half-beast to match his face, his claws. He stood, red-eyes glowing, saliva stringing between deadly sharp teeth, his claws longer, glistening with an oily black that shifted and swirled.

'Mine,' he growled around his teeth. Then he came at her.

The need for flight surged through her, shoving movement into her limbs. She ran towards the Dance even though she knew she wouldn't make it. He was too big, moving faster than she'd ever seen a Were move before. She stumbled, the power inside her nothing but a stutter, her energy almost gone. She couldn't pull any more from Ali, couldn't seem to access the bond to the pack, almost as if for some reason she was being denied her right to use it.

She glanced over her shoulder. Death came pounding towards her, so close—too close. She wasn't going to make it.

A howl from her left had her stumbling, turning.

Ali leaped into the clearing in his wolf form, coming between her and the beast that was Lachlan—how had he got here so fast?

In her head she heard the words, 'Use this,' as her mate shoved power at her through the bond.

The beast raised a clawed hand to strike Ali down as he closed with the wolf.

Morghanna pulled on the energy surge her mate had thrust at her, noting in the back of her mind that it tasted of the Dance and not him. Power drew up from beneath her feet, shoving into her, giving her more—she couldn't have stopped it even if she wanted to. It fired through her, burning every synapse and muscle and vein with a strength the like of which she'd never felt before.

She cried out, hands flung before her, gaze narrowing on the Darkness that surged in Lachlan's core and released the energies cascading through her.

She had no control over it—she'd not asked permission—so she couldn't monitor its strength, make sure it was enough to knock out, not kill. It simply poured from her, a raging flood of pure white energy, and struck Lachlan in the middle of his chest with a sound that made the leaves in the trees around them shake.

Lachlan wasn't thrown this time. He stopped in mid-stride, frozen, hand held high as the white lightning surged around him, outlining him before arrowing through him to the black presence in his heart.

A scream drove out of him as he shook violently, the lightning so intense her eyes watered. She could no longer see him.

Her head throbbed and spun, the green of the canopy above her fading.

The last thing she saw was the shadow of her mate's outline racing towards her as she collapsed.

18

Anna's terror slammed through the bond, punching the air out of Alistair's lungs. His muscles seized for the barest second and he stumbled. The speed he was going turned the stumble into a fall, but he went with it, rolling across the forest floor before springing to his feet again.

Without even a thought to tell the others what was happening, he spun around, and took off to where he could feel Anna; feel her terror. Every ounce of his being was with his mate, giving her everything she needed, trusting that his wolf would navigate the rough terrain and get them there as quickly as possible.

Her terror was a cold vicious slash in his mind, in his heart.

By all the hells, what was happening? She wasn't answering him through the bond. He cursed that it didn't allow him to see.

His wolf whimpered inside him, stumbling, and he realised he was letting that terror seep through and into his mind, clouding his thoughts. On instinct, he gave over more of himself to his wolf; he needed his animal's speed, the clarity of its thoughts, the violence of its teeth and claws to fight whatever it was she faced. But even so, frustration and fear sang through him—it was taking too long to get to her. Why did he have to go for a run with the others today? Why was the Dance so far away? If only he were trained, he might be able to transport himself to her right—

He almost fell over his paws as she pulled more of his power.

By the Gods, her fear. It was a sizzle through his nerves, racing through his veins, making his heart squeeze. But at the same time, she was standing so strong against her foe—her strength, it took his breath away.

The power of the Dance tingled through his veins as he drew closer, making it difficult to keep his wolf's form, but he had to keep it. It was his only way to protect her given she was sapping him of nearly every ounce of his power.

What the hell did she face?

He howled as he leapt into the clearing that was home to the Dance and then almost faltered.

A creature of nightmare bore down on his mate. She stood firm as she faced the monster in front of her, but desperation shot down the bond—after the last blast of power, she had nothing more in her with which to fight.

He couldn't understand why she wasn't using the power all around her. She had to use it. He wasn't going to be able to stop whatever this was. It was too huge, too rabid, energies surging and sparking through it, a power he had never come across before. He might keep it busy for a short time, giving her a chance to run, but he was certain it would make short work of him and then be on her moments later.

No!

He drew on the power all around him, as much as he could pull into him, and then pushed it down the bond to her, shouting with his mind for her to use it as he put himself between her and the monster.

He crouched, ready to spring as the half-man-half-wolf lifted a glistening black claw to strike at him. Witch-lightning shot above his head, startlingly white, tasting of Anna and of the earth, the wind, the trees, the air and the stars above. It hit the monster square in the chest, light cascading through him, over him, trapping him in place.

Eyes that had been full of possession and hatred a moment before filled with terror and pain as the creature began to shake. Eyes he recognised.

Lachlan.

Alistair growled, would have struck out, but something shot through the mating bond and he turned, just in time to see his mate crumple.

'*Anna!*' Her name was a howl and as he leaped towards her, the change came over him, rainbow light sparking all around, so that when he landed beside her, he was in his human form.

He lifted her gently into his arms, cradling her against his chest.

Her dress was torn, her face bruised in multiple places, blood on her lips and nose, cheek split open.

He snarled, both man and wolf, wanting to tear Lachlan to pieces but he couldn't leave her.

He glanced across the clearing to see what had happened to the Lachlan-beast. He lay on the ground, white lightning sparking around him, wisps of smoke rising from his skin; skin that was pink and black and glistening. Whatever Anna had struck him with had burned the bastard.

Good. He hoped it a killing pain. If not, Alistair would have to kill the bastard himself.

A gentle hand touched his face. He looked down.

Anna, her precious eyes so full of love, whispered, 'You cannot kill him, my love. It is against Pack Law.'

'He attacked you. He must be killed or exiled.'

'Not exile.' She clasped his face in both hands, fingers trembling. 'He will become rabid.'

'And then his fool of a father will have no choice but to hunt and kill him.' As he'd had to hunt and kill his little Sophie. A horrifying thing made even more horrifying when she'd gasped with her last breath, 'Sorry. I could not stop myself.' Her words had made him realise a part of her remained within the insanity-driven wolf she'd become, knowing what she'd done while being completely unable to stop it. But while such a fate was a horrific cruelty for an innocent like his sister, for someone like Lachlan ... 'It is the only fitting way to deal with one such as he.'

'Yes,' she said, her voice choked. 'But he is not a normal Were. There is something evil inside him. Who knows what he will do if separated from the one thing keeping him grounded?' Her gaze fixed on the Lachlan-beast. He had started to slowly change back into a man. Lightning zapped over him but seemed to be centred over the areas that were still primarily beast-like.

'Anna? What is it?' She was shivering.

'In his eyes I saw death. So much death.' She closed her eyes, the skin around them fragile with her tension. 'It was like seeing slices of a horrifying future.' Her eyes fluttered open, gaze meeting his. 'If he's exiled, I'm afraid of what might come.'

He wanted to deny what she said but there was something in her voice that reminded him of his nightmares. He still didn't believe it was a vision, but it did not matter. All he knew was she was right. Her fears and his nightmare could never come to pass. 'Then he must be sentenced to death.'

She shook her head, her chin trembling. 'Iain. I doubt he will sentence his only son to death.'

Given what he had found out from Dougal earlier about the Alpha's lack of action in regard to Lachlan, he feared she was right.

Ah hells.

He wrapped his arms around her trembling form, stroking her hair, kissing her head, whispering noises of love and comfort, needing to calm her before the others arrived. They were near. He could feel them through the Packbond. Had they followed him when they realised he'd run off, or were they called here, like him, by her distress and fear? Probably the first because if her bond with the pack was as sensitive and strong as her bond with him, they would have turned with him and been right behind him. Would have helped to defeat Lachlan.

Her fingers tightened on his back, clinging to him as she took in deep breaths. Hell. She'd been through so much, been attacked so suddenly, had fought so bravely, had exhausted everything in her, and in him, until she'd grabbed at the power he'd thrust at her; power that still trembled in the air all around them. It was probable she was also affected by it still; it had lived so vibrantly inside her only moments ago.

He'd only held it for a moment and yet it still zinged through his veins, made him more aware of every breath, every sensation, than he'd ever been in his entire life. In any other circumstance, it would have been exhilarating.

But he was too worried for his Anna.

A howl in the distance. Others in the pack had sensed their witch's upset. He hoped their Alpha had the clarity of thought to make them stay where they were. The last thing Anna needed was to have a crowd here, staring. By all the Gods, she was in no fit state to deal with the prying eyes of those who should have protected her.

Hells. He wanted to pick her up, to take her away from this place that should have been filled with peace and positive energy but was now tainted by the memory of betrayal and violence. Yet, he had to make sure Lachlan didn't come around and try to escape before the Alpha and his lieutenants arrived to take him away. Iain would undoubtedly be shocked by what his son had done, but he could not deny or turn a blind eye to it any longer.

A noise off to the right alerted him to the presence of the Alpha and Dougal. They came as men, not as wolves—had Dougal taken time to fetch his Alpha? Further proof he hadn't truly felt Anna's distress until it was almost too late—and ran into the clearing, the readiness of their change an electric charge around them. Despite the difficulties of changing in this space, they were ready for it, prepared to protect and defend their Head Pack Witch, even though they were too late. Sounds in the distance indicated more were holding back just outside the clearing, waiting to be called. Good.

They slowed as they took in Alistair, the way he held Morghanna protectively in his arms, and changed direction to join them.

Iain halted though as he caught sight of his son. He paled, mouth slack. Alistair had to admit it was a shocking sight. Lightning sparked around Lachlan where his hands were clawed and over his face where his mouth slowly changed from the monster's heavily fanged one back to his human visage.

Dougal stopped next to him looking equally as shocked, his gaze on Lachlan's hands. They were still the black-tipped and glistening claws of the creature, looking as if they could tear apart anything living with one deadly swipe.

'What happened here?' Iain asked, his voice hoarse as he took a few hesitant steps towards his son. 'Who wove yon magic?' He looked up at Alistair. 'Was it ye? Did ye do tha' to my son?'

Before Alistair could say a word, Anna pulled from his arms. Despite how battered, bruised and shaken she was, she held the force of a queen as she said, 'Alistair did nothing more than come at the first sign of my distress when Lachlan attacked me.'

'Lachie attacked ye?' Iain's gaze grazed over her bruised cheek, her split lip, the tears and grass stains on her robe before moving to his son. His mouth trembled, eyes darting as if trying to find some other meaning in her words that didn't implicate his son in such a treasonous attack. 'Lachie would niver—'

Dougal's hand on Iain's shoulder stopped the words that could have caused untold damage between the coven and the pack if uttered. 'Ye ken Lachlan's problems, my Alpha. We canna deny it any longer. Especially now.' He seemed to choke a little as he waved at Anna, the signs of an attack obvious on her. 'This goes beyond ought he did with his other obsessions.'

Obsessions? As in plural?

'There are others?' Anna said, voicing his thoughts. 'How is it you never mentioned those to me when we spoke about Lachlan? You made me feel like it was just me.' She shook with outrage.

As did Alistair. He glared at the Were he thought could be a friend.

Dougal had the grace to look away. 'I am sorry to ha' given tha' impression. But we hoped to keep his ... sickness ... hidden. We've always managed to stay abreast of it afore. Aside which, most of the females he obsessed o'er were happy wi' the attention.'

'Most?' Anna stiffened. Alistair didn't blame her. 'Which means there were some females at least who did not welcome his attentions. Who perhaps even pleaded with you for help?'

The look on Dougal's face showed Anna had struck a true note.

She obviously saw it too, the sizzle of her anger strengthening in the bond. 'Yet you did not give it, did you?' She made a hissing sound when they didn't answer. 'Your lack of action is appalling. It makes me sick.' She swallowed hard, gaze boring into Iain. 'What did he do to them? Did he rape them as he tried to rape me today?'

'Nae!' Iain and Dougal said together.

Iain shrugged off Dougal's hand, stepping closer to Anna. 'He niver showed inclination to do such afore. He just didna see their disinterest. Didna hear their rejections. His mind would twist it around until he believed they *were* interested.'

'And you did nothing to help them?'

'Nae. We did what we could.'

'And what was that?'

'If they didna want his attention, we sent them away.'

'You did what?'

'It isna as bad as yer makin' it sound. We had affiliations with smaller packs in need o' a larger breeding pool and those females were happy to go wi' more chance to find a mate. If it looked like he might search for them, we would divert his attention with a willing female and more responsibilities in the pack. It was niver a problem afore ye.'

Anna barked out a horrible laugh. 'I always wondered why there was a greater number of males than females in a certain age group and now I understand why. It also explains the weakness I have always felt in this pack.'

A weakness, Alistair saw now, that she had blamed herself for. His anger peaked again, but he did not need to spill it. Anna was taking them on without his help.

'You sent away critical members of the pack!' she snapped. 'And did everyone a disservice, all so that Lachlan would not be punished for the wrong he was doing? You should have locked him away years ago when you first realised he had this sickness. Instead, you played into it and made him worse until Alistair and I had to deal with him today.'

Iain took a trembling step towards her. 'I couldna,' he said, voice full of fear and tears. 'I couldna lock my son away. He's all I had after my mate died. The only reason I didna follow her in death. He is my only heir.'

'He is not your heir. He can never be Alpha!' Anna shouted. 'That would be an abomination.'

'Tha' we ken,' Dougal said, his voice calm and steady—admirable in the face of so much tension. 'We would niver ha' let it happen if he had a hint o' Alpha in him, but as it were, he niver showed any signs o' being our next Alpha. His eyes niver showed the slightest hint of blue.'

'He does not smell like an Alpha either.' Alistair's gaze arrowed on Dougal. 'But you do. In fact, you smell like more of an Alpha than him. And you have flecks of blue in your eyes. The same blue as him.' He nodded at Iain. 'Except, there is something not quite right in the Alpha-scent, or in the way your power fluctuates around him.'

Dougal blanched.

Iain hissed out, 'Ye canna know tha'.'

Alistair frowned and shifted his perception just a little so that he could see the auras surrounding the two Were opposite him. His eyes widened. 'You are feeding him Alpha power. How? Why?'

'What?' Anna stared between them. 'That is impossible.'

'Look.' He gestured at them and felt the moment she used the bond to see what he saw. A tear in Iain's soul where the mating bond had been, the essence of who he was slowly and inexorably leaking through that tear and fading away.

'Oh, Goddess. Iain.' She took a step towards him. 'You are dying.'

Iain's eyes filled with terrible sadness and pain before he dropped his gaze. 'Aye.'

'But why do this?'

'Fer my pack. And fer my son. They needed me too badly, so I forced meself to stay after me mate passed. Their need only became greater with the Pact. My son and the pack need stability through this time o' change. A change o' Alpha would ha' made it more difficult fer so many of our weaker pack members. And yer right. I did no' help the matter by sending some essential members away to safeguard them from Lachie's illness. But I had to give them the stability a known Alpha brings.'

'You drained yourself to keep them safe.'

'Aye.' He reached out and grasped Dougal. 'But my number one is a bonnie strong lad, and he's made certain nobody knew how sick I am. We planned to slowly change the structure of Pack MacCrae so tha' he could take o'er without there being the surge experienced when one Alpha cedes to another. But Lachlan's obsession with ye has made tha' far more difficult.'

Understanding dawned slowly on Anna's face. 'Because Dougal and your other lieutenants have had to spend a lot more energy dealing with him.'

Iain nodded sadly. 'We were hoping the fact ye were not Were, the obsession would quickly move on. He has niver shown interest in non-Were afore. We couldna ha' known he would go this far.'

She stared at him for a moment. 'So you do not know what he truly is?'

'What are ye talking about?'

'He is not simply suffering from a sickness. He is infected by the Darkness.'

19

Iain staggered as if hit. 'No.'

'Impossible.' Dougal's voice was a mere whisper. 'Bridgette said the Pact rid us o' the Darkness.'

'She did. We thought it gone. But I felt it in Lachlan just now. Its power signature is unmistakable. What I do not understand is why I did not see it until now.'

'It must ha' made its way back into the lad,' Dougal suggested.

'Or perhaps it never fully left him,' Alistair said quietly.

'Tha's no' possible,' Dougal said, his hand on Iain's shoulder as if to keep his Alpha upright.

Alistair gestured at Lachlan's prone form. 'You said it was not possible for him to have the Darkness in him because of the Pact, yet Anna said the evil entity is most definitely in him. Maybe it is the reason for his sickness.'

'Do we need to be afeard it is still in any o' the rest o' my pack?' Iain asked, eyes pleading with her.

'I do not know,' Morghanna said. 'Given no others have reacted to our Coven in the same way that Lachlan has, I would say no. But in regard to Lachlan, I think Alistair is correct. The Darkness used Lachlan's sickness somehow. Whether it caused him to be like he is from the time before the Pact, I could not say. But I suspect it somehow used that sickness of spirit and mind to stay with him somehow.'

'Are you sure it be in him still?' Iain's voice wavered.

She pointed towards Lachlan. 'You cannot deny what you saw when you arrived. Nor can you deny the evidence still there for all to see. Look at his claws. Those claws are not normal for even a partially shifted Were.' Black-tipped and glistening with something oily and writhing within. Just looking at them made her skin crawl. 'No Were should be able to turn into what he did.'

'Are ye certain twas no' the magics ye used upon him tha' caused him to be like tha'?' Iain asked.

Ali hissed out a breath and opened his mouth, but Morghanna grabbed his arm, shook her head and he subsided, his pride and confidence in her ability to stand up for herself shimmering down the bond. 'Your grief and shock will excuse only so much, Iain.'

The Alpha's jaw squared even more bullishly. 'But tha' thing he were when we arrived, with the claws and the hair and the ...' he gestured at his mouth. 'E'en when we had the Darkness inside, our wolves niver looked like tha'. We are larger than wolves, certainly, but nothing more unusual than tha'.' He shook his head and pointed at his son. 'Tha' wasna normal. Somat o'er than the Darkness had to have done tha' to him and if no' ye, then mayhap twas somat else.' His eyes narrowed as his gaze shifted to Alistair, a growl low in his throat. 'What did ye bring with ye, loner?'

Ali bristled, but he didn't do anything more than curl his fists at his side and take in a deep breath, his accent stronger as he spoke. 'I brought nothing with me. I have seen nothing of its like in all my travels. I have heard of nothing like it either. Whatever that was,' he gestured at Lachlan, his lip curling, 'was inside your son just waiting to burst out.'

'But this didna happen until ye arrived.'

'His arrival had nothing to do with it,' Morghanna said, anger a tight fist in her chest. 'He was that creature before Alistair even arrived in the clearing.'

'He coulda done something to me Lachie when he zapped him with his magic at the springs.'

'Lachlan turned into a wolf and leaped to attack us both. Alistair had no choice but to use his magic. It was the only way to protect me.'

'Lachie said ought about tha'. He only said yer mate attacked him.'

'And you believe him? After everything you know of him?'

Iain opened his mouth, florid pink deepening his pale cheeks, nostrils flaring.

'Iain,' Dougal said, his voice sharp. 'Ye ken the newcomer did ought to yer son.'

'How do ye ken tha'?'

'The old rhyme,' he said, his voice dropping to a harsh whisper. 'O' the Beast.'

Iain's face turned grey. 'The Beast,' he muttered. 'Nae. It canna be.'

'The Beast?' Morghanna's gaze searched first Iain's then Dougal's faces. 'What have you not told me?'

'Nought,' Iain said sharply. 'It is but a *sísceal*. A faery-tale. Something we tell our bairns to frighten them. Nought more.'

She gestured towards Lachlan. 'I think maybe it is something more. Most faery-tales have a grain of truth in them.'

'Not this un. We dinna need ye making up stories to turn the pack agin my son.'

'Iain!' Dougal placed a firm hand on his Alpha's shoulder. Something seemed to pass between them and after a moment, Iain dropped his head in his hands, making a moaning sound. Dougal stepped closer, his arm around the older man, and spoke for him once again—so obviously the true Alpha, she wondered she'd never seen it before. 'Our Alpha meant no disrespect, my Lady. It is simply part of a dark heritage we do no' like to think about. And to ken it might no' only be true, but here.' His gaze flickered to Lachlan and back. 'It's like being pulled back into a nightmare when we thought the nightmare o'er. Ye ken?'

Oh, Morghanna 'kenned' all right and it only made her angrier. Iain should have dealt with Lachlan and ceded his position to Dougal long ago rather than using up his power to keep his son as stable as he could, sending members essential to the pack's stability away and then acting like a leech on his second—the Alpha they should have —and his lieutenants. But allowing her anger to spill out would not get her the information she needed.

She needed to know what they knew of this faery-tale they spoke about. A shiver of knowing had swept over her the moment Dougal had mentioned the Beast. What they knew was important to what was going on now.

Alistair took her hand in his, fingers winding with hers, his comfort and support allowing her to push the anger aside. 'My people understand nightmares. We too have many dark periods in our past. Things we are not proud of. Things that began the mistrust that led to the Witch Trials and the burnings. They are cautionary tales told to our people, to our young. Tales told to keep them alive, so we will not forget. Because forgetting allows them to surface and threaten us once more.' Dougal nodded as she spoke, but Iain didn't look at her—he barely seemed able to lift his head. She ignored him and spoke to the male who should be Pack Alpha. 'So, tell me about these tales of the Beast.'

Dougal's brow furrowed as he rubbed his free hand on his leg. 'There isna much. Mostly a rhyme spoken to our bairns when they misbehave.'

'Tell me.'

'It's bin a while since I heard it. Let me see if I can ken it agin.' He thought for a long moment, his lip caught by his teeth, before he spoke.

'The Beast rises from anger and madness
Wi' serrated fangs, claws dripping darkness
The Beast hunts and kills through night and day
Sundering in two the Were who may
Stand betwixt him and the eternal dark
Losing the essence of man, wolf and mark
Blood and death are wha' the Beast brings
Blood and death and endless suff'ring.'

Morghanna shuddered. 'That certainly describes what Lachlan turned into. Looking into his eyes was like looking into blood and death and suffering.'

'I think I heard something like that from my mother when I was a child,' Alistair said, his voice distant.

'You remember your mother telling you that?'

'No. But she must have told me.' He turned to her, expression puzzled. 'It feels so familiar. So ... true.'

She twined her fingers with his. 'I do not think your mother told it to you. I think this rhyme is part of your heritage. Something you should never forget because it speaks a truth. It is why you acted as quickly as you did.' Pulling on the power of the Dance and throwing it at her. Something that was forbidden; hopefully they would both be forgiven for his transgression due to the circumstances. But it would be time to worry about that later; for now, she had more pressing issues at hand. She took a deep breath and continued. 'Deep in your subconscious, you must have known it was the only thing to subdue it.'

He nodded slowly. 'I think you are right.'

She touched his face then turned back to Iain and Dougal. 'Is there anything else? That rhyme only tells us of the horror of it, not where it comes from or how it can be vanquished.'

Dougal shook his head slowly. 'Only tha' if our bairns are naughty, we tell them the Beast will come to tear them apart.'

'That is even more gruesome than the rhyme,' Morghanna said.

'It is what they needed to know,' Alistair said slowly.

'What do you mean?' Morghanna and Dougal asked at the same time.

He stared down at her, horror dawning in his eyes. 'It does not simply refer to a physical tearing. It is a soul tearing. A tearing of wolf from human.'

'But tha' ...' Dougal shook his head, a growl deep in his chest. 'Tha' isna possible.'

'You think not?' Alistair pointed towards Lachlan where he lay, breath shuddering in and out as if the lightning was still cascading through him. 'The claws, the fangs. They look as such because they are full of ... evil. Destruction. They pulse and drip with the evil I saw in his eyes.' He shook his head as if coming out of a trance, out of a nightmare. 'Maybe the warning in the rhyme, in what you told your children, is more than just remembering a nightmare. If what Anna says is true, and this Darkness is in him, then what that rhyme is truly telling us is that the Beast was created to destroy the Were.'

'Nae ... nae ...' Iain said, the words almost a blubber of sound as he shook his head in denial.

'The Darkness was in us fer centuries,' Dougal said. 'Surely if it wanted to kill us, it would ha'.'

'Maybe it could not do so. Maybe it did not have the strength or the way. Maybe the Beast was an experiment that only worked under certain conditions—on those who were already sick in the mind and soul.'

'Speculation willna get us anywhere,' Iain snapped, evidently having gathered enough energy from his lieutenants to stand upright again. 'We need to concentrate on the now.'

'Looking to the past can inform the future,' Morghanna said, quoting her favourite teacher, her grandmama. 'But you are right. Figuring out how the Beast came to be in Lachlan is less important than figuring out what to do to stop it from coming into being again.' She paused, met Dougal's gaze. 'There have been no signs of it before?' Morghanna hadn't seen any signs of something so horrifying in Lachlan before this. Egotism, misogyny and narcissism sure, but never anything like this Beast. But she had only known the pack for a short period.

Dougal shook his head while Iain spluttered, 'Do ye ken if we had, we wouldna ha' done ought about it?'

'I do not know, Iain. At your own admission, you have done very little to curb your son's worst nature over the years.'

'Well, I wouldna ... I wouldna ha' ignored tha'.' His face crumpled as he looked at his son again. 'My puir lad doesna deserve this ... thing to infect him an' ruin his life. We need to get rid of it so he can be a normal Were once agin.'

She thought of the lack in him that had nothing to do with the Darkness. 'I am not sure he was ever a normal Were. Getting rid of it might not change his behaviour at all.'

'Aye,' Dougal said. 'But we need to stop it from coming into being agin and I dinna ken old myths and *sísceals* will help right now. We need to ken what the catalyst were.' Both Were looked at Morghanna with an expression of expectation.

'You think I can help you with that?'

'Ye were the only one h—'

'Ye did or said somat to bring it on,' Iain interrupted.

'You blame my mate?' Ali growled. 'Still? After all that has been said? What kind of Alpha are you?'

'Me precious boy is a victim of the Darkness according to her.' Iain jabbed his finger towards Morghanna.

'Were you not listening? He tried to rape her!' Alistair took a threatening step forward, the growl emanating from deep inside him growing louder.

Iain and Dougal immediately bristled, growls emanating from both their chests. Dougal stepped in front of his Alpha. The air bristled with tension and with the power of the change as the light started to morph around them.

Magic tingled through her as Ali pulled his abilities to him.

'Stop!' Morghanna stepped in front of him, turning her back on the other men to face her mate. She couldn't let him attack their Alpha. It would be taken as an Alpha-challenge—he had Alpha stamped on him in the same way Dougal did—and he wouldn't have to simply fight Iain, he would have to fight Dougal as well.

Even if he won against both Were, he would be horribly injured. If he lost, he would either be dead, or badly injured and immediately exiled. Given she couldn't live without him—she knew it as surely as she knew the Goddess fuelled her powers—the result of either would be the same. She would follow him, leaving her coven in a terrible position of weakness with a pack that suffered under the leadership of an Alpha who loved his son more than his people. If he was exiled, she'd go with him and the result to her coven and this pack would be the same.

She grabbed his arms, tried to imbue calm through touch and into the bond. The growling stopped—his wolf listening to her immediately, although his posture was still that of a male ready to attack at the smallest provocation, his power still a simmer inside. 'Alistair, please,' she whispered, fingers tightening on his arm. He glanced down at her, his eyes filled with such adoration, fury and pain that it made her breath catch. He hurt because he couldn't defend her, couldn't protect her due to the position they were in. He knew it—she could see that he did—but that knowledge did not sit easily with him or his wolf. 'I love you,' she whispered, sending him a caress and a kiss through the mating bond.

His tension softened under her touch and while he didn't move back, his posture changed to one less threatening.

She turned to the Were behind her. She hadn't worried they'd attack her. Because of the Pact, Were must protect and care for the coven members who shared their power with the pack they were bound to. Despite the fact Lachlan wasn't so constrained and Iain had almost let harm come to her because of his inaction, she was confident Dougal would not let anything more happen. Without the coven, the pack would revert to the state they were in under the Darkness' influence. No Were in their right mind would want that.

Morghanna staked her life on that fact when she'd brought her people here and tied them to this pack, just as she'd staked her life on it when she'd turned her back on them just now. Looking at the Alpha and his second, she saw her assumption was correct. Both Were had backed up, the power of their change having dissipated as fast as it had come.

A cry pulled her attention from them to Lachlan.

He writhed on the ground, his face full of a tortured kind of ecstasy, his claws elongating again, the poisonous black shifting and billowing in them.

The Darkness was fighting back.

She tamped down on her panic as Ali gripped her hand. Power

flowed from them to Lachlan, feeding the magics that had loosened their hold on the Darkness-fuelled Were. The lightning sparked, brilliant white once again, tendrils wrapping around him. He screamed, struggling against its hold.

She held her breath, waiting to see if it would hold—she and Ali were almost tapped out and they couldn't keep pulling from the power around them—she feared the consequences of them having already done so, let alone what might happen if they kept using it without asking for permission.

Slowly, his shift into the Beast began to reverse.

She let out a ragged breath, leaning a little against Ali.

'Why did he start to revert?' Dougal asked softly.

She was about to shake her head when the answer came to her. 'Your aggression. He is feeding on it. You all need to calm down.' She focused on Iain. 'Especially you. Your familial link would affect him most strongly.'

'Me puir Lachie!' Iain stumbled towards his son.

'No!' Morghanna moved to intercept him but Dougal and Ali got there before her, grabbing his arms, pulling him back.

'Let me go to me son.'

'Do not touch him,' Morghanna snapped. She softened her voice when he looked at her, face filled with worry and pain. 'None of us can touch him. Ali is right. I think his claws are poison. When he is fully man again, you can go to him, but not before. But you must calm yourself. I think heightened negative states act like energy to the Beast.'

'My Alpha. Breathe. The calming mantra.' Dougal grabbed the older male by the shoulders and leaned his forehead against Iain's. 'With me.' He closed his eyes and breathed in deeply, letting the breath out slowly as he counted back from ten, repeating it until Iain stopped struggling and joined him. Finally, the Alpha took a last breath and broke contact with his second, standing up straighter than he had since arriving. '*Tapadh leat*, Dougal.'

'*'S e do bheatha*, my Alpha.'

Iain touched the other man's face, the caress filled with care and love.

Morghanna blinked rapidly and turned her focus to Lachlan. He'd stopped writhing, his claws smaller, the poisonous clouds of ebony in them moving sluggishly now, fading. 'It is working,' she said. 'I think if we can all stay calm, he will soon return to normal.'

Iain nodded, but didn't say anything, his gaze pinned to his son, a look of such agony in his eyes that Morghanna couldn't help feeling sorry for him despite what his inaction had wrought.

Dougal faced her, his hand on the older Were's shoulder. 'Please. Help the lad.'

Morghanna bit her lip. She was afraid that nothing would help him except the full expulsion of the Darkness and maybe even then he would never be a trusted member of the pack because, the more she thought on it, the more she realised that the Darkness would never have retained its hold if there hadn't been something essentially rotten at Lachlan's core. 'I am uncertain what I can do.'

'Tell us wha' happened here,' Dougal said. 'Mayhap we can figure it out together.'

20

Morghanna took in a deep breath and closed her eyes, taking herself back, no matter how painful, to the moment her joy had turned to fear. Her words were slow, halting, as she relived those terrifying minutes.

Ali tensed at her side, his fingers tightening on her hip, his breath gusting hot against the side of her face as she told them the progression as Lachlan turned from peeping Tom to rapist, to the moment he transformed into the Beast, including her inability to use her magic to calm him down. 'I tried to reason with him, but he was beyond reason.'

'Then how did ye subdue him?' Dougal asked. 'Wha' is tha' lightning tha's keepin' him bound? I've niver seen its like used among the coven.'

'That is because nobody has used its like before. I did not even know such a thing was possible.'

'Then how?'

She glanced at Ali and he picked up the tale. 'I felt my Anna's terror and opened myself so she could use mine. But the power to keep him at bay drained us both quickly. Then, as I entered this clearing, I felt ancient power lying just under the surface. I did not know why she did not pull on it, but did not have the time to ask. I gathered it as soon as I got close enough and pushed it at her to use.'

'Tha' is agin the law!' Iain said.

Lachlan twitched and moaned.

'Iain,' Dougal said, his grip tightening on the Alpha's shoulder. 'Calm. Yer son needs ye to stay calm, ye ken?'

Iain gulped, took a deep breath and after a moment, said evenly, 'Bridgette told Alpha McVale when they bonded us to the Pact that ye could niver use the Goddess' power like tha' agin' us. There are rules about how ye take it straight from the source and wha' it can be used for. How could it ha' bin used agin' Lachie?'

'I niver learned about such rules,' Ali said, his voice rough. 'And even if such rules apply, surely law does not outweigh the need to keep my mate—and your Head Pack Witch—safe. I did what I had to. If there are consequences, I will own them.'

'Aye. There will be consequences,' Dougal said. 'I ken tha' from Leanna.'

Morghanna blinked at him. 'Leanna talks to you?'

'Aye. I noticed her standing alone at one of the pack ceremonies not long after ye all arrived. I wanted her to feel included and welcomed, so I went to talk to her. It took a few visits—and a few bribes of the sweet cakes she likes—but she did eventually start to talk back and tell me o' her life afore ye all came here.'

'Huh.' The young and powerful witch barely spoke to anyone since her parents were consumed by their power before the Pact was made. She'd been caught in the backwash of the explosion and bore many lash-like burns across her body, neck and face. She tended to stick with those she knew, and even then, barely talked. The fact she talked enough with Dougal that he was informed about the consequences of taking power that should not be used was ... interesting.

'Enough.' Iain swiped his hand through the air. 'I dinna care who talks to whom. All I care abou' is what can be done to help me puir boy.' He met Morghanna's gaze, his own full of pleading. 'Can ye use the power ye used to subdue Lachie to rid him o' the Darkness?'

Morghanna slowly shook her head. 'I do not think so. While it is more powerful than anything I have used before, given the way the Darkness so quickly fought back, I think it is most likely a temporary solution.'

'But surely the magics in this clearing are the power of the Goddess,' Dougal said. 'Wasna it power like this tha' Bridgette used to banish the Darkness from us when binding us to the Pact?'

'Yes and no. The power here is from the Goddess, but Bridgette did not only use the power of the Dance. She channelled directly from the Goddess, increasing and adding to her own power—and her natural power overshadows mine a thousandfold, even without the help of the Goddess. What is here,' she glanced around, lifted her hands, 'is droplets as opposed to the ocean that Bridgette used. Nowhere near enough to keep him fully contained or to rid him of the Darkness.'

'How can ye be sure?' Iain asked, his anger and desperation vibrating in his voice. 'Surely there's somat ye can do?'

She closed the distance between them and took his hands in hers. He shook, badly—a horrible indication of just how weak he really was, how much Dougal and the other lieutenants had been propping him up, hiding how close to death he was, all for the sake of protecting his rotten-at-the-core son. Despite her anger with him, she wished there was something she could do to give him what he wanted. But there wasn't.

He must have seen it in her eyes because his face crumpled as he said, 'I canna exile me own son. I canna.'

'No,' she said, fingers tightening on his as the knowing of earlier swept through her. 'You must not exile Lachlan.'

'It's the law,' Dougal stated from behind Iain. 'After what he's done, surely ye ken it's the only punishment.'

'They are right, Anna.'

'We must find another way.'

'Ye canna possibly want him to stay after wha' he tried to do to ye today?'

She met Dougal's surprise with a frown. She tried to feel out the knowing a little more. It wouldn't give up the words to her, just the feeling, like she'd felt earlier when Ali had suggested the same, that sending Lachlan away was the worst thing they could do. 'I have a horrible feeling that if we let him out there with the Darkness still inside him, it would be more dangerous—to everyone, not just our pack and coven.'

'He could die of grief-separation first. Some exiled Were do; saving us from hunting them down and killing them.'

She shook her head. 'It would be nothing so simple with Lachlan. He would turn rabid. And a rabid Beast is not something I think any of your Hunters could ever bring down.'

'What do ye suggest we do with him then?'

'We keep him contained until Bridgette can come back. She is the only one with the power to rid him of the Darkness forever.'

'Would she do tha'?'

'She will if I ask.'

'And ye will ask?'

'Of course.'

'Even after what he did?'

She frowned at Iain. 'Do not mistake my wish to take care of this for sympathy. I do not do this for Lachlan. I do this for my coven. For the pack. And for all the females who have been victimised in the name of his sickness.'

Iain's gaze filled with shame and, shoulders slumped, head lowered, he said, 'Do whate'er ye can. Please.' Then he turned and walked away.

Dougal's gaze remained on him for a long moment before he turned back to her and whispered quietly, 'Can *ye* keep him contained until Bridgette arrives?'

'We can.' She took Ali's hand in hers. 'With the coven's help. But not forever.' She glanced at Iain—his posture slumped, the vigour she'd always thought of as his completely gone, making him seem shrunken and fragile. 'I will contact Bridgette as soon as I recover my energies and ask her to travel home as quickly as possible.'

'When will tha' be?'

'Tomorrow. Maybe the next day.'

'It will take ye tha' long to regain yer powers?'

'No. But the fact we have to use some of our energies to keep Lachlan subdued means it will take double the time it normally would for me to gain enough power to do a sending.'

'Can no' one of the others do it. Leanna fer instance? Is she no one o' the more talented scryers?'

'Leanna is good at scrying, but Brionne is stronger. But I am not talking of scrying. Sending is different. Scrying only allows us to see and hear, to spy or pinpoint a location, but not communicate.'

'Well, could she or one of the o'er strong coven members do a sending?'

'No. I have been meaning to train some of the others, but there has been little time. The only other coven members with the knowledge and power to do a sending safely are Morrigan and Abigail. Morrigan is gone.' She swallowed hard against that fact. 'And I would not ask Abigail to risk it in her condition. Especially now.' The powers around the Dance felt strange; jumpy and erratic, pulsing in a way she'd never felt before. She wouldn't risk anyone to try to use them until they had settled down.

'Vera well.' He nodded. 'Is there ought the lieutenants and I can do to help?'

'Perhaps. I have never used this much power before in one go, and certainly not anything like it since we bound ourselves to the Pact. But maybe the Packbond might help.'

'How?'

'When I tried to pull power from Iain earlier to help defend myself, he shut me down.'

Dougal grimaced. 'That was me, I'm afeared.'

'Why would you do that?' Ali asked, eyes blazing as he stared down the other male.

Dougal's gaze flickered to Iain. 'I'm sorry for tha', Morghanna. I wasna prepared and when ye called for the power, ye started pulling it straight from Iain. He almost passed out. I threw up a block to stop the power drain from killing him. I had no idea the need was so great. I will ne'er do such a thing agin.'

'See that you do not,' Ali said.

Dougal met his gaze, then spat in his hand, holding it out to Ali. Ali spat in his then placed his hand in the senior lieutenant's. The air sizzled around their hands as Ali further sealed the vow with his magic, their gazes locked.

'Ali, you do not have to bond the vow with magic,' Morghanna, said, a little worried Dougal would take offence.

'No, it be better that he do,' Dougal said. 'This way ye are both in no doubt as to my veracity. I will no' let ye down agin.'

He nodded at Ali, who nodded back, then they let go their hold of each other.

'So, back to what we can do to help. Ye need to pull power from the Packbond?'

She nodded. 'I know we have only ever done it for Healings, but the conduit is supposed to go both ways, so theoretically, if there are no blocks put up on your side to stop me, I should be able to pull enough power through it to help me recover faster.' She frowned as she followed Iain's progress. 'Although, I am uncertain it will be enough. Iain is so weak, and it would do nobody any good if he were to die because of it. Perhaps it is best if I do without for now.'

'He should not be Alpha,' Ali said.

Dougal's jaw squared but he didn't meet Ali's eyes as he said, 'Tha' is no' yer call. We have done what we ken is best for Pack MacCrae in this time o' difficult transition. When the right time comes, he will step down and I will ascend, but until the pack is stable agin, this is the way it must be. Ye ken?'

Alistair glanced over at Lachlan, his hatred of the other Were a burning through the mating bond. 'Such a waste of energy and talent all to help his worthless arse.'

'Our Alpha loves his son. Tha' was enough fer me. It should be enough fer ye now yer a member of this pack.'

Ali narrowed his eyes. 'Being a member of the pack does not mean I should follow blindly or give my loyalty where not warranted. I have been packless and I 'ken' that much. As its next Alpha, you should know the truth better than any. If he cared about his pack as he should, this should never have been allowed to come to pass.'

Dougal's jaw clenched, a flash of anger flaring in his eyes.

'Dougal,' Anna warned, her gaze going to Lachlan.

Dougal gave her a short nod and breathed in and out deeply a few times. 'If ye need to use the power of the pack, then take it from me.'

'I am not bonded to you. I have only ever used the conduit through Iain.'

'As yer mate pointed out, Iain is no' truly Alpha. My link with him gives me power a lieutenant normally does no' have access to. It might no' be the straightest way through the link, but ye should be able to feel me there.' He held both his hands out. 'See if ye can sense it.'

Morghanna gripped his hands and closed her eyes, seeking out the bond. 'There,' she said after a moment, the flutter of Dougal at the far reaches of her consciousness. She concentrated harder and he came more clearly into focus. Through him, she could feel the other lieutenants, something she'd never felt through the bond with Iain. But still, it wasn't the strongly defined bond she had with the Alpha. She had no idea what would happen if she tried to pull power through it and said so.

'Mayhap if we do a blood binding, it will strengthen?'

She withdrew her hands from Dougal's. 'Mayhap. But if I blood bond with you, I do not know what may happen with my bond with Iain. It may circumvent it, given you are far stronger.'

'Why is that a problem?' Ali asked.

'Because it would flag to everyone what is going on with Iain.'

'I still do not see why that would be a problem.'

'It would destroy the pack,' Dougal said.

'I think you are overstating his importance. Would you not just step in to take over?'

'Ye dinna understand the importance o' the hierarchy in a pack?'

'Why would I? I have never been in a pack.'

'What about yer mother's pack?'

'My mother's pack.' Ali snorted. 'They chased us away, threatened to kill us, hunted us through the forests and across the mountains far from their lands. I learned nothing but fear and betrayal from my mother's pack.'

Morghanna put her hand on his arm, her gaze meeting his. 'They were afraid of what you were and what it meant. And there was probably not a little jealousy given you had control over your wolves and were not bound to the moon.' She turned to Dougal. 'He knows nothing of pack or how this could affect Pack MacCrae.'

Dougal's nostrils flared as he glanced over at Iain, who stood hesitantly a few metres from Lachlan, but then nodded slowly, let out a long breath and said, 'I dinna ken how ye could no' have been part o' a pack afore now. Pack is everything.'

'I had my brother and sisters.'

'It's no' the same. Did you no' feel an ache, a sense of loneliness, as if there were somat important missing?'

Alistair opened his mouth, his denial clear in his eyes, but before he could say the words, his eyes clouded over and he frowned. 'I ... yes. I suppose I did. I thought it was because I missed Mama and Papa and then Sophie. But since I joined this pack ...' He looked up at Morghanna in wonder. 'I did not realise until now. But that feeling ... it has gone.' He touched his chest, rubbed it with his knuckles. 'I feel full. Complete. Even though Frederique and Amandine are far away and I miss them, as I will always miss Mama and Papa and Sophie, that aching chasm inside me is gone. The mating bond filled most of it, but it was not until I ran with the other wolves that I felt truly fulfilled.'

'Tha' was when ye cemented yer bond to the pack.'

He met Dougal's gaze. 'Even though I do not trust our Alpha?'

'Yes. The Packbond is made up of more than just the Alphabond,' Morghanna said. 'It is made up of multiple threads to those you are most closely connected to within the pack, but also is bound into the hierarchy through trust and friendship.' She glanced over at Iain. 'If the pack found out suddenly that not only was Iain unfit to be Alpha, but his lieutenants had hidden it from everyone ...'

'It would be seen as a betrayal by the leadership,' Dougal continued. 'Packbonds that tie the various families together would begin to break down. There would be chaos an' anarchy. Even if we explained tha' we ha' done what we did fer the good o' the pack, and even if many saw this to be true, o'ers would see it as their opportunity to grab fer power.'

'What about loyalty to the Alpha? I thought that was sacrosanct.'

'There is loyalty, aye, but that loyalty does no' fly in the face o' a leader who would endanger the pack. Loyalty to pack is king. And there are those who would think we put our loyalty to Iain o'er the good o' the pack.'

'Is that not exactly what you did?'

'Nae. Iain is a good Alpha.'

Ali snorted.

'He is. Ye might no' see it now, but afore his mate died, he was one o' the strongest, most stable Alphas in the north. He and Ioan McVale kept all the packs in line and all o' us safe from the dangers many other packs suffered. He led us well through our darkening years afore Bridgette created the Pact, e'en while suffering fer the loss o' his mate. Ye canna ken the strength it takes to outlive yer mate. Ye have no right to judge him.'

Morghanna looked over at the male who bore no resemblance to the one Dougal spoke about. 'I wish I had known him then.'

Dougal nodded. 'He was a good Were. The best Alpha. So, while we did no' agree wi' his decision to cover up his son's sickness, we supported him as it seemed to cause no danger to the pack. By the time we discovered how much o' his energies he were giving to keep Lachlan stable and the pack strong, it were too late to do ought but support him. A change o' leadership just when the Pact was created would ha' destroyed our pack as surely as it would now if the pack were to discover wha' has been done. E'en the coven would be affected by the chaos and uncertainty. We canna allow anyone outside o' us and the lieutenants to find out. Fer the good o' Pack MacCrae, it must be so.' He looked between Morghanna and Alistair, his gaze intent. 'Ye must keep it secret. I will ha' yer vow now to keep it so.'

'We will keep it secret,' Morghanna said. 'But you must understand that keeping this secret will make it more difficult to keep Lachlan subdued because I will not be able to fully utilise the magical energies in the pack if I need them.'

'Are ye sure ye canna blood-bind wi' me?'

'Not and keep Iain's condition a secret from the pack. Can you speed up the transition in power from him to you?'

His mouth thinned as he rubbed his jaw. 'I dinna think so. We were working on it happening o'er the next eight to ten years.'

'What?' Alistair blurted. 'That long? That is absurd.'

'Things do no' happen fast wi' the Were. We are long-lived and change takes time, especially regarding the transition from one Alpha to the next. Only death o' an Alpha would speed up the transition out o' pure need. Fer our current situation, we had to take into account how long it would take fer our people to settle into our new existence wi' the coven; the setting up o' the new laws; the melding o' families with inter-racial matings and so on. No' to mention, the change wi' the coven leadership being a part o' the pack hierarchy. It has bin a lot fer our people to take on. A change in Alpha in anything less than eight years were stretching it.'

Morghanna sighed. 'Very well. We will just have to do the best we can. I will try to limit how much I pull from you and the lieutenants through Iain.' She glanced over at Ali. 'The next few months are going to be a challenge, my love. It is not the new mating period I had hoped to share with you.'

He touched her face, his expression softening. 'As long as I get to be with you, my treasure, I do not care how our time is spent.'

'We will have to speed up your training. As soon as my power is rejuvenated, I will bring you back here to do the testing.'

'Is that the wisest use of your power right now?'

She shook her head. 'It does not matter if it is or not. It is necessary. We need to know your strengths and start your training. I feel I will need to lean on you far more than I ever intended until Bridgette gets here.'

'My power is yours. You never have to ask.'

She went up onto tiptoes to kiss him, aware of every bruise and strained muscle from her altercation with Lachlan and the influx, then drain, of the incredible power her mate had pushed into her.

She trembled at the thought of what the consequences would be of their hubris in using that power without permission. A dark knowing shuddered through her:

It would not be good.

She shivered and pressed her lips harder against her mate's, ignoring the pain of her split lip. But she couldn't lose herself in his kiss this time. Her mind was too full of what had happened and of what she must do when she got back to their home. She would have to spend much of tonight praying to the Goddess, asking for forgiveness and lenience. Given she'd never done anything like this before, she hoped the punishment would be minimal for breaking the laws of the Dance.

She shivered again.

Ali pulled back from their kiss, gripping her shoulders. 'Are you sure you are well, Anna?'

'I am fine.' She managed a tight smile. 'Just tired. And a bit sore.'

'I will have a Healer sent to ye,' Dougal said.

'Thank you.' She turned around and looked over at the male who was partially responsible for the trouble she now found herself in. Iain hadn't moved from his position near his son, but it was clear he'd been sobbing. 'I think your Alpha needs you,' she said softly to Dougal.

He nodded, turned to go, but then turned back. 'Let me know if there is ought ye need and I will make certain ye ha' it.' His lips twitched. 'I be sorry fer all o' this. I will make up fer it. I promise.'

He turned then and walked over to support Iain. As he joined his Alpha, other Were walked silently out of the woods—they'd obviously been waiting there—going straight to Dougal and Iain. The lieutenants. All eight of them.

They gathered around Lachlan. Thankfully, he was back to his normal appearance. She did not know how they were to keep this all secret from the pack if what he'd turned into got out. Particularly if she wasn't able to use her magics in time to keep him unconscious.

Perhaps she should ask Leanna to concoct a strong sleeping potion to give to him. She and her mentor, Abigail, had been working on ones that would work on Were physiology and had one that had proved successful when setting the broken bones on a youngling the other day. Anything she could use that would keep him unconscious and give her time to recover would be good.

Hells, she needed more time. She needed more strength.

She needed ... more.

21

Alistair wanted to draw his mate into his arms, wanted to shield her from the probing eyes of the other Were, to carry her away, but fought against his need. His Anna needed to stand firm before these strongest members of the pack. She didn't need him undermining her.

Not that he truly could even if he wanted to. Even now, despite the pain of her injuries he felt simmering along their mating bond, she stood tall and sure, holding off the shakes that were sure to grip her as the adrenaline surge that had helped fuel her abated.

She didn't flinch when interested gazes flickered her way as Dougal spoke to the lieutenants, telling them that Lachlan had fallen prey to an illness that had made him attack her because he did not recognise who she was. The lieutenants simply nodded; he couldn't tell if they believed the story or not, but it didn't matter. They would make certain this was the story circulated through the pack.

Lachlan was unconscious as they lifted him, his body floppy, head needing to be supported by one of the men. He would probably stay unconscious for some time. Good. It would give his mate time to recover before she used more magic on him to bind the Darkness so it couldn't turn him into the Beast again.

Soon, everyone had departed, leaving them alone in the clearing. His mate turned to him, but as she did so, her knees gave way. Alistair grabbed her, pulling her to him before she fell. 'Anna? You are not fine.'

'I am. Just some dizziness. It is passing.'

They stood, still and silent, his arms around her, holding her close. He breathed in the scent of her, his fingers playing in the curtain of her hair. He kept his touch light, comforting, but rage still roiled inside him. When he thought of what could have happened today just because Iain was too weak to do what should have been done ...

The bruises and cuts on her face alone were something that shred him just to look at. He wished he was a Healer so he could at least take away that pain.

'What is wrong, my love?'

He touched beside the bruise on her cheek. 'I want to hurt our weak Alpha for what he has done.'

She stroked his face. 'I know. I did not think it possible an Alpha could be so selfish in the face of his pack's needs.' She pulled his face down and kissed him. He kept it gentle, worried about her split lip. She pulled back. 'Please, do not focus on what has been. We must focus on what is and what can be done.'

He nodded, brushing his fingertips over her cheeks. 'You are so wise, my treasure.'

'I am glad you think so.'

'It is not only me who thinks so. Dougal respects you and your leadership.'

She smiled, winced as her lip stretched. He wished he could offer her part of his shirt, but he was naked after the change. Instead, glancing to her for permission, he tore off a piece at the hem of her dress and held it against her bleeding lip.

And as he tended to her, he couldn't help but sense her doubts. About herself. About her ability to do what must be done. He knew she didn't believe him that Dougal truly respected her. Her next words proved him right.

'If Dougal did respect my leadership, would he not have told me the truth about Lachlan? Perhaps even asked for my help with him?'

'I suspect that has nothing to do with his respect for you and more to do with the fact that, until recently, they took care of their own. He respects you. More than you could know.'

She stared at him for long moments as he blotted carefully at the cut and blood on her cheek. 'Dougal is a good man. When they finally transition the leadership, I am sure the pack will begin to return to what it was.'

He frowned, wanting to discuss her doubts further but knew now wasn't the time to put forward his argument. Those doubts were obviously deep seated and it would take more than one session of talking to get to the bottom of them. Besides, despite her strength, she'd been through a trauma and a shock, and he didn't want to make that worse. So he nodded slowly and said, 'Let us return home. You need these wounds taken care of. And you need to rest.'

'We both need rest.'

He held her close to his side as they began to walk slowly home. Nobody came near them, a fact he was grateful for. He hoped the Healer Dougal said he would send wouldn't arrive until he got Anna home and changed into something not ripped and blood-stained. And had a chance to get a few cups of the mulled wine that she was so fond of into her. She did not need to have any of her people see her like this. She would think it a show of weakness, even though the way she'd held up showed the true nature of her strength.

'We need to speak of what we will do with Lachlan.'

She glanced at him. 'That is decided. I will gain back my strength and then I will use the aether to contact Bridgette.' She frowned. 'I am a little worried though that I will be denied access to the Dance so soon after we used its powers without permission.' Her fingers gripped his arm a little more tightly. 'If only you knew how to travel through the aether, I could guide you to do it.'

'I still do not understand why there is nobody else who could do the sending? I felt some powerful talents at the meetings I attended with you. And as I have passed through the village. It makes no sense you take this on yourself entirely.'

'As I said to Dougal, they are not trained. Besides, I am not taking it on myself. I have you to help. And Dougal offered his help too. And very soon we will have Bridgette back among us to rid us of this evil.'

'You could do it yourself.'

Her head snapped to him, eyes wide. 'No. I could not. I do not have the power necessary.'

'Yes, you do. With the power of the Dance, we could set a spell to help us channel directly from the Goddess as you said your friend did when she first fought the Darkness.'

'We cannot do that. It is forbidden.' She swung around to face him, stopping him from walking. Fear on her face, she clutched his arms, his shoulders, his chest, her fingers flexing and shaking. 'Promise me you will not do that.'

He took her hands, stopping their frenetic movement. 'Surely the Goddess would not have an issue with you using her power to rid her people of her nemesis? After all, she helped your friend, did she not?'

'That was different.'

'How?'

'Because Bridgette has a power I do not and could channel more of the Goddess' power than I could ever handle.'

He frowned down at her. 'So, this is not as much about permission as it is about you thinking you are not strong enough.'

'Oh, you do not understand, and I do not have time to teach you.' She pushed away from him and almost ran the short distance to their cottage.

'Anna.' He caught up to her just as she reached the front steps. 'Anna, stop. I did not mean to upset you. I am just trying to make sense of all of this.'

She glared up at him, her eyes full of worry and fear, showing a vulnerability he'd not seen in her before. 'I cannot give you any answers. I am not the powerful person you seem to think I am. Your power far outstrips mine. If life were fairer, you would be fully trained and in charge of this coven, not I. But life is never fair, is it?'

She broke from his grip once again and almost tripped up the steps to their front door.

'Then use me. Oust this Darkness using my power.'

Her mouth worked as tears filled her eyes. 'I do not have the skill. I am afraid that if I tried, I would kill you. And your death would kill me. If I had time to train you, then maybe we would be able to do it without calling on Bridgette. But even if I began right now and worked solidly with you for the entire two months it might take her to travel back to us, it would not be enough. Bridgette was only able to do what she did after years of study and devotion to the Goddess. You do not even believe in the Goddess. How can I teach you the devotion necessary to channel her powers without burning you up in such a limited time? Let alone teach you all the basics of magical energy transference and the advanced cantrips and incantations you would need to master so as to prepare for the undertaking? And there are some things only Bridgette herself knows, as she is the only one who has spoken directly with the Goddess in hundreds of years.'

'She would not share those secrets with you?'

'Of course she would, but they are not her secrets to divulge. Besides, that is not the point.'

'But Anna—'

'No,' she made a short, sharp chopping movement. 'The best option is to call Bridgette home. I will work with you so we can both help her when she arrives, and we will of course work together to keep Lachlan subdued and stop the Darkness from coming out, but as to the rest ... I will ask Bridgette to begin your training properly when she returns.'

'You will not train me?'

'I will do all that I can. As will any members of our coven whose power set might be similar to yours. But after what you did at the springs and then again today, the incredible strength you showed, I am certain there are things that only Bridgette can teach you.' She turned and, shoulders slumping, opened the door. 'I am tired. I need to lie down. Are you coming?' She did not wait for his answer, just went inside, disappearing into the dark of the room, the scent of their burned dinner wafting out.

Swearing, he rushed inside and over to the hearth as Anna trudged upstairs, seemingly unaware of the tragedy that was their dinner. He stared into the pot, the edges a mass of burned meat and sauce, the middle a dark sludge. None of it was salvageable. '*Merde.*'

He grabbed some towels and wrapping them around the edges of the hot pot so as not to burn himself, took the pot outside and scraped the contents out into the pig-pen that edged on the forest.

'*She is right.*'

He lurched upright. 'What?'

'*She is right. She does not have the ability to do what must be done.*'

'Shut up.' Why did the voice choose to come back now and talk to him? 'What do you know?'

'*Many things. Including the fact your mate does not think much of herself. Which means she is right. But only because she believes she is less. You must make her believe she is more.*'

'I am trying. But she will not see it.'

'*Try harder. It is crucial if we are to succeed.*'

'Succeed with what?'

'*With a future where Were and magical beings survive.*'

'What do you mean? What have you seen?'

'*I have seen what you have seen.*'

'I have not—'

'*Do not deny what you know to be true. See to your mate. Her light is the only thing that will enable us to make it through the dark.*'

A shove of wind made him stumble a few steps back towards the cottage. He turned, ready to give the voice a piece of his mind about its pushiness, but the wind was gone, and with it, the voice's presence.

He wanted to rail at the sky, at whatever the voice was, demanding it give him more than the bare essentials he had at his command, but he had no idea how to summon it back, or if it even could be summoned back.

Anna was right. He was untrained and that lack of training was a massive problem, more so than he had ever thought. He needed to learn quickly so as to help Anna in the way she needed. He had been happy to put off going to the Dance to discover more about his powers, powers he'd never really wanted to use because they reminded him too much of all the tragedies in his life. But his reluctance paled in the face of his Anna's need for him to be a strength at her side.

He would go to the Dance with her, let her do her testing, then would insist she begin his training, because, despite what she said, she was the only one who could train him properly. And in taking on the task, he hoped to show her just how powerful and special and worthy she truly was. That she was a match to anyone else in this world, including the lauded Bridgette.

Perhaps the first thing he should do was learn how to travel the aether so he could talk to Bridgette himself. If anyone knew what lay behind Anna's lack of belief in herself, it would be Bridgette. Or her sister, Morrigan. Maybe he would learn how to contact her as well.

But first, he needed to go inside and take care of his Anna. She needed care and feeding. Feeding he could take care of, but she needed a Healing as well if her powers were to rejuvenate quickly and not be wasted on her injuries.

If the Healer had not come by the time Anna had washed and changed, he would head down into the village to fetch her.

He had just walked in the door when Morghanna raced down the stairs still in her torn robe, hair wild, eyes wide in the darkness. 'Ali, there is something wrong.'

He grabbed her shoulders, steadying her. 'What? What is it?'

She lifted her hands to stare at them as she took a shuddering breath in, as if trying not to cry. 'I tried to use my power to light the candle by our bed but could not.'

He gripped her hands, desperate to calm her panic. 'Well, that is not unusual if you have used too much power. Is it?'

'No, but I did not flame out. If I had, I would have passed out, and I did not.'

'But you have never used power like we used at the Dance before. Perhaps—'

'No! You do not understand. It is not simply the candle.' She stared up at him, her eyes luminous and filled with a desperate panic he'd never thought to see in his strong, powerful mate. 'I cannot feel or sense any spirits around me. I have never had a moment in my life when I have been unable to sense them.'

He ran his hands up to her shoulders, holding tight as she began to tremble. 'That is not unusual given you used up too much power at the Dance.'

'No, no, you are not listening. I did not flame out. But even if I did, I would still be able to feel my power—the embers of it—and see the spirits. But now, I cannot feel it at all. I cannot even feel yours. The spirit world is closed to me. I cannot even feel the Packbond.' Her lip wobbled and she sucked in a shaky breath. 'This is it. The consequence.'

'The consequence for what?'

'This is the Goddess' punishment for using the power of the Dance without permission.' She swallowed hard. 'How can I keep the Darkness in Lachlan at bay if I cannot access my powers?'

22

Ali squeezed her hands gently, his thumbs sweeping circles across her skin in a motion that was oddly soothing. 'What about our mating bond? Can you feel that?'

Her eyes widened as she choked back a sob. 'I do not want to check. What if it has gone too?'

'It has not gone, my treasure.' He flattened her hand against his chest. 'It is vibrant and alive inside me. I can feel you as strongly as I felt you before.'

Somehow the beat of his heart under her hand made her feel a little less panicked. But ... 'Are you certain?'

He lifted one hand to stroke her hair back from her face, and despite her fear, she couldn't help but nuzzle into the warmth of his palm. 'Close your eyes and look. I know you will see it too.'

She did as he bid, her breath a catch in her throat. At first, she saw nothing and then ... 'Oh!' The relief was so vivid she would have collapsed on the floor except he caught her, pulling her into his warm embrace.

'See. If you can feel our mating bond—which has a strong element of magic about it—then your power has not gone. And neither has mine. You are exhausted and in pain. That is all. You need a Healing, some food and then a good rest, after which you will be back to normal by morning. I am certain of it.'

Morghanna nodded, even though his argument wasn't one-hundred percent solid—they really didn't know what created the mating bond as it didn't proscribe to any magical laws they knew. Just because they could both feel it didn't mean they had access to their magics. Also, she knew exhaustion wasn't entirely to blame for why she couldn't even feel the ember of power that was the very heart of who she was. She'd flamed out a few times when she was travelling around Europe, helping Bridgette to bind the European packs and covens to tie them into the Pact. All of those times it felt more like her power was behind a thick wall she couldn't get through—while she couldn't use them, she still knew they were there, could still feel them as part of herself.

This didn't feel like that.

However, she couldn't argue with the need for a Healing and sleep. She was tired and sore.

A knock sounded on the door. Alistair helped her to a chair and then went to see who it was.

Abigail entered, leaning heavily on Leanna's arm. Morghanna frowned as they entered. 'Abigail? What are you doing out of bed?' The old Healer hadn't recovered properly after helping Leanna with young Alex's leg. Morghanna had been very annoyed to discover that she hadn't simply advised Leanna but had been filtering power into the younger Healer to use whenever Morghanna wasn't there. Add to that her already fragile state ...

Morghanna glowered at her. 'Surely you do not mean to do a Healing on me? You are not well enough.'

The older woman waved her arm. 'Do not fuss so, child. The herbal poultice you made for me has helped with my breathing, and my heart is not thundering in my chest today. I am well enough to help Leanna do a Healing on you.'

She narrowed her eyes at the stubborn woman. She couldn't allow the old witch to give too much of herself again—she wouldn't have got as sick as she had in the first place if Morghanna had not relied on her as much as she had in the first months here. Morrigan had picked up much of the Abigail's work when the old witch's heart had almost given out on her, but now her sister was gone and in the pain of that and the thrill of her mating, she simply hadn't watched her old mentor close enough to make sure she wasn't doing anything foolish.

That wouldn't happen again. Not after Alex.

'You know you should not even be doing Healings—your role now is to teach any of the coven who show an inkling of Healer power. I wish I did not even need you to do that—'

'Pshaw!' Abigail said, waving her hand in annoyance. 'I cannot be useless in entirety, so do not take that away from me!'

'You are far from useless, Abigail. Your advice to me on Council matters alone has been invaluable. I could not be Coven Leader without you.'

Abigail pointed a crooked finger at her. 'That too is a piece of rubbish I do not wish to hear from your mouth again.' She raised her hand before Morghanna could argue with her. 'But I am not here to make you see sense. I am simply here to lend Leanna the benefit of my experience. Although, I assure you, I *would* have enough energy for a Healing to help you with those cuts and bruises if it were necessary.'

'And you would make yourself ill in the process. I will not allow it.'

'I told you, did I not?' she asked Leanna.

Leanna smiled shyly. 'You did.'

'Told her what?'

'How terrible a patient you would make. Too busy looking after everyone else to take time to look after yourself. I hoped your mate might help shift some of your burdens from your shoulders.'

'Looking after my people is not a burden.'

Abigail blew a heavy breath out of her nose, shaking her head sadly. 'See, stubborn. You are your mother's daughter.'

Leanna and Ali snorted.

She glared at them. Ali ignored her, just laughing louder, but

Leanna looked away, face paling. Damn. She hadn't meant to make the young witch pull back into her shell. So, despite the fact she didn't like being told she was stubborn like her mother—because she wasn't. Morrigan was the one who took after their mother in every aspect, good and bad—she forced herself to smile. 'I promise I will not be a bad patient today. I just did not expect Dougal to ask you to come.'

'He did not. He asked me,' Leanna said, glancing up quickly before looking back down again, the scars on one side of her face hidden by her hair. 'It was I who asked Abigail to come with me. I thought ... well ... I am not fully practiced in Healing a witch like you ... with your powers ... who has flamed out. The spirit energies ... I just ... I ... Perhaps I should not have asked?'

Morghanna touched the young witch's arm. 'I am so glad you are here, Leanna, and the fact you are wise enough to ask for Abigail's counsel when you are uncertain and want to learn more, brings me relief. Thank you both for your help.'

'Enough buttering us up,' Abigail said, a smile twitching her lips as she hobbled over to the table, waving at Leanna to hand over the basket of medicinals she carried. 'Alistair, can you please put the kettle on and boil some water? I wish to make a healing tisane. Leanna, put those candles in a circle on the floor around the room and light them east-north-west-south. We need to ensure the spirits stay away for the night.'

'Do not bother with that. I cannot sense them at all right now.'

'Right now being the operative word. But the spirits will be back the moment there is enough of your power to ride on through the veil, making your recovery take twice as long.'

'They use her power to communicate with her?' Alistair asked.

'Of course they do. They may have their own form of power but they need like power on this plane of existence so as to exist here for any length of time. It is why they flock around Spirit-talkers as they do. And why so many Spirit-talkers are driven to madness. The constant drain on their power in that way is insidious.'

'What about their shields? Do they not hold the spirits back?'

'Yes. However, holding shields against the spirits becomes more and more difficult over time. Our Morghanna is stronger than most though, and now she has found you, a slide into that kind of madness for her is more unlikely than it ever was.'

'Is there something I can do to help?'

Abigail patted his cheek. 'Just do what you are doing. That is all she needs. And for us to keep the spirits away tonight with the candles.'

'I am sitting right here,' Morghanna grumbled. 'I can speak for myself. If I need further assistance dealing with the spirits, I would ask for it.'

Abigail made a snorting sound, brows raised at Morghanna's slumped form at the table. 'Yes. I can see that is true.'

'If the candles help,' Alistair asked, frowning at her, 'Why do you not use them all the time?'

'How do you suggest I carry them around with me? Or do you suggest I remain locked in a room all the time so as to keep myself safe from the powers that are my birthright?'

'Of course not. But if lighting them as Abigail suggests would give you some relief while you are indoors, why not light them more often?'

'How would I gain the spirits' trust if I hid from them all the time? The knowledge they hold is a help to the coven, and now to the pack, and is far more important than my need to be left alone. Besides, them using my power as they have means there is less likelihood I would ever have the kind of dangerous power build that destroyed my parents and so many others. Spirit-talker powers rarely build enough to hurt anyone but themselves. So that is a bonus.'

'Not now that you have the Packbond to filter your power through.' He shook his head. 'I had no idea they drained you of power. There has to be some way of changing that dynamic.'

'Witches and warlocks have searched for centuries to try to discover a way to help their Spirit-talkers,' Abigail said softly, her calming voice stopping Morghanna from any further argument. 'To no avail, I am afraid. Not that we will cease searching, but I doubt we will discover anything tonight that will be more effective than the candles. So, light them, Leanna, and we can continue this discussion at a later date.'

Despite the fact she was a little annoyed still that Abigail had got out of her sick bed to come fuss over her, she was glad the old witch was here. She was right. It was pointless to argue about this now, especially given she didn't truly have the energy within her to sustain any form of argument against her worried mate.

She sat silently as Abigail instructed Leanna and kept Alistair busy with requests for what was needed for the Healing. Her knowledge was unsurpassed in regenerative cures and Leanna could continue to learn a lot under her tutelage. But despite the steel in her, the older witch's voice wasn't as steady and sure as it had been before this latest bout of illness.

Morghanna wished there was something she could do to heal the damage done to Abigail's heart. Morrigan had been researching spells on healing damaged organs before she left. Maybe there was something in her sister's notes that might give her a clue as to how to reverse what was done. Not that Morrigan had been looking at it from that angle—she wasn't aware Abigail's issues stemmed from the spell she'd done to save Morrigan's life when they were young. And she couldn't know. She'd think herself responsible for injuring their mentor and never forgive herself. Morghanna herself hadn't known until recently when Abigail caught the infection that hit many of their elderly but didn't get better as the rest of them had, her heart almost failing.

Abigail admitted the issue only to stop Morghanna from running herself ragged trying to find a cure. Morghanna had been so upset with Abigail, and with herself. She should have known, should have seen what taking on extra responsibilities within the coven was doing to her.

Fingers tapped the back of her hand, making her look up into Abigail's softly crinkled face. 'Stop blaming yourself for what ails the world, girl.'

'I am not doing that.' Well, not blaming herself for what ailed the world—just the woman in front of her.

Abigail waggled her finger. 'You need a little more of your sister in you. Any word from her yet?'

Morghanna shook her head.

'Stubborn. Runs in the family. But I am certain she will come back when she hears about this one.' She pointed at Ali. 'I am looking forward to her theatrics when she discovers you have mated.'

'There will be no theatrics when she realises the gift Ali is to us. The proof.'

Abigail chuckled. 'If you think there will be no theatrics, then you do not know your sister very well. She will not like the idea a male has come along and swept her sister off her feet with no "by your leave".'

Alistair's brows shot up. 'Morrigan would wish me to ask her permission to mate with her sister? Does she not understand how a mating works?'

Abigail snorted at Ali. 'That matters little when it comes to Morrigan and those she cares about. She will no doubt put you through the ringer, handsome male though you are, to ensure you are the right choice for her sister.'

'A challenge I will happily take on as long as she comes back.' He smiled softly at Morghanna before turning back to the fire and the pot of water.

'I just hope she comes back soon.' If she truly knew how sick Abigail was, surely she would want to help. She had been hiding the truth from Morrigan, afraid what she might find out and how that would make her feel. But maybe it was the answer to make her come back. Her sister was bound to pick her research back up and turn it towards helping Abigail. Time was running out though; the older Abigail got, the worse her condition became. And Morrigan had continued to block anyone scrying for her.

Surely she had to give in soon though. And come back like she'd always come back?

What if she didn't though? What if she'd truly given up on them? Given up on her?

A sharp tap on her hand had her looking up at Abigail.

The older witch wagged her finger at Morghanna. 'Now, now. I already told you none of that. You are not responsible for what your sister chooses to do, or any of us for that matter.'

'How did you know—?' She broke off as Abigail chuckled.

'Are you a thought reader?' Ali asked.

'Nothing of the sort, young warlock.'

A choked sound from Leanna had them turning to look at her, but she hung her head quickly and continued setting out the candles and other spell paraphernalia.

Abigail clucked her tongue, a smile dancing on her lips when she turned back to Ali. 'Despite what others might think—or snort—it is not mind reading that allows me to know what is going on in your mate's head. I helped rear Morghanna and her sister and I can read the creases in her brow and the shadows in her eyes better than anyone. I know when she is beating herself up over things she cannot change—especially when it comes to either her pigheaded sister or her need to fix everyone and everything.' She cupped Morghanna's face and looked deep into her eyes. 'You worry too much about things you cannot change.'

Her lips trembled. 'I need to change it.'

'No. You do not.'

'Listen to her, Anna,' Ali said, placing the pot of boiling water on the wooden board in the middle of the table. Abigail shifted away to give him room as he came down to kneel at Morghanna's side, taking her hands in his. 'I may have only been with you a week, but I cannot help but notice you expect more of yourself than you expect of anyone else.'

'Of course I do.' She pulled her hand from his, waving around her and to outside. 'I have been designated Coven Leader since my parents died and then Head Pack Witch for one of the strongest packs in the British Isles. There is so much to do, so many people to ensure are safe and well and have all they need to become who they are meant to be. I have to expect more of myself than I do of anyone else.'

'I understand that and your dedication is remarkable. It is one of the things I saw in you almost immediately, it is so strong. And I love you for it. But unreasoning dedication where you do not ask for any help and take everything on yourself ...' He shook his head. 'I saw that kind of dedication in my father and mother and they died because of it. I do not want that for you. You need to stop taking everything on yourself. What happened to Lachlan is not your responsibility. You could not have known about the—'

She shook her head minutely at him, thankful that both Abigail and Leanna were looking at him and not at her.

'—way his illness would make him behave,' he continued, thankfully not giving away the secret of the Darkness being in Lachlan. She did not need either Abigail or Leanna worried about that right now. If ever.

'Your mate is right, dearest,' Abigail said, turning back to her. You cannot do it all. And nobody expects you to. Not me, not the coven, not the pack and, no matter what she might have said before she left, not your sister.' She patted Morghanna's hand. 'What you are, what you do for us all, it is too much. Now you have a mate, I hope he can make you see that more clearly than I have ever been able to.' Her canny gaze turned to Ali.

Morghanna shook her head. 'I am Head Pack Witch and Coven Leader. The problems of the coven and pack are mine and mine alone. I cannot put that on anyone else's shoulders.'

Ali made a hissing sound as he recaptured her hands. 'Of course you can. We want you to. I am here for you now, Anna. I want you to lean on me and share everything with me, especially the things you think are yours and yours alone to deal with.'

She stared into his glorious eyes that were glowing with the fervour of his words and his love for her.

Was it true? With such a strong mate at her side, maybe she didn't need to be more than she had the talent to be.

The Fates had matched them for a reason. Perhaps he was the

strength and magical power she didn't have. Yes. It made sense now. She twined her fingers with his and smiled at him. 'I am so glad you are here. You can make up for everything I lack.'

'That is not what I meant.'

'The candles are lit,' Leanna said, interrupting him.

He opened his mouth to continue, but Abigail tapped him on the shoulder. When he looked up at her, she said softly, 'Later.'

'But—'

She shook her head at him. 'There is no argument that cannot be kept for later. Right now, we need to do a Healing and get some food into our girl. Will you help with that?'

'Of course. Whatever I can do.'

'Seeing as you are flamed out as well, perhaps you can take care of getting her some food. Leanna and I will take care of the rest. Then I will get Leanna to do a little rejuvenating Healing on you so your powers will come back more quickly too.'

'That is not necessary—'

'It is. No more arguments, or I will think you as bad as your mate.'

He smiled fondly at said mate. 'Never that.'

Morghanna snorted. 'You are as driven as I am to do right by those you deem your responsibility.'

'Then we can learn of sharing responsibility together. A perfect pairing.' He leaned down and kissed her briefly then whispered, 'Let us take care of you.'

'Okay.'

He kissed her once more then went to the hearth and set about preparing something new for dinner.

23

Leanna came forward, smiling shyly at Morghanna through the strawberry blonde hair that always hung over the scarred side of her face. She put her hands over the bruises on Morghanna's shoulder and uttered the first words of the Healing spell. The amber flecks in her cinnamon-coloured eyes glowed as her magic bloomed to life.

'Place your hands a little closer,' Abigail instructed, shifting to show Leanna exactly what she meant. 'Good. Now, as your powers begin to surge, widen them to encourage the flow of curative magic to spread through Morghanna.'

'Oh,' Morghanna sighed as the magic's warmth spread over her skin and into her muscles, much faster than she'd ever experienced in a Healing before. 'That is a neat trick. How come I have not heard of it before?'

'Your Healing lends itself more to treating injuries one at a time. Leanna's is different and therefore requires a different technique.'

'Of course. She is stronger than me.'

'It is not only that—and do not pull that face at me. The flow and pulse of her magic is different to yours, as is mine to hers and yours to your mate's. That difference has little to do with the strength of the power and everything to do with inherent abilities. And to a lesser degree, a person's strength of will. Even some of those with the smallest amount of Healing ability have gone on to become great Healers because of the way their power was harnessed and utilised and also because of their will to become so.'

'That is not necessarily true. I wanted to be a great Healer but can do no more than cure cuts, bruises and certain broken bones, and help calm patients and lessen their pain.

Abigail shook her head, her lips pursed. 'Yes, but that has more to do with the fact I could never figure out how to engage your magics with something more than our general techniques. The failing is not yours, but mine.'

Morghanna snorted. 'That is very kind of you to say, but it is utter rubbish. You are one of our most talented teachers. I was simply a poor student.'

'Now it is my turn to say that is utter rubbish. If you were a poor student, you would never have been able to learn to use the power of the Dance like you do. Only Bridgette is more proficient than you.' She tutted as she shook her head. 'Your father has a lot to answer for in regard to how you think about yourself and your powers.'

'My father? He loved me.'

'Yes. But he showed his pride in Morrigan's accomplishments and not in yours. He never saw what a talent you truly had.'

'What talent? Are you talking about my weak Healer abilities or my reasonably useless ability to see and talk to the spirits that I cannot seem to keep at bay despite all the work we have done on my shields and banishing spells?'

Abigail pointed at her. 'That is your father talking right there. As I said to your mate earlier, nobody has ever found a way to keep the spirits from a Spirit-talker for long. What I did not say is there has never been a Spirit-talker more proficient at keeping the spirits at bay than you. Besides, it is due to no weakness in you that they are drawn to you in droves; it is because your powers are the strongest I have ever seen or heard of. They are drawn to you in a way they are not drawn to others with your talent. You are wrong to see that as a negative.'

'When I need you and Leanna to set candles to keep them away so I can heal, I think that is a negative.'

Abigail blew a hard breath out her nose. 'You can do things with spirits nobody else with that talent has been able to do for more years than I can remember. And you have shown no indication of instability at all.'

'That latter is the only positive in all you have said.'

Abigail's firm gaze fixed on her. 'Your abilities have kept knowledge with us that would have otherwise been lost because you are able to speak to our ancestors no matter their language or dialect. You hear them clearly despite the noise most Spirit-talkers hear that exists between our plane and theirs. And you control them more effectively than any other Spirit-talkers I have ever heard of—and I am certain, if not for the fact that you have had nobody of significant talent around to teach you in the particulars, not to mention precious little time to truly practice and get to know your gift and all its quirks, you would have mastered how to have them come only at your beck and call. The fact you have become as proficient as you have despite the fact you have had nobody to teach you in the way I am able to teach Leanna about her Healing powers is simply remarkable. Imagine what you could do if you had someone to train you who truly knew what they were doing.'

'My aunt tried.'

Abigail waved her hand. 'She was not anything close to you in strength, and even then, her powers took her mind before she could truly be of any use to you. Your strength and the fact you have kept your mind intact is something that everyone in the Coven admires you for. And now, you have done what few Spirit-talkers before you have done: you have found true love.'

'That was hardly a choice. Although I am eternally glad for the fact the Fates deemed me worthy of mating with my Ali.' She glanced over at her mate as he prepared their supper; the angle of his head told her he listened to every word.

'If you were not worthy,' Abigail answered. 'If you were weak or sickening in some way, I do not think your Ali's wolf would have mated to you.' She waved Morghanna quiet as she opened her mouth to argue. 'And your mating promises to strengthen your mind and soul further if I understand these things correctly. Which means that you will be able to delve more into your talents in a way none have been able to do before you. And as a result, you will be able to teach those who come after you, so that no more Spirit-talkers suffer as your aunt did. Your father was wrong to make you think your talent an affliction. For I think it will come to be regarded as one of the greatest blessings we have known.'

'He had reason to think it so,' Morghanna protested, focusing in on Abigail's former statement rather than the latter. 'He lost so many in his family to the curse of the Spirit-talker.'

'Maybe that was so, but it is no excuse for him to have given you such a low opinion of yourself. Why your mother did not put him in his place and lift you up to where you deserved to be in their esteem, I do not know. Morrigan often spoke of her frustration with how they talked of you and to you.'

'She did?' She shook her head. 'She never said.'

'Of course she did. You simply did not listen.' She gestured to Leanna, her piercing attention moving to the younger witch, who had studiously been attending to the Healing as Morghanna and Abigail spoke. Morghanna almost sagged in relief to have the canny witch's attention on someone other than herself.

'Move your hands in a slightly circular motion now, Leanna. There, that is good. See how the orange of your power brightens and pulses when you do that?'

Leanna nodded. 'It feels more fluid through my veins.'

'Good. Concentrate on that feeling and keep moving your hands. Do you see the change in her aura too as you do that?'

'Yes. It looks brighter.' She frowned. 'But there is still that muddiness around her head and chest.'

'Yes, that is strange. Here, let me help.'

'Do not dare!' Morghanna said, pushing upright and stepping out of the old witch's reach. 'You promised you would not use any of your energy on me.'

'If I do not, then Leanna will not see what I mean.'

'She is doing fine without it. Are you not, Le-le?'

Leanna nodded quickly. 'I can do it if you explain what you wish me to do.'

Abigail pressed her lips together and grunted, and for a moment, Morghanna thought she would argue. But then Ali came to her side with a slather of fresh bread covered in the plum spread he'd made the day before and handed it to the older witch. 'Can you taste this? I am uncertain if I have added enough sugar and I hear you are the coven's expert jam-maker.'

Morghanna tried not to let her lips twitch into a smile as Abigail took the slice and bit in. Her eyes closed in obvious bliss as she chewed. When she swallowed, she smiled up at Alistair. 'This is excellent, young man. Tangy and not too sweet, just like our plums. How do you come to make jam so well?'

He shrugged. 'It was a family thing. This one is a recipe handed down through my father's family. They were vintners, but they also made cheeses, jams and spreads and sold them alongside their wine. His village was known for it. He taught me before ...' He shook his head, glancing away.

Morghanna grabbed his hand and gave it a squeeze. He smiled down at her, but it didn't reach his eyes. Such pain still lived inside him over the loss of his family—something she understood all too well. But hopefully soon, Bridgette would be able to help bring two of them back to him.

'Well, this is excellent jam. I look forward to seeing what you can do with cheeses and spreads. It will be good to have other produce to ship to market.'

'You wish to ship this to market?'

'Of course. We must look to markets other than lavender if we are to fully prosper. It is one of the things Morghanna has been trying to push in Council, is that not right, dearest girl?'

'It is. Abigail is right. Your jams and spreads will be a great addition to what we can sell and trade with, along with your artwork.'

She told Abigail about Ali's talent and his willingness to teach others in the pack.

'Marvellous,' the older woman said, clapping her hands together. 'I might join one of your classes. I used to enjoy sketching when I was younger.' She looked at her gnarled hands. 'Although, I am uncertain these will allow me to excel. But that is a problem for another time. Well, I can see already you are quite the addition to our family.'

'He is, in so many ways.' Morghanna smiled brilliantly up at him. 'And if you wish to make cheese to sell as well as the other things, I can talk to Iain and Dougal about extending our cow and sheep herds to supply the milk.'

'Goats and cows would be my preference.'

'Goats and cows it is. And perhaps we can look at planting some vines as well. I am certain Iain would not be averse to making our own wine.'

Ali frowned. 'I would have to look at the soil here. Vines do not grow just anywhere. Also, the weather might be something of a problem.'

'The McVales grow vines,' Leanna said softly.

'Do they?' Morghanna asked her. 'Where did you hear that?'

'Dougal told me. He has been researching if we could do so as well.'

'Perhaps you can talk it over with Dougal then?' Morghanna said to Ali.

'Yes. I will. But jams and cheese first perhaps. The vines will take many years to get started.'

'Of course.' Morghanna beamed at him. 'Iain will have to change his attitude to you now. You are bringing knowledge and skills we do not have. You are an even greater blessing than I thought.'

Ali actually blushed. 'I do not know about that. I am simply glad to be able to do something that will help you and the coven's standing in the pack.'

'In more ways than one.' She took his hand and kissed it, then looked cheekily up at him. 'May I have a piece of that bread and jam? And I think Le-le would like some too.'

The younger witch nodded enthusiastically.

'I would not mind another slice,' Abigail said. 'It will do me for supper.'

'Let Leanna continue your Healing,' he said, giving her a quick kiss, 'and I will make a plate of bread and jam for you hungry women.' Leanna bent over Morghanna to continue her work, and he returned to the bench near the fire to cut bread and slather it with butter and jam.

Morghanna sighed as the magics flooded through her again. She hadn't realised how tense she was or just how much she hurt from her fight with Lachlan. Her bruises began to fade and the cuts quickly knit together and became nothing but pink marks on her skin.

'That's remarkable,' she said. 'I think you're getting stronger every day, Le-le.'

'I'm not sure about that,' the young witch said, her voice husky and low.

'I am. Look at your eyes.'

Leanna glanced up at her, the proof of her growing strength there for anyone to see. 'I cannot see my eyes.'

'I can. And more than just the amber flecks are glowing.' Morghanna could barely see the cinnamon colour of her irises below the golden glow.

'Oh. Maybe it's just today. Nobody has mentioned it before.'

'Well, maybe that is so, but it is something to investigate further, right Abigail?'

The older witch nodded sagely. 'No need. It is a sign of growing power. We are so lucky you decided to bring Leanna and the remainder of her coven into this one after ...' Her gaze flickered to Leanna as the younger witch made a little sound of distress. 'Yes, well, we are lucky she is one of us. I think she is going to be one of the most talented Healers we have ever known.'

'You are the greatest Healer,' Leanna protested. 'Nobody could be greater than you.'

Abigail smiled softly. 'We will see.' She nodded at Morghanna. 'Finish up now. You still have Alistair to tend to as well.'

Leanna settled back into her work.

Morghanna sent a smile of gratitude towards Abigail. The older witch just nodded and turned her attention to what Leanna was doing.

She was glad she had Abigail to mentor her and that she didn't just have to rely on Morghanna's tutelage. Despite what Abigail had said before, Morghanna knew both her talent and her knowledge was lacking. She was a good teacher, but she wasn't the kind of teacher Abigail was simply because she lacked true talent and ability.

Imagine what you could do if you had someone to train you who truly knew what they were doing.

Abigail's earlier words flashed back to her. Was she right? Did she truly have an extraordinary power?

No. She knew it wasn't so. Leanna was the only witch in this room with extraordinary power. Morghanna was well aware of her limits. But it did make her feel better to think that she might be able to help those who came after her simply because she had not lost her mind and had mated. That was something to feel positive about at least. And she very much had Ali to thank for that fact. She'd have to make certain to thank him properly after Leanna and Abigail had gone.

Ali looked up then, as if he could feel the heat in her thoughts through the mating bond. He probably could. Her feelings and desire for him were so powerful, so heated, she was surprised the other two witches weren't fanning themselves.

'Thank you,' Morghanna said, gripping Leanna's hand as she finished. 'You are so talented. I am grateful you have Abigail as your mentor.' She stretched, smiling when none of her muscles twinged. 'More glad than you could know.'

'It is my pleasure to serve you, Morghanna. It is nice to be able to give back for once.'

'What do you mean? You give back all the time. Look what you did for young Alex the other day.'

'I mean, give back to you. You do so much for everyone. It is nice to be able to do something of significance for you for once.'

Abigail snorted. 'Out of the mouths of babes.'

'Leanna is hardly a babe,' Morghanna said before returning her attention to the young witch. 'And you do things for me all the time.'

'Not anything major.'

'The value in small, constant tasks done well is more than you can know, Leanna. Do not undervalue what you give to me or anyone else.'

'Good advice,' Abigail said. 'Now if only you would listen to yourself.'

'Do not make this about me when it is about Leanna and her confidence in what she brings to coven and Pack.'

'Why would I do that? You are right. Leanna is valuable. I tell her so every day. But I have as much chance of her believing me as I have of making you believe the same.'

'I believe Leanna is valuable.'

Abigail angled her a look, but before Morghanna could bite back, she gestured to Ali. 'Now it is your turn. Sit, sit.' He did so and Abigail gestured for Leanna to stand behind him. 'Start with his head, Leanna, then move down.'

As Leanna did the Healing, Abigail ate bread and prepared the tisane for Morghanna. 'Drink this now and then again in a few hours. You should drink some too,' she said to Ali.

He nodded and, as Leanna finished, turned and smiled up at her. 'Thank you, Leanna. I have never experienced a Healing before—it was remarkable.'

'It is my pleasure to serve.' She dipped her head, not looking at him.

Abigail pushed to a stand. 'Thank you, Alistair, for your delicious bread and jam. It has quite revived me. Come Leanna, it is time we left these two to rest.'

'What about the candles?'

'Leave them. They will last out the night and give Morghanna some respite from the spirits as her powers return.' She pointed at Ali. 'I look forward to hearing your proposal for extra trade in Council.'

Her mate nodded and, arm slung around her waist, saw them to the door with Morghanna. Despite the Healing, she was glad to have his solid warmth to lean into. Her injuries may have been fixed, the soreness taken away, but she was still exhausted. Probably due to flaming out. Her powers were wound so intrinsically into her body, giving it a constant source of energy, that the absence was doubly felt.

'To bed?' she said as Ali closed the door.

'Not yet. Let us go to the springs.'

'Oh, I would like nothing more, but I do not think I could make it there. I am exhausted.'

'I will carry you.'

'No. I would not ask you to do such a thing when you must be as exhausted as I.'

'I still have energy enough for that,' he said, raising his hands, flicking his thumb against his middle finger. A flame sprang to life in the middle of each palm.

'How can you have your magic back already?' she asked, gaping at him, not a little jealous of this proof of just how strong he was.

'Leanna's Healing helped. It is not much power, but it is enough to make me feel more rejuvenated than you do right now.'

'Still, you should not waste it.' She put her hands over his fingers, folding them into his palms, the action dousing the flames. 'Certainly not on me.'

'If not you, then who?' He untangled their fingers to capture her face in the warmth of his hands. 'Please, let me do this for you. Leanna and Abigail might have seen to curing your outward injuries, but I know you are still hurt by the attack. You need to wash away the memory of Lachlan's touch. We will take fresh clothes with us, and when we come back, we can burn this gown he ruined with his violence. I think only then will you be able to properly rest.'

Her lips trembled. She hadn't realised until he'd spoken the words how uncomfortable and soiled she felt in her torn and bloody ceremonial dress; how much the memory of Lachlan's hands and lips on her made her feel like something awful was shuddering across her skin. 'Okay,' she said softly, turning to kiss his palm. 'But only if you join me in the springs.'

'Of course. I intend to wash you thoroughly.'

'How thoroughly?' Her mouth curled up on one corner as she stared into his remarkable eyes, glowing now with sexual intent.

'I plan to be extremely thorough.'

'Good.'

She laughed as he picked her up, carrying her upstairs to collect clothes. She held the clothes and the lavender soap he picked up from the stack she kept near the hearth and he held her, carrying her out of their cabin, his energy reserves seemingly endless as he ran through the woods and up the hill to the rocky outcropping where they had first met.

They found the springs empty when they got there—it was the kind of evening that often saw coven members come up to bathe and rejuvenate and chat. Perhaps Abigail had figured it out and warned them off. Whatever the reason, she was thankful.

He lowered her to the rocks on the edge of the hot springs, her body sliding against his, the bundle of their clothes between them. She leaned up to kiss him, but he only let their lips brush lightly against each other before he set her back a little, took the clothes from her, put them on a rock out of reach of the lapping water, then came back to undo the sash at her waist and push the torn gown from her shoulders. She kicked it aside and watched hungrily as he undressed.

He put the bar of soap on a ledge next to the spring then picked her up and walked them down the rough steps that allowed the more elderly to get in and out of the springs.

She sighed as the water rose around them, the heat of it a balm as it lapped against her skin.

After he settled her on a step, the water lapping around her middle, he began to wash her, even wetting her hair and soaping it thoroughly.

Then it was her turn to wash him. She took her time, enjoying the way his skin trembled and twitched at her touch, the little moans that escaped his lips.

When she was done, he swam them over to the waterfall to wash the soap from their hair, the pound of water massaging her muscles.

When they were both clean, he pulled her close and kissed her, all tongue and heat and wet, the taste of him filling her up and clearing away the last of the horror of Lachlan's attack.

They made love in the water and then again on the edge of the springs in the soft grass as the moon rose above them. It was glorious and just what she needed.

With the night cool on their skin, they dressed quietly before he scooped her into his arms and carried her back to their home. He took her straight upstairs to their bed where he held her in his arms, his big body spooned behind her.

She stroked his arm, hugging it to her. She would never have got through this if not for him.

Thank you, Fates, for bringing him into my life, she thought as his breathing slowed.

Finally, with her mate soundly asleep, his arms around her, the beat of his heart a steady thump against her back, she fell into sleep too.

24

Morghanna awoke close to noon, hungry and surprised she'd slept so long, even more surprised to find Ali in bed next to her still asleep.

Pulling on that power in the clearing and throwing it at her had obviously exhausted him more than he'd let on. She'd have to watch that in him—his propensity to look after her even to his detriment.

Instead of getting up to deal with her hunger, she decided to stay where she was, wrapped in her mate's arms, taking comfort from him and letting him sleep a while longer. The Healing last night had done more than mend her cuts and bruises—perhaps Leanna had been uncharacteristically sneaky and used her gift of Soul Healing on her, as she felt remarkably well-balanced in mind, body and spirit today.

Or, maybe her mate and their interlude last night was the cause for her feeling of well-being. She had to admit, it was rather lovely to be looked after, especially by one's mate. She didn't want to give him many more reasons to do so to the extremes he had yesterday, but she probably wouldn't mind letting him look after her more than she was used to.

She sighed blissfully, letting herself drift in the joy of being mated before she had to be sensible and get down to what mattered.

Could she access her powers?

The question grew larger in her mind until she wasn't able to ignore it any further. Sighing again, she closed her eyes and reached out to connect with her power, wanting to feel it out to see what damage had been done.

There was nothing.

She tried not to let the panic shoot through her, concentrating on keeping her breathing and heartbeat steady. Behind her, Ali made a small sound of distress, his arms tightening around her. 'I am fine,' she whispered, sending waves of love through the mating bond. It was so strong and bright inside her, that despite not seeing the glow of her power beside it, she couldn't help but smile.

The mating bond sparkled.

No. That wasn't the mating bond. The colour wasn't right. The mating bond didn't have any purple in it, and yet, she was certain the sparkle she'd seen right at the edges of the bond was deeply amethyst.

Oh! Her power. It was there, hiding.

No, not hiding. It was aligned next to the mating bond, almost as if it drew strength from the bright surety of it.

A surge of love came through the bond to her, and with it, the amethyst sparkle pulsed again. Although, it was more than a sparkle. It was a thin thread, wound around the mating bond.

That was strange. Her power shouldn't be doing that. Maybe it really was pulling some form of energy from the mating bond, trying to come back to her.

Intriguing. She wondered if this had happened to other witches and warlocks mated to Were. She would have to do some research into it. Although, it did make sense that the two powers, no matter that they were very different, would align and succour each other. After all, wasn't that what she'd sensed in Alistair the very first time she'd met him? A strange twinning that she couldn't quite put her finger on.

Even more proof that the Pact was a blessing to both Were and the covens if it made these matings more likely; and mating bonds helped a warlock or witch to strengthen themselves and heal after flaming-out. It would explain why she felt so very good this morning; more so than Leanna using her special gift on her without asking would normally have given her. Maybe it wasn't about the Healing and everything to do with Alistair.

Her miracle. Her joy.

Unable to stop herself, she reached out to touch the power, to test her hypothesis. If she was wrong, she wouldn't be able to access it, but if she was right ...

The power flared a little when she made contact with it. The warmth and familiarity of it brought such relief. It wasn't strong by any means, and after that first contact, it responded sluggishly as she pulled it inward, but it did respond. And it did keep a tendril of attachment to the mating bond, one that pulsed every few seconds as if shooting power through that tendril to her.

Her own source of fuel lighting the fire of her power.

Remarkable.

Excitement fluttered in her chest at the possibilities. What would Bridgette and Abigail and Ali say when she told them. She turned to wake Ali, to share her discovery, but stopped herself. She was putting the cart before the horse. Before she could get too carried away, she must test it.

She took in a deep breath and reached out for the tendril of amethyst once more.

As she handled it, letting it sink into her, she noted there was something different about it. Maybe it had something to do with how she had flamed out. Maybe it had something to do with the fact it had tied itself into the mating bond. Whatever it was, she would figure it out; it wasn't yet cause for concern. This could help so many others if she could just find a way to apply it to other forms of bond.

She wished she could start looking into it right away, but she couldn't. She had Lachlan to deal with first. Keeping him under-wraps, and the Darkness from breaking out again in the form of the Beast, would take up much of her time and energy until Bridgette arrived to rid Lachlan of it. And then, she would have to help Dougal figure out how to handle whatever Lachlan became after it was gone. She had a notion he would still be a danger to many of those he deemed weaker within the coven and pack. But if they sent him away or locked him up, what would happen with Iain?

Despite Alistair's anger over the entire affair, Morghanna had to agree with Dougal's assessment: they had to go slowly with the transition of power from Iain to Dougal in this critical time when everything was so new. So, she would have to do everything she could to find a solution with Lachlan that wouldn't give away what Dougal and his lieutenants had been doing, or cause Iain's death in the near future.

What a mess.

Alistair woke at her sigh. His hand stroked down her hair to her shoulder. 'Good morning, my treasure.'

'Good morning, my love.'

He moved onto his back, pulling her with him, then cupped her face, brushed his thumb over her brow. 'Stop worrying. Worry never made anything better.'

'Oh? What does make things better?' she asked, brow arched as she ran her hands down his bare stomach to the erection twitching against her belly. 'This?'

'If wielded by a master.'

'A master, hey?' She laughed as he grabbed her and rolled her under him, but the laughter soon turned to breathless pants and moans as he used his hands and mouth on her, driving her to the edge before pushing inside her and taking her to the heavens, ridding her of any last dregs of what Lachlan had tried to do yesterday.

The Darkness-touched Were may have tried to take away her sense of power by using his strength on her in the most brutal of fashions, but she wasn't going to let that touch what she shared with her mate or affect any other aspect of her life. And she *would* find some way of making certain nothing like that ever happened again.

An hour later, after they'd made love twice more—and after she'd noted how the intimacy had fed into the mating bond, which fed into her powers, making them far stronger than they should have been even with the Healing—they headed downstairs to break their fast. They were just finishing up when the sound of footsteps pounding down the path to their cottage had them both leaping up from the table. She reached the door just as the runner banged on the door.

'Oh, thank the Goddess.' Leanna grabbed Morghanna's hands, eyes wide with fear. Her hair was uncharacteristically pushed off her face, the tracery of silvery scars almost seeming to glow against her too pale skin.

'Leanna. What is wrong?' She tried to pull the young witch inside.

Leanna shook her head violently and didn't budge. 'No. You have to come. Now.' Tears began to stream from her eyes. 'Lachlan has gone insane. Dougal and his soldiers have tried to hold him, but it is not working. They need you. They need you now.'

Oh Goddess, no. She wasn't ready for this. Her powers might have strengthened far more than she'd ever thought possible so close to a flame-out, but they were still not right. The fact that she hadn't felt the disturbance in the Packbond was proof of it.

But she had no choice. She had to try and help.

Ali reached for her hand, the warm steadiness of him enabling her to say, 'Where?'

'The Alpha Hall.'

They took off, Leanna leading them to the centre of the village. As they drew near, howls and cries of pain and struggle reached their ears.

They ran into the central square of the village, then came to a halt. A crowd of Were and coven had been drawn to the commotion, blocking their path. 'Clear the way,' Ali yelled, Alpha-tone in his voice. The Were instantly obeyed, the coven members not far behind as they felt the tug of authority through their bond to the pack.

Morghanna searched for the strongest witches and warlocks she could see as they passed through the crowd, calling them to her. Quickly, she told them she needed their help in subduing Lachlan, telling them only he suffered from a mysterious illness that made him incredibly dangerous.

'Defensive spells, my Lady?' Timothy McCleod, Claud's elder

brother, asked. She was glad to see him here as he was one of their strongest warlocks, his affinity to the earth and fire giving him strong defensive magics.

'It may not be enough,' Ali said. 'She may need to pull on your power and use it with her own to access the magics she used yesterday at the Dance.'

Some of the coven members gasped. 'That has never been done outside the healing sphere,' Timothy said. 'Will it not be too dangerous? What if the power becomes too much and you—'

She gripped his hand. 'That will not happen. I have the Packbond to filter into if the power gets too much. Besides, I have to risk it. What is in that hall is far more dangerous.' Ali was right. Their defensive spells would not be enough against Lachlan if he had turned into the Beast. But if she could tap into what she had yesterday when she'd only had Ali's power as a booster, and add their powers to it, then they might have a chance. 'If you are not willing, say so now.'

'We are with you, Morghanna,' Timothy said, the others quickly muttering their assent.

She swallowed hard then turned, and with her powers—still feeling a little strange but curiously strong with it—sparking inside her, ran up the stairs.

The sound from inside the hall was ferocious and violent, as if a war had broken out. Lachlan's voice, strangely rough and echoing with power that wasn't his, rose above the noise.

'She's mine! That bassa stole her from me. But he canna have her. Morry is mine. I claim her. He tells me I must claim her.'

She drew up at the doorway, Ali a steady, strong presence at her side, coven members ranged behind them, ready to lend her their strength even though it went against everything they'd been brought up to believe.

The scene inside was bedlam. The trestle tables and long wooden benches that usually graced the hall were bits of kindling scattered on the floor, lying broken against the walls. The cage that had stood against the far wall at the back on the left, used to hold transgressors against pack law until they were brought before the Alpha and his senior soldiers for judgement, was destroyed. The cage door lay on the floor halfway across the hall, the bars bent and torn. Bodies lay strewn on the floor between the cage and the Alpha chair that stood in the middle of the raised platform at the head of the hall.

Iain sat on the chair, his face streaming with sweat, skin deathly grey. He had his eyes squeezed closed as he shouted words of command that were obviously having little effect on his son.

Lachlan strained against Dougal and another dozen lieutenants and other strong members of the pack who were giving their all to try to hold him back. It looked like he was winning.

'Help them,' Leanna said from behind her. 'They cannot hold him.'

As she spoke, there was a grunt of pain and Killiana, one of the lieutenants, went flying through the air to smack against the wall. She didn't get up.

'Go. Get the sleeping draught,' Morghanna told Leanna. 'The one we use on bears. And one of the darts as well. Hurry. We will only be able to hold him for a little while.' Leanna dashed away. The scars on her upper body, arms and face had never stopped the young witch from being one of their fastest runners, regularly winning sprint races at coven gatherings. It was one of the only things that ever made her truly smile.

She wasn't smiling now though. And with good reason. Morghanna was concerned she wouldn't be fast enough despite how fleet of foot she was. Though there was no sign of the Beast on him, Lachlan was stronger than she'd ever seen a Were and growing stronger by the second. She wasn't even certain she could hold him at all, let alone long enough to allow Leanna to return with the potion and dart.

But she had to try.

'What do you want to do?' Ali said in her ear. 'I am yours to command.'

She wished he wasn't. She wished he was far away where he couldn't get hurt. Or even better, wished she'd done what she should have done, what Bridgette would have done. Bridgette wouldn't have left Lachlan to the Were alone to secure, no matter what they had said. She would have realised the true danger the Darkness presented and taken steps to ensure everyone's safety last night.

But she couldn't turn back time, and despite his incredible power, neither could Ali, so it was little help right now to play games of 'what if'.

Ali's power pushed at her, offering itself up for her use through the mating bond. He might not be trained, might not know what should be done here, but that didn't matter. She knew. And with his help, she was going to do it.

Or die trying.

She stepped into the hall, gathering her mating-bond infused power, ignoring how it shifted and pulsed strangely. Then she pulled on her mate's power through the bond.

Oh Goddess, she hadn't realised he'd been so drained by yesterday. He barely had a half of his power reserves returned to him— although, it was still more than any of the other coven members ranged behind them, and more than enough for most situations. But this wasn't most situations. She wasn't sure it would be enough, even if she drained him. And she didn't want to drain him.

'Take it,' he said, gripping her shoulder and staring into her eyes. 'Use up every bit. We have to keep them safe.'

'Take all of mine, too,' Timothy said.

'And mine,' Brionne said, appearing at Timothy's shoulder. Behind her were her brother Thomas, Stephen Samuel and more than half of the coven. All of them were nodding, indicating their willingness for her to borrow their power to use now.

It was humbling.

And frightening.

She had no idea if she could even manage it, but she had to try. There was no choice.

She reached for all their energies and took them inside herself.

Her eyes flared wide, everything in her feeling like it was filling, expanding.

The power! It was incredible, lighting up her synapses, making all seem possible. Different from yesterday but so strong. She hadn't had time to think about it yesterday, but now she wondered in one part of her mind if this was how Bridgette had felt when she'd first taken the Goddess' power to fight the Darkness and make the Pact. No, this was only one-one-hundredth of the power Bridgette had used, but even so, it was glorious.

She turned back to Lachlan, staring across the hall into the eyes of dark madness.

Hells.

The power inside her faltered. Her coven was full of strong witches and warlocks, many with defensive powers, but even so, she was afraid it wouldn't be enough. She wished she could pull from the pack but Iain, Dougal, as well as the remaining lieutenants and senior soldiers were using all the power and strength they had just to hold Lachlan where he was, and they were failing.

Somehow, despite the fact there were at least twenty Were ranged around him, creating a barrier between him and his goal—his father, their Alpha—he pulled them forward, an inch at a time. And despite the strength and concentration it had to be taking for Lachlan to do this, he still had enough energy to swipe at those closest to him, throwing whoever he could grab aside.

Goddess help them. He had to be stopped.

She bore down and pulled more power, aware of the grunts of those behind her. Ali gripped her hand, squeezed. She squeezed back then began to pull together the strands of her spell.

A simple spell in truth, but one that needed far more behind it than what she usually used if she was to succeed.

Sweat prickled on her brow as she tried to grasp more of the steadily strengthening power and pull it into her. She had to increase the flow into her normal channels so she could use it. Why hadn't she thought to figure this out when lying in bed rather than muse about the research study she would embark on?

Stupid. Stupid—

Ali let go of her hand and gripped her shoulder. The power steadied, became manageable, unfettered and pure.

Of course. Her power was taking strength from the mating bond, so it needed to be channelled from both of them, something that, somehow, he'd intuited.

She glanced at Ali, marvelling once again at the strength and purity of his gifts. Thanking the Goddess for it, she centred the suddenly free-flowing power and wrapped it in the energies she took from the others, then tried to take aim at Lachlan.

There were too many bodies in the way. 'You have to let him go!'

Lachlan's head whipped around at the sound of her voice. Avaricious delight bloomed on his face. 'Ye heard my call! Ye came for me.' He turned, and catching the Were around him off-guard, managed to take a half-dozen steps towards her before they rallied to slow his progress. He screamed, a sound that was closer to a roar than a howl. 'Ye canna do ought to keep me from her. She's here for me. *Mo ghràdh.*'

'Lachlan, I command ye to stop!' Iain's voice, weak and yet still ringing with Alpha power, rose over the noise of struggle.

Lachlan's head whipped around, the whites of his eyes wide, his pupils so large the colour of his irises had disappeared. 'Ye canna command me. I am Alpha-born too, old man. I will vanquish ye and then she will be mine. There is ought ye can do to keep me from her.'

'You are not Alpha-born,' Ali said, his voice ringing with his own Alpha energies. 'You are less than any male here. Less than the weak thing that has become your father.'

Lachlan's head snapped around again, gaze arrowing in on Ali, fury-tinged hatred turning his handsome face vicious. 'Ye are no' her mate. She is mine! Mine! Ye will pay for taking wha' is mine.' He surged forward, killing madness in his eyes, dragging the Were who barred his way across the floor. They strained and struggled but couldn't seem to stop him. In fact, as they weakened, Morghanna sensed his strength increasing. Another one of them fell aside. But Dougal and most of his lieutenants still stood in the way. She had to release the witch-lightning that may possibly hold Lachlan at bay even though Leanna had not returned with the potion-filled dart.

'You have to let go. You have to get out of the way,' she cried out to them.

'Ye ken? She wants me. She wants me to come to her!' Lachlan pulled the Were forward another few steps.

His movement gave her the gap she needed. She lifted her hands and released the spell she'd created. It hit Lachlan, freezing him in place.

'Clever,' Ali said. 'A spell of stillness like I used on him the other day.'

It wasn't clever. It was the only thing she had that might stop him. She didn't want to use what she used on him yesterday, fearful it might make the Beast come forth. But this, she could do, the spell having been imprinted on her mind when Ali had used it. They used something similar with patients when setting bones or stitching cuts, but his spell was far stronger; now even more so with all the power at her disposal from Ali and the coven. The only other thing she could use would require her to channel power into the spirits around her so they could manifest enough to help hold Lachlan in place. Except ...

She jerked a little in surprise.

'What is it?'

She glanced at Alistair. 'The spirits. They are not here. Usually there are at least a dozen hanging around me. But right now, there are none.'

'Is that a problem?'

'I do not know.'

'You will figure it out.'

His trust in her made her chin tremble as love and power flared through the mating bond.

Someone gasped. 'Look at that. How is that possible?'

Her eyes widened as light bloomed around Lachlan. Her power. It was strengthening somehow, even though she hadn't done anything.

Those who'd been holding Lachlan fell away, hands raised to protect their heads, their eyes. Lachlan gasped and shuddered; a bug caught in amber.

She sighed heavily. Had she done it?

Then he began to fight her.

She grunted as he hit out at the magic holding him still.

By the Goddess, he was so strong. Stronger than he should be. The full brunt of her immobilising spell should have felled a creature twenty times his size, but somehow, he began to move against it, even as she channelled more and more borrowed power into the spell. She didn't think she could hold him for much longer.

Where the hell was Leanna?

One of the coven members behind her cried out before crumpling to the floor. Damn. She wanted to check on them but couldn't risk turning her attention from Lachlan to look. She wished she had more practice at this, but none of them, aside from the hated witches known as succubi, ever trained to take power from others unless it was to help in Healing—but that was a very different thing from this offensive magic. She couldn't have known that at some stage she would need to do this. Yet here she was.

She only hoped that there wouldn't be any long-term effects from draining her fellow coven members in this way. Succubi often killed their prey—

She choked on bile at the thought, her skin pebbling with icy shivers. No, she wasn't a succubus. She was doing this for the greater good, not for her own power and glory.

She wasn't taking power from her Coven to feed herself. She was channelling it straight into a spell to stop Lachlan from hurting others and himself.

'You are strong. So strong and good, it blinds me, my treasure. Do what you must. We stand with you.'

Her mate's words were followed by a caress, a kiss, covering her, wrapping around her, lifting her up, succouring her. For a blissful moment she was light and peace.

Then Lachlan pushed forward; one step.

The Were who were still able tried to grab him, but the light-power seemed to be making that impossible.

Oh Goddess. What if he got loose?

'You can hold him.' Ali squeezed her shoulder, his love and trust a warmth urging her on through their bond. 'You can hold all of their power. Only you can do this.'

She nodded, wanting to believe him.

But feared his faith in her would prove to be wrong.

If only Bridgette was here. She'd be able to handle this so much better. If only Ali knew more and could take her place. With the extra power from the coven, he'd be able to use his lightning to hold Lachlan at bay for weeks if he was at full power. But it was no use wishing for things that could not be. She had to deal with the now.

And the now was all about keeping Lachlan at bay until Leanna arrived with the sleep potion. She just had to hold on.

Lachlan moved within the amber of her spell, taking a small step.

She pulled on more power from those around her and bolstered her working.

Lachlan grunted, anger riding across his face alongside pain. He glared at her and took another, struggling step forward. 'Why do ye keep me from ye, *mo ghràdh?*'

That endearment—one Malcolm, Bridgette's mate, used with such love for her—coming from Lachlan's mouth was like poison. She wanted to tell him to stop calling her that, but the power riding through her was excruciating now, too much after yesterday's exertions. She didn't know how long her body would hold up, even if she could maintain the level of power that was—just—holding Lachlan at bay.

'*Leanna—where are you?*'

'*I am coming.*' The younger woman's voice was an agonised shout in her mind. She almost stumbled in shock at the sound, so clear, so true. How? Leanna was not a mind-talker; and she most certainly wasn't.

Lachlan took another step and she refocused on him, pushing aside the questions that had distracted her and pulled on more power.

A cry of pain slashed in her mind: Leanna.

Hell! She was pulling from the younger witch too. She couldn't, hadn't meant to, but Leanna now struggled to remain conscious because of her ineptitude.

'*I'm sorry*,' she said in her mind, trying to pull back, to reach Leanna again. But it was too late. The power drain had been too much.

She'd had to pull from too many and now there was nobody left. All those who had entered the hall with her were now lying on the floor, unconscious, as were all the other witches and warlocks in the village. She sucked in a horrified breath as she realised she'd pulled from the children as well. Oh, Goddess, no.

'They gave willingly,' Ali whispered beside her. 'They would again if you called.'

She nodded, knowing he was right, but still horrified by the necessity.

Then the reality of it dawned on her. Now it was just her and her mate—and it wasn't enough. He was almost drained. And soon she would be too.

As if the thought brought on reality, her power stuttered.

Lachlan howled in triumph, throwing the final few Were, including Dougal, aside as if they were nothing but a cloak. He leaped towards her. '*Mo ghràdh*.'

'No!' With a cry that became the growl of the animal that was the other half of him, Ali's grip tightened on her arm. 'Take it,' he shouted and pushed power into her, power greater than what he'd channelled to her outside the Dance, greater than the power he and the coven had gifted her just now. Greater than any power she'd ever felt before.

For a split second she couldn't move, the shock of it holding her frozen. Where had he pulled it from? It wasn't from her or any of the others.

Then she knew.

Oh Goddess. No. How had he done it? Nobody had ever pulled on the power of the Dance outside the clearings they were found in. But that's what the power was; Goddess fuelled. 'Alistair, you cannot. The consequences are—'

'Consequences be damned. If you do not use it, we are lost.'

He was right. By the Goddess, he was right. There was no time to pray to that Goddess now to forgive them for their hubris, only time to harness the power and use it.

She gathered it in, something inside her sighing at its rightness. At how it belonged, expanding on the strange difference inside her, filling it. She raised her free arm as Ali raised his, ready to use the twinning power alongside her.

Lightning streaked from their fingers to hit Lachlan square in the chest mid-leap.

Screaming his rage, the insane Were was thrown across the room to smash up against the broken chairs and tables in front of the dais.

Dougal and the few remaining Were in the room who were able to stand leaped in front of the chair where their Alpha sat, claws out, their growls vibrating through the air as Lachlan pulled himself from the wreckage.

Snarls tearing from his throat, the insane Were pulled a piece of wood from his shoulder and turned away from those protecting his father.

The thing that curled inside Lachlan wasn't interested in them at all. With a roar, he began to change.

25

As he ran at Morghanna, Lachlan's features contorted, hair pushing out of his skin, jaw and nose elongating, teeth lengthening. His claws snapped out, tipped with glistening, pulsing blackness.

The Darkness.

'Alistair!' she cried.

'I know.' He sucked in a breath and somehow managed to push more power into their bond.

Ye Gods. The glorious electrifying blaze of it. It filled her, making her whole in a way she'd never been before.

'Ready,' Ali cried, his fingers tightening on hers as he pointed with his other arm at Lachlan. She mirrored his action then as one, they released it, all of it, at Lachlan as he changed before them.

The lightning hit the transforming Beast square in the chest, making him fly back, up into the air, holding him there. The white brilliance that was their combined lightning danced around him, growing brighter, almost blinding. Those still conscious in the room cried out, shielding their eyes, skittering away from the enormity of it. She didn't blame them. It was frightening. She'd felt the Goddess in her before, but this was different.

It was as if this power was hers. Hers and Ali's. And they could do anything they liked with it. As she held Lachlan in place, her mate used part of his share to create a bubble of protection around them as they worked to stop the Darkness. But they could do so much more. They could expel the Darkness. They could put a bubble of protection around the Packlands.

More.

They could conquer anyone who stood against them. They could reshape the world with this power if they wished.

She was a Goddess.

And it was magnificent.

She laughed, the sound ringing around them. Were who were still conscious covered their ears, cowering.

'No. Morghanna. Cease.'

Her laughter stoppered in her throat as the desperate voice rang through her mind.

'You are a Healer,' it continued, the echoing sound overtaking all other thoughts. *'This is not what you want. It is not what you do.'*

The voice in her head—was it hers? Alistair? Bridgette? Morrigan? It sounded like all of them, and it sounded like none.

She gasped as realisation struck. The Goddess. Was the Goddess communicating with her? As she did with Bridgette?

The Beast took her moment of distraction to fight back against the power aimed at it. It dropped down a few inches from where it hung, claws extending, the black darkening, swirling. It roared, a deafening sound felling those still standing upright in the room. All except her and her mate.

She pulled back from the brink of losing herself in the enormity and grace of the magical energies she wielded and glanced at Ali to see if he'd felt the same thing.

He hadn't. He'd kept on fighting while she was distracted by her own glory.

Blood trickled from his ears and nose—her laughter, the Beast's roars, all too much for his sensitive Were hearing. But where all the

Were, including Iain and Dougal, were down and writhing on the floor, he stood strong.

'Ali,' she said through the bond. 'Are you alright?'

He nodded. 'You?' His gaze went to her nose, her ears. She became aware of warm fluid on her skin, tasted and smelled the copper of it.

Not that it mattered. Couldn't matter.

All that mattered was stopping the Beast. Saving her coven, her pack.

More power surged into her—the strength in her mate that allowed him to do what he was doing floored her even as it frightened. She pushed the worry aside and arrowed her concentration on the fight before them.

Using the extra power, she pushed out more lightning from her deepest core—lightning that wasn't Healer orange or Spirit-talker purple, or any of the colours Ali wielded, but the brightest blinding white-gold.

Beautiful. Frightening.

Not her power. Not his. And yet, somehow it was both.

But this time, she didn't lose herself in it. She turned her mind to putting every ounce of herself and this power behind the greatest need:

To stop the Beast. To expel the Darkness.

The Beast rose higher. He howled in frustration. 'You have power you did not barter for, witch.' The voice was of the Beast, of the Darkness, echoing and horrible, all signs of Lachlan, his accent, his humanity, gone. 'You will pay for this.'

Ignoring its words, she pooled every single bit of energy and knowledge she had inside her, and began to chant, 'I tear you out. I tear you out. I tear you out.'

The power taken from the Goddess exploded in a light so bright, she could see nothing but the golden-white of it and the Darkness that was the Beast at its core.

Ali chanted with her in his native French. *Je vous arrache, je vous arrache.'* With this kind of magic, it didn't matter that the words were different. All that mattered was the intent. How she knew this suddenly did not matter—all that mattered was its truth.

The Beast's roars and struggles intensified, the lightning not just winding around it this time, but pushing into it, entering through its mouth, eyes, nose, ears. Black began to drip from its orifices as more and more of the white-gold power pushed inside it, pushing the Darkness out.

The Beast began to retreat, as if it were sucked inside, into oblivion, its snarls and roars fading until all that could be heard were Lachlan's screams. Screams that were ear-piercing and full of so much pain and fear it made the Healer in her want to cry. But she didn't, she simply kept feeding the witch-warlock lightning into him.

It was working.

It was actually working.

She and Ali were vanquishing the Darkness.

Power surged through her at the realisation and briefly the thought flitted through her mind once again, 'I am a Goddess.'

But as soon as the thought came, it left her with a rush, rejected by the soul of who she was, what she wanted, the love that filled her for her mate, for his goodness, for her coven, her family, her friends and pack. Her mate did not falter once. Did not let the eternal breadth of the power overwhelm him. He had a job to do, and he stood steadfast, unaltered, uncaring of the consequences.

He was magnificent.

She did not want to be a Goddess. She simply wanted to be here, with him. Sharing her love with him. Creating a family with him.

'I love you,' she whispered across the bond.

Je t'aime. D'ici à l'éternité.'

The return answer was a warm embrace she never wanted to do without.

The power pulsed brighter, a golden-white as bright as a sun.

A shriek of rage tore through the air around them.

She hunkered down, Ali her strength, and bore through the pain of it.

· · ·

ALISTAIR COULDN'T STOP his flinch as the shriek turned into a high-pitched noise, heard clearly above Lachlan's screams, building, growing louder and louder, making it harder and harder to concentrate. He pushed through, continued on. The strength of the witch at his side made anything else impossible. He would have faltered long before if not for her. For the special twist to her powers that allowed her to be the arrow to his crude bow. He'd never been able to grab and use the energies that powered his magic like this before.

Something inside her had opened this gift within him, allowing him to be a conduit to the Goddess' power. Anna was both gateway and channel, amplifying what he took tenfold. He had almost been swept away before the enormity of it, had felt her start to do the same, but then she pulled back, pulled him back with her. By the Goddess she was strong. By her own admission, not every witch or warlock who entered the Dance could tap into the Goddess' power the way she did. And yet, she didn't seem to be aware of this part of her gifts. Seemed to think it was all him. But it wasn't. He was able to pull on the Goddess' heavenly energies because she had opened the gate to him upon their mating.

He wanted to tell her, wanted to convince her, but now wasn't the time. Right now, he had to find a way to save their people.

The noise coming from Lachlan, from the Darkness, grew louder. He didn't understand how he could hear it—his eardrums damaged by the first piercing cry—but its pressure was almost unendurable. The room began to shake and tremble. Dust rained down on the bodies lying on the floor. He glanced up at the roof—was it going to come down? He could sense the same worry in his mate. Worry for the Were and coven members in the room. They would be crushed by the falling timbers if that roof fell.

He had to find a way to protect them. His treasure would never survive the loss of so many under her protection. He could almost hear the thoughts in her mind as she tried to find some way of saving them, but she couldn't do it. She had to keep her energies concentrated on Lachlan and the Darkness; but he could feel her wavering, her doubts.

He had to do it. But how?

'Your shield-bubble. Extend it.'

He had no idea why the voice suddenly decided to be useful, but he grabbed its idea and began to channel power into his shield.

'Ali? What are you doing?' Her voice came to him through the bond.

'I will save the others. You protect us all.'

'I cannot. Not without the fullness of your powers.'

'You have the strength, my treasure. You are the only one who can truly vanquish the Darkness. Let me protect the others.'

She glanced at him, but didn't question, simply trusted. The gift of her trust strengthened him further as he slowly enlarged the shield-bubble.

The room shook, dust and debris raining down on the unconscious. Too slow. He pushed harder. Sweat joined the blood trickling from his nose and ears as he manipulated the energies. The immensity of it threatened to break him if he didn't expend it quickly. In his mind, he pictured the shield-bubble enlarging, but also pictured tendrils of magic pulling all who lay within the room under the protective dome. And as he imagined it, the power made it so.

He pulled Iain and Dougal—the last two as they were the furthest away—under the dome.

Just in time. The timbers above them buckled, breaking as the sound—the horrible wailing, protest of noise that seemed to be from the darkest heart of evil—rose around them. Wood and thatch and the dirt of ages rained down, hitting the protective bubble, making him grunt with the impact. But none of the rubble made it through, simply bouncing to slide off the invisible force-field and join the rest of the rubble of tables and bench seats on the floor.

'Well done, my love,' Morghanna muttered through the bond.

Wind suddenly picked up, whirling around the outsides of the room, pulling in tighter and tighter until the rubble lifted, surging around Lachlan, pelting against the barrier.

The Darkness was fighting for its life.

But Morghanna stayed strong. And he stood with her as he always would. He trusted her to make the world right.

Hands gripping tighter, they infused their thoughts with their love, with their wish for the Darkness to be gone, with their wish to keep those they loved and belonged to safe.

He might belong because she belonged, but it was more than he'd had for a long time, more than he'd ever expected, the acceptance from the coven, the tendrils of friendships forming with Dougal and the lieutenants, finally being at one with his wolf; and he would fight with his last breath for all of it.

The howl of noise rose, heard only now inside his mind, his eardrums completely blown. Rubble and dust filled the air, whirling tighter and tighter in the centre of the room.

Lachlan shook harder, faster. Debris tore out of the tunnel of wind, smashing into the barrier, pounding against his mind. But he didn't falter, his strength Morghanna, as he was hers. They stood against it.

One. As they always had been. As they always would be.

The black seeping out of Lachlan's nose, ears, mouth, eyes began to quiver and shake, pouring out of him faster, lifting away as he glowed brighter with the light now thrumming through his skin. The blackness rose, pooling above him in a glowing sphere of moving, pulsing dark. Something in its movements showed a desperation to escape the power of their lightning.

'Nae! Nae! Dinna leave me. Dinna leave me!' Lachlan cried.

The lightning grew its own tendrils, whipping up to grab the black pool whirling above him before it could escape. This blackness was only one small piece of the Darkness, but still so powerful. The fragment of the Darkness screeched in protest as the tendrils of light wrapped around it, constricting, choking, obliterating.

He felt more than heard Morghanna's instruction, her need. He mirrored her actions as, with a final push, they closed their outstretched fingers and released everything inside them.

Lightning more blinding than before exploded against the

constricting, pulsing ball of Darkness before enveloping it completely. A cry, intense rage-fuelled desperation, filled the air, so great, it threatened to knock them down. Somehow they stood strong in its wake. Then, with a final push from his Anna, their power exploded.

The Darkness vanished in the flare of blinding pure white. Walls and furniture evaporated. The bubble and everyone in it were flung back.

Protect!

The thought was the last one as they fell to earth, the power he'd used to create the shield-bubble cushioning their landing just long enough before being completely expelled.

Exhaustion pulled at every part of him. Pain throbbed in every pore. The pull of unconsciousness threatened. But he held on—for Anna, for the people she cared for. He had to make certain the Darkness was truly gone, that Lachlan was no longer a threat. That everyone was safe.

He pushed up to a kneel and surveyed the damage. They'd been flung back into the square. The Alpha Hall was rubble spread across the square and beyond. A body lay on a pile of debris where the hall had once stood, flares of lightning sparking around him.

Lachlan.

His body bowed up, spasming as the lightning licked at him then sank into his skin. He lay still. Was he dead? No. His chest moved.

Alistair's wolf growled deep in his throat—it would have been better if the bastard had died, but at least it seemed the Darkness was gone and no longer an immediate threat. He turned from Lachlan— he could wait. Others needed him more.

All around him, Were and coven twitched and groaned, some coming to consciousness, some lying still but alive. Where was his mate?

'Ali.'

He turned to see Anna, trembling and covered in dirt, blood streaked on her face. She pushed up and began to crawl to him over bits of stone and wood. She glowed with power. 'Anna ...'

She nodded. 'I know, but we need to see to our people firs—' She heaved and vomited blood.

'No, get rid of it now,' he said, scrambling over to her. 'Please, get rid of it now.' She'd taken in the greater portion of the power, and while she'd used most of it in that last push, some of it still lived inside her, too large to be contained. She had to get rid of it or she would die.

She nodded and closed her eyes. He felt what she was doing through their mating bond, releasing the rest of the power still inside her through the Packbond, the purpose of the Pact. Even though he'd heard about it, it was remarkable to experience an external representation of what lived inside of him.

Rainbow glows sprang up all around him. Were—no matter if conscious or not—used the power she expelled to change into their wolf form, a change that would help in their healing.

He felt the tingle of the change come over him, his wolf responding to the urge that seeped into it through the bond that tied him to the pack. It was eager to be let free, to help him recover and rest as it took care of them both.

He smiled, stroking his wolf lovingly with his mind, happy to change right now, especially if taking some of that power would help their Anna. But first, he had to ensure she was somewhat comfortable.

He somehow managed to pick his mate up, then settle her against the wall of the nearest building as she expelled the dangerous power inside. That power prickled inside him through the Packbond, expanding out, out. He took two steps back to allow the change to occur without disrupting her. Rainbow colours glowed around him. He smiled, the relief and release a blessing he never wanted to live withou—

'You will pay.' The screeched words were followed by a lash of pain that wrapped around him, squeezing him tightly in its grip. He choked, fell to his hands and knees, his change halted abruptly. He heard Anna cry out as the thing dug its tendrils inside him, burning, icy cold daggers. Blood poured from his eyes, nose, ears and mouth.

He coughed and choked, struggling against the thing that tore into him.

But he couldn't fight. He had no power left. He'd expelled it all. He couldn't even tap into the energies Anna had been expelling—they were somehow blocked from him, what she'd already given him sucked deep inside him, drawn to the tendrils that sliced at his mind, his soul. He cried out as the roiling, tearing pain increased, then coughed and vomited—blood and something black and ugly.

Merde! It felt like he was being rent in two. The tearing came to a crescendo. He was going to die.

He could hear screaming—his? Anna's? His wolf howled in pain.

The howl ended abruptly just as the tearing pain ceased.

Coughing, panting, spitting blood, trembling on his hands and knees, he couldn't believe he still lived. Pain, bright and alive inside him, told him something terrible had been inflicted upon him. Perhaps he should continue the change, let it and his wolf heal him a little before allowing the Healers to have their turn.

He tried to pull the change around him, but nothing happened.

He stilled, breath caught in his throat.

No. No. That couldn't be.

He tried again but ...

There was nothing inside him.

Nothing.

His denial tore through the air as he heard Anna scream in his mind, 'No!'

Loss. Grief. Pain. They speared through him as he clutched at his chest, his middle, that place deep inside that had once been so full and was now so empty.

Was this what his nightmare vision had been about? Ye Gods. If only he'd known. If only he'd known ...

Anna's face appeared above him, agony tearing at her features.

'Ali.' Her voice, even heard through the bond, was hoarse, barely a whisper.

He reached for her, his anchor, hoping she could somehow help. But she couldn't help. She couldn't help. Not with this.

'Alistair,' she managed to whisper, her voice full of his loss. The horrifying chasm of it.

He made a choking sound and then, 'My wolf. My wolf.' He'd suppressed it for so long, misunderstood it, blamed it for things that were not its fault, and now, when he'd only just begun to accept it, to feel joy in it, to understand what the symbiosis meant to him ... 'It has gone.'

'I know.' She choked on a sob. 'Oh Goddess, I know.' She pulled him to her, holding him close, as if in doing so, she could hold him together. But it was too late.

Too late.

You will pay, the voice had said.

He had used the Goddess' power without seeking the proper permission, not once but twice. And in punishment, she had exacted a terrible price.

Anna lifted her head to the sky. 'Why not me?' she shouted, confirming his thoughts. 'Why punish him and not me?'

'To punish him is to punish you,' the wind whispered all around them, whipping up the dirt and flinging it in their faces before being sucked into a vortex and away, the words a nasty fading echo around them.

He closed his eyes, but he didn't need to have them open to know that she had heard—of course she heard, for she was more powerful than anyone could ever have conceived. He felt her agony, the deep shame and the blame she laid on herself for what had been done to him.

No. No. He made a sound that was meant to be a howl but came out as a shout filled with agony for the thing that was missing.

'Alistair.' Tears streamed down her cheeks as she tipped his face up to kiss him, to share in his grief. But nothing could help, the pain of his loss so great, it dragged him away from her, into unconsciousness. Into death.

Because how could he live without half of his soul?

This was what the ancient rhyme and warnings spoke of.

But why had her Goddess punished him with the curse of the

Beast? Why would the Goddess do such a thing when all they'd done was protect what she wanted protected?

No answer came as he slipped into the black of unconsciousness, finally unable to stand the pain of the loss in his heart, in his soul.

His wolf. It was gone. And soon, so would he be.

26

Morghanna wiped a hand across her eyes and stared blindly across the cottage. The material covering the windows flapped in the breeze, bringing with it the scent of roses and the sounds of a flourishing coven and pack. Just weeks ago, she would have looked out, and then, if she had no work to do inside, join the goings on and enjoy the glory of the day.

Now, all she wanted to do was close the shutters against all the things that reminded her of just how useless she was.

Sure, she'd helped stop the Darkness, stopped the Beast from manifesting, but most of the credit for that could be laid at her mate's feet. It was his power, his talent, that had saved them all.

And now despite his power, despite their bond, he was dying. And there was nothing she could do.

Was this the nightmare vision that had tormented his sleep? Had he seen this? It would explain why he'd not wanted to tell her about it —who would want to face this? But if he'd only told her, maybe ... maybe ...

Maybe what? She could have stopped it? Her mind had turned over the events every which way and had found no way around what they had done. They would be dead if Ali had not taken power from the Goddess and shaped it for her to use. The coven would be dead. The pack would be dead. And Lachlan—the Beast, the Darkness— would be free to ravage, destroy and kill his way across the world. There had been no other way. Ali had always been meant to do what he'd done to save them all.

She clenched her fingers, her rough nails digging into her palms.

Why had he not shared his burden with her if this is what he'd seen? It could have helped her prepare. They could have looked for a solution together, a way to get his wolf back.

How, she didn't know. Everyone had been looking for something, anything, to help, but so far, they'd found nothing.

Nothing.

She turned her blurry gaze from the flapping material, back to the male who lay in their bed. So still. Too still.

His eyes were closed as if in sleep, but it wasn't sleep. It was unnatural. Of course it was. Half of him had been torn away. And now, he fought for his life.

He was losing.

With Brionne's help, she'd scried with Bridgette and Malcolm again that morning. He was one of the most gifted pack Healers she'd ever met, and he'd promised to search through every resource he could lay his hands on as they travelled, asking all the pack Alphas and their Healers as well as the covens and their Healers they'd met if they had any histories that could help. But once again, he had nothing new to add. His sorrow and worry had sung through the connection, making the water in the scrying bowl ripple. Bridgette, feeling her desperation and the black shroud enclosing her, had sworn to find a way back to her quickly, but she and Malcolm were still a month away; two if the weather did not hold. She told Bridgette to continue her travels—her work was important—and that she would be fine.

A lie, but what was the point of Bridgette rushing back here only to find her gone, her body ashes alongside her mate's.

'Please, my dearest friend, do not lose hope,' Bridgette had pleaded before signing off, the same words Abigail and the other

Pack Healers had said every day over the last weeks alongside, 'He is strong. He can survive this.' But she knew their words for what they were: false.

They had tried everything. Leanna had driven herself to exhaustion every day as she tried to utilise her Soul Healing gifts to heal his soul—but even her burgeoning powers couldn't heal a soul when half of it had been ripped away and eviscerated. She couldn't create a patch when there was such a wound; Goddess knows she'd tried. But every time she attempted to mend the torn edges of what remained, they tore open once more the moment she was done, the reality of the missing part of him a knife cutting the wound anew.

Even though she hadn't wanted to, she'd told Leanna just that morning when she'd arrived to try again, not to attempt any further Soul Healings. Her efforts were doing him no good and were hurting the young witch. The simple, horrifying fact was, he faded more and more every day—the mating bond so much colder than it had been even yesterday—and she was helpless to stop it. But at least she could release the young witch from the burden of continuing to attempt what was impossible.

Tears streamed down her cheeks, a weakness she would never have allowed her coven or pack to see before now. But she was beyond caring that Leanna and Dougal were here now, or that others had been here earlier to help, to offer support. She was beyond the ability to lift her hand to wipe them away. What did it matter if she was crying when her heart, her soul, were being torn from her?

All because her mate had been so strong, he'd been able to wrest power from the Goddess without permission, and this was his punishment.

'He did not know. He is not trained. He did not know.'

The words tumbled from her mouth as they had repeatedly for the last two weeks as she sat watch, waiting, hoping against hope as her mate slowly declined.

He'd had moments of waking in the first few days, where he'd stared at her, the raw grief in his eyes breaking her heart as he murmured, 'I never knew. How much I needed my wolf. How important he is. I want him back. I only just started to know him. He cannot be gone. Please bring him back. Please.'

If he'd cried, it would have been more bearable, but his grief had been tearless, stricken. After those first few days, he'd stopped uttering those words, simply stared at the wall, legs curled up, arms wrapped around them as if to hold himself together. Then a week after that, he stopped doing even that. For days he'd lain flat on his back, eyes closed, as still as the death that threatened to take him.

Leanna appeared at the head of the stairs to the loft with a bowl of soup in her hands. 'Please, Morghanna. You need to eat.'

'I am not hungry.'

Dougal appeared behind the young witch, his expression grim, fierce. 'If you will not let her continue trying with Alistair, you can at least let her help you.'

She would have snapped a reply at the infuriating Were, but Leanna's lips trembled, her shoulders bowing. Morghanna hated herself for worrying her young friend like she was. So rather than yelling at them to leave as the fury inside her wanted her to do, she took the proffered bowl and forced herself to take a spoonful, choking it down, then another until Leanna, smiling shyly in apparent satisfaction, headed back downstairs to clean a cottage that couldn't possibly get any cleaner, Dougal stomping behind her to lend his help.

The moment they were gone, Morghanna put the barely touched bowl aside and picked up the mug of water. She had to keep Ali's fluids up. He'd long since stopped sipping the water she offered from the mug. She picked up the bored-out piece of reed she'd had Dougal fashion a few days ago, sucked up some water, slipping the other end between her mate's lips and released the water, trickling it via the reed into Ali's dry mouth.

His throat moved and she sighed in relief. At least he still swallowed what she gave him. She repeated feeding him the water on and off over the next few hours when she wasn't wiping his brow or holding his hand, begging, pleading with him, with the Gods, with her Goddess, to please bring him back, even though she knew her words fell on deaf ears.

The light in the cottage had begun to fade into the dark purple of twilight when Leanna came back upstairs, placing a plate on the bedside table. 'Dougal and I must leave now—Dougal has pack business to take care of. I would stay until Thomas and Brionne arrive, but I have a shift at the school.'

Morghanna pulled herself together enough to wave her hand. 'Of course you must go.'

Leanna nodded. 'Thomas and Brionne will not be long, I am certain. And I will be back tomorrow.' She placed a trembling hand on Morghanna's shoulder. 'Please, eat some of that bread and jam. Then try and get some sleep.'

'I will try. Thank you for all you have done.'

'I would do anything for you, Morghanna. I just wish there was more I could do to help.' Her voice broke. 'I am sorry. So very sorry.'

Morghanna couldn't look at her, couldn't dredge up any words to make the young witch feel better as she normally would, her throat too full of grief and rage. All she could do was nod.

Leanna's soft steps sounded on the stairs, followed by the gentle rumble of Dougal's voice as he obviously tried to comfort her. Then a few moments later, the front door closed.

For the first time in weeks, Morghanna was blessedly alone with her mate.

The silence pressed on her. She bent over Ali, kissed his forehead. A tear plopped down on his cheek—hers. She wiped it away gently, then looked up towards the heavens. 'Please. Please do not take him from me. He did not know. He did not know he was breaking the law.'

Her words rang, echoing and hollow in the stillness of the cottage. She waited—for what, she wasn't certain. Why she thought crying out the same words she'd been chanting inside or whispering for the last two weeks would make a difference, she had no idea. The Goddess was many things, but deaf wasn't one of them. Nor was she forgiving. She wouldn't care that Ali was untrained, that he'd made no promises to her of sacrifice, fidelity and service. From her point of view, his ignorance of the rules didn't make him innocent of breaking them.

The law was for all wielders of magic without exception.

Morghanna had once thought that law fair. It was for their protection from the unscrupulous and power-hungry. Now, she found it cruel and unjust. Especially as Ali hadn't used the power for personal gain. He'd done it to help her stop the Beast and vanquish the Darkness before they sank their claws into Lachlan irrevocably and sewn devastation and destruction. They'd saved Lachlan, the pack, the coven and who knew how many others beyond Packlands.

Ali might have been the one who'd reached for and taken the Goddess' power to fight the madness in front of them, but it had been done out of a shared desperation. She too was to blame.

And the Goddess hadn't put up a fight. If she'd not wanted him to use her power to defend her peoples, why hadn't she intervened? Why wait and send down punishment on them both for doing what they had to do to save the village?

It was no wonder Morrigan had turned away from the Goddess' plans and struck out on her own.

Morrigan!

Morghanna bolted to her feet, scurrying over to the small table Dougal had carried up here weeks ago so she could participate in the scrying with Bridgette and not be away from Alistair. She needed to contact Morrigan. Why hadn't she thought to try to contact her sister before now? She needed her strength, her indomitable will, to help her cope. She also needed her intelligence. Her sister always saw things in ways nobody else did—a curse as much as a strength. But if Morrigan were here now, she would figure out what could be done to bring Ali back, to see him through this.

Her fingers clenched on the lip of the bowl as she pulled it towards her. Nobody had been able to do a successful scrying for Morrigan, but maybe today would be different. Her desperation might get through and make her sister take down the barriers she'd put up.

Thankfully, the candles Leanna had used for the Healing she'd done a few hours ago on Alistair's body to keep him as healthy as possible despite the fact he was not eating were still lit, although guttering. That meant she had use of the other witch's power for a few moments at least. It was enough to boost her powers so she could do this without waiting for Brionne.

Words of the casting on her lips, she halted. Would Morrigan help Ali when she found out he was part wolf? She so hated the Were. A misplaced hatred, because the Were were as much a victim of the Fates as the powered. The Darkness was to blame for it all.

'The Goddess is to blame as well.'

The voice whispered in her head as it had whispered to her since Ali's wolf had been torn from him. She'd thought at first it was her own wicked thoughts, then had thought Ali spoke to her, but it was neither of those. It was like the voice that had spoken to her after she'd realised what had been done to Ali, the one that had said, 'To punish him is to punish you.' She wasn't sure whose voice it was, but it felt like it spoke truth. It certainly had spoken the truth when it had uttered those words. And it was true that the Goddess was to blame for punishing Ali with no trial, no recourse; just punishment meted out regardless of relative guilt or innocence.

'It should have been me!' The bowl clattered to the table, water sloshing over its edges as she let go and swung around to face the room. She thumped her fist against her chest. 'It should have been me.'

'No, Anna. The punishment ... is fair.'

She whipped around to see her mate staring at her, his eyes bloodshot and open.

'Ali! My love.' She leaped across the space between them but stopped herself from clambering on the bed with him—sometimes even the smallest of movements hurt him—and instead knelt on the floor. Taking his hand and holding it to her cheek, she met his gaze, drinking in her fill. 'Ali, my love, you've come back to me.'

He moved his head a little, swallowed hard. 'I am trying.' His voice was a harsh whisper, full of exhaustion and pain. He moved his hand, brushing his fingertips across her cheek, his touch so soft, fingers shaking. 'No tears.'

She choked back a sob and kissed his fingertips, his palm, then leaned over and kissed his forehead, his nose, his cheeks, then his lips, lingering there for a moment before pulling away.

His bloodshot eyes glittered as he whispered, 'Lie beside me.'

'Are you certain? I do not wish to hurt you.'

'You could never hurt me. Besides, when you hold me, it helps.'

She climbed onto the bed next to him, lying down, facing him, one arm over his waist the other cupping his cheek; she didn't want to stop staring into his incredible eyes—those fractured bits of sky seen through a green canopy of spring leaves. She could never get enough of looking into them.

He lifted his hands, tried to hold her, but trembled so hard they slipped away to fall back to the bed. She wanted to cry, but she didn't. He'd said no tears.

'Kiss me again,' he said, his voice barely a whisper.

She touched her lips to his, wanting to be gentle, but then he opened his mouth and—oh, the taste of him! She could never get enough of it. She was drawn into him, his kiss, for a mad moment before pulling back. His breath was too shallow, his skin too pale, but the mating bond had warmed a little at the contact between them, and she could feel him through it in a way she'd been unable to for days.

'Ali?' she whispered, then kissed him again. 'My love.'

'My love.'

'Do not leave me.'

'I am trying.'

She knew he was. But would his trying be enough? She had to find some way to help—to stop the inevitable from occurring.

Her mate deserved no less.

27

Over the next week, Ali gained back a little bit of his strength, while everyone who could, searched for a way to save him. But even with the little bit of hope his being able to get out of bed gave Morghanna, it quickly faded. There were simply no answers forthcoming on how to fix this, to fix him. And she was afraid, so desperately afraid, that the gain in his strength was a result of how they clasped onto each other through the bond—so hard and tight it was almost painful and draining her of energy; a fact she would never share with him.

The energy he received from their bond should have been enough, but it wasn't. The awful wound inside him, open and bleeding soul-energy where his wolf had once been, inexorably dragged him towards death. They knew it as they ate together. They knew it as they strolled around the cottage—twice was all he could manage. They knew it when they lay in bed at night, wrapped in each other's arms, and spoke of their pasts, and perhaps foolishly, their hopes for the future. They knew it when they kissed and looked into each other's eyes and when she took him inside her gently, their need to be joined too great, and rocked each other to completion.

He would die. And when he did, she would go with him.

He'd tried to talk to her about that, but she refused to allow him, refused to even think about staying as Iain had done. She knew it was selfish, knew her people needed her, but the grief, the aching hole of loss was so great, she couldn't imagine living past it once he was finally gone. He tried to make her promise she wouldn't follow him, his agony at the thought of her dying because of him a writhing pain inside him, and she wanted to, to take away at least that pain, but she didn't want to give a false promise. Not to him. Not when she had no idea how to hold on without him.

It was why, when they weren't spending his waking hours together, she sat over her scrying bowl, using power borrowed from anyone who would let her tap in, trying to contact Morrigan, to say goodbye, desperate to make amends with her sister, to make certain she was safe and happy; to beg, perhaps futilely, for her sister to come back and take her place.

At the end of the week, after she and Leanna helped Ali to bed—their single turn around the garden after breakfast had exhausted him—she turned to the scrying bowl that sat on the little table near the bed. 'Can we try again?'

Leanna simply nodded, lit the candles and said the blessings over the water in the bowl, whirling her finger through the liquid counter-clockwise until it began to spin and a cloud began to form. She stepped back, allowing Morghanna to take her place.

An image materialised; shadowy hills skirted by a forest. A river ran out of the forest and the image followed it, all the way to the rolling waters she knew to be the ocean. But her sister's face did not show.

She pulled on the magics Leanna had worked into the candles for her to use and tried again, her heart aching with her need.

She no longer thought to seek Morrigan's help—there was nothing her powerful sister could do. She also no longer sought to change her sister's mind with the proof that Alistair had provided—proof the Pact was their only chance to survive and thrive. He would soon be gone, and even if Morrigan answered Morghanna's pleas and came back, and Ali was still alive, the wolf was gone and the proof with it. She had even given up on the stupid idea of asking Morrigan to come back and take her place when she was gone—what had she been thinking? Her sister would never do that, especially when the reason for her to have been here in the first place was dead. Her stubborn sister would no doubt blame the Were as the cause of Morghanna's death.

No. She just wanted to see Morrigan once more before following her mate into the hereafter.

But her sister didn't answer.

She pushed the bowl away and stared blindly into the darkening room.

'We can try again later,' Leanna said softly. 'I can call Brionne back. She is better at this than I am. But for now, you should rest.'

Morghanna didn't answer, barely aware as the other witch doused the candles and left.

She knew she should lie down on the bed with her mate, but it was too hard to get her muscles to make the movements necessary even to crawl the few paces to the bed and up onto it.

Spirits crowded around her as her thoughts darkened. They had gathered around her night and day since the battle against the Darkness. Normally, she would have pushed them away, too exhausted and heart-sore to think of listening to their needs, but quite frankly, she didn't have the energy or will to make them go. Besides, strangely, they asked nothing of her, were there to offer only their help. In the first days after the battle, she'd managed to ask some of the older spirits of Were and covens to search their memories for any lore, any knowledge they might have of the Curse of the Beast, the rending of a soul. A few knew bits and pieces of lore, some old Healing spells that hadn't been tried because nobody had memory of them.

She tried them all. None worked.

They then went in search of others too, older than them, with more knowledge.

It came to nothing.

Nothing.

She rubbed her eyes as she thought over the last bit of nothing an old, wiry Were Knowledge Keeper had brought to her, a piece of the puzzle that suggested the Beast had indeed been amongst them before, but never so powerful as the Lachlan-Beast had been. She would have been fascinated by the story, but other than adding to their knowledge of the lore, it didn't help.

The Beasts the old story spoke of had not managed to fully rend a wolf from its Were. They had injured the wolves they had tried to rend so that they were unable to change, turning them rabid, which was bad enough, but not a full rending. And there had been no cure found; only death, served by the Alphas and Pack Hunters, had ended their agony.

Tired, so tired, she looked over at Ali as he slept. She had to stay positive for him, try to hold onto the hope that his waking had brought rushing back—but with every report indicating there was no way to repair what had been torn asunder, it was becoming more and more difficult to keep up the pretence. Watching him struggle against the wake of a powerful loss there was no recovering from, watching as he was reminded of the loss every moment of every day, the aching chasm of where his wolf used to be too great to ignore—it was the hardest thing she'd ever done, especially when she was so helpless to fix him.

His torn soul was bleeding and there was no way of staunching the wound. Not when remembering the loss tore it open afresh over and over. No amount of pretending was going to make that fact go away.

The only surcease he had was when they made love or in those few hours of broken sleep every night when he lay in her arms and the love between them fed the bond just enough to keep him alive, to keep him going.

And every night, she wished, futilely, that the bond could do more, wished it could make up for what he had lost.

As day and night passed, she stopped wishing and began willing it to be true, trying to push everything she could into the bond, to fill in the aching loss, but no matter how much she tried, when he woke and remembered, the chasm opened and began to pull him into its maw all over again. He was holding on as hard as he could—she could feel his determination to stay, to be with her—but it was no good. He was slipping away from her, and she was being forced to watch, knowing there was nothing she could do.

No other punishment could have been more brutal.

A few spirits crowded around her, manifesting just enough that they could push her to her feet and towards the bed. She didn't fight them, allowing them to help her onto the bed so she could spoon up behind her mate, her love.

Holding him tightly, she drifted into an exhausted sleep.

WEEKS after the battle with the Darkness, Iain came to ask if she would help waken his son. 'Lachie has no' recovered consciousness since the battle. The pack and coven Healers don't ken what else to do. I thought ... I thought ...'

Her eyes burned as she glared at him. How dare he come to her with this request!

He glanced down at his feet. 'Dougal said I should no' come to ask, but I had to try.'

'Did you?'

He winced at the cold snap of her voice. 'I am sorry. But I am desperate. Will ye help?'

'No. Your son can sleep forever as far as I am concerned. At least he is not a danger to anyone in his current state.'

He gulped, nodded. 'I should no' ha' come. I'll let ye get back to yer mate.'

She watched him go, her entire body thrumming with anger. She couldn't go back inside feeling like this. She did not want to upset Ali. Calling back through the door to Tru, one of the Lieutenants who was her current watcher, 'I am just going for a walk,' she stalked out through the front garden, rounded the cottage and entered the forest.

She walked aimlessly, trying to still her thoughts, her emotions, breathing long and slow until she was settled enough to return. That she had to do it—to spend precious time away from her mate—angered her further, but she pushed the emotions down, slamming them behind a roughly built wall in her mind.

When she returned, Tru had just put a bowl of stew on the table for her. She raised her brows at him. 'Dougal watched you,' he said, cheeks pinkening. 'He told me through the Packbond you were returning.'

She didn't respond, just sat and ate, shovelling the food into her mouth so fast she barely tasted it.

As she ate, she realised this night marked two months since their mating.

It should be a celebration, but Ali hadn't risen that day, too weak to do more than pick at the meals she brought him.

The end was close now. Her chest ached with the knowledge, like the breath was being squeezed out of her, but she didn't know what else to do.

Hours later, Morghanna lay in their bed. She stared at the ceiling as moonlight dappled across it, her mate sleeping peacefully—finally—cradled in her arms. He'd been tossing and turning and moaning for the last few hours, his body shaking with fever.

A tear slid down to wet her hair. He couldn't endure much more, and they'd found nothing, anywhere, to help him survive this.

She stared into the shadowed room, her thoughts a whirl, grasping for an idea. For anything. But there was nothing. Nothing. She wanted to wail into the night, to cry and scream and rave at the unfairness of it all.

More tears stung her cheeks, but she forced herself to keep all sound inside, thrusting the emotions back behind the wall she kept in place between her emotions and the mating bond. She could not wake Ali—he needed his rest.

Despite her efforts, he shifted at her side, murmuring, his face contorting with stress and pain. 'My love. My love,' he muttered.

'Shh,' she murmured, stroking his hair back from his sweaty brow, kissing him. He began to settle. She relaxed and began to stroke his brow, trying to fill her thoughts only with her love for him to keep him settled, but her thoughts soon returned to their hopeless cycle. His face contorted again and he cried out, 'No. My love. It burns. It burns.'

Ah Goddess—the pain of his loss was like a burn, blistering and hot. It flared through the bond, blazing, agonising. She had tried over and over to use her powers to put a Healing balm over the pain, but it never lasted. Even so, she did it again, kissing his brow, smoothing his hair, as she wound the spell around him, soothing him as best she could.

After what seemed an endless time of agony, he finally settled.

She let out a shuddering breath and collapsed beside him. He would sleep for hours as long as he wasn't disturbed by her negative emotions and the tension she just couldn't seem to keep at bay.

Ah, Goddess! It hurt to let go of him—they had such little time left together—but she had to put some distance between them so he wasn't disturbed by her. So, even though it was an agony, she slipped from their bed.

He muttered something, but it was only a brief protest before he fell back into settled sleep once more.

She threw on her cloak and padded silently down the stairs, thankful one of her 'watchers' who always seemed to be around even in the middle of the night, wasn't there—possibly seeing to the call of nature? She didn't care. All that mattered was that nobody would question what she was doing, where she was going, when she'd be back, or try to follow her.

She needed to be alone.

She shoved her feet into her clogs and stole into the night.

Spirits gathered around her as she wandered, but they didn't bother her with their needs, or their efforts. They too knew it was hopeless and had nothing to offer but their mournful presence.

She waved them away. 'Go. Go. Do not bother me this night. I wish to be alone.'

They faded away.

Her breath puffed in the chill air as she walked, autumn starting to give way to winter. The carpet of fallen leaves crunched under her feet as she walked blindly, her mind a whirl of thoughts; black, hopeless. Something skittered away in the undergrowth, and she tripped over a dead branch.

She needed to concentrate on where she walked or she could hurt herself. She looked around and shivered. The forest surrounded her, the sounds of night creatures going about their business, something that usually would have delighted her. As would the roll of thunder in the distance and the vibrant scent of the coming storm. But it didn't settle her. The life of it all seemed to laugh at her, to taunt her.

Cursing, she walked on. She needed to meditate, to sink down into her inner-self, commune with her magic and the pure essence of it. If she could do that, she would be able to settle herself, fortify her shield and return to Ali.

She looked up, meaning to seek a place where she could disrobe and prepare to meditate, only to find she was standing before the Dance.

She blinked at it, her mind blanking before a laugh was torn out of her. 'Of course,' she said to the sky. 'Of course I would come here.' Because normally, when she was this distraught, when she was this torn apart with questions and no answers, she would come to where she felt closest to the Goddess and ask for her guidance and help.

But that was most definitely not an option this time. Apart for the fact this was the Goddess' punishment, she hadn't felt the Goddess since the words 'To punish him is to punish you' had rung in her ears. The Goddess had withdrawn from her—although, why she hadn't taken Morghanna's magic too, she didn't know.

Morghanna wished she had. Wished the punishment had been to take her powers rather than Ali's wolf. 'But then, that would not have been such a severe punishment, would it?' she shouted at the Dance. 'You knew I could live without my power—it is not like it is truly essential, is it? Not like I am Bridgette or Morrigan or Leanna. But Alistair cannot live without his wolf.' She snorted. 'Losing my power would have been like the loss of a limb. Ripping Alistair's wolf away is like tearing out a heart. It is a death sentence. How is that fair? We protected life and you mete out death.'

Silence was her only answer, but it didn't stop her from stumbling forward and shouting at the stones again. 'In punishing Ali the way you have, you pronounced a death sentence on us both.' Her voice caught on a sob. 'Why? Have I not served you well? Have I not been faithful and patient and done everything you have ever required of me? Why would you bring me my soul mate then take him away? Why would you give me such joy and then tear it asunder? What is the point? Why would you be so cruel? Why?' She struck the stone in front of her, barely feeling the impact of it against her palm. 'Why?'

'I did not do this thing of which you accuse me, but even if I had, you have inside you that which you need to solve the problem and survive.'

Morghanna stumbled back, away from the stone she'd just slammed her fist into. 'What?' She whipped around, peering into the dark of the night. The voice was so close, like a breath across her cheek, but the clearing was empty. 'Who is there?'

'It is I.'

Warmth tingled on Morghanna's back, the hairs rising at her nape as power surged around her.

So much power. It swept over her, around her, covering her, sucking the breath from her lungs and the strength from her limbs with the unforgiving essence of it. She collapsed to the ground, clutching at her head, at her stomach, uncertain if she would pass out from the pain first or throw up.

A golden light flickered into being, growing in strength. A light so bright it made her eyes water. She snapped them closed but it didn't help. She couldn't stand it. It was so intense, it burned through her lids.

She threw her arms up around her head, collapsing on her side, pulling her legs up to her stomach, lungs aflame with the need to breathe.

But it did nothing. Everything was on fire. She was going to burn alive.

'*Morghanna!*' She heard Ali's cry in her mind. His struggle to rise, to come to her. Even though he didn't have the strength. Even though there was nothing he could do and he'd be burned alive too in this last form of punishment. Of their Goddess' justice. *'Ali! No. You cannot save me. She will kill you too if you interfere. Please. Leave me. Do not come. Do not come.'*

The roar in her mind shattered what was left of her thoughts. What was left of her soul. They were going to die. Now.

She couldn't believe this was the end.

28

'I'm sorry, my child.'

Morghanna whimpered, curling into herself further at the terrifyingly beautiful shriek piercing her skull.

'Once again, I apologise.' The voice gentled, a lullaby weaving around her. 'I did not mean to hurt you.'

The shriek might have stopped driving into her head, threatening to burst her eardrums, but the burning didn't stop. Not that she cared, her only thought for ... 'Ali!' she gasped.

'I do not wish to hurt your mate either.' The voice became echoing, distant. 'Sleep, my son. Sleep.'

Ali's presence softened, a shadow in her mind, just like when he fell asleep every night. The voice had put him to sleep. Thank the heavens. He now wouldn't come; wouldn't see her burn and be burned in turn.

The rasp of breath scorched, a blazing in her lungs, eating away until they were nothing but ash.

She curled even more tightly into a ball, fingers digging into her head, knees up to her chest, but the fire, it didn't abate. The agony ...

'I'm sorry, Morghanna. I forgot how sensitive humans are to my light on this plane. There.' The light faded and the power pulled away enough that Morghanna managed to suck a breath into her aching lungs. It hurt, but she took another breath, and another, trembling all over, a fine layer of sweat prickling on her too-hot skin. The throbbing, slicing pain in her head and behind her eyes made her stomach roil again even though there was nothing left in it.

'Here. Let me help.'

A coolness touched her forehead—the briefest touch—and the pain, the raging heat, the nausea, began to slide away. She sucked in a breath, expecting the blaze of fire to still burn her, but instead, the night air was cool, soothing. She gulped it in, her limbs unfolding to let more air in, cooling the remainder of heat from her skin.

'Breathe slowly or you'll pass out.'

The voice was a tinkle of music that both comforted and caused shredding fear. 'Who ... are ... you?'

'You know who I am. I have spoken to you before.'

'Goddess?'

'Who else would it be?' Soft material brushed over her arm as the Goddess knelt at her side.

She wanted to open her eyes but was too afraid, knowing what happened to those who set eyes on heavenly beings. 'Why would ... you come to ... talk to me?'

'You called out to me, asking me questions. I thought they deserved an answer.'

'You are here to ... answer my questions? Why?'

A hand brushed over her forehead. 'Because you are my faithful and honest servant. You helped in my fight against the Darkness. You deserve to know some of what is going on—at least in how far it pertains to you. Here, let me help you sit. I can't talk to you with you lying on the ground.' Arms reached under her, lifting her to a sitting position. She rocked unsteadily, but the arms held her upright, firm, supportive, strong beyond reasoning, the touch as comforting and healing as it was terrifying.

A sound filled her mind, like a soft lullaby and the shushing of a warm spring breeze. Her head swam.

The arms withdrew, as did the sound. Morghanna fell forward, but caught herself this time, her hands slamming into the warm earth beneath her, fingers curling in the grass. She opened her eyes, staring at the green fronds, the dirt beneath, breathing in the scent of the woods and something else that was like summer and spring and winter and autumn all at once.

Intoxicating.

It sank inside her, filling her, warming her in a comforting, steady way, soothing away the rest of the pain, the dizziness and nausea, filling her with strength and calm the like of which she'd not felt for weeks; if ever. 'Thank you,' she said, her voice still rough. 'Thank you for not burning me alive.'

'I'm sorry for that. As I said, I forgot how my light manifests here —it's been a while since I made an appearance on this plane of existence. Forgive me?'

Morghanna nodded—what else could she do? The Goddess sat at her side and was healing the damage she'd wrought. She also sounded sincere. But still, there were so many questions. She wanted to lift her head, to look the Goddess in the eyes and ask them, but fear sliced through her. She swallowed, noticing there was no burn or pain now. 'What did you do to Alistair?'

'Nothing but send him to a peaceful slumber. When he wakes, he will have no memory of this. Which, as it happens, is what I came to talk to you about.'

Morghanna sucked in another breath and dug her fingers a little more into the grass and the earth—relief had made her a little dizzy. She stared at an earthworm as it poked its head out of the soil and wriggled across the grass towards the Goddess. The grass grew taller around the heavenly being, the green a little greener, the fronds more succulent. A scent of freshness and the ocean lifted from them as they shifted in the breeze that wafted around her. Out of the corner of her eye, she noticed the Goddess' skirts were the colour of the ocean, green and deepest blue, and like the water, sparkled in the sun.

She snatched her gaze back before she could look higher.

Laughter burbled around her. 'You can look at me. Looking at me won't hurt you. I promise.'

She shook her head. 'That is not what the histories say. Truly looking upon heavenly beings usually leads to death or madness.'

The Goddess made a sound of disgust. 'Fables put around by some of my brothers and sisters—they prefer humans to be pious unthinking fools. I do not. You should know this about me. You have served me all your life. Please, look upon me.'

Slowly, Morghanna lifted her gaze and gasped. She'd been expecting something heavenly, something unthinkably glorious, but before her sat a woman. Beautiful certainly—breathtakingly so—but no more beautiful than some human women Morghanna had seen; her sister for instance.

Then the Goddess' features shifted, the colour of her skin and eyes and hair changing along with her dress: Celtic warrior maiden— in long flowing robes covered with a leather breast-plate with a bow slung on her back, a sword at her side—morphed into an Amazonian warrior then to a Nubian princess. She changed again, taking on the aspect of an Asian Empress, then her appearance flowed into that of a Viking shield maiden. Her skin began to turn blue and arms sprang out of her back where her weapons had been, her hair as black as night—Morghanna had seen nothing like it before and gasped at her fearsome beauty. Had she thought her no more beautiful than a human woman? She was wrong.

The blue multi-armed form faded into a Grecian Goddess then changed again and again, a dizzying array of faces and nationalities until she stopped on a gentler version of the Celtic warrior maiden form Morghanna had first seen—the bow and sword were gone and the long flowing robes were no longer cinched in place by the breast-plate but by a simple golden rope tied around her hips.

The Goddess nodded slightly and patted at her oceanic skirts. 'I think we might stay with this one, don't you think? It feels more … comfortable … in these surroundings. In this form, you may call me Arianrhod.'

Morghanna nodded dumbly as she stared in wonder at the heavenly being before her.

There was a slight glow emanating from beneath her creamy skin, and her red hair was a little more vibrant than any Morghanna had seen. Swept back by a circlet of green and gold leaves, it fell in an abandon of curls that moved and shifted with a life of their own. Her eyes still weren't normal; colours shifted in them, as if they couldn't decide on what shade they should be, and there was a knowledge so old and ancient in them, it would have made Morghanna shudder and look away if not for their warmth.

The Goddess smiled—it was like being caught in a sunbeam on the darkest of days. Morghanna couldn't help but return the smile, the remainder of her fear and anger floating away.

She took a deep breath of the heavenly scented air, calm settling over her, so blissful it felt as if she were floating.

'Okay, I think that's enough.' The Goddess waved her hand and the breeze disappeared, as did most of the glow from her skin, and Morghanna came back to her body with a thud.

'What was that?'

'You were so relaxed your soul rose towards the astral plain. Another unfortunate side-effect of my powers on the human mind and body. I simply pulled my glory in closer to my manifested body. Do you feel better?'

'I feel glorious.'

'Good.' The Goddess frowned. 'Are you still angry with me?'

Morghanna was about to say 'no' but then remembered what had brought her here. 'Yes.'

'Good.'

She stared in surprise. The heavenly woman waved her hand. 'If you are angry with me, that means you are fully here, in control of yourself, body and mind. That my power is not unduly influencing you. I need it to be so if we're to talk about what you must do. What is to come.'

Morghanna's lips trembled, tears burning her eyes. 'Death, my Goddess. That is what is to come. For when my mate dies, I will die.'

'That is something that will occur, yes, but not in the way you think it will. And certainly not now.'

Her breath caught in her throat and she rasped out, 'What? How?'

The Goddess shook her head and gestured around her. 'I cannot speak of that sitting here. *He* finds ways to listen, even when he's been banished as you and Alistair so successfully did to save that Were.'

'Are you talking about the Dar—'

The Goddess raised her hand and shook her head.

Morghanna frowned, unable to understand why one so powerful would shy away from saying a name out loud. Names were power, but still ... Not that she would question the Goddess on her aversion. Instead, she said, 'If you are talking about banishing that ... Beast ... We did it to save the village. Lachlan could have died for all I cared. I wish he had.'

'Yes, well, you will wish it again in the times to come, but that is as it must be for my plan to run its course.'

She frowned. 'What plan? What are you talking about, my Goddess?'

The Goddess held out her hand. 'Arianrhod, please.'

'Arianrhod,' Morganna said, the saying of the name somehow filling her with a sense of power.

Arianrhod wiggled her fingers. 'Come. We must go through the Dance. There we can talk properly; and I can give you a solution to help your wolf-less mate.'

'You will help save Alistair?' Hope springing to life once more, Morghanna took the proffered hand. A frisson of power skittered up her arm from the point of contact and twined with her magics, making her gasp and stumble as she was pulled to her feet.

Arianrhod simply steadied her and let go, answering her question. 'Of course. It was not me who tore the wolf from your mate. That was my nemesis' doing.'

'What? If not punishment from you, then why?'

'The Curse of the Beast.' She waved her hand as if it were obvious, but when Morghanna did nothing but shake her head, Arianrhod said, 'He created it centuries ago to pay me back, trialling a few versions and waiting to lash out with various iterations in the moment that would hurt me the most. He somehow knew I needed your mate to be part Were. But never mind, we can still fix things so they work.'

Her heart pulsed hard in her chest. 'You can give him back his wolf?'

'No. The Curse of the Beast is not something I can reverse. The wolf is destroyed. There is nothing I can do to change that and make your mate whole in the way he once was.'

Morghanna cried inside for the loss of the wolf that had been hers too. 'But if you cannot give him back his wolf, then how—'

Arianrhod lifted her free hand and light danced inside the ring of stones. 'This is not the place to talk of these things. Come. I will answer your questions when we are inside the Dance.'

Morghanna let herself be pulled into the Dance. As she stepped into the wavering circle of light within the stones, her ears popped. The world spun and wove around her, tumbling her every which way.

'I've got you.'

Hands grasped her shoulders, and she was suddenly still, standing on the grass in the centre of the Dance, light all around her —not the blinding light of earlier, but sunlight, pure and gentle as on a spring day. Beyond the wall of light that surrounded them, the stone monoliths that made up the Dance were but dark shadows sitting just outside the construct of the light, the clearing beyond them darker still.

'Come, sit.' Arianrhod patted the altar.

'What? No.' It was a sacrilege to sit on the altar. Except, the Goddess had taken a seat on it, pulling up her feet to sit cross-legged in the middle, her flowing skirts spilling over the side like a waterfall.

Arianrhod chuckled. 'I give you permission to sit here, Morghanna. In fact, I insist. Although I will ask you to remove your footwear. I do not want mud on my altar and I'm sure you don't want mud on your clothing.'

Morghanna toed off her clogs then edged over to the altar and gingerly climbed onto it, mirroring Arianrhod's position. Once settled, she met the Goddess' gaze. 'So, how can you help save Alistair?'

Arianrhod chuckled again. 'I see you've picked up a few traits from your sister—no mucking around with pleasantries, always straight to the point. It's about time.' She smoothed her skirts over her knees. 'However, before I answer your question, I must tell you a little about what is to come for you and your mate. And then I will give you a choice.'

Morghanna swallowed hard. 'Of course.'

'You and Alistair have always had a hard road ahead of you. Not by my design, but as the Fates decree. However, I have been known to nudge the Fates a little here and there when there is need; and there is need here and now.'

'What need?'

'You and Alistair must survive long enough to have a child. I can make sure that happens. I cannot guarantee what happens after.'

'We will have a child?' She placed her hand over her stomach, looking down at it as her heart beat faster, a strange sensation of longing rising within her. 'Am I ...?'

'No. Not yet. That is why I have come to you now. Why it is necessary for me to intercede, even though it is forbidden. That is why I brought you into the light of my Dance. I can hold time at bay for a short moment here so that we can talk without anyone—heavenly or earthly—becoming aware of what we speak.' Her brow furrowed a little. 'It's draining though, so we need to hurry.'

Morghanna's mind spun sickeningly, but she nodded. 'Okay.'

'As I said, I need you and Alistair to have a child.'

'Why? Why us?'

'Because of whom you are and what that means for the future. Your child will bear other children and those children will have children down the generations, until twins are born of another Were and warlock. These children are essential for the fight ahead.'

29

Morghanna shook her head, not certain she'd heard correctly. 'Fight. What fight?'

The Goddess shifted, her jaw stiffening before she made a little gesture of impatience. 'That I cannot elucidate on. Your mate might be able to tell you—he has been carrying the burden of your visions for you this many a year as you come to terms with your other talents.'

'What visions? I do not have visions.'

'Of course not. As I said, he's had them in your place.'

Morghanna stared into the dark beyond the stones. 'I ... He never told me.'

'I am certain he did not wish to burden you, or even fully understand what he was seeing or why.' Arianrhod waved her hand. 'That matters little now. If he can tell you after this, then I will leave that up to you to pursue. What matters now is the little I can tell you; your line will bring the fight to a head and hopefully, if the fates align, to a most glorious end.'

With those words, it was if the universe opened up in her mind. Images and knowledge of generations to follow and lines of destiny and fate that took them in many and varying directions rushed into her mind, tumbling over one another, calling for attention. The more that came, the more pressure came with them, until there was nothing but a screaming pain that made her feel like her head might explode. 'I ...' She clutched at her head. 'It is too much ... too much,' she gasped.

'I'm sorry.' Cool fingers touched her head, imprinted on her mind.

The sensation eased, most of the images fading away; but not all. What was left was bearable, but still left a pressure clamped around her head, a slight pain that threatened to expand at any moment if she took on even one more image. 'What was that?'

'Knowledge. Of the future. I thought you could bear at least this much but I was wrong.' She sighed, a tight frustrated sound. 'You see. This is why I can only tell you so much, and even then, it might be more than you can stand. I can take a portion of it away, but there is a need for you to be aware of some if you are to follow my instructions. I'm afraid that means there will always be pain.'

Morghanna blinked tear-filled eyes. 'As long as you can save Alistair. As long as we can have children, I will bear anything.'

'Child.' Arianrhod held up a finger. 'One child. Not children. I can promise no more.'

It was a stab to the heart but, 'It will be enough. More than I ever dreamed of before I mated.' Her mating had given her so many gifts she thought never to have. 'I still do not understand why you have chosen me. Surely Bridgette would be a better choice. Or my sister, Morrigan? They are far more powerful and resourceful, their magics so much more useful than mine.'

Arianrhod shook her head. 'Even after all you've done, all you've accomplished, and with the love of your mate shining through you, you still do not see yourself clearly, do you?'

Morghanna clutched her fingers tightly in her lap. 'I see myself clearly enough.'

'No, you don't. Look at yourself through your mate's eyes. Then take a moment to look at yourself through the eyes of your friend, your sister, your coven, your pack.'

Morghanna snorted. 'My sister? She left because I was too weak-willed to truly stand up for myself, for her, for our people. If I had been stronger, Ali might not—'

The Goddess put her fingers over Morghanna's lips. 'What happened with that Were would have occurred even if you *had* pushed the matter with his father and the pack leadership. You are not responsible for the Darkness being inside him. He was the one who invited it in.'

'He invited the Darkness?' she said against the Goddess' fingers.

Arianrhod smiled gently as she lifted her fingers away. 'Yes. Because of the banishment your friend did with my power, it cannot enter a Were without invitation. Unfortunately, there are those who will always seek more power, no matter the cost.'

'I ... that ...'

'Exactly,' Arianrhod said, sighing heavily. 'But let's get back to the point I was making. Your sister left because she has her own path to follow, not because of anything you may or may not have done. And certainly not because of this purported weakness of which you speak.' She cupped Morghanna's cheek. 'You are the light that pulls them together, the calm island in the storm, the one everyone comes to for advice, to talk to and share thoughts and ideas with. You have all that, which in itself is remarkable. But even more extraordinary is the strength you carry within that means you have never let your Spirit-talker powers overwhelm you like so many have before.'

'That is due to my dual powers, not because of any particular strength within me.'

Arianrhod dropped her hand from Morghanna's face as she made a little hissing sound between her teeth. 'You are wrong. You have a special kind of strength. It is what drew your mate to you. Were rarely mate with those who are not of their kind, and certainly never with those who don't have strength and something extraordinary inside. But it is not simply the fact you have mated with a Were that tells me exactly who and what you are. You are not the first Spirit-talker with a dual power, but you are one of the few who managed to access that duality. Your love of family, of friends, of people, your devotion and empathy are so drilled into the core of who you are that you would do anything to keep them safe and happy. You used that determination to access your duality and keep yourself useful and sane. You are extraordinary. Your mate knows it. Bridgette knows it. Your sister knows it. Your coven and pack know it.'

The tight feeling in her chest started to unfurl as the Goddess spoke, the truth in her words winding around her; but a lifetime of self-doubt still had her shaking her head.

Arianrhod cocked her brow. 'You shake your head, but deep inside, you know my words speak truth. Bridgette would never have been able to bring the Pact about if not for your help and support. Alistair would never have been able to pull my power to him to help in your fight against the Darkness if you were not so full of empathy —you created the key to unlock the door inside him, then changed what was needed in your own powers to become the bridge he used to channel the power to and through. And the most astonishing of all is that you did it unknowing, the instincts within you so steady and sure.'

She leaned forward, catching Morghanna's chin, raising her face until she met the Goddess' gaze. 'You are the strongest of them all, more so because you do not know all that you are and yet you still try. You still manage to do what others of your kind cannot. If you do not believe me, then consider your mate. If what I say is untrue, he would never have so quickly accepted his wolf and his life in the pack and would never have lasted this long without his wolf if not for you and your abilities. And you would never have been open enough to accept the mating bond.'

The last bud of self-doubt bloomed into understanding as Arian-rhod's lips curled knowingly. Ali's love was proof—but her love of him even more so. Those with her gift could rarely open themselves up enough to love, their heads too full of the madness of their powers, but she not only loved, she loved enough to move mountains. She loved enough to wield power she never dreamed was hers to use. She loved enough to change the inevitability of death. She was the one who'd been keeping Ali alive by buoying the strength within him. It was a losing battle though—his strength being eroded by his grief, and slowly, inevitably, eroding hers, but she'd kept him alive until now, which was something. A something that had brought her here, to this moment, with her Goddess.

She had never been less than Bridgette or her sister or anyone else she'd ever loved. She was at the very least equal to them, if not, in some ways, more. 'I never thought ... I never saw ...'

'Of course you didn't. That is part of the wonder of you. What makes you one of my favourite children.' Arianrhod's hands fell from Morghanna's face, her eyes filling with devastating sadness. 'It is why I am sorry for what I must ask. Of what I must make sure you do. Sorrier than I am for any other I must use to win this war. Sorrier than you can ever know.'

Tears slipped down Morghanna's face as a sense of horrible sadness replaced the growing wonder of moments before. Why did she suddenly feel so sad, so bereft? The Goddess was about to show her how to save Ali, had promised they would have a child. Had shown her the truth of who she was and what she was capable of being.

She was being given the world—joy should fill her, not a sadness so eternal it felt it might never end.

Arianrhod shook herself suddenly and tapped Morghanna on the knee. 'Enough of that. You may be strong, but your empathy is not enough to encompass all of who I am, what I was and what I must be.'

Morghanna blinked and the bleakness that had threatened to swallow her was gone as fast as it had come. 'I felt you?'

'Yes. Nobody has done that with me for a very long time.' Arianrhod's expression softened. 'And while I appreciate your wish to share my hardship and grief, I cannot let such a burden sit on your shoulders. I already ask too much.'

Morghanna looked away for a moment before turning back to meet the powerful gaze of a being so far beyond her, she had no chance of ever understanding even a thousandth of who Arianrhod was. She took herself in hand and focused on the now. 'What must I do to save Alistair?'

Arianrhod, her smile still a little sad, brought her hands together to clasp in her lap. 'You must make him forget.'

'Forget? Forget what?'

'That he was ever Were. In fact, you must make everyone forget.'

The words echoed in her head, endless, impossible and for a moment, she couldn't talk, could barely breathe. 'What? How?' she finally managed to ask around the chasm opening before her. 'How would that help him?' And how in the heavens and hells was she supposed to do such a thing?

The Goddess waved her hand as if the answer was self-evident, but when Morghanna continued to look at her as if she were crazy, Arianrhod lowered her hand and fixed her gaze on Morghanna's. 'It is not the fact that he has lost his wolf that is killing him. We can all survive without part of our soul if needs must.'

'That is not true. I—'

The Goddess raised her hand again. 'You know nothing. It is as I say. A person can survive with part of their soul gone. They can even survive with their entire soul missing—Lachlan is proof my words are true.'

'Lachlan has no soul?'

'His soul was always a cracked and warped thing, but what he did have was burned away by the Darkness long ago.'

That would explain much of the 'lack' she'd always felt in him. Then her gaze flew up to the Goddess. 'If Alistair is missing part of his soul, will he become like Lachlan?'

Arianrhod placed her hand on Morghanna's knee. 'No. Lachlan is like he is because he is soulless. Perhaps, if he had not succumbed to the Darkness the way he had, what was still there of his damaged and withered human soul, alongside his equally damaged wolf-soul, might have meant he could learn to be a decent Were, if not empathic and caring. But the Darkness ate away his human soul and warped the wolf-soul into the Beast, which means it no longer has a soul either in the way we understand these things. So there is truly no hope of him being anything close to decent; or that he will be anything less than a constant danger if allowed to live.'

'Then what should I do about him?'

'Nothing for now.' She waved her hand as Morghanna went to protest. 'I did not come to talk to you about Lachlan. I came to talk of your mate. His soul was always good and strong. With a soul such as his, even part is enough to maintain empathy, true caring and kindness. Most beings would not even notice that part of their soul was missing. However, when the part of the soul that is gone is its own identity—like that of your mate's wolf—the loss is more. The sundering will not kill them, but the loss ... It is like losing a mate. And we all know what happens to Were when they lose a mate—few ever survive the severing of that bond.' She took Morghanna's hand as she sighed. 'Your mate is grieving, and that grief is killing him. However, take the source of the grief away and he will cease to tumble down the path to death.'

Morghanna stared at the Goddess, silence stretching between them. 'That's ... that's ...'

'A simple truth most people do not consider. Remove the memory of what has been lost and you will remove the grief.'

'But if you remove the memory of what he was, then what will be left?'

'What does that matter if he is living and no longer tortured?'

She stared at the Goddess, horrified. 'Of course it matters.'

'How? If he is alive, what matters what he remembers?'

'But ... If you remove the memory of his wolf, will he remember who he is? Will he remember where he came from? Will he remember his family?' Panic began to rise. 'Will he remember why he loves me? Will we even be mated?'

Arianrhod lifted her shoulders. 'He may remember his journey here, falling in love with you, agreeing to build a life with you here and join your coven and pack. He may not. I cannot say with any certainty as this has never been done to this great an extent before.'

'Oh Gods.'

'In regard to his family, I am afraid those are memories he cannot keep. Nor can they.'

'But ... why not?'

'Because so much of what they remember about him is tied up in him being Were. He protected them with his wolf. Hunted for them. Guarded them while they slept. He even killed their younger sister in front of them when she lost her mind and tried to attack them. And so much of his memory of them is tied up that way too. There would be too much to alter, too many gaps that would bring questions. The only way to leave any of their memories intact is to leave memory of his wolf there.'

'But surely we could leave Frederique and Amandine with their memories of him? What would be the harm in that?'

'Harm? Think of what would happen if they came looking for him with those memories intact and questions on their lips about why he did not know them or remember who he was. Imagine if they brought up his wolf. He would either spiral into madness or repudiate them in a way that would be painful to all of you and certainly destroy any possibility of them having a relationship with him. This way is far more merciful.'

'But ... but Bridgette and Malcolm know all about him, as does everyone here. They've been trying to find a way to help him, talking to every pack and coven they see. And they were to find Frederique and Amandine and offer a new home here if they so wished.'

'But most of them have no memory of Alistair as his wolf, and those that do, it is one memory, maybe two, so fleeting as to be no loss at all. So ridding them of any memory pertaining to Alistair's wolf is comparably easy. Bridgette and her Malcolm will remember nothing of him being a Were, and neither will anyone they have spoken to. Nobody here will remember him as anything other than a warlock who came to seek shelter a few moons back, then fell in love with and married you.'

'But what about the battle that caused this? His sickness?'

'They will remember he fell sick after helping you banish the Darkness from Lachlan, a rare complication of flaming out so spectacularly like he did.' She sighed. 'And as for Alistair and his siblings —they must be as strangers with different parents and different paths.'

'Is there no other way? What is the point if he has no memory of who he is? No memory of why he loves me?' She gasped in a shuddering breath. 'What if he never loves me again?'

'That will not happen. I am certain of it.'

'How? When you said earlier you did not truly know what he might or might not remember of us?'

'If he does not remember who you are, he will still come to love you. Even without my recent encouragement in compelling him to come here, you would have found each other in time. I simply needed it to be sooner rather than later.'

'It *was* you who brought him here.'

'Of course.'

'But why?'

'I do not always know the exact why, nor would I share it with you if I did.' She made an explosion gesture around her head.

'Oh.'

'What I will tell you is that your mating is no simple mating. It is an eternal soul-binding; bound that way by the hands of Fate. In every incarnation, you will find each other. It is an immutable fact, as immutable as the power that made myself and my brethren.'

She had never heard of such a thing—but why would the Goddess lie? And it did bring comfort. Except ... 'How can I choose something that will make Ali forget those he loves? Who will remember the love his parents shared? Who will remember his sister?' She trembled with the enormity of it; of making such a decision for him, for them all. 'He would not want his sister, or his parents, forgotten. He lived his life in the memory of them. How can I wipe them from existence? How can you expect him to agree?'

'It is too late to seek his agreement.'

'He is my mate!' She fisted her hands at her sides, head throbbing, prickly heat rushing over her. 'If he were to find out about this it will tear him apart.'

'How would he find out?'

She gaped at Arianrhod, unable to come up with a reply.

'So, you would choose for him to die rather than lose memory of his wolf?'

'I ...' She lowered her gaze, tears plopping in her lap. 'No.'

'There is no need to feel shame simply because you treasure life above all else.'

'There is. When my want is a selfish one.'

'Is it selfish to want to be with your love and he with you in this life? To bring joy and harmony to another being? Is it selfish to bring a new life into the world, one whose line will be instrumental in the fight against the Darkness?'

30

Morghanna stared at the Goddess for long moments before answering softly, 'No.' She wiped the tears away that had fallen at Arianrhod's words. Those words, they should be like icy daggers but instead, they filled her with an idea. Looking up, she said with steely resolve, 'No. It is not. But there has to be a way his parents and his sister, Sophie, will not be forgotten. Even if only his siblings remember them and not him. I have to make certain they are not wiped from existence.'

The Goddess tipped her head as she looked at Morghanna. 'It is a waste of our time and energies.'

'Please.'

'Hm.' She tapped her finger against her chin as she stared into Morghanna's eyes, then bobbed her head. 'Maybe we could cast the spell so that his remaining brother and sister—'

'Frederique and Amandine.'

'Yes, them. I think it is possible to cant the spell so they remember their parents and their sister. But ...' Her ever-changing eyes filled with firm resolution. 'He will not remember them and they will not remember him. Is that acceptable?'

'Is that acceptable? How can tearing everything he has ever loved from him be in any way close to acceptable?'

'He will not lose everything. He will have you. And his new family here. And you will remember.'

'I will?' It seemed unbearably cruel that she would remember what she'd agreed to have taken from him. Cruel but just.

'I am sorry for it, but yes. You must. There are things that must unfold that will not if you have no memory of what has transpired and what we talked of today.' Arianrhod settled her hands in her lap, her expression firm. 'But we waste time with these worries. A decision must be made and it must be made now. Even if it is not acceptable, do you agree?'

'I ...' Her mind scrambled. She knew she had to agree, could see the urgency in her Goddess' eyes, in the tension around her shoulders, but there were still questions she wanted answers to. Worries she needed to air. 'What of Alistair's gifts? He has not been tested, but I am certain he carries the gift of prescience—'

'As I said earlier, that is not his gift. It is yours. He has been carrying it for you.'

'Even so, he is still carrying it, right? And I am fairly certain he can mind-talk—which means he might be able to read this in my mind. What if he sees things in these visions he has for me, or reads something in my mind that gives away what has happened, what he once was?'

Arianrhod waved her hand. 'Now you are aware of it, and that the strength you always denied having makes you perfectly capable of carrying the burden of visions, the gift of the Sight is truly yours. There is now no need for him to channel those visions into himself.' She tapped Morghanna on the chest. 'You of course will need to train yourself in this gift, to ensure you never give away to him or anyone else what they cannot know of what you see. But your acceptance has made it a certainty that he will never see anything of what has transpired here.'

'I ... but ...' It was so much to take on, but she had to rope her thoughts in and concentrate on getting the answers she needed before making such a huge, shattering decision. 'That might be true—'

'It is.'

She waved her hand. 'Fine. But me being strong enough to take on the Sight does not have any bearing on his ability to mind-talk. He could still read my mind.'

'No. he can't. His ability to mind-talk was tied into the wolf side of him so he could communicate with his Were and non-Were family when in wolf form. Now the wolf is gone, that gift has no purpose to function. But just in case, you should keep your memories of what we do here shielded from everyone around you. You should do that anyway because we do not need your powerful friend Bridgette, or your sister Morrigan, finding out things they should not. I will help.' She touched her finger to Morghanna's brow. There was a tingle and then a snap. 'Done.'

'Ow.' Morghanna blinked at her. 'Did you just create a shield?'

'Once the spell is canted and released, all that pertains to your mate's wolf will move behind that shield. Your innate strength will keep it going in perpetuity. Nothing will be able to get through.' She tipped her head, looking upon Morghanna as a parent does a recalcitrant child. 'So, enough excuses. There is a choice now before you. You choose to save Alistair's life and wipe the memory of his wolf from existence, or you let him keep his memories intact and watch him die.'

'Not much of a choice. I might lose him either way.'

'But one choice gives you hope. To me, hope is everything.'

Morghanna stared at her for a long, tense moment before saying, 'As it is to me.' Even if he didn't remember her, he would be alive. Arianrhod had read her well: she was prepared to give up everything to make certain he lived.

Arianrhod clapped her hands. 'I knew you would make the right choice.' She reached out, palms up. 'Take my hands. Let us bind the spell.'

'Now? But why do you need me to help you do this?'

The heavenly being, her gaze eternally mysterious, said, 'Because you are you and I am not. Because I cannot bind the spell to myself. Because your strength and love and empathy will make it stronger than anything I could ever achieve as I don't understand those things as you do.'

'But I—'

'Enough questions. Come now. The spell must be canted in this frozen moment in time so that nobody knows what we have done.'

'But can you not give me a day to prepare and say goodbye to Alistair as he is now?'

'No. The mating bond might allow him to figure out what we are about and he cannot know. Nobody can know. Also, there is a limit to how many times I can create this bubble in time without my brethren sensing it and coming to see what I'm up to. If we are to do this, it needs to be now.'

Morghanna gulped. She wished she had more time. Wished there was another way. Wished to hold Alistair as he was in her arms one more time, to kiss him and his wolf, his Were side, goodbye. But she couldn't. His wolf was already gone. And this was the choice she had to make to save him. To give him a future. Them a future. She had to follow it through, no matter the pain it might bring in this moment. She had to concentrate on the two brilliant points of light the Goddess had told her in all this bleakness:

That they would have a child. And that their love would last through all time.

'Well then?' Arianrhod held out her hands and waited, brow raised.

Morghanna blinked back a tear as she stared at the outstretched hand before her. It was cruel and unfair but ... 'Alistair must live. I will do what must be done.'

'Good.' Arianrhod smiled. 'If you have not believed it before, believe it when I say to you now; your strength is enough to carry you through what must be done now and in the future. It has always been enough.'

Morghanna swallowed hard, but before she clasped hands with her Goddess, she met her ever-changing eyes. 'Thank you for hearing my need. Thank you for helping me to save my mate—my soulmate. We promised each other forever and you have given us a chance now for that to come true.'

Arianrhod's expression hardened, the alien, unknowable being in her coming to the fore, making Morghanna pull back a little. 'Do not thank me. For even after your days are done, your service to me will not end. Now we are on this path, I cannot relinquish you from this service until the fight to come is done. I do promise you will be with Alistair for what remains of this life, but you will not have your forever with him until your service to me in the future is ended.'

Morghanna trembled, her certainty faltering. 'When will that be?'

'I cannot tell you. My foresight is blocked past a certain point and by the lack of clarity of certain choices and events. But I do promise that I will help you towards your forever with your soulmate, whether in another life or in the hereafter. Even if it takes centuries. Do you understand?'

Morghanna clenched her fingers, her toes, was about to say no, but then thought about the alternative.

She was strong. Arianrhod was right about that. She would not die when her mate did, despite her thoughts on the matter over the last few weeks. There were too many people counting on her—Ali was right in that—and no matter how she grieved and wished she could die too, there was a part of her that would never let her take the easy path. She would suffer and grieve for her mate for as long as she lived—and her life would be long if she let him go now.

She had a knowing that was as certain as the Goddess sitting before her.

No matter what she did, there would be pain. But one choice at least gave her the option of happiness for a time. That was more than many people ever got to ask for. And besides, she knew, if Alistair had a choice, knowing this sacrifice would help in the fight against the Darkness, he would take it.

She knew her love that much at least.

Slowly, she nodded and placed her hands in the Goddess'. 'As long as Ali does not die now, as long as we get time and have a child, as long as there is hope for our forever, I will serve you for as long as necessary. I will play my part.'

Arianrhod's nod was short, sharp, her eyes full of respect and a strange kind of kinship. Suddenly Morghanna didn't feel quite so alone. 'Now, close your eyes and let my words and power flow through you. Let them expand out, growing from you as you did the power Alistair sent to you.'

Light began to glow brighter around the heavenly being, and Morghanna quickly closed her eyes, trying to let go of her doubts, concentrating only on Arianrhod's voice, her words, as they wove around her, the power in them once again terrifyingly apparent.

'Hear me the powers of time and space. I bid you bind the elements between to our use, from now until my fight is won. Bind this spell of forgetting to the one known as Alistair Sinoir. Let it flow out from his essence to touch all and everything he has ever known and loved. The Were will forget he was once Were. His friends, the covens will forget he was once Were. As will all those he has met and those he left behind. His blood family will forget him even while they remember those already passed from their line, but he will not remember them or anything that may make him remember what he has lost in his fight against the Darkness. All will be bound by these words I say, except those who sit here. Forget. Forget. Forget.'

The light brightened, a red and orange aura seen through closed lids. Power skittered over Morghanna's skin, through her fingers and into her veins, lighting up everything inside her, burrowing deep, finding a path to the bonds that tied her to everyone in her life, testing them, twining around them, then shooting down them, lighting them up with the power inside.

A power that was the Goddess. A power that was her.

Arianrhod's voice wound around her, calm and sure, stopping her panic as the power found the soulmate bond and began to caress it, to enter it. 'In the forgetting, your soulmate will feel no pain. He will waken as if nothing bad ever occurred.

You will go to him and you will start your lives anew. Now let's gather the final words of the spell and release it into the universe.'

A prickle ran over Morghanna as Arianrhod first intoned their spell then told her to make it her own:

'It will be as the Fates command
Bind this spell from hand to hand
Everyone but I will forget
From this day, my future set
To solely have knowledge of what has been done
The powers in the heavens bind these words to one
The spell of forgetting is bound to me
So I say it, so mote it be.'

The final words of the spell fell from her lips.

For a moment, all was silent, then the light and power intensified, so bright, it was painful. Even so, she clung to her hope, to her belief, that what her Goddess had promised was real and true, that Alistair and she would find their way back to each other regardless of what she did now. That they would always find their way back to each other.

The power increased, pushed and shoved at her, threatening to tear her skin from her body, make her joints fly apart, but she held on, clinging to her hope, to her love until it expanded in one brilliant moment of pleasure and pain.

Then it was gone and she was falling, falling, so far, so fast, she knew she would die upon impact.

She braced for it, mind crying out for all that would be lost ...

She landed softly on a bed of grass.

The soft sound of water tinkling filled the air around her.

Her breath was a burst in her lungs. She let it out then breathed in the cool air in great gulps.

Where was she?

What was she supposed to do?

Had it worked?

Had she been as strong as the Goddess said?

'*Of course it worked. As I said, you are exactly as strong as you need to be.*'

'Thank you,' she whispered to the voice of Arianrhod ringing in her mind. 'Thank you.'

'*Now, open your eyes and face the future we have wrought.*'

Morghanna opened her eyes.

31

The Goddess was gone. So was the Dance. And the walls of light. And apparently, the night had passed too.

Dappled light danced on the grass around Morghanna.

Not the slightly grey light of early morning or the bright light of midday, but the mellower light of late afternoon.

And the air, it was filled with the fragrance of cut hay overlaid with a salty-sulphurous smell. And there was that tinkling sound.

She was at the hot springs?

How had she got here?

Spirits appeared, whirled around her, brushing against her, their joy a frisson of shivers along her skin before they disappeared—gone to report to Abigail, who had a very, very light touch of Spirit-talker power, where she was, no doubt.

Tattle-tales, all of them. Ah well, she supposed she best pull herself together. Abigail would have to find someone to report the news too and then it would take them at least a quarter hour after that for them to get here at a quick march. So she had time to figure out what had happened after the spell was cast.

Morghanna sat up. The source of the tinkling water—the spill from the upper spring over the rocks that fell into the lower one— hove into view.

Even though she'd known she was at the hot springs from the smell and the sound of the waterfall, the visual proof cut at her heart. Tears sprung to her eyes.

This was where she had met Alistair. This was where her life had inexorably changed.

This was where she'd fallen in love instantly with the male who was her forever.

But without his wolf, would she be *his* forever?

The question sliced through her mind despite Arianrhod's promise. What if the Goddess had been wrong about the kind of bonding she had with Ali? What if she had lied about it just to ensure Morghanna did as she wished. It wouldn't be the first time a God or Goddess lied to one of her kind to get their way.

But no, there was something in Arianrhod's expression that spoke of truth. But what did that truth really mean? It was all very well to talk of soulmates, but would it be as strong as a Were-mating? Would it be the same?

And what if their great working hadn't worked?

What if it had and he was gone from her forever?

The reality of what she'd done was a punch in the gut.

She collapsed back on the grass, clutching her arms around her, rocking, a wail working its way up from her chest. No! Her Goddess had promised that one day they would have their forever. But what if that was something she couldn't promise? What if it was one of the things she truly couldn't see? What if—

'Are you unwell, *mademoiselle*?'

The wail stuck in her throat. She stopped rocking.

'*Mademoiselle*?'

She unwound enough to lift her head.

He stood there looking down at her, too thin, but alive.

He was alive.

There was colour in his skin and a light of interest and concern in his beautiful spring green eyes that were shot with fractured sparks of vibrant blue. His eyes had always reminded her of looking through a canopy of leaves into a summer sky.

Summer sky. A vibrant blue summer sky.

He still had the mark of an Alpha on him? How did that work now he didn't have his wolf?

The thought was shoved behind the shield, becoming muted and hard to concentrate on. She frowned.

'Mademoiselle? Are you unwell?'

Her gaze shot back to him, the sight of him once again taking her breath. Hands trembling, she reached out to him. 'Oh. I am fine. I am more than fine. Oh, Alistair, it is so good to see you.'

His eyes widened in surprise. 'You know who I am?'

His words were like an arrow through her gut.

Her hands dropped into her lap.

Oh Goddess. This was the worst of what she'd imagined. He didn't know who he was, let alone *who* she was.

She squeezed her eyes shut, begging the tears not to fall. Strength —the strength Bridgette and Morrigan and Abigail and Arianrhod and Alistair, dearest Alistair, had believed was in her but she'd been too blind to see until now—rose up and kept her steady.

She opened her eyes and smiled at him, remembering the story Arianrhod had told her of what others would remember of him. The story they had woven in the spell. 'Yes. We have met.'

He took a few steps forward, his expression so confused it was heartbreaking. 'I woke up on the floor in a strange cottage. I did not recognise anything. I could not recall how I came to be there. I cannot even seem to recall who I am. Can you tell me? Who I am? Where I am? Why I am here?'

Somehow she managed to keep the gentle smile on her face as she said softly, 'I can tell you a little.' She did not want the very first thing she said to him to be a lie, especially given a part of everything she said to him after that would be. She swallowed hard. 'Let us go and sit over on that log and I will tell you what you need to know.'

She pushed to her knees and had to catch herself as dizziness rushed over her. He made as if to help her up but she waved away his help. She didn't know if she could bear to take his hand, to touch him, and not see that flare of awareness in his eyes that had occurred the very first time they'd met. His wolf had known her; had known their bond.

Would there be a part of him that would know the soul-bond, that would accept it like his wolf had accepted the mating bond?

The thought fogged and slid behind the shield before it could become a danger.

Was this what it was always to be like? Knowing what she knew but not being able to truly think about it? To reason through it? To come to terms with it? Just a pain as deep and turbulent as the deepest ocean in a storm, one that she could never find a way to Heal?

A sound of distress slipped from her lips.

'You are unwell,' he said, brow furrowed, something beyond concern burning in his gaze.

She looked away, not wanting to build hope that would prove weaker than a house of sticks. 'I sat up too quickly. But I assure you, I am well. You are the one who looks like they are about to fall over. You should sit down before you do.' His walk here had leant colour to his cheeks when she'd first seen him, but now he had caught his breath, the colour had faded and he once again looked as pale as he had when she'd left him in their bed last night.

He glanced at the log she had gestured to but didn't move. Then when he did, it was to take an unsteady step towards her, hand stretched as if to touch her, as if couldn't help himself; as if he were drawn to her, like there was nothing more important than to get closer to her.

But no. That was just wishful thinking on her part. Wishing and hoping. She needed to stop such useless emotions before he started to think there truly was something wrong with her.

He was different—she could sense it already—but he was possibly as perceptive as he ever was. Besides which, his warlock powers were intact and she needed to be careful, regardless of Arianrhod's assurances about his mind-speech and the prescient gifts that were apparently hers.

'Please, take a seat, Alistair, before you fall down. I promise, I am fine.' She pushed herself up, brushing grass from her skirts as she stood.

ALISTAIR. Was that his name? Yes, he thought maybe it was. There was something about it that felt like when he'd dragged this shirt on this morning, like it was his. Like it was home.

Just like he felt when he had laid eyes on her after climbing all this way.

He felt he knew her even though he could not remember ever having met her before.

His vision swayed a bit and he staggered a little.

'Alistair!' she said, taking an unsteady step forward as if she too were a little dizzy.

'I am fine,' he said, righting himself before he fell. 'But I think you are right. I think I will take a seat.'

He backed slowly to the log, unable to take his eyes from her, even as he plopped onto the wood that had been shaped by many arses into a fairly comfortable seat.

He wondered if she'd join him. He hoped she would but didn't want to ask her in case it scared her away. There was something hesitant and careful in her manner towards him.

Whatever it was, it was obvious she wasn't in any rush to join him. She seemed to have gotten over her dizziness and was once again making busy with brushing and straightening her clothes. And while she seemed capable of taking her gaze from him to mind what she was doing, he did note that she kept looking back up at him, an expression there that seemed like relief to see him still there.

Almost as if she were worried he would disappear.

Strange.

But not as strange as the sense that was growing stronger with every second that passed; the one that he knew her. It wasn't simple familiarity, as if he'd seen her somewhere before. It was something more than just casual acquaintance too.

He *knew* her. Like she was important to him in some way he still couldn't fathom.

It was confusing, but even so, he was certain of it.

Just as he was certain that she was the reason that he'd been driven to come here. When he'd woken, he was so confused, everything muddy and unclear—except for one thought. The thought that had brought him here.

Find her.

Find her.

He had followed that urging, that need, that ... instinct ... despite the weakness that so quickly overwhelmed him, making it so he stumbled rather than walked the winding path through the woods and up the hill. He would have fallen many times except for the need to keep going, to get here and ... find her. See her.

Then he had staggered out onto this landing where water rushed and tinkled and the smell of sulphur mixed with the brighter scents rising from the forest and fields below. He'd thought to go to the spring, to fall in and let the warm waters work on his tired and exhausted muscles.

But his gaze had landed on her.

And somehow in that moment, everything that was a jangled confusion of conflicting thoughts and emotions raging through him had settled and most of his exhaustion fled. And the only scent he could smell was one that, he realised now, he'd been smelling all the way here. She had been the source of that delicious, heavenly scent, somehow a mix of sunshine and lavender in the rain. It had filled him instantly, like a balm, making him want to breathe in nothing but her for the rest of his life.

It was crazy, wasn't it? To feel like this? To think these things?

And yet, nothing had ever felt more right than what he'd felt upon seeing her.

He watched her closely, the way she twitched her skirt, the way she wrinkled her nose, the little flick of her long black hair back over her shoulder, the warmth that flashed in her beautiful violet eyes as she glanced up at him, cheeks heating every time their gazes tangled.

He wanted to go to her, to hold her face in his hands, to feel the soft warmth of her leaning against him, to breathe in the scent of her. Except, despite the energy that had surged through him on seeing her and the balm her scent was to his mind and senses, he truly was weak. His muscles were soup and he was afraid if he tried to stand right now after he'd exerted himself to get here, that he would fall over.

He wished she would come to him though, because he wanted to run his hand through that mass of black hair and feel the warmth of the fire that hinted within its strands. He wanted to run his fingers over the outline of her lips, feel the bow of the top one with the pad of his finger. He wanted to lean in and pull her pouty bottom lip into his mouth and suckle a little before encouraging her to open to him, sweeping inside to taste the womanly sweetness of her.

Strange, familiar, intimate thoughts to have about someone he could not remember, but they seemed natural.

Of course, he would not know if they were natural or not while she stood over there and he sat here.

She finished straightening the faded blue blouse and its matching skirt and finally—finally—looked up at him, the slight wariness gone from her expression for a fleeting moment.

Oh, by the Gods, those eyes. And her face. The expression as she watched him. It was all so familiar. Everything about her was so familiar. No. Familiar was the wrong word. Dear. She was dear to him.

Acceptance of that settled on him like a warm blanket. He held his hand out.

She swallowed hard and trembled—was she frightened of him? By the Gods, what had he done?—but then she straightened her back and walked to him, bare feet brushing through the grass.

Why were her feet bare? It was a wonder they'd not been hurt on the walk up to these springs.

She took a seat at the opposite end of the log, keeping a careful distance between them.

The urge to move closer pushed at him, but he ignored it. He didn't want to spook her. 'Who are you? What is your name?'

'My name is Morghanna,' she said, smiling softly.

'Morghanna.' He frowned a little, a word whispering in his mind. A name. 'Anna.'

'Yes.' She nodded, swallowed hard before licking her lips.

'You know me?'

'Yes.'

'And I know you?'

She swallowed again, as if the words were somehow hard to say. 'You arrived two moons hence. You told us your name is Alistair Sinoir.'

She spoke French and for some reason that didn't seem strange, even though he knew he was not in France. 'Alistair Sinoir.'

'Is the name familiar?'

He tipped his head to the side. 'Strangely, yes, although I cannot remember ever hearing them before.' He fisted his hands on his knees. 'What else?'

'You are a warlock and have been travelling for some time, coven-less, looking for somewhere to settle down and call your home. I am our coven's leader and head Pack Witch, and I thought you might be a good fit with us. You agreed, so the Alpha of Pack MacCrae bound you to the pack. Then together, we bound you to the Pact.'

Her words seemed strangely right—despite not remembering who he was, he knew he was a warlock, knew he was able to command magical powers, knew of covens and Were packs, although he was certain he'd never belonged to either before. The only thing that seemed unfamiliar was ... 'The Pact?'

She smiled briefly as she outlined the extraordinary magical undertaking she and her friend, Bridgette Colliere, had executed to ensure the safety of the powered and the Were in one stroke of genius.

'Your gifts must be great to accomplish such a feat.'

She blushed and smiled softly. 'Yes. Although, I think perhaps you are more actively powerful. But from what you told us, you never received formal training, and so it was difficult to ascertain just how much power you hold. Unfortunately, before we got to the testing, you fell deathly ill.'

'I did?'

'Yes. You helped me to fight a terrible enemy by combining our magics and thanks to you, we defeated him. But you gave too much. A fever took hold of you. We were afraid ...' Her voice choked and her fingers clenched white in her lap. He wanted to grasp them in his, pull her close and wrap his arms around her, to comfort her, but stopped himself—despite the strength he could sense at the heart of her, something about her seemed so fragile. He was afraid one touch would break her apart.

So he clenched his hands on the log either side of him and waited for her to find her voice.

She cleared her throat. 'I was so afraid we would lose you. But thankfully, I have dual skills of Spirit-talker and Healer, and I was able to call on a spirit who had the knowledge to save you. I was also helped by other Healers in our coven.' Her eyes filled with a sad kind of happiness that tore at him, made his breath catch. 'And here you are. Up and about. At last.' She took another shuddering breath, looking down at her hands where they knotted her skirt.

'Thank you, Morghanna,' he said, but his voice caught in his throat, so he tried again. 'Thank you, Anna.'

Her gaze snapped up to his, longing so clear in her eyes that he felt it in his core.

'Ali.'

Ah. The word echoed inside him, filling him. Right. So right.

He moved across the log—keep his distance be damned—and took her hands in his, stilling them as they twisted and knotted in her skirts. Her hand in his, it felt right. It felt like his world, his universe, his everything. Something settled inside him. 'Anna.'

'Yes?' She seemed to sway towards him. He pulled her closer, one arm slipping around her shoulders, the other hand pushing into her hair, his thumb sweeping over her cheek. She closed her eyes, but not before he saw the ache of longing grow in them.

'What were we to each other before I fell ill?'

Her eyes snapped open again, looking into his deeply, so deeply he wondered he didn't feel her in his soul. Although, come to think of it, he thought he did. He could feel something there, something he had never felt before—he didn't know how he knew. He still couldn't remember much of what came before he'd opened eyes this day and headed out to search for her, but he did know. They were linked. He was certain of it. And not just because she'd saved his life and invited him to join her coven and been instrumental in linking him to their pack and the Pact.

He knew her. Better, it seemed, than he knew himself. There was an eternity of comfort in that fact.

And longing.

And need.

He looked deeply into her eyes, his thumb tracing the outline of her lips. 'Why am I here?'

'To find somewhere to belong,' she whispered, her voice raw, erotic.

'To find the person I belong with.'

Something flared in her eyes. 'Yes.'

'You.'

Her lip quivered. 'Do you remember me?'

'No.'

'Oh.' The flare of light—hope?—died.

'But I *know* you. It is as if I have always known you. It is what drove me here today—to find you. I woke up and all I knew was I needed to find you.' That spark was back in her eyes, her body shaking, lips wobbling into a smile as bright as day. 'I think ... no, I am certain that I travelled from my homeland to yours to find you. I have always been meant to find you.'

'Yes.'

She leaned up as he leaned down.

Their kiss was an explosion of light and joy, of longing and passion, of love and coming home, the like of which he'd never known before and never wished to forget again.

'Ali. My Ali,' she gasped between deep, drugging kisses, the desperation, the terror, a shadow in her tone.

'I am sorry. I am sorry I almost left you,' he said against her lips, before sinking in to her taste again. She met him, kiss for kiss, touch for touch, giving him everything he needed, as he gave in return.

When they both pulled away, panting hard, staring at each other, she smiled at him—a big goofy smile—and he was damned certain his smile was the same. 'I am sorry I do not remember what we started.'

She winced and shook her head. 'No, Ali. Do not blame yourself. You could never—'

He kissed the words from her lips before pulling back again. 'No. Let me apologise. My forgetting hurts you and I hate that it causes you pain. But I never truly forgot you. I knew I needed to find you and that when I did, everything would be well. I promise I will never forget you again. And I promise, I will never be responsible for hurting you like that again either. I will never leave you. Never.'

Her hands—the warmth of her palms on his cheeks—tensed. Her breath puffed over his skin, the scent intoxicating. 'You cannot promise that. I cannot promise that.'

'I know. I know. But I want it to be promised. It needs to be promised. Our bodies may part but our souls are bound. Together. Forever.'

Her breath hitched and he thought her mouth moved over the words 'soul bound', but then she said, 'I want that more than anything.'

'Then it will be ours. Always forever.'

'Yes. Always forever.' She kissed him again. 'I love you, my Ali.'

'I love you, my Anna. My treasure.'

They began to tear at each other's clothing and were soon on the grass, naked under the sky, hands and lips worshipping, their bodies connected. There was blissful familiarity in this too and he sought for a memory to explain why, but then she moved against him and all thought flew from his head.

Pleasure rose, up and up until finally, it exploded around and within them.

Something snapped tight inside Alistair and he cried out at the pleasure-pain-rightness of it. Her cry joined his and he was certain she had felt the same.

But then he was carried away on the bliss of the twining and with it, all thought.

It was a long time before he was able to gather his thoughts back to him and form words, before he was able to move enough to brush his Anna's hair from her face, stare into the heavenly glow in her eyes and ask, 'What was that? What just happened?'

She smiled, a soft, seductive smile. 'The Were would say we are mated.'

'But we are not Were.'

'No.' He could have sworn her smile flickered, sadness shattering the joy in her eyes for a fleeting second, but she kissed his chest before he could be certain.

'Then what happened?' He cupped her face, lifting her gaze to his.

She looked up at him. 'The Pact changed many things. It seems that we too can have mates. A one true love who is bound to our soul.'

'One true love,' he said slowly. 'I like that.' He pulled her to him and kissed her softly. 'And what does this soul-bond mean?' he asked, using the word he thought she'd whispered earlier.

'It means you are truly mine as I am truly yours and the heavens help anyone who gets in between us.'

He laughed, loving the ferocious growling sound in her voice. 'I love that you are mine. I love that we are soul bound.'

'I love it too. It is everything.'

'Yes.'

They made love again on the banks of the spring, then again as they swam in the warm waters under the rising moon. She seemed as unwilling as him to leave this place, and they slept wound together under the vastness of the stars, waking numerous times before morning light lit the sky to share their bodies, their love, over and over.

It was hunger that finally drove them to wander back down to the village in the early hours of the morning. He had not expected for anyone to be around and was surprised to find what looked to be the entire village up and waiting for their return.

'They knew through the Packbond,' his Anna whispered to them before they were swamped by well-wishers.

Cries of wonder and joy lit the air as they exclaimed over his sudden recovery. Many hugged him, others slapped his back, the need of the Were and coven to touch him a need he shared.

Then they were being pulled towards the centre of the village where a breakfast feast had been prepared to celebrate the return to health of their newest coven member and pack warlock; he who had helped them face and banish a terrible evil, had survived a brush with death and had come home to them all.

The breakfast feast turned into a day-long celebration that stretched into the deep of the night.

THE JOY of the Were and the coven, and of two of their members in particular, reached out to touch a certain Goddess in the heavens.

She smiled sadly and whispered, 'It has truly begun.'

32

Deep in the woods, in a hut guarded by ten of the strongest Were, Lachlan was pulled from the violent dreams that spoke of things that were no longer his and opened his eyes.

'Wha' is tha' noise?' he asked the Were leaning against the wall nearest his bed.

'Lachlan? Ye are awake?' The Were—Callum, Dougal's second—started upright.

'Obviously,' he said, gesturing to himself as he sat up. He felt curiously weak, but given they'd torn his Darkness from him, that was no surprise. His mind was strangely fuzzy around the circumstances of that, but he was certain the Darkness was gone. Not that it mattered. He didn't need the Darkness to help him get what he wanted. He was perfectly able to do that himself. He was the Alpha's son, after all; the next Alpha by rights. 'Ye dinna answer my question. Wha' is tha' noise?'

'Mayhap I should fetch Dougal and yer father.'

He grabbed Callum's wrist as the senior lieutenant went to move away. 'Tell me. Now.'

Callum removed his wrist from Lachlan's grip—too easily. Damn it, how come he was still so weak?—and with a sneer on his lips, said, 'No' that it is any of yer business as ye will ne'er be allowed anywhere near them e'er agin, but Alistair has woken. He and Morghanna art soul bound. It's like mating fer witches and warlocks.'

'Ye bassa. Ye lie,' he growled as fury exploded inside him. 'She's mine. She's mine.'

Callum huffed out a laugh. 'Yer aff yer heid, ye insane scrote. All ye have to do is open yerself to the Packbond to ken it's true.'

Lachlan grasped for that link inside his mind—so weak, too weak. What had the Darkness done? But even though it was weak, he could saw the truth in Callum's cruel words.

Morghanna—his Morrie—was soul bound to that bloody insolent warlock.

He lifted his head and howled his rage to the night, the light of change gathering around him. He sprang from the bed, knocking Callum against the wall, hard. The cabin shook.

Were burst in through the door and charged him, tackling him, taking him down before he could pull enough power to force the change. They subdued him, pinning him to the bed.

He howled and raged but couldn't free himself.

Minutes later, Dougal arrived with a witch—that little scarred whelp the first lieutenant showed a ridiculous amount of interest in, Leanna—close on his tail. The bitch began to cant a spell he knew was used to send patients to sleep.

Fighting the Were holding him down, he managed to free a hand enough to hit the mug that sat on the table beside the bed towards her, breaking her concentration as she stumbled out of the way of the missile.

Dougal growled, capturing his hand, pinning it to the bed and adding his might to those holding Lachlan down. 'Leanna. Now.'

She lifted her hands, but before she could start the spell again, he shouted, 'I vow this night to seek my revenge. On Morghanna and her Alistair. On every Pack member who brought me this low. May the dark Gods ken, my Were-vow never be forsworn, I will have my revenge.'

Outside, a roll of thunder rumbled across the sky, finishing with one knocking clap above the hut.

A flash of lightning and a crash of thunder quickly followed. Then another flash lit the sky, the white flare hitting the hut, sending wood and thatch and Were and witch flying.

As Lachlan was sent hurtling through the air, he wondered if this be the night he met his maker.

But at least one dark God smiled on him. One dark God had accepted his vow, for he landed on a patch of softened turf as the hut went up in flames behind him. He got to his feet, unharmed as the cries of Were filled the air as they ran to protect Dougal and their pack witch like good little puppies.

Strangely rejuvenated, he glanced one last time at the flaming cottage he'd been kept prisoner in for weeks then ran off into the night.

He did not know where he was going. He did not know what he must do next to outwit them and survive. He did not even know how he was going to manage to do what he had sworn. But none of it mattered.

He smiled as he ran.

One dark God had accepted his vow.

It was enough.

I HOPE you enjoyed Morghanna and Alistair's story as much as I enjoyed writing it. If you did, I hope you will continue to follow them and their friends in *Alpha Bound*, Dougal and Leanna's story, the next novel in the **Dawn of the Curse: A Pack Bound Prequel Series**.

You can read the first few chapters of *Alpha Bound* right here. Just turn the page ...

ALPHA BOUND

DAWN OF THE CURSE: BOOK 2

1

'I willna change my mind,' Iain said to Dougal and the other lieutenants ranged in front of him on the other side of the long table. 'I dinna understand why ye bring this argument to me again today. I gave my answer yesterday, and I meant it.'

Dougal managed not to clench his jaw—or punch the table in front of him—even though his anger was a raw, wild thing inside him. Somehow he managed to say evenly, 'My Alpha, I beg that ye listen to what Cal has said.' He gestured to his second in command and oldest friend, who stood beside him, tension in every inch of his tall frame. 'The pack is unhappy about this ruling. They dinna think it is sufficient after the death, destruction and injury that Lachlan caused. If ye canna sentence him to immediate death by hanging, then his Packbond should be broken and he should be banished. It is the fitting punishment fer what was done.'

Iain's jaw squared dangerously and he thumped his hand down on the table in front of him. 'My son's punishment has been handed down. He will be put into the dreamless sleep by one of our Healer witches.'

'Neither Morghanna nor Abigail have the time or energy to do such a thing right now,' Cal said, standing firmly beside Dougal even while some of the others—including Cal's brother, Bram—took a step back.

'Then the other one ye have been sniffing around can do it,' Iain said briskly, blue eyes pinned on Dougal as he waved his hand in the direction of the Healer Hall. 'Although why ye show interest in such a mousy, scarred thing, Dougal, I dinna ken. A Were like ye needs to mate with another strong Were.'

Inside him, his wolf saw red—and he didn't blame him. How dare anyone, even their so-called Alpha, talk about their future mate in such a way. He wanted so badly to let his wolf have its way, to burst out of him and take the selfish, narcissistic Alpha by the throat, but that would create more chaos and right now, he was unlikely to win. Even with others by his side like Cal. Their Alpha was still too strong —something he was to blame for more than any other.

So, instead of attacking to avenge the slur on his future mate as every muscle and fibre inside him longed to do, Dougal viciously shoved his rage down, telling his wolf everything he had been telling himself this last month to try to make it remain calm. He clenched his hands at his sides, desperately trying to stop his claws from clicking out—at this point, even something so small would shout a challenge to the increasingly paranoid Iain. The pack desperately needed stability. He couldn't be the thing that tore it apart. Not during this difficult time.

Cal shifted, briefly bumping his shoulder, the touch offering his support physically as he sent it down the part of the Packbond that connected them to each other. At the same time he said, with a calm Dougal was striving to feel, 'I am certain ye are aware, my Alpha, that one doesna choose who the Fates deem ye are mated to.'

'Hmph.' Iain folded his arms across his chest before saying with a smirk, 'Shame. But I suppose it canna be helped if she is who ye want, Dougal. At least she is a strong witch despite her mousiness and the ugly burn scars on her face.'

Dougal just managed to tamp down his wolf again before it could burst out and take what was theirs. He didn't manage to cut off its growl, though he did manage to squelch it. Iain's brow rose—he'd heard it—and leaned forward, as if preparing for the challenge he was obviously trying to provoke.

Swallowing down hard on his fury, Dougal pushed his wolf back with as much force as he could, pleading with him just to hold it in. *'Fer the pack. And fer Leanna,'* he said inside his mind to his wolf. *'She doesna need the stress of our injury or death, especially now. We have to hold back on our challenge fer her.'*

His wolf subsided, but remained on high alert. As did he. It was hard not to be when the Were in front of him kept insulting his mate. She was so much more than those scars on her face. The thought helped him to keep it together and say in her defence, 'Leanna is stronger than she appears. Morghanna says she is the strongest Healer we have aside from Abigail, and soon will surpass her with a little more training.'

Iain's shit-eating grin widened as he waved his hand. 'Which is why I said she can take care of carrying out the sentence on my son.'

Dougal gritted his teeth aware now that Iain was definitely trying to bait him. How had he ever given all his loyalty to this Were? He was so uncaring of his people and what his decrees did to them. Despite the fact that Iain, being the Alpha, should already know it, Dougal pointed out, 'It will hurt her to do such a thing. Ye canna ask it of her.'

'I will do more than ask. I demand it.' Iain smacked his hand on the table once more, his eyes darting around, taking in who else was in the dining hall that was standing in as their temporary Alpha Hall after it was destroyed by Lachlan when he tried to take over the pack and falsely claim Morghanna as his. As his eyes landed on the dozen or so kitchen workers setting up for the midday repast, he straightened his shoulders and roared, 'All of ye, get out!'

The workers immediately dropped what they were doing and scurried out of the hall like a cur with its tail between its legs. Hating to see his packmates so cowed, Dougal said, 'My Alpha, they were only doing their jobs.'

Iain's gaze snapped back to Dougal, and he said with the full hardness of his Alpha voice, 'I remind ye, I am still Alpha of this pack. Unless ye or anyone else here has something to say about that?'

Those around Dougal lowered their gazes and Dougal had to force himself to do the same so their angry Alpha wouldn't take eye contact as a challenge. He needed time and a plan on how to cut off the flow of power between him, the lieutenants and senior soldiers, and the Alpha—especially important given too many of them were still blindly loyal. Until they'd stopped feeding Iain their power without giving their intent away, Iain would be strong enough to fatally wound him in a challenge even if Dougal could manage to take him down.

There was a tense silence as everyone waited to see which way Iain would go.

'Good,' Iain said finally. 'That is settled then. As is my decree. The scarred Healer will take care of putting my son into the deep sleep until the Healers find some way to fix him. Once asleep, he will be kept where I can visit him regularly. Those are the last words I will say on this matter.'

'Aye, my Alpha,' Dougal intoned along with the others, their words ringing in the empty hall. Hopefully it wouldn't be long until the pack's Alpha Hall was rebuilt, because having these meetings in such an open space where there was no true privacy was making it impossible to reason with Iain. He'd always been stubborn but now ...

He shoved that thought aside as it only made the anger inside him rise again. Something neither he nor his wolf needed more of right now. They needed clear-headed thinking. The timing for a challenge had to be right. Especially given too many of their people were still scared and hurting from the aftermath of Lachlan's attack. And unlike his Alpha, he wasn't going to be accused of putting anything before what he owed to his pack—except for his mate of course.

Mates were the only exception to the 'pack first' rule.

Not that Leanna was his mate yet. But she would be. Soon if he had his way. He'd been slowly bringing her around—a necessity given her past—and he wasn't about to hurry her along now. It must be her choice. Despite his and his wolf's need to hold her in their arms and claim her as theirs, they were both firm on this one point.

Leanna needed to choose them.

So he'd given her time and space and had gently courted, allowing her to get to know them. To trust them. He thought she was almost there. He just needed to—

'Well? What are ye waiting fer! I have given my final word. Go see it done!'

'Aye, my Alpha,' Dougal said, his bow deep and as subservient as he could make it. Then he backed up, Cal at his side, the others already making their way out of the door.

He couldn't believe he had let his mind wander like that while standing in front of his Alpha and the other lieutenants and senior soldiers. The degree of his distraction due to the unresolved nature of his mating was another reason why the time was not right to challenge for Alpha.

As he closed the door behind him, he straightened and let the life of the Pack Village surround him. He and his wolf needed the calm familiarity it always brought to stop him from turning around and going right back in that room.

The sound of construction filled the air, as did the sounds of pack and coven going about their work. The scent of freshly baked bread wafted out of the kitchens beside the hall, as did the smell of blood and viscera from the deer the Hunters had brought in this morning. The cooks planned to turn some into Iain's favourite venison stew and the rest would be salted and dried for use through the colder months when prey was scarce.

Hopefully the stew would be ready soon as he knew Leanna liked it and it would tempt her to leave her work to fill her stomach— something that was becoming increasingly difficult to do in the month since the attack. She lost herself too often in reading through the ancient grimoires and diaries Bridgette Cantrae and her mate, Malcolm, were sending back from their travels through Europa to continue to unite packs and covens. New packages arrived by magical means every week it seemed and Leanna was fascinated with them—

she said they were showing her how much had been lost through the centuries.

Cal cleared his throat, bringing Dougal's attention back to the present. He glanced at his friend who stood at the bottom of the stairs and saw that Cal was looking at him as if waiting for a response. 'I am sorry. I was lost in thought. What did ye say?' he asked as he jogged down the stairs.

'I can see ye are worried. So I was asking do ye wish me to go and tell Leanna?'

Dougal sighed heavily as he shook his head. 'Thank ye fer the offer but nae. It must come from me.'

'Ye are a good Were,' Cal said, slapping his shoulder as they began to walk towards the Healer Hall.

'I try to be,' he said softly. 'I dinna think I am doing much of a job of it right now though.'

'Hogshite. Ye are the only reason our pack is still as strong as it is.' Cal looked around as if checking to see who might be near, then leaned in and said quietly, 'Ye should be our Alpha now.'

'Cal,' Dougal said warningly.

'What? It was always meant to be ye when Iain was ready to stand down.'

'He doesna want to stand down yet though, does he?'

'Nae. More's the pity. He has let us down too often. And used us fer too long to strengthen himself. Now with this latest decree about Lachlan's punishment ... The pack are nae happy.'

'Whist,' Dougal whispered, leaning in close to Cal and speaking in an undertone no other Were should be able to hear, especially given there didn't seem to be anyone around. 'We canna talk like that —not yet.'

'But when?'

'As ye said, it would hurt the pack right now and I canna be responsible fer that.'

'Iain is hurting the pack with his selfishness.'

'Aye. But we need to be certain all the lieutenants and senior soldiers would back my challenge or we risk causing a schism we would struggle to rise from. I canna do that to the pack.'

'Most of the pack are ready fer ye to be leader.'

'That is an overstatement, Cal. There are still too many who dinna see him like we now see him.' He looked away, towards the mountain peaks across the loch. 'I am ashamed. I was so blindly loyal fer so long that I didna do aught even though deep down the wrongness of what he was doing was a bitter whisper inside me. That I let him weaken me to the point where I couldna stand against him with any certainty of winning ...' He sighed and shook his head heavily. 'I truly thought I was doing the right thing in following his lead, his instruction, so blindly. I am ashamed it took Lachlan trying to rape Morghanna to ken just how wrong Iain was in how he handled his son. And just how blindly loyal we all have been to go along with it.'

He looked back at Cal, the shame and anger—with himself as much as with Iain—swirling like nausea inside him. 'It is a struggle to do aught about it now, but it would be even more wrong to make a move when the pack needs stability. Even the stability of a leadership that does not place them first, as it should, is better than the trauma an Alpha challenge would bring right now.' He patted Cal on the shoulder. 'I am sorry to have to ask for ye to swallow yer anger and pride too, and continue to follow Iain's leadership, but if we care fer the pack, we canna do aught else. Do ye ken?'

'Aye. It goes against the grain, but I ken the need to wait. Especially with this latest decree causing so much difficulty fer ye with yer mate.'

'I thank ye, *mo bràthair*, fer yer concern. But I am not worried fer myself. I am more worried about her reaction when I ask this of Lele.'

'Will she refuse?'

'Nae. It isna in her to refuse to do something to help, even if it hurts her to do it.'

'How do ye cope with that? I would want to take my mate away from everything that caused her pain and never let her out of my embrace.'

Dougal chuckled wryly. 'It is a struggle for both sides of my nature not to do exactly that. But Le-le has been smothered and treated like she isna capable her entire life by people who should have known better. Morghanna told me some things ...' He shook his head, the words sticking in his throat because not only were they private things Le-le did not want to share with many people, but it was hard to think about how she was treated by her mama and other members of her family and former coven before coming here. He swallowed hard and looked down at the ground as Cal stood silent by his side, waiting for him to continue.

'She has been through so much. She simply needs trust and love and support from me and no more.'

2

Dougal took a deep breath in and looked towards the Healer Hall where he could feel his future mate even now. Given they weren't mated, he should not feel so strongly and with such certainty where she was. Nor should he feel her emotions with such clarity as she went about the work of Healing that she loved. But it had been like this from the first moment he'd seen her when a small piece of the bond had snapped into place even though that shouldn't have been possible.

He shouldn't have been so surprised though given the strength of the pull that had drawn him towards the edge of the village that day when the caravan of travelling witches had arrived to be bonded by the Pact to Pack MacCrae. Leanna had been there among them, hiding in the back, and he'd instantly known it was she whom he had been drawn to see. He hadn't been able to take his eyes from her as Morghanna had taken her under her wing and ushered her away to the temporary bunkhouse that had been set up for the new arrivals.

He'd followed at a distance, not wishing to spook this witch who was going to be his mate. Even without that little thread of bond that improbably attached them upon the moment of seeing her, he could sense he needed to be careful with how he approached her.

Thankfully Morghanna, having seen him waiting outside the bunkhouse, had asked him to be her *Sgàth*, her Shadow, and oversee her safety. She hadn't said it then, but he knew now she meant to keep Lachlan far away from the shy and damaged witch. And as he'd gotten to know the gentle strength that was his mate, he understood exactly why the Fates had matched them as they had.

She was the other half of him, the part that reminded him why he should care for others, not just that it was his duty because he was Alpha born. Knowing her, working alongside her, had made him a much better Were and first lieutenant and had made him ready to see just how wrong he'd been in blindly following his Alpha, despite the fact he'd been brought up to believe that was his duty.

He understood now that the strength in other packs, like the McVale Pack, wasn't in the strength of their Alpha and his lieutenants, but in the way they worked together, in the way they didn't follow blindly, but questioned and pushed their leader to be better, to do better.

That's what he wanted for their pack.

And what they wouldn't have under Iain's leadership. Especially with him continuing to put his son first.

He sighed as his thoughts came back around to the main issue that plagued him. And the conversation ahead of him. He turned to Cal and said, 'Thank ye fer yer considerate offer, but I need to tell Lele about Iain's decree and help her prepare for what she must do. But we will talk more about the issues plaguing our pack after Lachlan is taken care of and everyone has settled down to routine once more. I warn ye though, I willna make a move until the pack is more settled and ready fer such a change.'

Cal nodded. 'Aye. I agree. But do ye wish me to begin wording up some of the pack that see things as we do?'

'Nae. Not yet. We need to be more certain who is seeing the truth of the situation, especially among the lieutenants and senior soldiers.' He scrubbed his fingers against the roughness of whiskers that shadowed his chin and cheeks. 'Let us get through dealing with

Lachlan first. Then we will be more certain about who is with us and can talk about what needs to be done.'

'And hopefully by then ye will have the strength of a mating to a powerful witch behind ye.'

Dougal couldn't help the smile that quirked his mouth. 'Hopefully. But that is up to Le-le. Which, after asking her to do this today, I am uncertain she will be ready fer any time soon.'

Cal patted his shoulder and smiled knowingly. 'By the scent that surrounds her—yer scent—I ken that time is sooner than ye think.'

He didn't say anything to that because the hope for it was too tight in his chest. Instead, he nodded and said, 'Get on with yer assigned tasks then. I will get to mine.'

'Aye. I will go straight to the cabin and see Lachlan is properly secured. I will await yer's and Leanna's arrival.'

'Very good.'

He turned and continued on to the Healer Hall where he knew Le-le would be pouring over the old diaries or creating Healing potions and tisanes—one of her favourite things to do.

As he entered the hall, he couldn't help but think about how he was going to tell her what had been decided. He really didn't want her anywhere near Lachlan, but he couldn't protect her from this. She was the strongest Healer they had aside from Abigail and it was her duty to do this.

But truthfully, no Healer should be asked to do this. Even to stop such an evil from hurting the pack and coven again. The sentence for such an evil should be banishment if not death—a sentence Iain would have brought down without hesitation on anyone else had they done what Lachlan had.

Dougal sighed angrily and shook his hands out. He couldn't face Leanna with such anger and disappointment in his heart. Because she was too empathetic and would be unable to cope with such extreme emotion. Especially now when he was here to take her to do something he knew she would not want to do.

But there was nobody else who could do it. Even if Morghanna was as good at sleep spells as Leanna, she was too busy with her duties as head of their coven, not to mention helping her husband with his memory loss and retraining him in his powers—powers he'd used to save them all. And Abigail couldn't do it—the old witch's health had already been fading before Lachlan had tried to destroy the pack and coven, but since then, having given her all to Morghanna and Alistair in the fight, she really hadn't recovered.

Morghanna was afraid the old witch wouldn't be with them for much longer if she couldn't find some way to help rebuild her strength.

But that was a worry for another time. Today's worry was all centred on Leanna and getting her up to the prisoner cabin where Lachlan was being held. He had to support her in the difficult task ahead. And he couldn't do that if he showed up with this anger in his heart.

He took a moment to pace the space outside the door of the herbal stillroom, breathing slowly in and out to calm himself and his wolf. And only when he was certain he could face her with some semblance of calm, did he open the door.

She looked up immediately, not hiding the scars on her face behind her strawberry blonde hair like she used to do with him— and still did with most everyone else. It was as if she had known it would be him. But there was no sign of the shy smile she'd begun to give him every time she saw him. No sign of true welcome in her eyes.

She knew.

Of course she did. She would have been told of Iain's decree yesterday the same as everyone else. Undoubtedly Morghanna would have already spoken to her about it. Morghanna had told him earlier that he would not change Iain's mind—and she had been right, as she most often was about these things. By the looks of the shadows under Le-le's beautiful brown eyes, she'd had the conversation with her mentor last night.

He could wish Morghanna had kept the news to herself until this morn so that Le-le at least had a good night's sleep under her belt. Not that she wouldn't be capable of the magic required of her with no sleep—she was so strong and could go without sleep for days without faltering in her Healing duties. But the emotional toll of what was ahead would be better faced if she were well-rested.

'He said no to your request,' she said solemnly.

Dougal's brows rose. 'How did ye ken I asked Iain to rethink his decree?'

She tipped her head towards him, her plump lips twitching into something close to a smile. 'I have spent enough time around you, Dougal, to realise you would not agree with such a decree. But you should not have bothered. Iain will never change his mind where his son is concerned. And this is the best solution given everything.'

'Not fer ye, it isna. Ye ken ye are the one who will have to put him into the sleep?'

Leanna nodded briskly, her hands moving nervously over the herbs in front of her. 'I know. I knew as soon as I heard. I told Morghanna and Abigail I would do it.'

'Ye did?'

'Yes.' Her brows rose. 'You do not expect me to ask them to do it just to save me the difficulty of such a thing, do you?'

'Nae,' he said, smiling fondly at her. 'I didna expect any such thing.'

She tilted her head, her pointed chin lifted stubbornly and she pulled her shoulders back. 'Let us not dally then. It is best we simply get on with the task. The sooner done the sooner it will be over.'

'Very wise.'

Her eyes flashed with a little hit of temper. 'You are not laughing at me are you, Dougal MacCrae?'

'I dinna dare, Leanna Finnigan.'

'Good.' She took a deep breath and put the rosemary down she'd been running through her fingers. 'Well, let us go then.'

'Ye dinna need to take aught with ye?'

She looked around her as she shook her head. 'It is not that kind of spell. Although, maybe if we can get him to drink a calming tisane, it would make the entire process easier.'

'Given he has refused anything magical to help with his pain, I dinna think we will have any luck with that, but we can take some and try if ye wish.'

She paused for a moment, her gaze roving over the stills and jars in front of her, and then shook her head. 'No. Best I simply do the spell and put the poor Were to sleep.'

'Dinna feel sorry fer the bastard, Le-le. He doesna deserve yer sympathy.'

'No. Maybe not. But he will get it none-the-less. He is a lost soul who has been horribly affected by the Darkness. Despite what he has done, I will not allow my anger and hatred to override my ability to feel pity for such a retched creature. He will never know true happiness and for that reason alone, he has my sorrow.'

'Ye are a wonder, Le-le.' He had drawn close as she'd spoken and reached out to brush a lock of hair behind her ear, the silken strand like warmed sunlight against his skin. Her scent—like sun-warmed lavender and the sweet tang of a just-ripe apple—wove around him, making him want to stand there and simply breathe her in.

She looked up at him as his fingers grazed against her cheek, her skin pinking a little, the flecks of amber in her brown eyes glowing a little in the sunlight streaming through the window behind her. 'Dougal,' she breathed out.

He leaned in a little. 'Aye?'

Confusion and uncertainty swam through her brown eyes, the amber flecks in them flaring brighter for a moment before she swallowed hard and took a step back, embarrassment a flush over her skin.

He let his hand drop to his side even though he longed more than anything to reach for her again, to cup her face in his hands and take her mouth in the kiss he was certain she wanted as much as him. But she obviously wasn't quite ready for that, besides which, now wasn't the time. To cover up his obvious arousal, he stepped to the side and held out his arm. 'Shall we go?'

'Yes,' she said, her voice huskier than usual. He heard her swallow before she said, 'You will not leave my side, will you?'

'Never,' he said. 'Not unless ye wish me to.'

She nodded and said softly under her breath, 'I would never wish that.'

He wasn't certain if she'd meant him to hear that, so ignored it and gestured towards the door. 'Shall we?'

To her credit she lifted her head and marched steadily out the door at his side, never wavering as they headed up the hill towards the cabin in the woods where the pack's greatest enemy was being held.

I HOPE you enjoyed that little taster of *Alpha Bound*. If you want to read more, you can buy your copy here:

https://books2read.com/u/bzyNın

If you don't want to miss out on news about books in this series or in the original, modern day set **Pack Bound Series**, as well as special giveaways, sales, book signings and information on my other books, then sign up to my newsletter.

As an added bonus, when you join, you will get a FREE ebook copy of **Witch Bound**, a novella set 40 years before *Pack Bound* in the original series. Just keep reading to find out more:

LOVE A FREE BOOK?

YOUR FREE BOOK IS WAITING

One Fate, one mate, a bond too strong to deny ...

Paul Collins, duty-bound Pack Warlock and seer, must marry a strong witch for the good of Pack McVale. But his hidden feelings for his best-friend's sister, maternal wolf Ivy McVale, make this a more difficult pill to swallow every day. Especially when they begin to mate.

Then Paul has a vision: If they mate, Ivy will die. Desperate, Paul uses his powers to change destiny and make Ivy think she's always hated him. He can deal with any punishment the Fates make him pay for tampering with destiny, as long as Ivy lives.

After recovering from a bewildering month-long illness, Ivy notices her nemesis, Paul, is tormented by something. And strangely, she is the only one who can feel it. Unable to endure such unhappiness—even if he does call her Poison Ivy—she is determined to help him, no matter the cost. Because Pack McVale cannot survive without him, and curiously, neither can she ...

Simply sign up to my newsletter and I will email your free copy of Witch Bound to you. You will also receive the latest on upcoming books, sales, giveaways and relevant bookish news.

Get My Free Copy of Witch Bound Here:

But wait! There's more ...

If you're not into newsletters but think you might be into subscriptions that give you serialised content, exclusive chapters to new books, exclusive bonus content, signed print books and much more, then turn the page to find out about **Leisl's Legends** ...

JOIN LEISL'S LEGENDS

Subscribe to (or follow) me (via the QR code) at my Leisl's Legends page on REAM—a new subscription app like Patreon except it's designed especially for readers and authors for an amazing reading experience—and you will get early access to *The Huntress and the Vampire King,* my hot enemies to lovers, witch-and-vampire-licious urban fantasy romance that readers over there are already in love with. It's the prequel novel to the first book in the Blood-Rites Series - *The Blood of the Seer.*

Be the first to find out where it all began with Anita and Hei's love story.

BECOME A LEGEND NOW!

https://reamstories.com/leislleightonauthor

You will also find serialised chapters of the next book in my popular **Gods Cursed Series** there and can comment on the story as I write it! Not to mention you will also get extra bonuses like exclusive NSFW Bonus Epilogues, Bonus Prologues and cut scenes and chapters from all of my books.

Be part of creating the stories you love AND get exclusive access to a whole range of goodies including other WIPs, bonus content, voting rights, signed books and more.

Read on to find out more about The Huntress and the Vampire King PLUS read the opening chapters ...

The Huntress and the Vampire King

She hates the vampire who saved her; he holds the key to her fate ...

Hunter-witch Anita Middleton wants revenge against the violent vampire cults that murdered her father and has worked hard to become one of the best vampire hunters there is. But on a difficult hunt she is caught in an ambush and is mortally wounded ... only to be saved by a mysterious warrior. A warrior with brilliant blue eyes and long silver-blonde hair who fights with a grace and violence like nothing she's seen. It is only after she wakes in the heart of his palazzo that she realises her saviour is a vampire - and according to her brother and mentor, this vampire king is their ally.

Lord Hei rules over an empire of witches, humans and vampires who have been trying to keep the vicious vampire cults, the Wild and Dark Brethren, at bay for centuries. Then he saves Anita and knows with one look she is the prophecied Huntress who could be his downfall or his salvation - and she is also his fated mate. But she struggles to trust him as her hatred of vampires is deep-seated. And she *needs* to trust him because only he can offer the specialised training a Huntress needs so her power won't overwhelm her.

But with the Dark Brethren mysteriously amassing, he has little time to win her over. And Anita must go on a crash course to learn how to control her Huntress magic ... or go slowly and violently insane.

The Huntress and the Vampire King is the exciting action-packed prequel novel to *The Blood of the Seer*.

If you love your vampires hot with a bit of The Witcher thrown in and your heroines as kick-arse as Buffy and even more tortured, if you love fated mates, enemies to lovers, chosen ones and epically hot romance mixed with action and mystery, then *The Huntress and the Vampire King* is what you've been waiting for.

Sign up to Leisl's Legends and start reading exclusive early release chapters of it now!

BECOME A LEGEND NOW!
https://reamstories.com/leislleightonauthor

ALSO BY LEISL LEIGHTON

PACK BOUND SERIES

Pack Bound

Moon Bound

Shifter Bound

Wolf Bound

Witch Bound

(A Pack Bound Series Prequel Novella -

FREE ebook copy to Newsletter Subscribers)

BOX SET

Pack Bound Series Collection Books 1-4

DAWN OF THE CURSE

A PACK BOUND PREQUEL SERIES

Soul Bound

Alpha Bound

Hunter Bound

Fae Bound

(Coming in 2027)

GODS CURSED SERIES

A Love Cursed Christmas Wish

Love Cursed

Soul Cursed

Blood Cursed

Hearts Cursed

Fates Cursed

Witch Cursed

Dragon Cursed

(Coming 2026)

BLOOD-RITES SERIES

The Blood of the Seer

The Blood of the Sire

The Blood of the Son

(Coming 2027)

BLOOD-RITES PREQUEL AND BONUS MATERIAL

The Huntress and the Vampire King

The Middleton Manifesto

(Available now via Leisl's Legends subscription)

ANTHOLOGIES

A Perfectly Paranormal Valentine

A Perfectly Paranormal Halloween

A Perfectly Paranormal Easter

A Perfectly Paranormal Christmas

A Perfectly Paranormal Prophecy

(Coming in 2027)

As well as writing sexy, epic and romantic paranormal novels, I write mysterious and emotional romantic suspense novels too. Check out the following titles for amazing, suspenseful reads:

STORM HAVEN SERIES

Need You Tonight

The Devil Inside

COALCLIFF STUD SERIES

Climbing Fear: Book 1

Blazing Fear: Book 2

ECHO SPRINGS SERIES

Dangerous Echoes: Book 1

Books 2-4 in this series, (written by Daniel deLorne, TJ Hamilton and Shannon Curtis) are also available now at all ebook retailers.

You can find all the buy links for Leisl's Books at her website:

ABOUT LEISL

Leisl Leighton is a tall red head with an overly large imagination. As a child, she identified strongly with Anne of Green Gables, and like Anne, is a voracious reader and born performer.

It came as no surprise when she went on to a career as a performer, script writer, script doctor, stage manager and musical director for cabaret and theatre restaurants.

After starting a family, Leisl stopped performing and began writing the stories plaguing her dreams. She now writes emotional stories mixed with mystery and a little bit of what goes bump in the night.

Her novels have won and placed in writing contests here and overseas. She is a passionate advocate for the romance genre, was President of Romance Writers of Australia from 2014-2017 and when she's not writing romantic stories of redemption, she is helping other authors reach their dreams with her Author Services.
You can contact Leisl through her website via the QR Code above or here: https://www.leislleighton.com

And if you want to stay in touch and be the first to find out about new releases, appearances, special deals and exclusive content and give-

aways, sign up to her Newsletter and pick up your free copy of *Witch Bound* via the QR code.

Or sign up to *Leisl's Legends* via this QR code to get *Witch Cursed* plus serialised early access stories and bonus content including a bonus NSFW ending for Love Cursed.

You can also follow her on social media:

f facebook.com/LeislLeightonAuthor

instagram.com/leislleightonauthor

BB bookbub.com/authors/leisl-leighton

a amazon.com/stores/Leisl-Leighton/author/B00DBYRGZY

ACKNOWLEDGMENTS

Soul Bound marks the first in a new arc of the Pack Bound Series. I am so excited to be writing the stories of the witches, warlocks and Were who started the Pact and get to delve further into the beginning of a world that has been endlessly fascinating to me - and thankful, fascinating to all the readers out there who have loved the Pack Bound Series and begged me for more.

I do intend to write a total of 4 books in this prequel arc (Dawn of the Curse) and then hope to return to the present and take up the story of the witches and Were who helped bring the first arc to its conclusion. It is thrilling to have the privilege of being able to spend more time with these characters that I love in this world that they helped me to create. I wouldn't have been able to do it though without certain, essential people in my life.

So, firstly, thanks go to all the usual people: my hubby, my boys, my mum and dad, my siblings, my writing group friends—Anita, Marnie, Chris, Laura, Frana, and most recently, Sam and Helen—for all their love and support through the good and bad, especially in these very terrible last few years.

Thanks to Helen and Liz—your counsel and amazing friendships will always be missed.

To all my writing friends, past and present—your part of my journey has helped me get to this point and I am for ever grateful. Especially huge thanks to everyone in Romance Writers of Australia who have helped me gain the knowledge and courage to try this hybrid publishing thing.

Thanks to my agent, Alex Adsett, for encouraging me to go off and pursue getting these stories out there myself and by always having belief in me even when I doubt myself (you are the Goddess Arianrhod to my Morghanna!)

Thanks to my editor, Marnie St Clair—working with you is always a joy.

I have to stop and marvel once again at the amazing cover Samantha Marshall created for Soul Bound—you are an artistic Goddess among us mere authors who only have the writing thing going on. I thank all the deities I get to call you not only my cover artist, but my friend. Thank you.

Finally, thanks to all the readers. I hope you enjoy this story as much as I enjoyed writing it. I would not be doing this without you and just the thought I might bring you a little bit of joy in these difficult times makes all the hard work and toiling (almost always) alone on perfecting the writing-thing, worthwhile.

Happy reading.